JULIAN CLARY

MURDER MOST FAB

EBURY
PRESS

3 5 7 9 10 8 6 4 2

This edition publishing in 2008

First published in 2007 by Ebury Press, an imprint of Ebury Publishing

A Random House Group Company

Copyright © Julian Clary 2007

The Random House Group Limited Reg. No. 954009

Addresses for companies within the Random House Group
can be found at www.randomhouse.co.uk

A CIP catalogue record for this book is available from the British Library

The Random House Group Limited supports the Forest Stewardship
Council (FSC), the leading international forest certification organisation.
All our titles that are printed on Greenpeace approved FSC certified paper
carry the FSC logo. Our paper procurement policy can be found at
www.rbooks.co.uk/environment

Printed in the UK by CPI Cox & Wyman, Reading, RG1 8EX

ISBN 9780091914486

To buy books by your favourite authors and register for offers visit
www.rbooks.co.uk

In secret we met:

In silence I grieve

That thy heart could forget,

Thy spirit deceive.

If I should meet thee

After long years,

How should I greet thee?

With silence and tears.

'When We Two Parted' – Lord Byron

ACKNOWLEDGEMENTS

With special thanks to Kirsty Fowkes, my editor, who encouraged and restrained me with great skill and diplomacy.

Thanks also to Andrew Goodfellow at Ebury for giving me the chance to write my first novel, Ian Mackley for telling me to get on with it, David McGillivray and Brenda Clary for helping me select poems, Frankie Clary for the Spanish translations, and Valerie for kind looks late at night.

PROLOGUE

Dear Timothy,

I am sorry about this book, in so far as it implicates you. My story is so interwoven with my love for you that it is impossible to separate the two.

It is time for me to explain my life, to demystify my feelings for you and spell out exactly how fame and murder took over what might otherwise have been a harmless, insignificant existence.

Guilt grows like a tumour inside me. The idea of telling my true story, thus squeezing the spot, expelling the poison and cleansing my soul, is not only a solution but a compulsion – writing down the truth in all its grisly detail will be chemotherapy for my moral anguish.

You know the real me, the me that existed beneath the famous television persona, Mr Friday Night. Fame is such a strange thing, Timothy. It transforms you and everyone who knows you. Only you, my beloved, remembered the innocent boy from Kent whose heart you stole and broke and mended – and broke again. Even while I was the darling of the tabloids, the king of television, doyen of the party scene, I was just Johnny to you … But even you didn't know the full story.

If we were being picky we might describe me as a serial killer. But I don't think of myself like that. There was no bloodlust to quench, no orgasmic satisfaction in dispatching any of my unfortunate victims.

I was forced into a situation by circumstances beyond my control, obliged to make a choice between my survival and other people's deaths. It sounds trite to say 'one thing led to another' but it's true. I wasn't acting under any uncontrollable urge. Please don't think of me as a psychopath, sociopath or schizophrenic. None of those is applicable. I'm a normal, balanced, contributing member of society. And I love you. It couldn't be worse, really, could it?

As for the rest of my dreary life, I'm done for. But, strangely, I don't mind. I'm a different man now, after everything that's happened. I had it all, lost it all, and now I'm surprised to find that I don't want it back. Been there, done that, got the bloodstained T-shirt. My juices don't flow at the thought of publicity like they used to. The thrill of being in the papers has long since been replaced with dread, but the final feeding frenzy of tabloid adjectives and lurid headlines has been a fine exit. And if one is, however unwillingly, to enter that arena, it's best to be cast in the role of bad boy. The language of journalists flourishes much more imaginatively when they take the moral high ground.

I'm sorry. I love you. I hope you understand and that you forgive me,

JD x

PART ONE

CHAPTER ONE

I was no ordinary prostitute, I liked to think. I was high class. I had a number of tricks up my sleeve, as it were, to ensure my client's satisfaction. I was twenty-two and my enormous, proud and ever-ready member had the ability to throb and twitch on command, and – most exciting of all – could ejaculate by the beakerful at a moment's notice and not before. If required to play the passive role, my sphincter could squeeze and tug, vibrate and undulate in a frankly unnatural manner. I was more of a circus turn than a common trick. I claimed I could peel a satsuma with my arse, but that wasn't strictly true – although I did once crack a Cadbury's Creme Egg.

Believe it or not, back then in the early nineties, I was a straight-looking boy-next-door type who specialized in rough sex and humiliation. The image was part dominant master and part horny straight boy, up for it when paid, yet – wouldn't you know? – bad and dirty with it.

Although I was British, my grandmothers had clearly had exotic tastes: people speculated that I'd had one Indian grandfather and one, maybe, Hawaiian. While Grandmother Rita assured me that

Grandfather Norman was good, solid British stock through and through, she had to admit that there was no knowing what might have come through on the other side. I was dark-haired and olive-skinned with inscrutable Buddha-like brown eyes. You couldn't tell what I was thinking when I kissed your forehead any more than when I tightened my hands round your throat.

I am a modest five feet nine inches, smooth and naturally toned from my youthful participation in athletics. My aura, I'm told, is the same dark green as an empty Louis Coudenne claret bottle held up to the sunlight: menacing and mesmerizing all at once.

My working name at that time was simply JD (Johnny Debonair being my real name) but I also answered to 'sir'.

JD – floating your boat, whatever the weather! read my business card, and it was true. If being verbally or physically abused was your desire, I could deliver. I could transport. I could bring joy. As my ad at the back of *Gay Times* stated (beneath a torso shot with a digitally blurred face): 'Totally active type. Versatile if need be. Horse hung.'

I wasn't boasting. The look of gratitude on my punters' faces said it all – they were misty-eyed as they said goodbye. It wasn't love, of course, but I knew I could induce infatuation in a single visit. I was the font of happiness. Besides offering them my magnificent body, with its awe-inspiring genitals, I could give them emotional satisfaction too. I told them that I hoped to see them again. I did extended eye-contact and dealt with the financial transactions quickly and dismissively, never counting or questioning. I remembered their quirks and preferences, knew how and when to trigger their orgasm(s) and held them tight in my arms afterwards, evaporating their loneliness for a few blissful moments. I was worth it.

I was also discreet, punctual, clean and enthusiastic. I did what it said on the packet.

In retrospect, my path to the unusual career choice of high-class hooker seems straightforward, but I had no idea I was heading in that direction even as I took each step along the road. Generally speaking, enrolling at the Lewisham School of Musical Theatre isn't always a sure-fire fast-track entry to a life of vice. It might not be as prestigious as some drama schools but it has still launched one or two limp little careers of vague interest, if only to those closely related to the people concerned. Nevertheless, that was where it began for me.

I hadn't craved a life in musical theatre but I applied for a place because my grandmother had decided it was the best possible career for someone like me. I was an extrovert youth, with a mother who wore gypsy skirts, so it was agreed I would be a natural. As I wasn't sure one way or the other, I went along with it. Apart from anything else, I had to think of something to do with myself and most other possibilities seemed too much like hard work. There was no way I was going to spend my life in an office, if I could help it; singing and dancing for a living were better than that.

I charmed my way through the audition, giving it my all with a hearty, thigh-slapping rendition of 'Michael Row the Boat Ashore', thrusting my funky groin at the panel during the alleluias. I couldn't sing, but I had charm that made people smile and that translated, somehow, into stage presence.

I was offered a place on the year-long course and assumed that, in exactly twelve months' time, my name would be in lights above the door of some West End theatre. My mother would have to come to terms with the fact that the fruit of her loins was very probably the next Michael Crawford. Not an easy realization for any woman.

I had a rather rude awakening when I arrived in the big city and promptly found myself a long way from the glitz and glamour of the West End. My bedsit was in a dreary lodging-house on Brownhill Road, one of sunny Lewisham's less salubrious addresses. I began to wonder then if leaving the cosy little cottage I shared with my mother in a beautiful corner of Kent had been the right decision. But then I remembered all the reasons why I'd had to get away and determined to make the best of it.

I pretended that everything in my new life was perfect. 'The bedsit is beautiful,' I told my mother on the phone. 'It's a nest of luxury.'

'Oh, good. Clever Grandma to find it for you.'

Grandma had told me it wasn't exactly the Dorchester but I hadn't been expecting quite so much in the way of peeling wood-chip wallpaper, damp, and electrical sockets that buzzed.

'Are you looking forward to college?'

'Oh, yes. I can't wait to learn how to do jazz hands properly.'

'You'll have a fabulous time, my sweet.'

She firmly believed it was now only eleven months and twenty-eight days before I burst into the world of showbiz in a blaze of glory.

'I'm saving up for the trip to New York,' she said gaily. 'I expect you'll be wanted on Broadway, too, once they hear about you.'

To be honest, I agreed with her.

My illusion that a life in the public gaze awaited me after a year at drama school was rudely shattered on my first day at the college when I met the other students. Every single one believed that fame and fortune were the inevitable outcome of our course and, even with my ... *rural* grasp of mathematics, I could see that this was a statistical impossibility. And so, almost at once, I started to lose faith. Which, of course, was fatal.

In our first class we were made to sit in a large circle, then took it in turns to say a little about ourselves and why we were there. A large proportion of the other students – particularly the women, I noticed – were suspiciously thin.

A very slender girl with long auburn hair, which she flicked and stroked and twirled round her fingers, said her name was Stephanie Dalton – 'But my stage name is Darryl Streep. I've been acting since I was three and my mother says I could sing before I could talk and dance before I could walk.'

That didn't seem likely to me but I kept my thoughts to myself. By now she had taken to sucking a strand of hair into a wet rat's tail and stroking her cheek with it playfully. 'Just give me a songbook and a dance routine and I'm happy!' she exclaimed.

Everyone clapped, and I joined in dutifully, wondering why this merited applause.

The only black person in the group was next. He had an American accent, was tall and leggy, dressed in jogging pants and a faded blue singlet with 'POW!' written across it in jagged yellow lettering.

'I'm Larry, how you doin'?' he said, then dissolved into self-conscious giggles. A moment later he pulled himself together with a mock slap of his face. 'Okay, here goes ...' He took a deep breath as if he were about to dive off the top board. 'I'm Larry, I'm from Phoenix, Arizona, come to London cos it's the best place on the planet for a hoofer like me to learn his trade, lovin' it, lovin' it, so excited.' He spoke as if he was reading a list, intoning downwards at the end of each item. It was difficult to know when he'd finished speaking. 'I'm seventeen, but ya gotta start young in this business, youngest of five, I'm gay but it's not an issue, missin' my folks like mad, been here a week and seen *Cats* six times, er, er, oh! And I'm black! Surprise!' He flung out his arms, smiled a dazzling white smile and raised his eyebrows to signify he was done. He got a much bigger round of applause than Darryl, who tried to smile but looked more than a little put out.

My heart sank. It was early days, but I knew I didn't fit in with these people. I didn't have their weird enthusiasm for singing and dancing. But worse was to come.

The boy next to me identified himself. 'My name is Sean,' he said, in a posh Glasgow accent. 'I'm a Pisces and I'm Scottish, as you can probably tell, and I just live to sing. I'd like to be playing a lead role in the West End in about five years' time. *Cabaret, Guys and Dolls, The Umbrellas of Cherbourg* ... I don't really mind in which order.'

I gave him a sideways glance. He was painfully thin and his cheekbones were accentuated by his constant pouting. He wore a tight red cap-sleeved T-shirt, baggy jeans and the inevitable leg-warmers.

'I'm here in Lewisham to hone my craft and get my career on the road,' he told us.

Now it was my turn. 'My name is Johnny Debonair and I come from a village near Ashford. I'm here to see if I like it. It was my grandmother's idea ...' I trailed off to an embarrassed silence.

'Well done, Johnny,' said Larry, giving me a reassuring pat on the arm.

A decidedly restrained spatter of applause began, then stopped almost immediately. I wasn't bothered. I couldn't bring myself to pretend I was one of the kids from *Fame*, as everyone else in the room seemed to want to do.

There were fifteen of us in the class. When everybody had introduced themselves, our tutor, Francis Grey, told us it would be a tough year, we were going to work really hard, but it was a start of a new life, a life on the stage, the most demanding but also the most rewarding life there is, and so on. I perked up when he lowered his voice and added, 'The sad news is that not all of you will make it. Some of you will fall by the wayside ...'

There was hope, then.

The first class of the day was, as it would always be, a general warm-up for voice and body. We began with an exercise of sticking out our tongues as far as they would go. This we alternated with forcing air through our lips so we sounded a bit like horses snorting. We chanted 'ma, ma, mas' and 'moo, moo, moos' and then moved on to vowel sounds. Then we sang scales to the piano.

'Who's not giving me that C sharp?' asked Francis. We sang the scale again as he walked up and down, cocking his ear at us. He stopped suddenly and looked accusingly at me. 'Quiet, everyone.' He stared at me as if I'd stolen from the poor. 'Give me a C sharp, please, Johnny,' he demanded.

There was a hush of expectation. I made an intelligent guess and confidently sang the note.

'Oh, my God!' I heard Larry whisper. 'That was a C!'

'Hmm. Well done, Johnny. Good effort. We'll work on that in your individual class,' said Francis. 'It was completely wrong, of course, but you're not to worry about it now.'

Larry looked at me as if I had herpes.

'However,' Francis continued gravely, 'I have to tell you now that without C sharp you can't ever do *Oklahoma!*.'

Maybe I should top myself now, I thought – but I didn't have the nerve to say it.

*

By the end of the first week I knew for sure that I didn't fit in. Everyone seemed neurotic, intense and a trifle self-obsessed. I was a country boy, excited to be in London and wanting to have fun. I didn't yearn for a life on the stage as badly as the others did. Some of the girls amused me, but even they insisted on humming musical numbers mid-sentence as we scurried between classes and there was a whiff of vomit about the more slender ones.

My initial impressions of Sean had been correct. At first he appeared to take quite a shine to me, and spent the first week fluttering his eyelashes and being heavily flirtatious. He even sang 'Some Enchanted Evening' to me one day while I was eating my lunch, and rather good it was too, although I would never have admitted so to him. Someone who worshipped so devoutly at the shrine of Rodgers and Hammerstein didn't seem quite right to me, and it felt cruel to encourage him. And as for the flirtation – well, my heart was well and truly elsewhere and there was no way skeletal Scottish Sean could compete with the man of my dreams.

Once he'd got the message, Sean went on the turn. He began a laughable but vicious whispering campaign about me, which all stemmed from a chat we'd had in the college refectory one morning about his hopes and ambitions.

'I just pray I'll be good enough, that this gift I've been given by God, *my voice*, will fulfil its potential,' he said, as if the alternative was global catastrophe.

'I think anyone can sing and dance,' I said provocatively. He needed shutting up.

'How can you *say* that?' Sean looked aghast. 'How can you *disrespect* your colleagues in that way?' He had raised his voice and begun to gesticulate. 'You want to start *appreciating* the talent that surrounds you in this place, for God's sake. The blood, sweat and *tears* of your fellow performers!' He was wild-eyed and passionate.

After that outburst (of which this was but a short excerpt), he did a lot of neck stretching whenever I came into the room. We never spoke again, but a conspiratorial atmosphere would descend upon any group of fellow students I attempted to engage in social interaction. Eyes would roll, lips would purse, and colleagues would suddenly remember they had left their jazz pumps in the studio and scurry away from me. Sean had got to them.

'I hear you and Sean are, like, handbags at dawn,' said Larry, with glee. 'I just love all this bitchin' – it's so musical theatre!'

After that it was a lonely life for me at drama school, as we went about the endless rounds of singing lessons, play rehearsals, fencing classes, elocution, and so on. I was beginning to regret the day I'd ever thought I might be able to spend my adult years as a chorus member in *Les Mis* even if it was as good as a job for life.

By the end of the first term, I was disgruntled. For our first term 'show case' (which was themed round the songs of Nancy Sinatra and Lee Hazlewood), I sang 'Elusive Dreams' with an anaemic Welsh waif, the only person still speaking to me. I finished to a luke-warm response that, almost at once, petered out to nothing. Sean sang 'Been Down So Long It Looks Like Up To Me'. Everyone clapped and whooped. Sean shot me a look of terrible triumph as he took his fifth curtain call. As far as he was concerned he had won a great victory. It seemed I would never be among the people who truly believed that a well-honed musical could save the world.

I didn't care. As far as I was concerned, a far more amusing lifestyle had presented itself back at Brownhill Road.

CHAPTER TWO

I first encountered Catherine on the landing at Brownhill Road when I had been living there for about three weeks. We came out of our rooms simultaneously, she on her way to work, me to the bathroom, and we almost bumped into each other.

'Oh, sorry,' I said. 'Didn't see you there.'

It took me a moment to register the vision in white. The woman I had almost knocked to the ground in my desire to bag the bathroom was in her nurse's uniform, the small starched hat nestling in her lacquered blonde hair like a paper chalice. A smouldering cigarette hung from her glossy lips as she stared at me for a long moment. I had left music playing in my room and the sound drifted out into the corridor.

'Hi, there,' she said, in a clear Essex accent. 'Like a spot of Dusty Springfield of a morning, do we? I strongly suspect you're a homosexual.'

She had a face like that of a porcelain doll, with fine, delicate features and a rosebud mouth. Her makeup was a perfect mask. Pale foundation and frosted blue eye-shadow clouded seamlessly into white beneath a finely drawn eyebrow. Her lips were baby pink, and smiled knowingly. She resembled an extra from *The Rocky Horror Show*. Her cloud of perfume hit me and my nose twitched.

'Don't think I've overdone it with the Chanel, do you?' she said.

'No, it's nice. It's No. 5, isn't it? My favourite. I'm Johnny. I moved in a few weeks ago.'

'Yes, I've heard you. Are you a student at the drama school by any chance? Only I heard you attempt 'On The Street Where You Live' sixteen times in a row the other night. Much more of that and you'll have to find another street. You're way out on the C sharp, too.'

'Sorry if I disturbed you.'

'Oh, I was already disturbed, darling. Welcome to the madhouse, Johnny. My name's Catherine and I'm off to slop out some bedpans and see who's pegged it in the night.' She dropped her cigarette on the lino and stepped on it, swivelling her ankle three times to ensure it was extinguished properly.

'Have a good day, then. See you later,' I said.

'It will be a good day if Mr Pickering's passed on, that's for sure. His shit stinks.' She clacked off down the stairs.

I giggled. This was the first glimmer of hope I'd experienced since I'd arrived in Lewisham that I might meet a kindred spirit to keep me amused. Perhaps Catherine was the friend I'd been waiting for.

Later that night I was in my room rehearsing my part in the class studio production of a musical about Wendy Richard. At about eight thirty there was a knock on my door. I opened it and there stood Catherine with a bottle of wine in one hand and two glass tumblers in the other. She was wearing a dark blue embroidered kimono and smelt strongly of jasmine mixed with Benson & Hedges. 'Enough of that shit. Party time!' she announced, and minced into my room.

'Mr Pickering's still with us but Mr Lawson's shuffled off, thank the Lord and sweet baby Moses in a basket.' She set the glasses on my cluttered yellow-Formica dressing-table and clumsily poured us each a glass of warm Chardonnay. 'To the life hereafter!' she said, raising her glass.

I grabbed mine and we chinked. 'Bottoms up!' I said.

It transpired that Catherine worked on the geriatric ward at Greenwich Hospital. 'Fucking coffin-dodgers,' she said. 'I don't mind the ones who can wipe their arses and know their names, but I've got some who can't do a thing except eat. Well, it's a waste of food, isn't it?'

I giggled again. Something about Catherine was refreshing after all the fake luvviedom of college. Her honesty and openness were a blessed relief.

Almost immediately, we charmed each other and found immense enjoyment in each other's company because we laughed so much and so hard, and there is little as seductive as laughter.

'Ooh, you're a scream, you are,' said Catherine.

If we were in the mood, we could howl at a blank sheet of paper. Mostly, though, it was the absurdity of human behaviour that amused us: the stiffness of a nervous newsreader, a man at the bus stop unaware of the bogey hanging from his nose, or the gauche bartender trying to make a pass at one of us.

Apart from my mother, I had never been so entranced by a woman, and before long we were meeting up every night to drink, talk, tell each other stories and make each other laugh hysterically. She helped me cope with the hostility I was enduring at college and I saved up incidents and anecdotes for her at the end of the day.

'That Sean erased my face with his biro on a lunchtime-production poster on the noticeboard. Imagine!'

'No!' said Catherine. 'The evil bitch. I say we push her emaciated frame under a train!'

I had never met anyone like her. I found myself rushing home from college and waiting for her to come in. I could soon recognize her three-taps knock and would hurry to answer.

'Cup of tea, Cowboy?' She nicknamed me 'Cowboy' because of my Kentish Lad background. 'Or are you too immersed in *Grease*?'

One night she tapped and swanned in without waiting for an answer. She handed me four Valium. 'Listen, babe, these are for you. Wesley's coming over shortly and there might be a bit of noise. They'll help you sleep. Good luck to you and your family.'

The door swung closed.

I adored her for the exquisite campness of such encounters. She provided me with quality comedy on a daily basis. I loved the idea of the nurse off to work in full slap, reeking of alcohol; I thrilled to her casual announcements of tragic deaths, and admired the tough, ever-present survival instinct that ensured she always came out on top in any situation and by any evaluation.

That night she entertained Wesley so royally she should have handed out Valium in Deptford, too. Imagine a hyena giving birth to a pineapple and you're getting close.

'You amaze me, Catherine,' I said to her once, when she showed me the black pearls she had liberated from a confused pensioner. 'You really are the most unusual nurse I've ever met.'

'I have to keep my sense of humour, Cowboy. I work in God's waiting room. When one of my patients dies and the relatives, if there are any who can be arsed, have said their goodbyes, we pull the curtains round, strip them naked and wash them head to foot, inside and out, before they go down to the morgue. Most of the other nurses don't like doing it so I always get the job when I'm on duty. I don't mind. I take a pride in my work. My stiffs are spotless. I'm the last hand to touch them, probably the last person to look at them. I clean their nails and comb their hair. I talk to them, tell them what I'm doing, and how nice and clean I'm making them. Hygiene's important, I think, especially when you're dead. And as I do it, I wonder what sort of lives they've lived. I'm far nicer to them once they're gone, really. They scratch my back and I'll scrub theirs. And with each old penny dreadful, I make the sign of the cross. Rest in peace, in the name of the Father, the Son and the Holy Ghost, Amen.' She looked at me solemnly. 'And then I see if I fancy any of their jewellery before I send them down to the freezer.'

Being with Cathcrine was never boring. As well as her dark and dangerously hilarious anecdotes about life and death on the geriatric ward, she would, without premeditation, make sure that every evening had a beginning, a middle and an end. She had a gift for creating a well-structured social occasion. Frequently, after we had downed the wine she provided, we ended up in our local pub, the Cocky Sailor.

Out of uniform, she dressed demurely in black and burgundy blouses, perfectly pressed skin-tight jeans and kitten heels. She insisted we drink white wine, favouring the oaky, rich Chardonnay that rolls down the throat like Spanish semen but gets you drunk and tired all the same.

We'd talk the whole evening, getting drunker and drunker. Occasionally a Lewisham lad would saunter over and try to chat her up. She gave them very short shrift, usually, and would send them packing with admirable efficiency. If they offered to buy her a drink she'd say, 'Yes, thank you, I'll have a large Chardonnay and so will my friend Johnny.' And when the unfortunate chap delivered the glasses: 'Ta. Now fuck off and take your button-mushroom cock with you.'

I loved her wry take on life, and I think she was amused by my naïvety. Besides calling me 'Cowboy', she never missed an opportunity to refer to me as a country bumpkin. 'This must be quite a shock to your system, coming to London. Electricity and cutlery, washing more than once a month! Quite a steep learning curve for a teenage sheep-shagger from Kent ...'

The 'middle' of the evening might be an altercation with a parked car as we staggered home, or Catherine's sudden need for a wee behind a wheelie-bin parked on a busy junction. The end was always the same: Catherine and me screeching with laughter back in my room as we reviewed the night's highlights.

If we weren't at the Cocky Sailor, we stayed in for what Catherine called 'girly nights', enjoying cheap white wine or Tesco's vodka with a Chinese takeaway while we applied menthol face packs and talked about our futures.

One night, Catherine produced a joint from her designer handbag and we lay top to tail on my single bed, smoking until we were nicely high.

'What is it about you, Cowboy?' she asked. 'It doesn't take Sigmund Freud to spot sadness in your aura. I wish you'd cheer up. From what I understand about gay life, you'd all shag a sleeping policeman if it was dark and you'd had a few Bacardis. But you're not like that so there's only one explanation. You've fallen in love, haven't you? Or you think you have, probably with someone unattainable, like a cartoon character or a nameless shadow you met in a bus shelter.'

Catherine could usually prise anything out of me but this time I wasn't giving anything away. I knew what she was like. She'd make a joke of all that had happened in my past, and I wasn't sure I could take it. It was still a tender wound and I could hardly bring myself to think, let alone talk, about it. I wouldn't allow anyone to mess with the man who lived in my head.

'Oh no. There's no one,' I said carelessly.

Catherine gave me a meaningful look. She knew me well enough by now to guess that I wasn't being honest. 'Well, love, if you want to keep it to yourself, that's fine. But you shouldn't dwell on these things. If it's all come to nothing, move on. That's what I'd do. You know what my motto is? "Eat life before it eats you. Or you're a loser." And the best way to get over someone is to get under someone new. I'll send Wesley over, shall I?'

Wesley sounded like an experienced and memorable lover. But I couldn't – wouldn't – betray my true love. As tacky as it sounds, I was keeping myself nice. I answered ironically, with a poem by Robert Herrick:

'Gather ye rosebuds while ye may,
Old Time is still a-flying;
And this same flower that smiles today
Tomorrow will be dying.'

'Whatever. I catch your drift,' she said.

My mother had raised me on poetry almost before I could talk, and my photographic memory meant that I could recall a wealth of popular and metaphysical verses, so it had become my habit to quote pertinent couplets or stanzas when they popped into my head. Sometimes it seemed the best way to express what I was thinking. Certain poets squeezed a lot of meaning into a few words, and I liked their economy.

'What about you?' I asked, handing back the joint as swirls of aromatic smoke floated up to the ceiling. 'What are your dreams? Are you going to stay a nurse all your life?'

'I'm twenty-six, Cowboy. Time to find a husband. I want a doctor or a lawyer. Three kids, big house, swimming-pool. I want the whole lot, even love.' The next sentence she spoke with uncharacteristic vehemence. 'And I'm going to have it, too.'

We paused to absorb her slightly embarrassing display of ruthless ambition. Catherine's laugh rumbled first, but I wasn't far behind. Within thirty seconds we were rolling around on my rusty bed, holding our sides. Eventually we peaked, and our laughter died slowly, bar the odd reprise, to a giggle that did not prevent talking.

'And you?' said Catherine, picking up where we'd left off. 'What in the name of Terry Wogan do you want?'

'Oh, I'd like to live with my gorgeous, faithful, well-balanced, sexually insatiable boyfriend, of course,' I said, without hesitation. 'Next door to you, if that could be arranged. I want to live happily ever after, too. He will be remarkably earthy and Neanderthal but a rock in every respect: sober, fit, self-contained, yet madly in love with me and happy to dedicate his every waking hour to my continued happiness. And hung like a draught-excluder, natch.'

'Dream on,' said Catherine, yawning shamelessly. 'And if you think you're getting your grubby mitts on my Wesley, you can go fuck yourself.'

'Charming.'

Not long afterwards, I discovered another side to Catherine.

There was a communal telephone by the front door and several times I answered it to an Oriental-sounding woman asking for her.

Once summoned, Catherine would take a pen and pad to the phone and write down some details. Thirty minutes later she would be off, dressed to the nines, in a cloud of Chanel.

After this had happened three times in quick succession, I asked her whether she was being invited to parties.

She laughed. 'I suppose that's one way to describe it. Parties for two. If they pay, I party. Snatch for cash. I thought you'd twigged by now, to be honest. Most nurses are lucky if they can afford a polyester skirt at the market. I've got a Gucci tampon case. Did you never wonder? Think about it, Cowboy.'

She explained that she was registered with an agency that allowed her to supplement her modest nurse's wages with occasional escort work. She made no bones about her activities. 'It's business, isn't it?' she said. 'Pay to lay. Very discreet, though, none of your rubbish. All done through the agency. Foreigners, mainly, in need of a little feminine company. I get wined and dined, keep the conversation going, laugh at their stupid jokes, and I'm paid for it. If they want any extras – and they always bloody do – we make our own arrangements. I can't live on a nurse's pay. It's not a wage, it's a fucking tip.'

I was fascinated by and impressed with her business-like attitude to her sideline.

'I've seen a lovely pair of boots in Dolcis. Time to shag an Arab. Quote me a bit of Shakespeare, honey, while I put my cap in.'

'For sweetest things turn sourest by their deeds;
Lilies that fester smell far worse than weeds.'

'Oh, really? I do hope so.'

We laughed about it, because we laughed about everything,

but her mercenary approach was clearly a means of emotional survival. If she'd had a particularly unsavoury encounter she would flinch in telling the story, shuddering as she recalled the misshapen penis or the bitter semen she had been tempted to swallow for an extra fifty quid. She would sit on my bed and stroke the wad of grubby twenty-pound notes to comfort herself.

'In for a penny, in for a pound. His wife should be very grateful to me, if that's what she has to do to keep him happy,' she said sadly, gazing into the distance. Then she snapped out of it, switching into comedy mode in the blink of a mascaraed eye. 'Still. Down the hatch to grab the cash!' She gave one of her rare but beautiful smiles, and threw herself back on the bed, tossing the money into the air and laughing as the notes fluttered across and around her.

I was in awe of her. She made prostitution seem glamorous. I even loved the horror of it. It appealed to me, in my secret agony, that such an activity could deaden the spirit.

Catherine burrowed, expanding and bewitching, further and deeper into the territory of my mind without my realizing it. My life revolved round her, and although there was no sexual attraction, on my part at least, there was every other variety.

CHAPTER THREE

One evening Catherine called me from the Grosvenor House Hotel in Park Lane. 'Get your arse down here,' she said urgently. 'I'm with Prince Howsaboutit, or whatever his name is, from Bahrain. He's got a friend who's in the mood for a nice English boy. What's more, he's gorgeous – think Brazilian footballer wearing a sheet. They're handing out Rolex watches like they were after-dinner mints.'

I didn't need to think twice. 'I'm on my way,' I said. 'I'll meet you in the foyer in forty-five minutes.'

'Attaboy,' she said, with satisfaction. 'I knew you'd be up for it. No jeans or trainers, Cowboy. Wear your suit.'

I hung up, excited. Her secret world as a hooker had seemed so enthralling when she talked about it. Now I would see for myself what it was like.

As arranged, Catherine met me in the foyer and led me through to a luxurious, expensively lit bar. 'Just stay calm and act cool and you'll be absolutely fine,' she muttered, as we approached a discreet, leather-lined booth.

Inside sat two handsome, exotic men in their mid-thirties. Catherine introduced them to me as Assam and Shazad, and they stood up and shook my hand. Assam cast an approving glance at Catherine, then patted the seat beside him, beckoning me to join him. They were drinking peppermint tea and his breath was fresh and sweet. He was undeniably handsome, built like a sportsman, with limpid, dewy eyes that lingered on my face, then scanned my body approvingly.

'Very pleased to meet you,' I said.

'You are handsome boy,' said Assam. 'Drink champagne, please.'

'If you insist, Assam.'

After half an hour of polite chit-chat, he whispered to Catherine that he would like to invite me up to his suite.

'Assam wants to show you his etchings. You'd love that, wouldn't you?' she said to me brightly.

'Love it!' I echoed, already relishing our recounting of the dialogue once we got home. I stood up boldly. 'Take me as I Assam ...'

Assam laughed politely at my 'joke' and bowed goodnight to Catherine and Shazad. He took my elbow and steered me towards the lift where he pressed the button for the top floor: the penthouse. 'You are nervous. Why you nervous?' he said, once we were inside the lift. 'I like you very much.'

He moved closer, but although I braced myself for a kiss, he reached behind me and squeezed my left buttock, almost to the point of pain. This wasn't romance, I reminded myself. It wasn't showbiz either – it was prostitution. Although I was scared, seduced by the unexpected handsomeness of Assam and goggle-eyed at the opulence of such a posh hotel, the like of which I had never seen before, I knew I mustn't let Catherine down. I must be a 'pro' and deliver the goods. Nothing else would do.

As soon as the door closed behind us, Assam let out a sigh and took off his jacket. The charm and politeness he had displayed downstairs in the bar took on a curdled, cynical tone. He fixed me a drink and said, rather curtly, 'Make yourself comfortable while I take a shower.'

I stepped on to the balcony and looked down at the traffic sailing along Park Lane and the shadowy expanse of Hyde Park disappearing into the night. Around it, London glittered and gleamed, a luxurious playground for those who could afford it.

I wasn't sure what was expected of me, but I made an intelligent guess. Back in the suite, I stripped down to my boxers, slipped the condoms under the pillow and arranged myself on the bed.

A few minutes later, Assam emerged from the shower, wrapped in a fluffy white hotel towel. He dropped it and joined me on the bed. He was warm, expensively scented and a little damp.

He didn't kiss me but pushed my head roughly away from him and bit the back of my neck. He was an inconsiderate but technically accomplished performer, and I displayed as much enthusiasm as I could, even though my mind was bubbling with a thousand thoughts.

I had never been paid for sex before. In fact, I had only ever had sex with one other person and I loved him with all my heart. Sex without love was a new experience for me.

I felt many different things. Assam's indifference was strangely erotic. The way he turned and pulled me made me feel like a rag doll, but it was not unpleasant. Intimacy with someone new broke my heart, but ultimately hardened it, too. Face it, sister, I said to myself, your heart is already broken. It's high time you toughened up.

As Assam forced himself inside me, huffing and puffing, telling me how much I wanted it, I told myself it was a healing experience. If I didn't want it, maybe I needed it, which was more important.

*

I was awoken in the night for a prolonged reprise that involved hair-pulling and what I presumed was Arabic dirty talk. (It seemed unlikely that Assam would be reciting sacred poetry at such an intimate moment.) A few hours later, as dawn was breaking, he had me perform a traditional sex act on him, then announced that the car would be waiting for me downstairs in ten minutes.

'Thank you very much,' he said formally, once I was dressed. 'I must sleep now. This is for you.' He handed me a promising envelope, so I said goodbye and trotted off, without so much as a mouthwash.

While I was waiting idly in the foyer for my car, Catherine sashayed out of the lift, all spick and span even if she was still in last night's clothes.

'Ah, there you are,' she said, linking arms and swinging me towards the rotating doors. She scrutinized me. 'Bit of residue in the right corner of your mouth,' she said. A manicured claw flew towards me and gouged out the offending material with a couple of layers of skin. 'Best not to give the hotel staff any more reason to be suspicious.' As she said this she smiled falsely at the concierge. 'Got the dosh?'

I handed her the envelope.

'Well done.' She peeped inside. 'Very well done!'

Catherine and I were delivered back to south-east London in a chauffeur-driven Mercedes, whooping childishly out of the window, our pockets bulging with twenty-pound notes. Soon she was sitting on my bed, counting our booty, while I made some tea.

'Ooh, Christmas has come early,' she said. 'Let's go and buy some champagne!'

I turned off the kettle.

Catherine handed me a fat wad. 'A very well-deserved two hundred pounds for your trouble,' she said.

I felt a distinct sexual thrill. 'Money turns me on,' I confided. 'I could get to like this.'

'Well,' said Catherine, 'I could have a word with Madame for you. I don't think she has any boys on her books. She really ought to. There's money in them there buttocks.'

'I'll think about it,' I promised. So far I hadn't been struck down by a bolt of holy lightning for my wicked behaviour and, in a strange way, I had enjoyed my night with Assam. Also, there was no denying that the money would come in useful – I was a poor student, after all.

The next day I put a hundred pounds in an envelope and posted it to my mother with a note explaining that I'd been paid rather well for a modelling shoot. I felt extremely proud of myself.

There was little to discourage me from renting out my body again. It seemed terribly easy and, as I was in cahoots with Catherine, rather funny. After all, I wouldn't be a common prostitute, I reasoned: I'd just help out when they needed me and, even then, only at the top end of the market. I asked her to take me to see Madame as soon as possible.

Catherine styled me in ripped jeans, black T-shirt and leather jacket, and escorted me to the HQ of Elegant Escorts for my afternoon appointment with Madame. She operated her small concern from a neat, minimalist mews house just off the Portobello Road and she was an inscrutable Oriental woman of indeterminate age, somewhere between thirty and fifty. Evidently Japanese in origin, she clearly had some background in rock-chick, groupie circles. She wore a top-quality leather waistcoat fitted to her child-like waist, and had the air of a rock god's mistress.

I quickly discovered that Madame's catchphrase was 'Make happy, make money!', and that she smiled and nodded a lot.

'Catherine tell me that you go to appointment with her, and Mr Assam very complimentary! Good, good. Make happy, make *money*!' She hung on to the last syllable of 'money' a little longer each time she uttered it, until *eeeeee!*s echoed round the room like escaped budgies. 'Most men like lady, but some men like *boy*!' she said, giggling bashfully, geisha-style. 'But it raining men. Do you suck and fuck to completion and how big your cock? It big, and make happy, make moneeeeeey!'

'I've had no complaints in that department,' I said.

'Mr Assam, he said it award-winning!' She nodded knowingly.

'Oh, well done, Cowboy,' said Catherine. 'I didn't like to ask but you've got the look of somebody with a big one. The donger of death.'

'Length and girth very satisfactory,' said Madame, consulting her notes. 'Ejaculation distance almost two yards!'

I lowered my head, feigning modesty.

'Shame there isn't an Olympic event for that sort of thing,' said Catherine. 'If they'd only bring in Synchronized Rimming and the Spunk Javelin I could imagine you with a bronze medal hanging round your neck.'

'Bronze?' I said, a little hurt.

'So,' said Madame, standing up to indicate that the meeting was over, 'I get you work. You make happy, make—'

'Moneeeeeeeeey!' Catherine and I chimed simultaneously.

And that was that. My career as a high-class prostitute had begun, though in those early days it was merely my sideline and, in some ways, my hobby.

*

A week later Madame called me and, inevitably, my second paid sexual encounter felt much more like work. A businessman awaited me at the Savoy Hotel. No dinner was involved, I just had to present myself at room 406 at ten o'clock that evening. 'Mr Smith' opened the door in his sizeable boxer shorts and was as sweaty as he was salacious. But the thrill was still there, as he handed over the money and lost himself in lust. 'Your body is my plaything,' he breathed.

I remembered Catherine's advice: 'If you can appear to be enjoying the sex even when it disgusts you, you've got it made. They'll come quicker and probably pay you extra.'

So I made all the appropriate noises and, sure enough, had Mr Smith spurting like a geyser within a couple of minutes. I was back on the tube within half an hour. I got my genuine thrills when he pressed a sizeable tip into my hands as I left. Money, it appeared, made everything worthwhile.

I continued to attend college, although my heart was no longer in it. One highlight was the Shakespeare's Sonnets workshop. I already knew the famous ones by heart and gained the momentary admiration of my peers for my faultless recitation of Sonnet 94 within minutes of the task being announced.

I declaimed with much feeling:

'But if that flower with base infection meet,
The basest weed outbraves his dignity.'

For an instant, I was in the sunshine but soon I was relegated to the shadows. I committed the cardinal sin of not showing up for rehearsals and, as a result, I was regarded as the devil's accomplice. I didn't care. My life outside was much more entertaining than anything drama school could offer me, and I regarded the other students as tedious neurotics lacking any real sense of humour.

Over the following months, after I'd turned a handful more tricks and was what Catherine called 'broken in', I felt relaxed about it. I seemed to have a bit of a flair for this career – perhaps I'd found my true calling. As an added bonus, it seemed to ease the pain of my aching heart – anything that did that was worth taking notice of. I'd been miserable for long enough, I told myself.

The money was wonderful, of course, but what I loved most was the gratitude I invoked. Like an acupuncturist or a hairdresser, I put a spring in men's steps and sent them smiling and happy on their way.

I explained this to Catherine late one night when we got in from our respective jobs. Catherine's Gucci handbag was bulging with the contents of her punter's mini-bar, and over a few neat Bacardis we reviewed our performances.

I had been to a private house in Chalfont St Giles, where I had been booked for a 'Mix and Mingle'. This turned out to be a geriatric gay orgy in which I was the central attraction.

Catherine had been wined, dined and taken roughly from behind by a visiting Italian diplomat. 'Unfortunately he was no stranger to a bowl of pasta. If I look a bit like a pug, it's because I've been face down on the shag pile for over an hour with nineteen stone of Italian porker on top of me.'

I was drunk and very pleased with myself. 'Do you know what, Catherine? I think I've truly developed as a human being from this line of work. Whatever sexual role I'm cast in, I feel completely confident I can play my part well. I've already learnt to watch for the defining moment when need is transformed into nature. The breathing, the biorhythms – even the colour of their eyes changes as something in their souls opens up and they lose themselves in the moment. You know, I'm *proud* of my work.'

'Steady, Cowboy,' she cautioned. 'If you start talking poncy bollocks I shall go to bed. Success in sex is measured by the grunts and the tip. Nothing else. Your development as a human being is of no interest to me – let's not pretend otherwise because you've got a few too many miniatures down you.'

'But don't you ever feel that way? As though you're truly helping another human being?'

'Of course not. And this isn't a support group for sex workers. At least, I bloody hope not. What shall we drink next? Whisky or Baileys?' She was only ever interested in facts and figures and what the next drink would be.

'Well, I do,' I said, a trifle sulkily.

'We've all been there, sweetheart. But never mind – in years to come you can say you were scarred by your reckless youth. Or that I lured you into it. I don't care what you say – just shut the fuck up about your vocation and your desire to heal the world before I kill you.'

I had learnt that Catherine couldn't tolerate serious conversation and always brought me back to earth if I started to bare my soul, but I was determined that, for once, we would have a proper conversation about the reality of our lives. Maybe now I would tell her about Kent and the things that had happened to me there. The time felt right.

'What would your mother say if she knew you were on the game?' I asked.

'"Snap", I expect,' said Catherine. 'Oh, God, here it comes. You're quite the public speaker tonight, aren't you? Remind me never to pour Bacardi down you again. You're going to force me to listen to the story of your life, and it's all going to be rather dreary. I can feel it in my water.'

'"So many worlds, so much to do, So little done, such things to be",' I quoted. 'That's Tennyson. And yes, I am about to tell you my life story. I insist. So listen carefully.'

PART TWO

CHAPTER FOUR

My mother looked like Julie Christie and I was her adoring only son. Her name was Alice and we lived alone in an isolated cottage on the outskirts of a tiny windswept village on Romney Marsh in Kent. My mother enjoyed a carefree life, smiled all the time and was always humming. In fact, she was so relentlessly happy that, as a child, I doubted any tragedy that might befall me would cause more than a hiccup in her joyful disposition. After all, this was the woman who had gone along to my grandfather's funeral in a floral dress and a straw hat with a broad smile. 'How lovely to see you!' she'd greeted friends and relatives. 'Beautiful day, isn't it?'

Because I was an only child and we lived in the middle of nowhere, my mother and I depended on each other for company. She played with me like an older sister and was never preoccupied with housework or any matters to do with the real world. We didn't have a television and she never listened to the news on the radio. Instead we played 'chase' round the house and garden, had dressing-up parties and midnight feasts. I remember we whispered, too, as if anyone might hear us. When the weather was good, she took me tramping across crusty fields, her long sandy hair blowing across her face.

My mother cooked wonderful food: big hearty casseroles in the winter and fresh fruit cocktail with real cream, served in the garden, during summer. After dinner she liked to lie on the sofa, or in the garden hammock if it was fine, and listen while I read poetry or novels to her by candlelight. We would lose ourselves in long, lovely books by Thomas Hardy, George Eliot and Charles Dickens. Sometimes we couldn't wait until the evening for the next instalment and would get up half an hour early to have a chapter after our porridge before I went to school. I think we'd read all of D. H. Lawrence by the time I was ten. Parts of *Sons and Lovers* made me blush.

My mother thought it was important to memorize poems. 'That way,' she explained, 'they're always in your head, and you can get to them at any time. What beautiful thoughts you can have as you lie in bed, waiting for sleep to come! Tennyson, Christina Rossetti, Oscar Wilde ...'

So, with her encouragement, I commited as many poems as I could to memory, and then it became our habit to recite couplets or sonnets throughout the day. She made it fun. The more our repertoire grew, the better able we were to pluck a poem from our heads appropriate to every mood or occasion. For example, if my mother was hanging out the washing and I hurtled down the path on my bicycle, she'd stop me by declaring:

*'Tread lightly, she is near
Under the snow,
Speak gently, she can hear
The daisies grow.'*

I had to guess that she was quoting from 'Requiescat' by Oscar Wilde, and reply with the next verse.

> *'All her bright golden hair*
> *Tarnished with rust,*
> *She that was young and fair*
> *Fallen to dust.'*

Or, if I couldn't remember the next verse or wanted to express a different point of view, I would quote from another poem that seemed apt, perhaps some of my favourite nonsense by Lewis Carroll:

> *'"Will you walk a little faster?"*
> *Said the whiting to a snail,*
> *"There's a porpoise close behind us*
> *And he's treading on my tail."'*

My mother's rustic image was hard to square with the few facts I knew about her own childhood. They seemed to imply a certain poshness. I knew that she had originally come from London, because that was where my grandmother Rita lived, and that she had been privately educated and brought up as what they used to call a lady. I also knew that she had turned her back on all that, running away from school and embracing a life that rejected material trappings and social status, which meant nothing to her. A pastoral existence had been trapped inside her, waiting to get out. Now she was a real country girl and happiest in our garden or pottering about our tumbledown Kentish cottage, which was always cheerful and clean.

One spring we took on an orphaned black-faced lamb, which we called Saucy, and she followed Mother around, nuzzling her and making her laugh even more than usual. Saucy nibbled at the lawn while chickens pecked their way round the yard; potatoes, beans, radishes and garlic grew in our half-acre of garden, protected from Saucy by a white picket fence. My mother wore gingham or white lace blouses, with the sleeves rolled up, pinafore dresses or flouncy skirts, the perfect picture of a country lass. She even spoke with a non-specific rural burr, which may have been Suffolk but certainly wasn't London or Kent; as she had never lived anywhere else, its origin must remain a mystery. She loved to be outdoors, tending the flowers or watering the vegetable garden, or trying to cajole Saucy into chasing her and being lamb-like and carefree once more. But Saucy, by the age of two, was a dour and boring sheep, refusing to play, just widening her eyes a little and glaring at my mother disdainfully. We loved her nevertheless, lavishing her with affection and attention that she blankly endured.

Mother gave the wild birds in the garden names. She greeted and recited Keats to every robin or blue-tit:

'You live alone on the forest tree,
Why, pretty thing, could you not live with me?'

She waved at departing swallows, wishing them a safe journey, and stretched her arms skyward to migrating geese. Young and enigmatic, she exuded earthy glamour and heads would turn as we cycled through the village to the shops or to church each Sunday.

*

I was seven or eight, I think, when I realized my mother wasn't quite right. Her consistently benign demeanour wasn't normal. A child needs to find the boundaries of acceptable behaviour, which are demonstrated by parents for the little one's ultimate good. Dear Mother couldn't have got cross if she'd wanted to but that wasn't the Utopia it might sound. I grew up more than a little confused about the difference between right and wrong, and I was terrified when other people were angry because I'd never known anything like it at home. I also had a sneaking feeling that my mother never got cross because she didn't care what I did. If I ever want an explanation for my later outrageous, exhibitionist behaviour, I won't have to look very far. I found it so hard to get a reaction from her that, in the end, I became frustrated – bored, almost – with her unchanging pleasantness. It was like living in a shopping centre and having to listen to Muzak twenty-four hours a day.

There was a secret at the heart of our existence, which always stood between us: the identity of my father. I didn't have a clue who he was. The subject wasn't taboo, but if I asked about him, Mother would squint dreamily at the sky, say something like 'You have his eyes, little man!' and no more. Any prolonged gaze skyward meant that informative conversation must stop.

Specifics were hard to get out of her, and even as a young child I registered the inconsistencies in the answers she gave me, and the picture I had in my mind of my father grew increasingly bizarre. I'm sure she wasn't deliberately evasive – I'd describe it more as creative ramblings. According to her, my father might be tall or short, black or white, musical or tone deaf, all in the same week. The only thing that never altered was her devotion to him, and his to her. It wasn't long before I grasped that she said whatever came into her head, never thinking I would absorb every word and dwell on it obsessively as I lay in my little bed gazing up at the ceiling where she had painted the stars and the planets for me, albeit in an order of her own choosing. There was no North Star, for instance, but a lovely green four-leaf clover instead. 'Much nicer!' she said.

That was typical of how she rewrote the facts of life to suit herself. In the entrance hall of our cottage, for example, she marked every six months how much I had grown. Except the latest pencil mark was a good three inches higher than I was. 'Well,' she said, 'that's how tall you would have grown if Renata Rabbit hadn't eaten all of my lovely, healthy spinach, the little minx. It's only fair. I don't see why you should suffer.'

It dawned on me that my mother would never reveal the definitive truth about my father, and the picture of him that I had lovingly built up crumbled into dust. I couldn't even be cross with her – she probably no longer knew what truth was. So, instead of asking for facts, I enquired why he never came to visit.

'He doesn't know about you, sweet-pea,' she answered, 'but if he did, he'd be very proud indeed.'

After that, I gave up trying and instead made up a new image of him: he was a soldier from the army camp in Dymchurch, perhaps, a brave and handsome man of the kind I read about in my favourite adventure stories. I filled in the gaps with my childish imagination, and if my friends asked about him, I'd say he died in action, fighting for his country, but I had no idea in what battle or country.

There was one person I could rely on to tell the truth: Alice's mother and my grandmother, Rita. She told me once that my mother had been just nineteen when she had fallen pregnant, and that it had all been 'most unfortunate'. But she, too, would say no more.

I looked forward to seeing my Grandma Rita. As far as I knew she was my only close relative, and she visited us every month, sweeping down from London in her big black shiny car, which all but blocked the lane outside our cottage. She wore lipstick, powder and chunky jewellery, but the effect was more formidable than glamorous. She'd peer at me disapprovingly, stroking her crucifix, then silently hand me whatever she'd brought for me, something unexciting but practical, the kind of thing it would never have occurred to my mother I might need – a grey jumper or a navy blue winter coat to replace the one that Grandma Rita had noticed on her previous visit was threadbare. She took no pleasure in the act of giving, seeming more embarrassed by it than anything, and I always thanked her politely: her presents were useful, even if they didn't set my pulse racing.

Grandma Rita never stayed for long. After an hour at the most she would glance at her watch and say, 'Goodness, is that the time? I mustn't catch the traffic. Goodbye, Alice, and goodbye, Johnny – be kind to your mother and work hard at your studies. Show me the flowers before I go.'

This was always a highlight. While my mother stayed inside to clear away our tea things, Grandma Rita took my hand and I led her down the passage to the back door. From there she'd peruse the flowerbeds.

'Blackfly on the rosebuds. I suppose your mother wouldn't hear of killing them?'

'Oh, no,' I'd answer, shocked. 'They've all got names.'

'How ridiculous! What's that one called?'

'Jeffrey.'

'And him?'

'He's a she. Claudia.'

We'd play this game for a while, until she broke away to point at some bindweed. 'Pull that out, Johnny. It'll strangle everything else. Never mind Alice, just do it, quickly.'

And I did. In what felt like an act of defiance to my mother, I tugged at the yards of weed that wove their sticky way among the cultivated plants and shrubs.

'Do that whenever your mother's not watching and your evening primrose will soon recover,' she said, then lowered her voice to whisper, 'and if you spray the blackfly with rosewater it doesn't kill them. They just fall into a deep sleep ...'

Abrupt and unbending as my grandmother was, I relished her visits. It was a novelty to have someone stiff and cross to talk to, such a refreshing change after my mother's Butlins brightness. I would sometimes force myself to misbehave just so I could hear a raised voice.

'Your shoes are muddy, remove them at once, you mucky pup!' Grandma Rita would shout, when I tramped in from the garden. My mother would have said, 'What a lot of mud! You *have* been having fun outside!'

I worked out later that the purpose of Grandma Rita's visits was to pay the rent on the cottage and give my mother her small allowance, which we depended on for our survival.

Nothing was ever said, but I sensed Grandma Rita disapproved of her wayward daughter and the bastard grandson she had produced. My mother never indicated that she had disgraced her family by having me, but I began to realize she had made great sacrifices for me – willingly and without condition, but still she had paid a price for bringing me into the world. There was a sense of banishment about our lives. Apart from Grandma Rita, no other family member ever showed their face. Our Christmas cards were few.

The mystery of my father hung round us like a mist, and I could never forget that this secret lay between us. When my mother smiled at the moon, or cried at the beauty of the Kent sunset, or stared for hours into the log fire, I imagined she was thinking of my father. As a child, I had learnt not to ask difficult questions; as I grew older, either my mother or I became a little more perceptive. Either way, I began to doubt the sincerity of her unstoppable, almost unnatural happiness. Maybe, I wondered, a torrent of misery lay behind it, held back with immense willpower. If she saw me uproot a weed or massacre the blackfly, it might come crashing in.

One damp October night when I was twelve everything changed.

My mother came into my bedroom to wish me goodnight. She sat on my bed, hugged me to her chest and said, 'Promise me one thing. Promise you'll live an interesting life. I don't care about success, happiness or dignity. Just make it a good story.'

'I promise,' I answered, not knowing what she was talking about. 'Are you all right?'

'Johnny, my little love, I don't live my life in the real world. I don't hold with it. I think it's for the best,' she said, as if that explained everything. 'I tried it once and couldn't hack it. Goodnight.'

She stood up, and her petticoats rustled as she walked to the door. Then she looked – not at me but at the clover leaf on my ceiling – and spoke:

'When I am dead, my dearest,
Sing no sad songs for me;

> *Plant thou no roses at my head,*
> *Nor shady cypress tree ...'*

For a moment, I racked my brain but then the next few lines swam into my mind. I answered obediently:

> *'Be the green grass above me*
> *With showers and dewdrops wet;*
> *And if thou wilt, remember,*
> *And if thou wilt, forget.'*

Christina Rossetti was one of the first poets I had memorized.

Later that night I awoke with a start. As I blinked into the darkness, I could hear my mother weeping. She sobbed quietly and without hysteria, the sound muffled beneath bedclothes but a relentless, soulful cry, pulsing into the night, unanswered and despairing. Then I heard the words she was repeating: 'I see him, I see him!'

Eventually she stopped and I fell into a disturbed sleep.

The next morning when I woke up for school there was no sign of her. She had started to lay out some breakfast for me, but had only got as far as leaving a grapefruit on the kitchen table with a knife sticking out of it. Beside it there was a note with another of Christina's couplets:

> *Better by far you should forget and smile*
> *Than that you should remember and be sad.*

I felt very strange about this but didn't know what to do other than make my packed lunch and set off to school on my bicycle.

Because my mother was as she was, I had always clung to routine, whatever the circumstances at home. It was a way of making myself feel safe. I could only assume she had gone out early to pick some berries or gather kindling.

That afternoon I was hauled out of class and taken to the head-master's office. He was behind his desk and Grandma Rita was sitting stiffly in a winged armchair by the fireplace.

'Hello, Johnny,' she said. 'You're to come and stay with me for a while. Alice ... your mother is unwell. Too much *Wind in the Willows*, I dare say.' She tried to sound carefree, but it didn't come easily to her.

'It's just a temporary arrangement,' said my elderly headmaster, Father Thomas, reasonably. 'I'm sure you'll be back here very soon.' He gave me what was intended to be a reassuring smile, and stood up, bent over like a turtle straining to escape its shell.

There was an air of embarrassment in the room, as if someone had made a nasty smell. I had encountered this before, the previous August, after the parish priest asked my mother to wear something more suitable than a bikini top and hot pants to Sunday Mass. Afterwards, the village's horror had been made apparent to me whenever I popped into the shop for a packet of crisps on my way home from school. People practically held their noses.

This current situation was very worrying indeed, though.

'Is she all right?' I asked, old enough to know that the truth was, once again, being kept from me.

'One doesn't often use the words "all right" in relation to Alice, but she is ... happy enough. Just indisposed. It would be unwise for her to attempt her motherly duties at present.'

'My son,' said Father Thomas (a term of address I longed to hear, if not from him), 'how was your mother last night?' He sat down again, indicating that this was no casual enquiry. They both leant forward, waiting for my answer.

By now I was most concerned about my mother. I had no idea what 'indisposed' signified, but it sounded grim, and I didn't want to betray my mother and get her into more trouble by recounting her distressed behaviour.

'She was fine. Great, in fact. Her usual happy self. We read some Sylvia Plath poems before bedtime. Where is she? Please can I see her?'

Father Thomas and Grandma Rita looked knowingly at each other.

'Sylvia Plath,' said Father Thomas, mouthing the name so I wouldn't hear, although I could see him perfectly well. Then he whispered loudly, 'Head in the oven. I'll say no more ...'

'Let's be off,' said Grandma Rita. 'We don't want to get caught in the rush-hour. Thank you, Father Thomas. We shall liaise with the authorities and no doubt be in touch.'

'Yes, indeed,' said Father Thomas, rather formally, rising from his chair a second time and offering an arthritic hand. He shuffled round the desk and his hand now hovered over my head. 'Bless you, my son. God go with you.'

Grandma Rita leant heavily on me as we made our way out of the school towards the Bentley.

'Not a word in front of Andrew,' she said, nodding towards a middle-aged man in a peaked cap who was needlessly polishing the windscreen with a chamois leather. 'He's such a gossip.'

As we settled into our seats, she said, 'Radio Four, please, Andrew. Shall we break into the Murray Mints?'

Apart from this, and the odd tut about the traffic or rude comment about the type of people who lived in Chatham, we travelled to London in silence. We reclined on the back seat, separated by a thick, log-like armrest made of creamy leather. 'Stop shaking, Johnny,' said my grandmother.

Until then I hadn't known I was.

She surprised me by reaching out across the armrest and taking my hand. 'Worry not. I think your mother will recover, and be able to look after you as well as ever she did. And I'm always here, you know. More of a soldier on guard than a guardian angel, true enough, but here all the same.' She turned her head to stare at me. Her shoulders faced front. 'You look so small. But you'll be fine – you *are* my grandson, after all.' She patted my arm, and reached into her bag for another Murray Mint.

At last we reached our destination.

My grandmother lived in a large Georgian house that sat sedately on the edge of Blackheath, like an old-fashioned, run-down hotel looking out to a calm sea. Inside, she showed me to a spacious, rather cold bedroom on the third floor, furnished with pungent, dark mahogany.

'What an amazing view of the heath,' I said politely, attempting to replicate my mother's optimism and say something I thought a grown-up would like to hear. 'It's so beautiful!'

'Beautiful? You don't know its history, Johnny. Have you any idea why it's called Blackheath?' She moved across the room to stand alongside me, eyes darting, scrutinizing every inch like an owl. 'Most of the people who died in the Great Plague of 1665 are buried here – communally, of course. Something like a million perished. This entire heath was one big graveyard. No one can build on it even now for fear of releasing, once more, the Black Death. Poke a stick in and take the consequences.'

'Black Death, Blackheath?' I said, solving the simple riddle.

The view curdled before my eyes. All I could see was the tangled skeletons of those who had died a terrible death all those centuries ago. The fresh blue sky turned yellow and septic.

'I tell you this because of what has happened today. Think of it as an aperitif. It is time for you to grow up and stop believing in Father Christmas. You need to come to terms with life a little. You and I understand your mother, do we not?'

'As much as anyone can, yes.'

'Well, this was once your mother's room,' said Grandma Rita, as if that explained everything.

'Is Mother in hospital?' I asked. I couldn't shake my horror at the thought of the plague and its victims buried just feet from where we stood. I felt more anxious than ever about where my mother was and how she was faring. I was confused, feeling displaced and anxious about her situation and my own, but I could rely on my grandmother to tell the truth. 'How is she? Please tell me.'

'She's having a rest. Sit down a minute and I'll explain.'

I sat down obediently on an overstuffed dressing-table stool. My grandmother walked to the fireplace, laid one hand elegantly on the marble chimneypiece and turned to me. She said gravely, 'There are some mushrooms that grow in the woods called fly agaric or, to give them their full Latin title, *Amanita muscaria*. They are bright red with white spots, very much as you would have seen in the pictures in your storybooks. The sort of thing a friendly elf would live in, if that helps. I'm not sure what ideas of botany twelve-year-olds have, these days. Anyway, those mushrooms contain hallucinogenic properties and are not recommended for consumption. It seems your mother may have forgotten this.' Grandma Rita regarded me with cool but intelligent eyes. 'It's rather painful for you, Johnny, but it's best that you hear it from me. The matter is, no doubt, the talk of your village. You'll have to put up with sniggers and gossip when you go back, but I expect you're used to that.'

High on nature's LSD, my grandmother told me, my mother had been discovered at dawn dangling naked from the clock tower of Hythe town hall.

'Alice has never been inhibited. A blanket was required. The police rescued her and decided that a doctor should examine her without delay.' Grandma Rita saw the look on my face. 'She will be fine. The effects of the mushroom are wearing off slowly but she's not quite right yet. Flashbacks, you understand.' She glanced at herself in the mottled old mirror and touched her grey hair with an unconscious gesture. It did not move. Like many women of her generation, she liked to have it set once a week into a style so rigid it could withstand a gale-force wind. She sighed, her mind clearly occupied with thoughts of her wayward daughter. 'It could have happened to anyone. That's the line I, for one, shall be taking. The countryside is full of dangers. A lamb once exploded next to me. Gas, apparently ... But perhaps some of it is my fault. I should never have called her "Alice" – I may have brought it all on. She'll be getting stuck down a rabbit's burrow next. Always blame the parents. Now. Dinner at eight.' She glided out of the room.

That, it seemed, was all the explanation I would get.

CHAPTER FIVE

I stayed for what seemed like months at my grandmother's house. Life in Blackheath was formal but unhurried. Grandma Rita had a butler, a cook and a housekeeper as well as Andrew the chauffeur, and everything ran like clockwork. She even hired a private tutor to make sure I didn't fall behind with my schoolwork. At dinner each night she gave me a brief report on my mother's progress.

'Alice had her restraints removed for fifteen minutes today. Apart from the chewed skirting-board there was remarkably little damage. Her doctor thinks this is splendid news.'

After lessons in the morning, I would join Grandma Rita for lunch in the conservatory, where she would ask how my studies were going. In the afternoon I would read, explore the house or go out for a long walk, discovering Greenwich Park, Deptford market and beyond, once I'd got the hang of the buses, to Peckham and Camberwell. Slowly I discovered London Town, and was dazzled by all it had to offer. I wandered wide-eyed, through the dark autumn evenings, past the bright lights of Shaftesbury Avenue and in colourful Chinatown. Strangely, my grandmother didn't restrict my movements. She gave me five pounds' pocket money each week. As long as I was home in time to change for dinner, she showed no sign of disapproval. Over dinner she would enquire about my activities and listen as I told her everything I had discovered.

'You've been to Trafalgar Square and didn't pop into the National Portrait Gallery? That's like going to Woolwich and not getting mugged. Shame on you!'

Slowly she thawed and we started to enjoy our time together.

'You have brought great joy into my life,' she said once, head cocked to one side. 'Yes. Joy is the word, I think. Such enthusiasm about the *Cutty Sark* … It's most refreshing.'

As it happened, my thirteenth birthday fell during this time. I was hopeful of a card from my mother, but it wasn't to be.

'There was one,' said Grandma Rita, that morning, 'but I didn't consider the contents appropriate.' She grimaced at the memory. 'She's still not at all well, poor Alice.' Then she smiled. 'Happy birthday, anyway, from me and your mother. Maria has made kedgeree to mark the occasion.

'It was the sixties that did for Alice,' she continued unexpectedly. 'All that permissiveness and whatever … it unleashed a great deal of trouble, unfortunately, and she is the consequence. A product of her time.' She seemed to be thinking aloud. I didn't make a sound for fear of stopping her. This was a rare insight into the past and their relationship. 'I should never have let her go to that music festival when she was seventeen. Before that she was quite a nice girl to have about the place. Clean and well spoken. Then, suddenly, it was marigolds in her hair and unexplained laughter in the middle of the night.'

Just then Maria knocked at the door and entered, carrying a steaming offering that smelt of fish in an elaborate Victorian dish. My grandmother snapped out of her thoughts and said, 'Ah, kedgeree! What a treat!'

Before it was dished up they both sang a high-pitched, vibrato version of 'Happy Birthday' with shrill harmonies for the last, prolonged 'you!'.

'Happy birthday, Johnny,' said Maria, once they'd done. 'You have a lovely day now.'

When she had gone my grandmother dished up the kedgeree, saying, 'This'll put a spring in your step.'

We ate a few mouthfuls, regarding each other as we chewed.

'Lovely,' I said truthfully. Kedgeree was delicious. It tumbled about my mouth, hot and salty, another new experience for me. So far, being a teenager was great.

Grandma Rita looked a little uncomfortable, then took a small box from her handbag and pushed it across the polished table to me. 'This is from me. I hope you like it.'

The box was made of worn tan leather. I picked it up and opened it. Inside, it was lined with grey silk, and nestling in the folds was a fine gold chain with a circular gold pendant about the size of a five-pence piece. On one side was St Christopher and on the reverse the Virgin Mary.

'It was your grandfather's and I'd like you to have it.'

'Thank you, Grandma!' I'd never had anything gold before.

She picked it up and put it over my head. 'He wore it all his life, and now you may do the same.'

'Gosh! Are you sure?' I felt different, a bit like being confirmed. Or maybe my grandfather's spirit was paying me a visit.

'I was looking through his things last night and I suddenly

sensed that he wanted you to have it. We never had a son, and he would have spoilt you, I expect. Now you are thirteen it's time for you to wear it. St Christopher will ensure you arrive safely wherever you go and Mary, the Mother of God – well, she can fill in the gaps Alice might inadvertently have left empty, if you know what I mean.'

'She does her best, Grandma,' I said, bristling at any criticism of my mother.

'Let me put it another way. Mary will take care of your spiritual well-being,' she compromised.

'Good. I feel indestructible now!' I said, clenching my fists and raising my arms in a heroic pose.

She smiled at me affectionately. Her eyes weren't exactly brimming with tears, but they were full of emotion. 'You're a very pleasing young man,' she announced.

'Thank you,' I said. 'And you're a very pleasing grandmother.'

'Shall we go to the theatre on Saturday? Would you enjoy that?' For a split second she looked and sounded a bit like my mother.

'Yes, please!' I had never been to the theatre before, apart from amateur pantomimes at Dymchurch town hall, and since I'd embarked on my afternoon trips to wander around theatreland, I'd been desperate to see a proper professional show.

'Jolly good. I'll have a look in the evening paper and see what is suitable.'

She picked up the small copper bell she kept beside her wine glass and flicked it twice. When the butler had delivered the paper she perused the offerings in the West End. '*Hair* is on, but I fear the nakedness on display may remind us of your poor mother's appearance in Hythe, so that would be an unfortunate choice ... *Hamlet*? No – Ophelia. She's one Liverpudlian short of an armed robbery. *Cinderella*? No, there's a clock in it.'

In the end we went to see the Chinese State Circus performing in a tent on the South Bank.

'As far as I know your mother has steered clear of Chinese men, so there shouldn't be any upset. We don't want any reminders of our mutual embarrassment,' Grandma Rita said, as we travelled up to Waterloo on the train. 'I've always thought that the best thing to do about Alice is not to think of her at all. Her father said that, too, you know, and she was only five at the time.' She gazed out of the rain-splashed window and said nothing more until we arrived.

'I hope there aren't too many children there,' said Grandma Rita, springing to life as we got off the train and pushed our way through the crowded station.

'Don't you like children?' I asked. She had never seemed to like me much before I came to live with her.

She considered the question seriously, then smiled almost apologetically. 'Well, if I'm being honest, not little ones, no. I don't consider you a child any more, by the way. Children expect you to be perfect and the pressure to fulfil this fantasy is too much. After thirteen years with your mother you should have realized the truth.'

The show was an energetic display of gymnastic tumbling and choreographed acrobatics. I was enthralled. From the moment the music started my heart was racing. I couldn't take my eyes off one particularly handsome young acrobat. I was rather surprised to find that whenever he came on stage I felt an exciting tingle in my loins. He was wonderful, I thought. Not only was he a splendid gymnast but he was very attractive. My eye was never drawn to the girl performers, I noted, no matter how dainty their ankles or bendy their spines.

We clapped and cheered our way through the show. As we watched a female contortionist dangling from a rope, pulling her legs up behind her and flipping a calf over each shoulder, Grandma Rita leant over to me and said, 'Goodness. I can't even get my tights on in the morning.'

Afterwards we travelled back to Blackheath and sat in the kitchen drinking tea and eating muffins with Parmesan.

'Mother always says that cheese before we go to bed will make us dream,' I said.

'And what will you dream about?' she asked me.

'Chinese men bouncing off trampolines,' I said, without hesitation.

'Then take off your St Christopher before you go to sleep. You never know where such dreams might lead at your age.'

'Thank you for a lovely day, Grandma.'

'You're very good company, Johnny. I shall be sorry when you go. The doctors say your mother's almost better. You'll be able to go home soon, it seems.'

She looked so sad it didn't seem right to be too thrilled at the news, but I was glad to hear I'd soon be seeing my mother again. I'd missed her desperately, despite the security, comfort and stability of life in Blackheath. 'Really? I can go home?' I thought of the cottage and my little bedroom, and longed to see them again.

'In about a week.' She reached across the kitchen counter and took my hand. 'I shall miss you. For all her faults, you're a credit to her.'

I saw my opportunity. This was the moment to ask the question that was never far from my thoughts. My heart thumping, I said, 'Am I a credit to my father, too?'

Grandma Rita stroked my hair, as if she were contemplating the purchase of an expensive fabric. 'Well, any man would be proud to have you as a son, I'd have thought.'

'Who was my father?' I spoke quietly and clearly, but my voice trembled.

'As far as his identity is concerned … we have narrowed it down to Kent, but there are the cross-Channel ferries, you understand. We can't rule out a European kitchen hand.' She gave a sniff. 'Is there anything else I can help you with?'

I covered my eyes with thumb and forefinger and pressed hard, willing the tears away. 'You really don't know?' It sounded more like a plea than I had intended.

'No. I don't.' She stood up and draped her arm rather awkwardly across my back. I could feel her bony forearm resting on my spine. She attempted a trio of comforting rubs, but I think it bruised her a bit because she stopped. 'Sometimes it's better not to know.'

She was thinking of the kitchen hand, I imagined, and tried not to feel too disappointed.

It seemed that my paternity was destined to remain a mystery.

CHAPTER SIX

By the time my mother's malaise had passed and I went home, I had
been away almost two months. I hadn't seen or spoken to her in all
that time, and our quaint country life had seemed a world away.
I had become used to formal dinners with my grandmother, polite
enquiries about each other's health and bland comments regarding
the weather. I felt older and more grown-up. I had seen television,
newspapers, the great metropolis. I knew of life outside our village.

As a mark of my new maturity I arrived by train, via Ashford.
I was to get a taxi from there. 'Don't hang about in Ashford, whatever you do,' warned Grandma Rita firmly, as she saw me into the
train at Charing Cross. 'You might slip into a coma. People do,
you know. It's a well-known fact.'

I kissed her goodbye. 'I'll see you soon, Grandma, and thank
you!' I didn't stop to discover if she was upset by my departure,
but hurried to my seat on the train that would take me back to
Kent. I couldn't wait to get home: would my mother notice my
new-found maturity?

As it turned out, my mother wasn't the same either. When the
taxi drew up outside our cottage, I was disappointed not to see her

standing on the doorstep waiting to greet me. Perhaps she's busy in the kitchen making our celebratory tea, I thought, as I paid the driver. I hurried down the side path and barged in through the kitchen door. The first thing I saw was that the plants on the window-sill were dead from neglect.

I found my mother in the lounge, wrapped in her overcoat before an empty hearth. She looked up as I tumbled into the room and smiled weakly. 'There you are, Johnny! Is the taxi driver still here? Why not invite him in?' She was pale and thinner than before.

'Hello,' I said. 'The driver's gone, silly.' I kissed her forehead. There was an antiseptic, hospital smell about her. 'How are you feeling?'

'Clean and scrubbed up. Full of antidepressants, antibiotics, and anything else with "anti" on the bottle.'

'Shall I light the fire to warm you up a bit?' I asked. My mother's robustness had gone, she seemed delicate and uncharacteristically bitter.

'I don't know where to begin,' she said, casting a bewildered glance round the room. 'Look at all the dust and cobwebs. And the garden! I know it's winter but it's so dismal. The birds have gone feral. Not one of them came when I called.'

'We'll soon get everything back to normal, don't you worry,' I reassured her, as I rolled up some newspaper to build a fire.

I was happy to be home and overjoyed to see my mother, but she wasn't her usual self by a long chalk. I was sure that if I could just get our cottage neat and tidy we would both feel more comfortable. I enjoyed the challenge and the responsibility. Mother didn't have much energy, it seemed, so while she rested I dusted and swept, cleaned windows and made the place as warm and cheerful as I could. I changed the sheets, aired the bedrooms and cycled to the village shop for some provisions.

From time to time I checked on my mother. She wasn't very chatty, but once she managed to quote Yeats to me:

> *'Move most gently if move you must*
> *In this lonely place.'*

It was from 'Long Legged Fly' and I couldn't remember the next line, but I thought it was something to do with being part woman and part child, so I felt it unwise to complete the poem anyway.

By eight o'clock that evening, when we sat down to a bowl of soup and warm toasted rolls, everything was cosy and clean. My mother had had a bath and changed into a cream lace blouse with a ruffled red polka-dot skirt. Sitting by a roaring fire, rubbing her hair dry with a towel, she gave a contented sigh. 'Ah, thank you, Johnny … thank you.' Her smile was wide and heartfelt.

I felt the warm glow of satisfaction at a job well done when, after tea, she looked into the fire and recited a poem of lighter sentiment:

> *'There is so much good in the worst of us,*
> *And so much bad in the best of us,*
> *That it hardly becomes any of us*
> *To talk about the rest of us.'*

I laughed. 'That's a new one. Who's it by?'

'My favourite,' said my mother. 'Anonymous.'

I felt relief wash over me. It seemed the worst might soon be over and we could begin to be happy again.

*

Over the next few weeks my sole concern was my mother's recovery. I cooked us a hearty breakfast before I went to school each day and rushed home afterwards. Then we would stay inside in the warm, reading together and occasionally listening to a play on the radio. Like my mother, the house plants filled out slowly and began to flourish again. A social worker from the hospital visited now and then, checking that medication was being taken and that family life was progressing along acceptable lines. I was delighted to see the colour returning to my mother's cheeks and to hear her laugh once again at the antics of a ladybird or the impertinence of a sparrow.

Outside our happy home, though, things were not so rosy. I already knew from the whispers and titters at school that my mother's naked ascent of Hythe town-hall clock had not been forgotten.

Boys on the bus, knowing of my fondness for poetry, would sing unkindly:

'Hickory, dickory, dock,
Whose mum ran up the clock?
Johnny's ma forgot her bra,
Hickory, dickory, dock!'

Within the village community it was less of a laughing matter. Mental illness was clearly regarded by some with great suspicion.

'I hear they've allowed your mother home, then,' said Mrs Brampton, one of our local busybodies, outside the post office one day.

'Yes, thank you. She's doing fine.'

'Don't thank me, young man. Our Bible-studies group has been praying for her – praying they'd leave her in there and throw away the key!'

I wanted to protect my mother from these malicious remarks, and that was easy while she remained at home in isolation. But within a few months she was as robust as she had ever been, and as spring came and nature began to awaken, there was an added glint in her eye. Late one night I found her standing by an open window, inhaling deeply. She held her breath for thirty seconds, then exhaled through her mouth, letting out an animal groan. 'Aaaeeuugh!'

'Are you all right?' I asked, afraid a relapse was heralded.

'Never better, sweetness. The marsh … it's calling me! Listen!'

Indeed, I could hear a strange, goose-like croak in the distance. My mother had always had a passion for Romney Marsh, and didn't much care for life outside it. Ashford, the nearest town, she declared dull and suburban, and she loathed supermarkets with a passion. We grew our own vegetables and got our eggs from the six new hens that clucked about the garden like mini Dora Bryans. Where possible everything, from logs to loganberries, was born and bred on the marsh. We were organic before the word had been invented.

The next morning Mother dusted down her bicycle and was off, as excited and bubbly as if she were to be reunited with a long-lost love. Our roles now somewhat reversed, I worried about her all day but, flushed and invigorated, she made it home about six o'clock, celery and watercress sprouting from the basket attached to her handlebars. She was back to normal. Or so I thought.

I enjoyed school and was moderately good at all subjects, but I had become so used to being responsible for everything at home that I was a little bemused by authority when I had the misfortune to encounter it. If I was told off at school, I raised my eyebrows and smiled – but I wasn't told off very often. It wasn't in my nature to be rebellious so I didn't clash with authority, which helped to disguise the fact that I had no respect for it whatsoever.

Besides, my mother's illness and curious behaviour were common knowledge. I sensed that the teachers were particularly kind and tolerant towards me on account of the 'situation' at home.

It took a while for the rumours to reach me – rumours that my mother would leave her bicycle in a hedge if a shirtless farmhand caught her eye. Then she'd trudge across the field to reach him, discarding her clothing as she went. The boys at school teased me about it, of course. I defended my mother's honour in a couple of playground scraps, but my informers were full of admiration rather than scorn. They were hoping I'd invite them over so they could see what a brazen hussy looked like.

Then she was said to have been spotted emerging from behind a haystack with three 'Folkestone-type lads'. That she had come home a few nights previously and asked me to help her pick out the straw clogging her bicycle chain seemed to back up the story. And there was straw in the bath plughole next morning, too.

It was true, then. Mother had rediscovered the free love and going-with-the-flow she had found in her youth – and after her breakdown she went with the flow in a big way, seemingly at the mercy of her sexual desires.

The village was scandalized. She had always had a reputation for strangeness, but now she was regarded as little short of a loose-moralled nutcase. The shops along our modest high street were abuzz with sharp intakes of breath and the hurried exchange of fresh information, and always fell silent when my mother and I walked in.

Mother wasn't bothered to find herself the subject of village gossip. 'I always have been. It's nothing new. Pardon me for not having a blue rinse and cobwebs between my legs.'

As a consequence, I wasn't bothered either. I knew that my mother was part of nature, so whatever she was doing must be natural. When the winter cold kicked in and the marsh was bleak and windy, she enticed men home to do the deed. 'This is Peter,' she'd say to me, or 'Meet Bob,' or 'Charlie's come round to inspect the joists,' while she pulled some bewildered-looking man into the sitting room. 'Why don't you go and change your library books?'

I was a bit put out that she didn't have as much time to spend with me as she used to, but I was of an age now when I wanted to lock myself away and play records anyway.

She applied the same come-one-come-all approach to men as she did to her garden. If it was green she'd nurture it, if it had feathers she'd feed it and now, if it wore trousers, she'd show it a good time.

I grew accustomed to my mother's menfriends and their frequent visits. I was fascinated by her never-ending quest and the variety of booty she brought back. After all, the village was agog and I had a ringside seat. I was even quite proud. If my mother did something, she did it well.

It was with a curious synchronicity that my mother's nymphomania coincided with my own sexual awakening. But while she was bright and blatant about her activities, puberty had darkened my private thoughts. They were as salacious as any other teenage boy's, but I was confused: was I going through a phase or was I a homo? I didn't think about girls sexually. I tried to, but nothing happened as it did when I thought of boys. Meanwhile hair sprouted in all sorts of places and my penis grew and grew. I locked myself into the toilet several times a day to check its progress.

Growing fast, clear-skinned and happy despite, or maybe because of, my secret gay fantasies, I was a sporty youngster, gregarious and handsome. Inspired by the outing with my grandmother to the Chinese State Circus and the lithe athlete who'd caught my eye, I spent what little spare time I had at the athletics club and found I was particularly good at the horse and the rings. I knew I enjoyed being among those well-honed young men, and I was aware that I looked forward to the showers – but I hadn't yet joined the dots.

I became best friends with a classmate called Vincent, the curly-haired, rough-and-ready, yet roguishly good-looking son of a family from Essex. They lived in a mock-Tudor house in a much-loathed new estate on the outskirts of the village. His mother – Vincent referred to her as 'my old lady' – drove a sports car while wearing a head scarf with dark glasses, and although he never said as much, I guessed that his father was spending a few years in prison. Together we talked about our absent fathers and the responsibility we felt towards our mothers. Most of all we talked about girls and sex. Or Vincent did.

'I can't wait to shag a bird.'

'Me too,' I said.

'Beverley Dean let me feel her tits.'

'Me too.'

'I'm gonna finger her next time.'

'Me too.'

'Do you want to see a dirty magazine? Look at this bitch. She loves taking it up the arse.'

'Me too,' I said, then hurriedly corrected myself. 'I mean, er, wow!'

Vincent gave me a suspicious look and put away the magazine.

With his cheeky grin and laddish swagger, Vincent had a starring role in my sexual fantasies, but although we sometimes stayed at each other's houses, and my mind was filled with all sorts of fruity scenarios, I didn't dare touch him. From his frequent comments about queers and poofs, I got the distinct impression that my attentions would be violently rebuffed.

My heart would sink when he suggested we hang out at the village bus shelter – a mecca for local teenagers. Vincent would chat up one of the girls, back her against the graffiti for a snog and a grope. I was so worried my jealousy would show that I would slouch off home before a girl made a move on me.

By the time I was sixteen I knew for sure where my feelings lay. I was gay and that was all there was to it. But how on earth was I going to meet a like-minded lad while I lived in a quiet Kentish village?

Little did I realize that an innocent stroll down to the post office one Saturday morning would answer that question, and awaken enough powerful emotion to last me a lifetime.

CHAPTER SEVEN

On that sunny spring morning, I was doing some shopping for my mother at the village post office and I took the opportunity to buy myself an ice lolly. I lingered outside the post office, working away at my raspberry Mivvi, idly seeing how much of it I could get into my mouth without gagging, when my eye was caught by a printed card in the window. There were plenty of others alongside – mostly scrawled in near-illegible biro and advertising an old fridge, a car or a cot for sale – but this one stood out. It was printed on thick cream card with a gold embossed crest at the top:

Wanted: Enthusiastic youngsters required to work as weekend gardeners. No experience necessary, training will be provided. Apply the Head Gardener, Thornchurch House.

My interest was pricked. I knew a lot about plants from helping my mother. Besides, Thornchurch House was the oldest and grandest residence in the village. Sitting high above us mere mortals on a majestic hill, it was painted a pale yellow, had a sweeping drive leading up to it, and grand pillars on either side of a large, oak double front door. The Thornchurches had lived there for generations, surrounded by their ample acreage of farm- and woodland. The current lord and lady were decidedly aloof, seen once in a while driving through the village in a Land Rover or Daimler; they never stopped for a chat with anyone. They seemed to think of us villagers as their inferiors and were so intimidating that if they ever pulled up outside the post office we would scatter out of their path like the pheasants they shot in the fields.

Every Sunday Lady Thornchurch was to be seen in church, sitting in the pew reserved for the family, and giving off the cold, heartless air of the fervently religious. After the service, she shook hands curtly with the vicar but never lingered, although some of the more aspirational village ladies bobbed hopefully into her line of vision, trying to engage her attention. She wore a fur coat – a mortal sin to my mother, who hissed whenever Hilary Thornchurch's name was mentioned. Lord Thornchurch was never seen in church but he once opened the village fête, and was a tall, stately, handsome man, as one would expect a lord to be, but brusque and standoffish.

There were two Thornchurch offspring, a son and a daughter, but they were not allowed to play with the village children and seemed to have been away at boarding-school since they were about five. They were posh and mysterious. Regina, the eldest, was now working in London at a Mayfair art gallery, and Timothy was finishing his A levels at Eton.

I read the card in the post-office window again. Here was an opportunity to get a glimpse inside the closed aristocratic world that lay behind the huge wrought-iron gates, and it appealed to me. Some pocket money would be welcome too, and I rather fancied the idea of myself as a son of the sod, sowing seed in the fertile earth.

I finished my lolly, dropped the stick into the bin and decided that I would write to the head gardener that very day.

Before long I was interviewed for the position, and the Sunday after that, I was set to weeding the flowerbeds adjoining the stables. It was a fresh, late-spring morning and I was chopping away dead daffodil leaves when I heard someone approaching. I stood up, secateurs in hand, and turned round.

I saw a tall, beautiful boy with curly blond hair, piercing blue eyes and full lips. His eyes flickered as he looked me up and down. 'Hello. I'm Timothy Thornchurch,' he said. 'What are you doing?'

'I'm Johnny,' I said. 'I'm gardening.'

He hadn't needed to say who he was – I already knew. I'd seen him once or twice, sometimes as a shaggy mop of blond hair in the back of a speeding Daimler, and once larking with his pals by the canal during the annual village raft race. He was fit and muscular, and I'd admired him from afar but never thought of talking to him. After all, I was a simple country lad and he was a sophisticated public-school boy, boarding at Eton in term-time and shut away in the grandeur of Thornchurch House during the holidays. Although we were almost the same age and hailed from the same place, I had barely given him a second thought. Before now I had never looked into his eyes. Even if I had, he was way beyond my reach – not that I was reaching.

Now he stood in front of me in all his patrician glory. We stood five yards apart but remained motionless and stared for an inordinate amount of time. Then, almost unconsciously, I imitated one

of my mother's flirtatious little tricks: I licked my lips, pushed out
my chest and half smiled. A moment later, Timothy said carelessly,
'See you around, perhaps, Johnny,' and walked off.

I returned to my work and started to hum with excitement.
Delightful chills were thrilling me all over. He was the most desirable thing I'd ever laid eyes. Steady on, I thought. Timothy
Thornchurch wouldn't be interested in me in a million years. After
all, I was a nobody, someone employed to weed the garden – and
not the whole garden at that. This wasn't *Lady Chatterley's Lover*,
I reminded myself.

But a few hours later, as I was walking down the poplar-lined
driveway on my way home, he pulled up in a battered Land Rover.
'Do you live in the village, Johnny?' he said, with a grin. 'Hop in,
I'll give you a lift.'

'Thanks. I live in Cherry Lane.' I climbed in next to him, and
we roared off down the drive.

Over the sound of the engine Timothy said, 'I'm going to
check the sheep on the knoll. Do you mind if we go up there first?
Then I'll take you home.'

'That'd be great,' I said, trying not to sound too enthusiastic.
The idea of spending time with this beautiful boy enthralled me
and sent quivers of pleasurable anticipation right through me.
'Sheep are … lovely, aren't they?'

He gave me a bemused sideways look. 'I don't know if
"lovely" is the word. One got her head stuck in a fence the other
day. They're too stupid to pull backwards.'

'You'd think Mother Nature would tell them to do that,'
I said, anxious to agree with him.

'No fences in the wild, I suppose,' he said. His voice was posh,
and with a languid, confident drawl that I guessed must come

from his school. My own accent wasn't as rural as it might have been – my grandmother's influence – so I didn't feel awkward. Besides, Timothy was friendly enough.

I had the curious tingling feeling that something was about to happen, though I couldn't guess what it might be.

He parked on the grass verge of a narrow country lane where the trees formed a green canopy overhead. We got out of the Land Rover, climbed over a stile and made our way across several fields.

'All this is ours,' Timothy said, with a careless wave. 'I don't know where the boundary is but it's pretty much as far as you can see.'

'Goodness.' I tried to imagine what it must feel like to own everything within sight, but it felt too strange. How could anyone own hedges and trees, fieldmice, clouds and the wind? I knew what he meant – the land itself – but he seemed to imply that every last thing on it belonged to his family and I didn't see how that was possible.

We walked in companionable silence until we reached one of the local landmarks: a craggy, ancient burial mound, grassed over and dotted with rocks, ferns and sheep droppings.

'Is this yours too?' I asked as we climbed up it.

He shrugged his shoulders. 'Not sure. Probably.'

When we reached the top we looked out across the woodlands to the marshes and the still, grey sea in the distance.

'So, Johnny, what about you? What do you plan to do with your life?' he asked. 'Are you going to be a gardener?'

'I don't know, really. I'm not very good at anything. If I was a sheep I wouldn't have to do anything at all, just eat grass all day and sit in the shade in the summer. That would suit me.'

'You could be a hippie. That's the nearest you'll get. Smoke grass and sit in the shade.'

'That sounds nice, but I suppose I'll have to earn a living somehow. Make some money to look after my mother. We live together, just the two of us.'

Timothy looked envious. 'You're lucky not to have it all planned out for you. You have the freedom to do anything you like, be anyone you want to be. I have to fulfil expectations, or else.' He gazed out to sea, then talked quietly, intensely, as if he was reciting a boring list. 'It's been drummed into me. Oxbridge, the law or politics, marriage, children, keep the family name going, inherit the estate, continue the lineage ... Everything must be just as it's always been. Nothing less will do.'

'But isn't it nice to have money?' I ventured. 'It must be lovely to be rich.'

'You'd think so – but it's strange how little it matters when you're unhappy.' He sat down suddenly on the grass. 'Do you have to rush off? Why not sit here for a bit and talk to me? I've got nothing to do at home.'

I'd have cancelled a date with Tom Cruise to be next to him for five minutes. I sat down, already alive to his physical nearness in a way I had never been to anyone else's. I inhaled surreptitiously. He had a grown-up smell, a combination of furniture polish and russet apples. 'I've got nothing to do either,' I said.

'What makes you happy, then?' asked Timothy, as if he already knew the answer.

'Oh, well ...' I was desperate not to say anything stupid.

'Have you got a girlfriend?'

'No.'

'Ever had one?' I shook my head, wondering where this was leading.

'Have you ever been kissed?' he asked softly, looking away from me, fiddling with a bit of flint and digging it into the ground.

'No.'

'Would you like to be? Because I've got the strongest urge to kiss you right now.' He spoke casually.

A delicious shiver ran right down me. 'Feel free,' I said. 'Try it.' At last he turned to me.

We were sitting close enough for him to kiss me from where he was, but he took his time. First he smiled, then an arm reached behind me and stroked the back of my head. He pulled me towards him, his face angling itself to the right slightly so our noses didn't bump. Just before his mouth touched mine, his blond curls fluttered across my eyes like a dragonfly. I shivered as the kiss began. It was the softest, sweetest feeling. At first his lips brushed across mine from side to side. Then they pressed against me as he held my head firm. His tongue darted quickly into my mouth, but once there it began to swirl and wiggle, cajoling mine into activity too, until they were writhing about like two lizards having a mudbath.

He pushed me on to the rough grass, and in the process slid down to my neck, which he bit and nibbled, not stopping even when I arched my back and giggled. Breathless, I opened my eyes and the sky was a brighter blue than it had been before.

After I don't know how long, he rolled off me and we lay panting side by side.

'That'll do you for starters,' he said, eventually.

Starters? I thought. Already I knew that my life would never be the same again. The implication that a main course might follow was, well, mouthwatering.

Timothy jumped to his feet, as casually as if we had been sunbathing. 'Come on,' he said. 'I'll drop you home, if you like.'

Once up and strolling across the fields, we were again teenage boys who had only just met. Back in the car I wanted to stroke his thigh or hold his hand, but somehow I didn't dare. The only hint of what had happened between us was the wink he gave me when I jumped out in front of the cottage. 'See you soon, Johnny,' he said with a big, open-mouthed smile.

Later that night I lay in bed drumming on my lips with my fingers to bring back the electrifying tingle I had felt on the knoll. I couldn't sleep and I couldn't stop smiling even when I did. I woke up with my face aching, my heart fluttering, after blissful dreams of Tim kissing me, then kissing me some more. He filled my thoughts. I could think of nothing but him. What would happen next? Had that kiss been a moment of madness or the beginning of something wonderful? Never having been in a romantic situation before, I didn't know the rules. I just knew I wanted another kiss.

The week passed with me dreaming of Tim and writing his name over and over again in biro on my school exercise books: Timothy Thornchurch, Timothy Thornchurch, Timothy Thornchurch ... or 'TT for JD', our initials enclosed in a heart. I was madly in love. I didn't care about anything else.

'You're looking bright and cheerful, my little fig,' my mother commented, the night before I was due back at Thornchurch House. We were doing the washing-up together and I felt as though I was floating a foot above the floor. 'Your eyes are shining, your cheeks are pink and ... hold out your hand – yes, you've got a tremor in your fingertips.' She threw down her dishcloth and gripped my shoulders. 'Are you in love, my sweet?' She searched my face for an answer and, finding one, declared, 'Praise the Lord!'

I blushed violently. While I longed to talk about Tim, I was agonized by the thought of admitting that I was in the grip of a full-flown passion.

'Who is she?' asked Mother. 'Anyone I know?'

I shook my head, still scarlet and unable to say a word. I knew she wouldn't mind a bit if I said it was a he, rather than a she, but I still couldn't bring myself to say anything.

She smiled kindly. 'Oh, darling, how lovely. Isn't it gorgeous? Like a delightful itch you just long to scratch, even though it's so nice it hurts. Well – enjoy it. And remember what Laurence Hope says.

> *'For this is Wisdom; to love, to live,*
> *To take what fate or the gods may give,*
> *To ask no question, to make no prayer,*
> *But to kiss the lips and caress the hair ...'*

The following Sunday I arrived at Thornchurch House at nine a.m. on the dot.

'You're keen,' said the head gardener. Little did he know. Clearly impressed, he asked if I'd like to work full-time during the summer. This seemed a very good idea and I accepted with alacrity. He put me to work clearing out an old barn and stacking some elm logs ready for winter. The barn was situated away from the main house, but although I kept a lookout there was no sign of Tim. It wasn't until mid-afternoon, feeling bereft as I swept the last of the sawdust and twigs into a neat pile, that I heard someone clear their throat behind me.

I spun round and there was Tim, wearing white cricket trousers and a creased grey and white striped shirt. He looked beautiful, of course, even more so than I remembered. He was squinting in the sunlight, and his skin was peach-like, with a dusky golden glow. He gave me a big, crooked smile with a sapphire flash from his eyes, and my stomach did eighteen somersaults in quick succession.

Despite my reaction to his presence, I tried to appear casual and not as though I had dreamt of him every waking moment – and sleeping moment, come to that – since he had kissed me.

'Oh, hello, Tim,' I said lightly, as though he was the last person I'd been expecting to see. 'How are you?'

'I'm good, thanks. Exams all done. It's holiday time!' He did a mad Aboriginal dance to show how happy he was.

I laughed. 'Holiday for some,' I said. 'I haven't broken up yet. And then I'm going to be working all summer.' Tim's face fell. That was a good sign, I thought, heart racing. I added meaningfully, 'Here in the gardens.'

'Cool,' said Tim. He gave a contented smile, as if a plan was falling nicely into place. He stepped forward and gave my shoulder a gentle push. I felt the heat of his hand, and the desire behind it. 'You finishing soon?' he asked.

'Five o'clock,' I answered.

'Meet me in the old summerhouse down by the pond?'

'Sure. See you then!' I smiled back at him. His touch had made me giddy with excitement. I turned back to my sweeping to hide my burning cheeks. I heard him chuckle as he left. 'See you later, Johnny.'

The next two hours were the longest of my life. I willed the time to pass but it seemed to take for ever. At last the head gardener dismissed me and I slipped away, not to the gates but towards the pond and the old summerhouse.

When I got there Tim was waiting, sitting on the creaking old veranda, swigging from a bottle of red wine.

'Try some of this,' he said, without any preamble. 'It's Daddy's Beaujolais. It'll put hairs on your chest.'

Nervously I sat next to him on the rickety wicker sofa and took a swig from the dark bottle. I'd never drunk wine before and I choked on the bitter taste, then pulled a face and wiped my lips on the back of my hand.

'It should be accompanied by venison or pheasant,' Tim pointed out. 'Would you rather have a cigar?' From his trouser pocket he produced an expensive-looking packet and shook it until a fragrant brown cigar popped out. 'Daddy's too, from Cuba. Rolled between a virgin's thighs, allegedly.'

I took the cigar and sniffed it. It smelt rather woody and luxurious, but I had the feeling it wouldn't be quite so fragrant when it was alight. 'No, thanks. I expect I'll only cough again.'

Tim took it from me and held it between his teeth while he lit a match. He sucked and chuffed on the cigar until we almost disappeared in a cloud of blue smoke. With the Beaujolais in his other hand, he smoked and drank alternately as we sat in silence. I watched intently, impressed by his expertise.

'Now you,' he ordered.

'I'm game,' I said uncertainly.

'That you are, Johnny-boy,' said Tim, handing me the bottle and the cigar. As he did so our fingers touched. He looked at me and smiled. 'Remember me?' he asked.

A few minutes later I was floating pleasantly, intoxicated for the first time in my young life. Tim seemed to pick his moment. As I sank into the damp cushions and my eyes began to close I became aware of him leaning across me.

'Now you've relaxed a bit, I can give you what you came for,' he said. Then he kissed me, far more urgently than the first time.

He pushed up my T-shirt and pulled down my trousers; two moves, swiftly enacted to seem as one. He dragged me inside the summerhouse where an old mattress glowed in the dull light. We kissed, caressed and unwrapped each other. I cannot deny that I gasped and cried my way through my first experience of gay sex. Tim was insistent and considerate, telling me to relax and announcing what was going to happen next, as if he were a doctor. Alarm gave way eventually to enjoyment.

'Good lad,' Tim breathed in my ear, as he built to a crescendo and my cries became sighs.

Now I understood, at last, what it was all about. With the sense of drama that only an adolescent can articulate, I wrote in my diary that I had 'discovered the meaning of life'. This much was sure: I had come home. There was no looking back now.

CHAPTER EIGHT

The summer holidays stretched before us, the whole glorious eight weeks.

'My parents are going to Scotland for the summer, to stay with relatives,' Timothy said. 'And Regina is in the South of France where some friends of ours have a villa. So, we'll have the place to ourselves.'

That was the start of what we called the 'Summer of Love'. Practically every night we experienced the hard vigour of youthful lust in exquisite combination with the frail wonder of first love. It was carefree, spontaneous and of the moment. Whatever was to happen later, no one could take this time away from us. Neither of us had any agenda or expectations, we just devoured each other. Evening after passionate evening, week after endless week, we would meet, our hunger fuelled by the need for secrecy. Even though Tim's family were away, we knew that plenty of others could discover us – there were servants in the house and gardeners outside. It was clandestine and dangerous – we understood that no one else must know – but Tim and I were carried away on a tidal wave of heightened emotion. I couldn't imagine my life without him.

With his family safely out of the way, we were able to extend our playground. Now, when we weren't in the summerhouse, Timothy took me up to the main house. He showed me around, casual about the vast hallway lined with marble busts and tapestries, the endless corridors, the grand rooms with their silk curtains, antique furniture and oil paintings. I was open-mouthed.

'I don't really like these rooms,' he said, hurrying me out, although I wanted to linger. 'Let's go to mine.'

His bedroom was tucked away high in the house, in a turret where a spiral stone staircase would give us plenty of warning if anyone approached. 'This is more like it,' he said. There were bookshelves, paintings, a four-poster bed and a small cast-iron fireplace. I thought it was enchanting, but I found Tim, pulling me down on to the hard mattress, more enchanting still.

After our initial bashfulness we soon felt comfortable and excited enough by each other's presence to waste no time on the build-up to sexual congress. The politeness of our encounters in the fields or the flowerbeds was in direct contrast to our animalistic inclinations in the summerhouse or in the exotic, tent-like confines of Timothy's four-poster bed and its green velvet curtains. We leapt on each other as soon as we were alone, hungry but happy, like ravenous arrivals at an overeater's banquet. I lost all sense of time and all sense of restraint. Sometimes I would come to, only to find Tim blinking at me in wonder. 'Welcome back to the planet, Johnny. I knew I was good but I didn't know I was that good ...'

I had never realized how extraordinarily sweet and transporting the pleasure could be.

I often got home after midnight and my mother would sing-song-shout through a glass of Viña Sol: 'Yoo-hoo, precious, who's a dirty stop-out?' from the sofa, but I said goodnight and hurried up to my room, where I would leap into bed as fast as I could. There I would lie, exhausted but glowing. I was sore, bruised and desperately tired but too ecstatic even to blink. To bring me down and envelop my emotions in cotton wool, I recited a poem to myself, Sonnet XXX from Spenser's *Amoretti*:

> *Such is the power of love in gentle mind*
> *That it can alter all the course of kind.*

'Why don't you invite your new friend to tea?' my mother asked one morning, as she handed me my sandwiches.

'What new friend?' I asked, blushing.

'The one you're spending all your evenings with. The one who's making you such a happy boy. I'd like to meet this person.' Her eyes flickered to the love bite on my neck. 'I'll make crab sandwiches and a pavlova, if you like. What do you say?'

'Er, I'll ask. Thanks, Mum. I'd better go. I'm late.' With that I trotted down the lane towards Thornchurch House.

That evening, during our post-coital chat in the priest's hole, I told Tim of the invitation.

'I expect she found a blond hair on you and put two and two together.'

'Well, romance is her specialist subject. She was bound to notice that something was going on.'

'Yes, but she'll have some milkmaid in mind, not young Master T. What will she say if she finds out?'

'My mother's unshockable. Trust me.'

'I'd be fascinated to meet her. From what you've said, she sounds quite a character. Not at all like mine.'

'Would your mother be horrified by me?'

'She'd have twenty-eight screaming blue fits. Her precious son fucking the gardening boy in the summerhouse?' Tim winced. 'Doesn't bear thinking about.'

'I thought your lot were all at it.'

'My lot?'

'Public-school boys. Aristocrats. Posh people. I thought you couldn't stay away from a tradesman's entrance.'

Tim laughed. 'Perhaps you're right. As long as it's done in private and doesn't interfere with the business of getting married and having children, the upper classes have no objection to buggery. It's not like you're doing anything unspeakable, like using the wrong knife and fork.'

'Nor do the lower classes, I think you'll find.'

'Only the middle class wouldn't have the imagination. That's what comes of living in semi-detached houses.'

'They've only themselves to blame. So, will you come to tea, then? Tomorrow? The pavlova's dreamy.'

Tim paused, then said decisively, 'Yes. I will. Please tell your mother I'd be delighted.'

'How funny!' I propped myself on one elbow to look at him. I was curiously thrilled at the prospect. For all her peculiarities I loved my mother, and part of me really wanted her to meet Tim. I didn't like having a secret from her. 'Just watch out, she may try to seduce you. She won't be able to help herself.'

'Maybe she'll succeed.'

I pushed him playfully. 'Don't you dare, Timothy Thornchurch!'

He grinned and raised an eyebrow.

'You don't really want to sleep with a girl, do you?' I asked. The idea seemed curious and rather repugnant.

Tim brought his face close to mine and stared deeply into my eyes. 'If I had to, I'd think of you all the time.'

'I don't know if that's a comforting thought or not,' I said, unsure whether I was being teased.

Tim shrugged. 'So don't think about it. Mind you, I've heard that the female body self-lubricates. Imagine!'

'How clever.'

'Come on, let's go and get some of Mummy's Russian cigarettes and smoke them out the attic window.'

That night when I got in I told my mother that my 'friend' would come to tea.

'Goody! What fun. And what should I call this "friend"?' she asked.

'Tim. It's Timothy Thornchurch.'

'No less!' she said, having choked slightly, clearly surprised more by the breeding than the sex. 'And would it be wrong of me to serve toad-in-the-hole?'

She didn't wait for an answer but hurried off to the kitchen where she was soon clattering saucepans and Pyrex dishes, humming, 'Food, Glorious Food!' as she did so.

I knew my mother well enough not to urge restraint: the table next day would be heaving with an unseemly spread.

After a day of harvesting beans and carrots from the vegetable garden, I was dirty and sweaty and left it too late to bathe, so I went down to the end of the lane as I was. Tim met me there all spruced up, his hair combed, wearing a smart blazer. We made an odd couple.

'Perhaps I can give you a bath before tea?' he joked. 'And afterwards can we go to your room to play Scrabble?'

Despite the jovial banter I could tell he was nervous. 'Does your mother know the score?' he asked, as we walked down Cherry Lane.

'She saw the love bite,' I said.

'Ah. Oh, shit.'

'Don't worry. She has no qualms about such things. I think she's rather pleased that I'm delving into an area of life that she's spent so long investigating. She understands these matters.'

'Does she have liberal views on abominable homosexual practices and licky-licky lesbians too?' For once Tim was wide-eyed.

'Oh, yes. No problem. She's a bit of a hippie. All love is good love.' It was nice to be impressing him for once.

'You lucky bastard. My parents would have me hanged, drawn and quartered if they knew what was going on.' Tim looked troubled. I saw he wasn't exaggerating. He shuddered, which seemed to snap him out of his darkening mood. He pushed me behind a hawthorn bush and began to kiss me, pulling at my clothes. 'At least I get to be a rebel.'

When we made it to the cottage my mother had laid a lavish tea on a table in the garden, in the shade of some hazel trees. As we walked down the side of the house she was flapping a tea-towel at the branches.

'Hello there!' she said cheerfully. 'I'm trying to explain to Mr Squirrel and his wife that the Waldorf salad is not for them on this occasion.'

I realized at once that my mother was not speaking in her usual *faux*-country burr. All trace of that was gone. She was speaking quite naturally in a posh voice, not unlike my grandmother's.

I could only guess that she had reverted to it in honour of Tim's presence in our humble abode.

'You must be Timothy,' she continued. 'How do you do?' She shook his hand and glanced at me, eyebrows bobbing as if to indicate her approval of my boyfriend. 'Very nice,' she said quietly.

'How do you do, Mrs Debonair?'

'Oh, please call me Alice,' she said graciously. 'I don't qualify for the title of "Mrs", I'm afraid. Shocking, isn't it?' She gave a silvery laugh that I had never heard before either, and held up her left hand to show she wore no wedding ring, then she waved it in the direction of the trestle table piled with goodies. 'Sit down, boys, unless you need to make yourselves comfortable first? No? Jolly good. Now then. Do tuck in.' Mother handed him a plate. 'So, you're the one who's making my Johnny so happy, then?'

'I suppose I must be,' said Tim. 'Unless he's seeing someone else on the side, but I'd be surprised if he had the time or energy.'

'I haven't,' I put in.

'Johnny's a darling, isn't he?' Mother gazed at me with undisguised pride.

'Mother ...'

'Well, you are, sweetheart! I'm only saying the truth. You're my absolute rock and I can't imagine life without you. You must take care of my precious boy, Tim. Do you promise?'

'Of course,' Tim said.

'Johnny's quite a catch, I'll have you know. Not only are you getting first dibs at him, in all his luscious, youthful glory, but he's a kind of special breed.'

'What are you on about?' I asked, worried about where this conversation was going.

'Well, just as Aberdeen Angus cattle are selectively bred for the supreme quality of the steak they produce, Jacob's sheep for their superlative wool, so it is with you, Johnny.'

'And what, might I ask, was I bred for? Am I going to start laying eggs when I'm twenty-one?'

'No. Don't be silly. You were born for love. Top-of-the-range, vintage love.'

'Is he very rare?' asked Tim, looking at me appreciatively.

'Oh, yes, dear. As rare as hens' teeth.'

'Here's to you, then,' said Tim, raising a glass.

'Cheers!' said my mother. 'Now, tell me all about yourself. Everything.'

'I think I was probably born to boogie,' Tim began, but he didn't get any further.

Just then a burly figure in soiled dungarees and muddy boots appeared at the side of the house. 'Hi, Alice, are you busy?' he said.

'Ooh, Frank!' cried my mother. 'I didn't realize it was Thursday! Do excuse me, boys. Needs must when the devil drives.' She got up. 'Let's go inside, Frank.'

A moment later they had disappeared.

'Well, this all looks delicious,' Tim said, helping himself to a crab sandwich. 'Your mother's a good sort, isn't she? I can't imagine my folks being quite so welcoming to you. And I'm absolutely starving ...'

I put some food on my plate, trying to act normally, but I couldn't help glancing up at the house to where my mother's bedroom window was open. I had seen the spark in her eye and knew exactly what was about to happen. Sure enough, just as Tim was sampling a piece of asparagus quiche, the sound of soft sighs, stifled giggles and deep, manly moans wafted across the lawn. Before long, they were accompanied by the squeezebox eeee-aww of my mother's ancient mattress as it was given a damn good pounding.

'I know our cottage must seem tiny to you, after Thornchurch House. It's only eight rooms, including the larder, if you can call that a room, but we've always lived here and I'm very fond of it ...' I was talking loudly, hoping to cover the noises emanating from the house, but Tim had already cocked an ear towards the open window.

'I say – what's that?'

'What's what?' I said, trying to pretend I couldn't hear anything. The game was up, though, when we both heard my mother say loudly, 'Oooh, Frank! Don't be in such a hurry! Ladies first!'

Tim was open-mouthed. He turned a sweet shade of pink. 'Oh, my God! Your mother is ... she's ... um – is this normal?'

Now that he'd guessed, I realized I might as well come clean.

'It is for a Thursday,' I said matter-of-factly. 'Frank is a farmer from Sellindge. On Saturday she has to make do with a supermarket manager from Maidstone. That isn't quite so noisy, obviously. Times are hard.'

'Clearly!'

My mother had begun her yelping routine. I was familiar with this. She sounded like a poodle having electric-shock treatment. It could go on for some time, then turn into a vibrating, meditative bleat and finally a crow's triumphant caw. The whole process generally lasted fifty minutes – I happened to know because that was how long it took to play my *Rocky Horror Show* album, which I reached for each week when Frank arrived.

We tried to continue eating, but it was hard. With every shriek from the bedroom, we giggled. As Frank and my mother reached the heights of their passion, Tim's thoughts were evidently turning in the same direction. 'Can we go to your room and play Scrabble now?' he asked suggestively.

'As long as you promise not to hog the triple-word scores ...' I breathed.

'I promise ... Now, come on!'

We went inside together.

Just under an hour later, four tousled heads and eight quivering legs met downstairs again.

'Thanks for a charming evening, Alice,' Tim said, with his smooth confidence, 'and a delicious tea.'

'Yes, hasn't it been lovely?' said my mother, hurriedly doing up her blouse. 'I'm awfully glad you boys are chums. You must call in again soon, Tim.'

'Thank you, I will.'

By the garden gate, in the deep blue of the summer night, we said goodbye.

'Sorry about Mother,' I said, suddenly awkward, afraid that my unusual home life might have horrified Tim.

'Don't be. She's charming and very funny. You don't know how lucky you are. See you tomorrow?'

'Of course.'

'Good.' He blew me a kiss and then sauntered up the lane, hands in his pockets, blond hair shining in the darkness. I watched him till he vanished from sight.

It was only towards the end of the summer that the mood changed. I had never thought about the future, assuming naïvely that we would stay as we were for ever. But now, as autumn approached, Tim became unusually serious.

'You're old before your time,' I said to him one night, after he had stroked my face. Suddenly he looked terribly sad. We were lying on the makeshift bed we'd constructed in the summerhouse, the old mattress covered with an embroidered counterpane and silk cushions. After the weeks of scorching sunshine and no rain, the musty, damp smell had gone, replaced with a dry herb-and-moth combination. (Face down on that mattress as often as I was, I had ample opportunity to inhale every subtle change.) A candle flickered in its brass holder nearby.

'Love is a drug,' said Tim. 'We're both destined to suffer withdrawal symptoms.'

'Why should we? Why can't we go on as we are?'

'Even if we did, and even if we never felt any differently from the way we do now, one of us would suffer eventually. Unless we happen to die simultaneously in a car crash – and what are the chances of that happening? – one of us will have to endure the pain of losing the other.'

'But that's years away, surely! We'd be old – over thirty at least. It's so far off I don't think we need to worry about it now.'

'It might not be as far away as you think.' Tim rolled on to his back and stared at the summerhouse ceiling.

A horrible pang of fear stabbed me in the stomach. 'What do you mean?'

'I don't know what I'm trying to say. Just that ... Listen, Johnny, our love is a natural disaster. It's no one's fault, no one's to blame, but make no mistake, the end result will be tragedy. For you, for me, for those around us. Maybe for everyone. You and I are bad news. Sad, bad news. That much I know for sure.' At the end of this speech Tim moved into the candlelight, and I could see that his eyes were full of tears.

'But ... why?' I said, suddenly desperately afraid.

'Things have to change.'

'Is it your family?'

'It's ... it's *everything*. It's just all too huge for the two of us to fight, that's all. And I don't even know if I want to fight it.'

'Perhaps if you told your parents, explained what we mean to each other ...'

Tim laughed. 'Yes, I'm sure that's all we need to do. I can just see Daddy being moved to tears by my plight. Oh, Johnny ... you don't understand even the half of it.' He was quiet for a while, then said quietly, 'I wish I could spare you, but it's too late now to stop it. I just hope you'll forgive me. I wish it didn't have to be me who made you miserable.'

'Wouldn't you be miserable, too, if we couldn't see each other any more?'

'Yes – but I'm much tougher than you are, Johnny. You're so vulnerable. You feel everything ten times more than anyone I've ever met.'

'So let's not part.'

Tim groaned.

'Don't dwell on the future. It's so far away,' I said. 'Kiss me. That'll make everything all right.'

'For the moment.'

'That's all I care about. Glorious, wonderful *now*.'

'Celia Johnson, eat your heart out.'

CHAPTER NINE

The following Saturday Tim's lovemaking at dusk was particularly vigorous, and we had barely caught our breath before he began again. There was an angry energy to his lust, as if he was trying to break and batter rather than pleasure me. When, finally, he finished for the second time, he got up immediately and pulled on his clothes. 'This is going to stop now,' he said, wiping his forehead with his crumpled T-shirt, then shaking it and putting it on inside out.

'What do you mean?'

'That was the last time for us, Johnny. I'm sorry, but it can't go on. On Monday I'm leaving for Cambridge. I'm starting university. It's a new beginning and it's the right time for us to say goodbye and get on with our real lives.'

My heart contracted with horror. 'Isn't this real, then?' I whispered. I couldn't begin to imagine life without him. For the last two months, Tim had been the centre of my universe, my whole reason for being. The idea of his leaving me was like the sun being put out – everything afterwards would be cold and dark and terrible.

'No, it's not real,' Tim said. There was a callous note in his voice that I'd never heard before, a roughness that made him sound like a stranger. He wasn't looking at me.

'How can you say that?'

'Grow up, Johnny! Did you really think we could go on like this for ever? You're a fool if you did.' Then he added quietly, 'It's been fun, though.'

I was still naked, lying on the floor. 'But I love you. Don't leave me. I know you love me too – I know it! What about all the times you've kissed me? What about the things you said the other night, about growing old together? Can't I come to Cambridge with you?'

Tim stood up and stared down at me. His blue eyes were hard. 'Don't be silly. I don't love you. This whole thing's been a bit of fun, that's all. I liked fucking you, but it's only what boys do before they grow up and get married.'

'I don't think it is, Tim ...'

'Everyone does it.'

'No they don't! Not like us, anyway! They don't love each other like we do.'

'Don't be so stupid. Shut up about love, for fuck's sake. It's like listening to a girl. It's over. I'm not like you, anyway. I'm not *queer*.' He uttered the last word with a contemptuous sneer.

'Don't be like this, Tim,' I begged. 'I know what you're doing but you don't have to be like this, please ...'

But he turned on his heel and walked out, slamming the flimsy door behind him. Peeling petals of old paint fluttered to the floor.

I lay there still panting, stunned into silence. Then, far too late for him to hear me, I said, 'Remember me,' and I began to cry.

It had been such an abrupt termination that the shock left me staggering aimlessly like a bomb-blast casualty who cannot recall his life before the explosion. I was bloodied and confused. My tears fell and fell, until the dry cushion I wept on smelt salty and damp again.

Eventually I found my clothes and wiped my eyes. I retrieved my bicycle from the hedge and free-wheeled down the hill towards home. The moon was full and high over the knoll. By the time I got to Cherry Lane I was dry-eyed but desolate.

I stumbled in through the door. My mother was sitting by the fireplace, staring at a moth on the lampshade. 'Hush!' she said, waving a hand in my direction. 'I think it's a Purple Prober. Very rare, these days.'

I sat in a chair, unable to speak, still reeling with shock.

Mother chattered on as though everything was normal. 'I shall name him Philip. What a lovely day it's been! Such a busy time of year in the hedgerows. That nasty Mr Jackdaw has been causing havoc. I went out there with my feather duster to shoo him away but I was too late to save the poor robins' nest. Now they're angry with me, as if it was all my fault.' She looked at me, as though seeing me for the first time. 'I wasn't expecting you home. Is everything all right?'

I tried to speak, but couldn't. I felt utterly distraught and the tears welled up again, spilling on to my cheeks to make way for more.

'Whatever's wrong, poppet?' She sat up and reached out towards me. I got up, walked over to her and slumped on the sofa next to her. 'Darling, darling,' she said. 'What's happened? Is it Tim?'

She knew where I had been spending my evenings, and although I had never told her we were lovers, she'd obviously guessed. I had caught her studying me curiously, as if she was watching a butterfly emerge from its chrysalis. She was pleased with me, I felt. I was continuing the good work on which she had made such an enthusiastic start.

'It's all over,' I said, through my sobs. 'He's going away. He never wants to see me again. And he said ... he said ...' My water-works display made it hard to speak. 'He said he's not ... queer.'

In the presence of my mother I became a child again, crying and burying my face in her chest.

'How ludicrous. Only a homosexual would make such a claim!' my mother said, stroking my head and face, comforting me as if I was a nervous dog at a fireworks display.

'But how could he say something so terrible?'

'Perhaps the only way he could deal with his pain was to hurt you worse. Perhaps he has to tell himself that. Perhaps it's true.'

'It can't be ...'

'If it's true to him, then it all comes out the same in the wash. He doesn't want to love you, even if he does. So he won't.' She hugged me tightly.

'But he does anyway?' I was confused.

'Yes. But he won't allow it. It's like dyeing your hair. In reality I might be an unfortunate shade of mouse, but to all intents and purposes I'm brunette. It's what I want that counts. The rules of nature can be manipulated. Love can be denied or impersonated. It's awfully complicated. No wonder Ted Heath's a confirmed bachelor.' We sighed simultaneously. My mother continued, 'Oh, it hurts, doesn't it? But pain is good for you, in a cerebral way. Think of the poets! Suffering is beautiful, you will come to realize. It lets us know we're alive. How else can we be sure? This is a coming-of-age for you, and I'm your proud mother.'

Her words made a strange kind of sense to me. I stopped crying and felt a calm serenity descend on me.

'You're so like me!' she said, as if my tears had been a cause for celebration. 'Far too intense, probably, but at least we experience life, you and I. We don't do bland, do we, darling?'

I shook my head and tried to smile. She had her arm round me and gave me a long, twenty-second squeeze, so tight I could only manage shallow breaths.

'Think of all the people who never feel a millionth of what you've felt for Tim. They're missing out. They're half-wits, effectively. The sort of people who end up reading the *Daily Mail*. We can only pity them. Think of Tim as a blessing in your life, not as a punishment.'

'I'll try.'

'Good boy.' Mother got up languidly. 'What a day for you! I've half a mind to crack open the paracetamol, but I think it's best if you work through the pain. How about something nice from the biscuit barrel? I should be able to lay my hands on an iced ring, if you're lucky. You'll be right as rain in the morning. Trust me.' She patted my knee as she went through to the kitchen. 'Your first broken heart. How thrilling!'

Mother was wrong as, sadly, she often was. It wasn't thrilling and I wasn't as right as rain. For forty-eight hours I cried until I vomited. I was unable to leave the house, sure that Tim would appear at any moment to tell me he'd made the most terrible mistake of his life and beg me to take him back. But he didn't come.

The following week, when I knew for sure that Tim had gone to Cambridge and that he had no intention of contacting me, I fell into a deep depression.

My mother tried to cheer me with little presents and my favourite food, but she couldn't lift me out of my misery. 'It's time to move on, Johnny. You're too young for such a *grand malaise*,' she said, as she cleared away another uneaten dish. 'You don't want to peak too early. Save yourself. The tortured, emaciated look works much better in your twenties.'

She might have been reading the last rites for all I knew. I wasn't listening. I was lost in a spiral of sadness. I couldn't speak.

'Is anyone at home?' asked my mother.

'What am I going to do with my life?' I wondered, when at last the mists cleared enough for me to form a sentence. I sat listlessly at the table, playing with the meal she'd prepared. 'I feel as though everything's over for me. I'm seventeen, I'm gay and I don't know what I want to do.'

'Hmm. That's the whole point of being seventeen. I don't know how much help I'm going to be, darling. I've not done anything with my life – except have you, of course – and I'm perfectly happy. Follow your instinct, that's my advice.'

'I can't stay here.'

'That's a shame. It's so nice, just the two of us. But I do understand if you need to see a little of the world beyond Kent. Maybe you'd like to go and investigate. Go somewhere you don't have all these memories of Tim.'

'Like where?'

'There's a place called London. Young people flock there, apparently. I'll phone your grandmother.'

The next afternoon I arrived at Grandma Rita's. I stood on her doorstep clutching my suitcase, feeling lost and emotional. The butler showed me into the drawing room, where she sat at her desk writing a letter. She stopped, took off her glasses and came over to kiss my cheek.

'Welcome back, Johnny. It's been a long time.' She looked me up and down, as if I were a piece of brisket in a butcher's window.

'Wipe your eyes, for goodness' sake. If you're choosing to be homosexual you'd better get used to being miserable. No need to cry about it. I met Noël Coward once. He covered his misery very well. Wrote a lot of silly songs to keep his spirits up. Let's have some sherry. It's rather good at deadening everything.' She poured two glasses and made sure I'd downed mine before she spoke again.

'Now. Your mother's told me everything that's happened and I think I've found the perfect solution. If you're going to be gay you'd better go into musical theatre. That's what Noël did, rather sensibly. I don't suppose you'll be very happy there either – none of them is – but at least you'll be able to do the splits, which will be a boon in your particular avenue of life, if you call it living.'

Through my fug of misery, I vaguely understood what she was saying. Why not? I was beyond caring. Life was over for me, anyway. She could have suggested I swim the Channel in a straitjacket and I would have agreed.

Within days I found myself filling in application forms for drama schools under my grandmother's careful supervision. I didn't show much enthusiasm so she took over. 'I'm going to say you were one of the chorus of *Oliver!* in the smash-hit Stockholm production. They'll never check.'

I spent the next few weeks sleeping and writing love letters to Tim that I never posted. I still felt grief-stricken, but my appetite returned and a sense of survival kicked in. I had to consider the future, however much I dreaded it.

'You've had some replies. We'd better learn some audition pieces,' Grandma Rita told me. 'I think you'll make a convincing Fool.'

Auditions were duly arranged. I went along nervously, tripped over my speeches and stumbled through my unaccompanied song.

The more prestigious ones sent me packing but eventually I was accepted. 'You'll fit in with us very nicely,' said a lisping tutor at the Lewisham School of Musical Theatre. I was on my way at last.

A week before my first term began, my grandmother announced that she had found me some lodgings near the school. 'Your room sounds a bit Anne Frank, but that's part of the experience. I've arranged a bank account for you and a minimal allowance.'

'Can't I stay here with you?' I asked. I wasn't sure if I was ready to leave.

'Oh, no, Johnny,' said Grandma. 'If you don't go and see what life has waiting for you it will be a waste of your grandfather's St Christopher. You'd better go and pack your things.'

PART THREE

PART
THREE

CHAPTER TEN

The day that my life was to change, I had no warning or sixth sense about it. These things just happen, as if by the decree of a higher force. Nor did I know I was taking the first steps towards my finest and darkest hours.

I had endured another gruelling day at college, tap-dancing, singing Bertolt Brecht songs and being sneered at by Sean, the evil anorexic. I had had enough, so I decided, rather recklessly, not to attend the evening rehearsals for *Oklahoma!*, which was to be our end-of-term show. There were so many brothers in that show I doubted that my absence would be noticed, and I was miscast anyway. Second husband from the left was never going to work for me. So, at five o'clock, I went home to the bedsit on Brownhill Road, intending to pass the evening quietly with a cup of tea and a book, and perhaps a cheeky vodka or two with Catherine later when she got in from her late shift. Now that I'd skipped my rehearsals, I had the evening off.

At about seven thirty the telephone rang.

'Hello, Johnny here!' I said cheerily, hoping it was Madame with some work for me.

'Johnny, it's Miss O'Connor.'

'Ah. Hello.' Miss O'Connor was the principal at the Lewisham School of Musical Theatre. 'Of course, Miss O'Connor. How can I help you?'

'Mr Grey has just informed me that you're not at this evening's rehearsals for *Oklahoma!*. Apparently, without the extra man, the barn dance is a complete shambles. Why aren't you there, Johnny?' The enquiry was polite, but there was a steely, over-enunciated edge to her voice.

'I'm not feeling terribly well, actually, Miss O'Connor,' I bluffed. 'I'm a bit snuffly and thought it would be best if I stayed at home. I didn't want to spread any germs and jeopardize the whole production.'

'That's very thoughtful of you,' said Miss O'Connor. 'But I've already written three times to warn you that your persistent absence from both classes and production rehearsals will not be tolerated. We've reached the end of the line with you. Tonight's absence means you no longer have a place with us. The contents of your locker will be returned to you in the morning. I'm sorry, Johnny. I always felt you had something but you don't have the necessary application. Others want your place who are prepared to work. I regret that things didn't work out for you at the Lewisham School of Musical Theatre, but I wish you every success in whatever path you decide to follow. Goodbye.'

'But, Miss O'Connor—' The phone was already dead.

I went back to my room. It was rather disappointing to be thrown out of drama school, particularly on a one-year course. It didn't say much about my staying power. Even though I'd felt I couldn't face another week in the company of a bunch of dysfunctional theatricals, I'd never thought of leaving. I'd planned to stick it out for the remaining few months, get my diploma and see what happened. And now, just like that, I was history. No discussion, no chance of appeal. I was out, with the briefest dismissal. I could only imagine how exultant Sean and the others would be feeling.

I sat on my bed, surprised to find I was rather hurt. In the minute it had taken me to go downstairs and answer the phone, I had lost my identity. I was no longer a musical-theatre student, just an aimless young man adrift in London and dabbling in the oldest profession.

I couldn't wait to confide in Catherine. She would put an interesting slant on things. My expulsion would appeal to her – she'd be thrilled by the drama. Anticipating our needs – particularly Catherine's, as she could drink like a fish after a late shift – I nipped to the corner shop and bought us a bottle of gin. As she wasn't expected back until ten, I called my mother to share the news with her.

She answered with the usual tentative 'Hello?' She didn't hold with telephones. She seemed to think they were on a par with battery farming and pulled a face whenever hers rang.

'Mummy, it's me.'

'My precious peacock, my boy! How are you?'

'I'm fine and dandy, but I have something to tell you.'

'What's the matter? I knew there was something. I can always tell from your voice if things aren't good. Not more love trouble, is it?'

'No, nothing that bad. They've dismissed me from college.'

'Dismissed you? How silly of them! Was it that tutor of yours? Go and see Miss O'Connor at once. She'll sort it out.'

'It was Miss O'Connor who gave me the boot.'

'Oh. How strange. She seemed such a sensible woman when I met her at your last production, that one where you were so brilliant as Salman Rushdie. Would you like me to call her and remonstrate?'

'I was Badger in *The Wind in the Willows*, Mother. There's really no point in you phoning Miss O'Connor. Her mind was made up. I'm afraid it's a done deal. Don't be upset.'

'Upset? Me?' My mother sounded incredulous. 'Always look on the bright side, darling, that's what I do. Are you going to come home and live in the village? I could put an advert in the post-office window advertising your services as a singing telegram.'

'Tempting, but no. I want to stay in London for a while. I like it here. Maybe I can get some bar work,' I said.

'Oh, yes. That would be lovely. I'll tell Grandma you've had a career change. Hostelry. It's all the rage. I'd better go because the bird table's empty and Sandra Sparrow isn't looking too happy about it. God bless.'

And she was gone.

Since I'd left home my mother had been her bright and breezy self on the phone, unruffled by my departure. She showed only a polite interest in my life and couldn't wait to fill me in on garden developments or village news. I think she thought of me as a migrating swan that would return in time. Nature would take its course. I was glad she didn't appear lonely or depressed and I was only slightly put out not to be missed, even vaguely. As usual with my mother, it was style above content. Everything seemed fine, but I had no idea how she felt about anything other than the local wildlife.

It was only eight o'clock when I heard a familiar knock on my door. I opened the door, puzzled. Catherine stood before me, her nurse's hat crumpled in her outstretched hand.

'Goodbye to Mr Pickering and his turds. I am, henceforth, an *ex*-nurse. Hello, world!' She sauntered into the room, tossing her hat into the bin, then throwing herself backwards on to my bed and shouting, 'Gin! Make it snappy!'

'By an uncanny coincidence,' I said, pouring her a potent G and very little T, 'I myself am now an *ex*-musical-theatre student. I've been informed that my services are no longer required.'

'Well, how's that for synchronicity?' said Catherine, chinking glasses with me. 'This is God's way of telling us to get a life and to ask all those miserable cunts to go fuck themselves.'

'What happened to you?'

'It was a fair cop, I suppose. I was caught red-handed in the drugs cupboard. You know I've always considered the odd bottle of diazepam a perk of the job – well, Sister didn't agree. "Show me the barmaid who hasn't helped herself to the odd Malibu," I said. "Find me a secretary who hasn't got a cupboard at home full of manila envelopes," I said. But Hattie Jacques didn't see it that way. Frogmarched me off the ward like a common shop-lifter. Don't tell me she got that fat without eating the leftovers from the anorexics ward. So I'm out. I'm supposed to be counting my blessings that no authorities were brought in. All for one measly bottle of pills! And a few packets of tablets. And all the other stuff they didn't find out about. Oh, well. There is a bright side, though – I've got enough to see us through to the millennium. What about you?'

'Sacked for failing to make up a set in a barn dance.'

'Pathetic, isn't it? Mind you, there is your handicap in the C-sharp department.'

'It's a wonder I wasn't run out of town sooner.'

'Let's forget them all, the whole dreary pack of them. I know what we need.' She took a bottle of pills from her handbag. 'Valium. Two milligrams or five, Cowboy? I think we deserve a five each for starters. Here you go.'

She tossed me a pill and we took our medicine with no fuss.

We pushed my bed to the wall to make some space, put on an Alison Moyet record and danced our troubles away, thrilled to be thrown together in adversity. What would become of us? As the Valium washed over us, it dissolved our anxieties. Our dancing became fluid and relaxed, and then it became more of a stagger to the bed.

After our fourth gin and tonic Catherine was a little less cheerful. 'You know, Cowboy, I love excitement and living on the edge and all that, but part of me still craves a straight life, a normal life. I like the idea of being a nurse – it's the perfect occupation for a future surgeon's wife living in Hazelmere. And, what's more, I've wasted the last six weeks making eyes at a skin specialist. He's called Alan, and he's single.'

'What a waste. So you've lost your only claim to respectability and my career as a West End Wendy is completely up the Swannee.'

'And there's my wage, and your grant. They've gone too. What are we going to do for money?'

We looked at each other.

'I'm going to say out loud what we're both thinking,' said Catherine. 'Fuck respectability. Let's do that when we're old and decrepit. Right now we're young and gorgeous. Why don't we go full-time on the game? At least for a little while. If we do that, we can easily afford a bit of the good life for as long as we want it.'

'You're mad, Catherine,' I said. It was all very well fooling about turning tricks now and then – but a full-time prostitute? That wasn't the future I'd dreamt of, to say the least.

She produced a copy of the *Evening Standard* and turned to the accommodation pages. In less than a minute, she'd found an advertisement for a swish rented flat in north London. 'Look, we could move in somewhere like this. Kit ourselves out, get expensive haircuts and pedicures. Start treating ourselves like a proper business. Ooh, I can just see it! What do you think?'

We were both sitting upright now, awakened by the startling vision of our future that Catherine was conjuring up.

'Well … I don't know …' I looked at the ad. The flat did sound lovely, and although it was expensive we could easily afford it if we turned a reasonable number of tricks each week.

'That flat's winking at us, Cowboy. I don't know why we're living in a shit-hole like this, anyway.'

She was serious, I could see. 'You're way ahead of me,' I said. It wouldn't do to tell her, but although I could imagine Catherine living the life of a full-time sex worker, I couldn't picture myself doing so.

'I've assessed our options,' she said. 'Yours as well as mine. The events of the day have given us the push we needed. We can do this.'

She was right. Apart from returning to my mother's or finding some poorly paid menial work, what else was there for me to do? I already had one foot in the door. I was young and Catherine would make it fun. 'Well, if it's just for a while, to see if we like it or not – yes.'

'More gin!' said Catherine, by way of celebration.

'No more Sean, no more bedpans!' I said.

'That's the way! You won't regret it.'

When we woke up the next morning, our heads pounding with gin hangovers, I had second thoughts. Did I really want to trade full-time in sex? It was different for a girl. Catherine just had to grease herself up and could lie there all day. I couldn't. I had to get an erection, perform, ejaculate. Young and virile as I was, I had my limits.

But Catherine had become even more convinced overnight that this was the way forward, the perfect occupation for the two of us.

By the time I'd got up, she was already phoning landlords and had alerted Madame to our new availability. She exuded a steely determination, an absolute confidence that we were doing the right thing. She was so firm about it that soon I'd put aside my misgivings and joined in wholeheartedly. After all, I reasoned, why not? It was time to live life on the wild side.

We signed up for a number of credit cards and immediately went shopping for a complete new wardrobe each.

'It's an investment,' said Catherine. 'Some people might request a slapper who buys his clothes at Deptford market, but not many. You need leather trousers, a dress suit, summer casuals and a balaclava. Something for every occasion. I need evening dresses and one of everything from Ann Summers. For the chic-but-still-a-bit-of-a-goer look, I'm going for Jasper Conran. I also need makeup, self-tanning cream and some expensive lotions. We'd *both* better get some condoms, flavoured, ribbed, extra strong, extra small and extra large, a whole box of lube, poppers, home-enema kits and some antiseptic wipes. It's important to be professional.'

'Masks?' I suggested. 'Dildoes, silk scarves, ropes?'

'Now you're talking! All of that stuff. Come on! Let's go and spend some money and have some fun.'

It was one of the best days we ever had. We began in Selfridges' luggage department, where we selected two large, matching pony-skin suitcases on wheels. Then we went to the designer fashion departments and filled them with our smarter clothes, accessories and shoes. Later we caught a taxi to Soho where we breezed through the grubby-beaded curtains of the sex shops and noisily perused their sex toys, butt plugs and dildo selections, then asked if they had anything bigger.

We bought all the equipment and tricks of the trade we could think of, and lots of small, expensive luxuries for ourselves. We peaked in Bond Street where Catherine declared we'd be considered half naked in our new jobs if we didn't have his and hers Rolex watches on our wrists. We finished the day drinking champagne in Claridges, surrounded by our heaving suitcases and supplementary bags of loot, toasting ourselves and our new lives.

We took a flat in leafy Gloucester Crescent, Camden Town, a spacious, Edwardian conversion, with high ceilings, ornate fireplaces and a bidet. It was a big leap from a bedsit in Lewisham, and we reinvented ourselves from the moment we moved in, as if we were Russian spies assimilating ourselves into an alien community. Play the part as we did, we couldn't help pinching ourselves and collapsing into giggles the moment our interior designer or Oriental-carpet specialist left us alone.

'This is a new beginning,' declared Catherine. 'You have dumped your dreary musical-theatre life and I have transferred my allegiance to a more hands-on aspect of the caring profession. From now on, we look after ourselves.'

Catherine was concerned from the start that our 'work' be secret. Our rule was 'No trade in the flat'. Landlord and neighbours were told we did promotional work. Even with me she referred to escort work and 'personal entertainment'. I didn't exactly lie to my mother when I told her I had a good job working for Help the Aged.

From the day we moved in we were determined to play the part to the hilt. It was like being in a film, we decided. Everything must be done for effect, as if our every waking hour was being watched and recorded. We drank champagne for breakfast, caught taxis to Bond Street and staggered into wine bars weighed down with designer purchases, always imagining we were the stars of our own documentary. But after the excitement of the move and our unrestrained shopping sprees, we had to get down to the serious business of finding the cash to pay for it all.

Slowly our earnings caught up with our expenditure. Catherine got plenty of work through Madame, but as there was only the occasional call for boys among her particular clientele I also advertised myself under the name 'JD' in gay magazines. It meant that I strayed from the safer environments of hotel rooms and private parties but in some ways it was better: as well as the transient foreign businessman who might remember me the next time he was passing through, there were the regular users of such services who booked me once a week or fortnight. Regular punters gave me job security and made the whole thing a lot less stressful – there was always the possibility of a nasty encounter every time I met a strange man in an anonymous room, but I was lucky: nothing worse than some stinging whipmarks ever blighted my working day.

I took to life as a full-time prostitute much more quickly and easily than I'd expected. Slowly but surely I gathered wisdom, experience and knowledge. I learnt, for example, that a man's mood might change after orgasm with alarming swiftness: sleep is often the next thing on his agenda. The married man might be overcome by guilt and in a hurry to pretend it had never happened. All this was fine, as long as I had witnessed their ecstatic flash in the pan. That was of ultimate importance to me. As long as they had experienced a moment of pure delight, they couldn't forget me, even if they wanted to.

As time went by I realized I was special. This is no place for modesty – I was a terrific fuck. Even gruff, dominant men couldn't conceal their admiration of my body and the delights it offered. Their eyes gave them away. More-expressive punters went into raptures over my genitals. 'I've heard of the Crown Jewels but this is like winning the lottery!' declared one, before diving in to enjoy his prize.

My beautiful face inspired others, who turned it to the light as if it was a piece of crafted Viennese crystal.

I prided myself on the pleasure I gave my punters, no matter what physical attributes they brought to the party. The appearance of an employer didn't concern me: if he was pig ugly, it gave my performance greater value. A doctor who resuscitates the dying gains greater professional kudos than the one who cures a headache with junior aspirin.

Outside work, I had no desire to enter into a relationship – in fact, I wasn't capable of it. I was still in love with Tim, who seemed to hover over me like some kind of holy spirit.

Since he had dumped me so cruelly in the summerhouse nearly three years before, I had progressed from the hurting and the longing to acceptance of our separation. I put him out my mind as much as I could, although I sometimes wondered what he was doing. His time at Cambridge would almost be over – perhaps he would make his way to London to take up some respectable career suitable for the heir of Thornchurch House. Sometimes I imagined meeting him by chance, in a tube carriage, a café or shop, but he had lived for so long in my imagination now that seeing him in the flesh would have scared me.

Instead, I kept the memory of Tim hidden, taking it out to treasure when I was alone. I trained myself to feel a cold indifference to any emotional stirrings when I met new people. I had confidence now, born of my skill as a prostitute, and found it easy to meet men who desired me for myself and didn't expect to pay for it. When I wasn't fucking professionally, I went to bars and clubs, then home with men who were eager to attempt more than a one-night stand, but I always got rid of them pretty swiftly. And even if, despite myself, I was attracted to someone, the sensation evaporated if he referred to his feelings. A bit of rapture, an occasional heartfelt compliment or plain old-fashioned expressions of lust were acceptable, but if there was a whiff of neediness or a hint of a meaningful stare it was curtains, I'm sorry to say.

As for declarations of love – they were most unwelcome. Any revelations of this nature caused a tickle at the back of my throat that was part suppressed laughter and part nausea. I couldn't get out of there fast enough. I didn't want to know. Love had caused me enough pain, thank you very much. Not only that, my love for Tim still had me in its grip and there was nothing left for anyone else.

I came to prefer my encounters with my clients. They paid for my time, so I was prepared to indulge any fantasy – even a romantic one. If they wanted to talk about love, that was fine by me because it was only an act. My body was their plaything and I would absorb their emotions with brilliantly disguised indifference.

But I had one little habit that had started during my very first encounter with Assam. My last words to every customer were always 'Remember me.' The punter never heard them – often they were asleep. I muttered them quietly under my breath as a parting gift.

'Remember me,' I would say, as I left another businessman snoring on his hotel bed, his great naked body supine on the duvet.

'Remember me,' I entreated the whimpering little man I had flogged to three different sorts of orgasm.

'Remember me,' I whispered, as I broke free of the loving married man who wanted to leave his wife and family for me.

If they remembered me, perhaps Tim did too. Maybe somewhere he was thinking of how great and indestructible our love had seemed. Did he ever recall our embraces, our love, and that it had felt like the most perfect, pure thing in the world?

CHAPTER ELEVEN

'Where are you off to this afternoon, Cowboy?' asked Catherine. 'I've taken the day off. Got to recharge the batteries. I've been fucked fifty ways in the last two days and, boy, do I need to recover. My fanny's like cake mix. Fancy a face pack and some cranberry juice?'

'I can't, I'm afraid. It's my Barnes afternoon. I won't be late back, though.'

'Oh, yes. Your dear old queen.'

'Sammy.'

'Can't let him down. He might be dead soon. Cornering the market in senior citizens, aren't you?'

'The market is there to be cornered. Sammy's one of my favourites. One of my best. And he's promised me a little surprise today.'

'Maybe he's going to shit himself.'

'Sammy's not the sort. He's a gentleman. And very educated. He taught me what talaria are. Do you know what talaria are?'

'I can't imagine.'

'Talaria, I'll have you know, are the little wings you see on the feet or ankles of the fleet-footed messenger god Mercury. And sometimes Perseus and Minerva.'

'Thank you, Stephen fucking Fry,' said Catherine.

In the early days, when I advertised in the trashy gay magazines, I was hired by all sorts. It was a tricky business: time-wasters, telephone-wankers and false-address-givers were commonplace. I learnt quickly to value my regulars.

Older queens soon became my preferred clientele. They had used such services before and appreciated my superior ministrations, the pride I took in my work and the seemingly genuine satisfaction I displayed. I didn't sigh or even appear to notice if they couldn't achieve an orgasm, and I greeted premature ejaculation with celebration.

Sammy was one such client. He phoned me one day and I liked his voice at once: he sounded gentle, well-spoken and polite. 'Might I possibly bother you to visit me at home?' he asked, after the preliminaries were over, lowering his voice as if someone might overhear such an improper suggestion.

'I'd be glad to. Where do you live?'

'Eighteen Castlenau Gardens, Barnes.'

'Lovely,' I said, writing it down. 'Any preferences? Shall I bring anything special with me?'

'Oh, no, no, no. I'm very easily pleased. All straightforward and no nonsense. Just bring yourself. Tomorrow afternoon might be convenient?'

'I'll see you about three, Sammy.'

The following day, a dreary Friday in February, I rang the door-bell of a red-brick mansion block, with a faded 1930s glamour, and

Sammy buzzed me in, then opened the door to his ground-floor flat. He was a tall man who stooped, as so many tall men do, and I put him in his late sixties. He had kindly eyes and a full head of silvery hair.

'It's very good of you to come,' he said, with a shy smile.

I followed him down the corridor, registering his pressed corduroy trousers and the welcome fact that he seemed sober, not psychotic. He led me into a clean but cluttered kitchen-diner and asked if I'd like a drink.

'Just some tap water, please,' I answered.

'I guess you've done this sort of thing before?' he enquired, then sneezed nine times in rapid succession.

'Are you all right?' I asked.

'Excuse me,' he said, then immediately sneezed another seven times. 'You're not wearing Angel, are you? It has a very unfortunate effect on me.'

'Yes. I am. Terribly sorry.'

'I'm the same with strawberries. You'd better have a shower while I clear my passages.'

Somehow this unexpected drama relaxed us.

'That's better,' said Sammy, when I walked naked out of the shower, rubbing my hair with a faded peach towel.

'I suppose it's one way of getting my clothes off,' I said, presenting myself to my clearly appreciative client.

'Most acceptable,' he said, in a deep, syrupy voice. 'Now come and lie down.'

The next hour went by perfectly pleasantly. His sexual demands were very straightforward, his kind eyes clouded only momentarily with lust. I gave of my heart and soul, as always, and the job was done in twenty minutes. After that, we sat chatting easily over cups of tea in his sitting room until my time was up. Sammy counted out my money in twenty-pound notes, adding two extra 'for your trouble'.

As he showed me out, he enquired, 'Would you be available again next week? Same time?'

'Absolutely,' I said. A repeat booking was always a compliment. I had warmed already to this polite, generous old man and felt that the weekly hour would be an oasis of calm in my otherwise frenetic diary.

I was right. Sammy was the ideal client. He was intelligent enough to know that our relationship was fuelled only by the financial transaction, which allowed him to enjoy his time with me without fear of rejection. We understood each other, the deal was mutually agreeable, and neither of us had any complaints.

'Everyone should have a JD in their life,' he mused one afternoon, a few months into our arrangement. 'You fulfil all of my needs, and I adore you.'

I learnt that Sammy was a retired English literature teacher and that, while modest and unassuming, he was proud of his silver thatch. 'Quite a feature, my barnet, in the sixties. I had long hair before the Beatles.' He seemed to be at one with his life, enjoying a comfortable retirement, busy with bowls, bridge and an active social life. But occasionally he felt the need of youthful company and sexual release. Booking me was the way he got it, and it seemed perfectly sensible, as far as I was concerned. I looked forward to my Friday afternoons.

'You're fond of that old man, aren't you?' said Catherine, as I got ready for my trip to Barnes.

'Sammy's as sweet as apple pie.'

'Bit of a father figure for you, perhaps?'

'There's no need for that kind of talk. Ours isn't a father–son relationship. More like a dear old uncle with fuck privileges.'

'Just don't waste too much time on him, that's all. I've spent all the time I ever want to waiting on the elderly. Most of them are as tight as a choirboy's arse. Now get going or you'll be late.' Catherine shooed me away, obviously keen to have the flat to herself.

When I arrived in Barnes, Sammy let me in as usual but instead of letting me lead him to the bedroom straight away, as he normally did, he sat down in the sitting room and gestured to me to do the same.

Was he calling a halt to our arrangement? I wondered, surprised. Or was he about to attempt something unconventional on the hearth-rug?

'Now, JD, do you remember what I said the other week – about how everyone should have a JD in their lives?' he began.

'Yes,' I said warily.

'Well this week, out of the kindness of my heart, I'd like you to visit my dearest friend, my neighbour, Georgie. Would you mind awfully?'

'I suppose not.'

'He's my oldest and best friend. He lives next door and we call each other sisters. A visit from you would do him the world of good. I've been worried about him lately. We've both been struggling with the ageing process, you know, but I fear it's been worse for Georgie. We were cruising companions when we were younger, and we know absolutely everything there is to know about each other. We were lovers very briefly when we first met – for about five minutes – and then became friends, helping and supporting each other through the trials and pains of love and life.'

'I could do with a friend like that,' I said, rather envious.

'Oh, yes, Georgie's the tops, he really is. But we're beginning to realize that the excitement is pretty much over for us. The thing is, though, we still have that gnawing itch for sexual happenings – it's just that the gay scene doesn't seem to want us any more. We're too old, washed up, finished. No, no, we are, JD.' Sammy put up a hand to silence me as I tried to protest. 'Imagine – we were once spoilt for choice, the toast of the underground gay world, and now … Well, we've been put out to pasture. At first we tried to outstay our welcome, lingering in the pubs and clubs, but eventually the snubs became too difficult to bear. We turned to videos, but there's only so much excitement you can get from those.

'In my opinion, sex is an area of life that has to be dealt with as any other, if a man is to stay healthy and sane. That was when I made the decision to hire boys like you, JD, just as I might a housekeeper or an accountant. And it was the best I ever took!'

'Thank you, Sammy, I'm glad I've been worthwhile.'

'You're most welcome. And that's why I'd like to ask you if you'd be terribly kind and consider offering your services tonight to dear Georgie instead of me. He's a bit livelier than I am, if you know what I mean, but he's a darling.'

'I'd be happy to,' I said, rather moved by the account of the friendship between the old men. 'Where does he live?'

'Right next door. There's the beauty of it. We've been neighbours for thirty years. If I knock three times he knows I'm on my way over.'

'How convenient. Well – show me the way!'

'Excellent, excellent. Oh, Georgie will be pleased! And perhaps you'll call in later and tell me how it went?' Sammy's eyes were sparkling.

'Will do.'

I left Sammy's, stepped over the flowerbeds to the front door of number sixteen and pressed Georgie's buzzer, as instructed. The door opened within two seconds. Georgie was a rotund, balding little man of around seventy who had clearly not enjoyed Sammy's blessings in the looks department. He wore blue linen trousers with a short-sleeved white shirt, also linen, and smiled nervously as he stood behind the door. 'You must be JD,' he said.

'And you must be Georgie. Very pleased to meet you.'

'Come in, my dear.'

We went into a flat laid out in exactly the same way as Sammy's, but the opposite way round. It was strange to be somewhere that felt so familiar yet looked so different. It took me only a moment to realize that Georgie had lived a theatrical life – the sitting-room walls were covered with black-and-white portraits of past theatre stars, many of them autographed – '*To darling Georgie, for making me look so fabulous! Much love, Vivien*' – and framed posters of West End shows from the fifties and sixties.

'I was a dresser,' Georgie said, watching me observe his photographs. 'I did all the big theatres, all the great shows. I had quite a following. Yul Brynner wouldn't let anyone else take his trousers off, you know.'

I laughed. 'Talking of taking off our trousers … shall we?'

I went up to Georgie, whose eyes became a little more bulbous and cheeks a little pinker as I approached. He smelt of aftershave, gin and toothpaste, for which I was grateful. A happy, clean punter was always a relief in my line of work: BO and smegma were hazards so difficult to cope with that I would make my excuses and a hurried exit.

(On the other hand, if someone with a fetish requested it, I could arrive sweaty and unwashed for their delectation. A nose would be thrust into my groin or my armpit. Sigh would follow sniff. For a while I sold my own soiled underwear to this specialized group in sealed plastic bags. A lucrative and surprisingly popular sideline.)

'Oh, yes, please ...' sighed Georgie, obviously thrilled, and we went to his bedroom at once.

On that first occasion, the sex would not have been classed as kinky. When he pulled off my boxer shorts he murmured, 'Oh, happy day ...' but I knew Georgie wanted more than was on the conventional gay-sex menu. I could tell almost at a glance the client who wanted it rough and the one who preferred vanilla.

'JD, you're manna from heaven,' Georgie declared, after forty wholesome minutes of wrestling, pumping, jerking and, finally, satiation.

'I might put that on my calling card,' I said. 'Delighted to have been satisfactory.'

'Oh, you were, you were. Sammy's been a very naughty girl, keeping you to himself for so long. I only managed to wiggle out of him what he's been up to when I saw you leaving last week – the wicked miss! Of course, it's shaming to have to pay for it. In his time Sammy's been wooed and won by lords and bishops,' Georgie confided, 'and I'm no stranger to the armed forces. We have tales between us that would have you panting like a queen in a lorry park.'

'I can well believe it,' I said, pulling on my clothes.

'I take it you cater for ... all tastes?' Another little blush crept over Georgie's fat cheeks.

'Oh, yes. All tastes.'

'Goody! Then perhaps we could come to an arrangement ... I'd love to do this again, you see, and if you're coming to see

Sammy anyway ... perhaps you could pop next door for a little rough-and-tumble with me afterwards?'

'I don't see why not. As long as I do Sammy first.' Sammy's impatience to reach his climax would mean I'd have a good half-hour to recover my resources – I had a feeling I'd need them with Georgie.

'Then here's your money – cheap at the price!' Georgie handed me a roll of notes. 'And I'll see you next week, you gorgeous thing.'

'Thank you. Until next week, Georgie.' He closed the mahogany door behind me.

I stood three inches from it. 'Remember me,' I whispered.

'Did Georgie enjoy himself?' Sammy said anxiously, his head poking out of his front-room window.

'Yes, he did. In fact, he wants the same again next week.'

'Oh.' Sammy's face fell. 'I don't suppose you'll be able to do both of us ... I've got so used to our Friday-afternoon encounters and I'm such a creature of habit.'

'You underestimate me, Sammy,' I said gravely. 'I'm perfectly happy to look after both of you. Stamina is one of my selling points.'

Sammy smiled gratefully. 'I'm so pleased! How lovely. Now we can all be friends together.'

The next time I went to Barnes, I spent the first hour with Sammy and the second with Georgie. This time, Georgie wanted me to tie him up and bite his neck. Just as Sammy had hinted, Georgie was much more adventurous than his friend.

As time went by, we fell into a routine. I visited Sammy first, as he was the least demanding. He rarely lasted long, I gave him a cuddle, we had a cup of tea together, I collected my cash and my thoughts, then popped next door to Georgie.

While Sammy was organized and business-like, almost in a hurry to get the sordid proceedings over with, Georgie wanted to savour every moment and made sure he got his money's worth. He'd be excited and a little tipsy when I arrived and I never knew what he'd have in store for me. He got into the habit of handing me a piece of paper with instructions on it when I arrived, and then he would go upstairs to prepare himself while I digested his requirements – burglar, pizza-delivery boy, sex fiend on the run following a prison escape, whatever the mood of the day demanded. It wasn't always sex as we know it. In fact, within a few months it was fairly full on S and M, with verbal and physical abuse, candle wax, clothes pegs, hoods, masks, and so on. Georgie always wanted to go one step further.

After we'd finished and tidied ourselves up, we would go next door to Sammy's for a drink and a chat, which became the part of the evening I most looked forward to. Often, when the weather was fine, we sat out on Sammy's veranda. The old boys would be giggly and relaxed in their dressing-gowns, telling me stories of their youth on the underground gay scene of fifties London and candidly (or, in Georgie's case, bitterly) analysing their current status in the spectrum of gay desirability.

Gradually, through these post-coital chats, I gleaned an insight into gay life in their heyday.

'There used to be a pub in Percy Street that was wall-to-wall guardsmen,' said Georgie. 'I was voted "Fuck of the Week" for two months in a row – and look at me now! Opening my purse before I can open my legs!'

'Do you remember that man called Rob?' asked Sammy, drunk but not delirious. 'He drove a cab, but if he didn't have a punter at the end of the evening he'd drive you home. "I'm not queer," he'd always say, "but I need some relief." He epitomized the type of man I liked in those days. Straight, but willing to engage if all else failed. After a come-on like that you were home and dry ...'

'The glass collectors were always up for it at the Marquis of Granby,' added Georgie, 'but you had to follow them out to the dustbins with two pound notes at the ready. No money, no honey. I remember seeing John Gielgud standing in the saloon bar with spunk on his bow-tie.'

'Do you remember the police raids?' asked Sammy.

Georgie groaned appreciatively. 'Constables in those days knew how to take down a girl's particulars! Those Bow Street boys spit-roasted me in the snug on more than one occasion.'

Sometimes their conversations escalated into animated spats that left me all but forgotten.

'I've been lucky in love,' said Sammy, 'but Georgie ... let's just say the hummingbird of love hovered over her upturned trumpet and moved swiftly on.'

'Excuse me!' protested Georgie. 'I'll have you know that more men have declared their love for me than have for you!'

'But isn't that my point?' argued Sammy. 'I deal in quality, not quantity. Your statement alone points to your foolish promiscuity. *You* cannot sustain a relationship so you move on. It's not a question of conquering and collecting hearts engorged with passion. The pursuit of real love means delving somewhat deeper into the bowels of an intimate relationship than you appear capable of doing.'

'Oh, do shut up. Just because you've wasted your life hankering after the unattainable it doesn't give you the right to pity me.'

'I have no right to pity you. I just have the inclination. Based purely on the observations of forty-odd years. Face it, darling, you're an emotional cripple!'

'You talk about the pursuit of love, Samuel ...' said Georgie. He stood up, moved behind my chair and cupped my head between his hands as if it was an exhibit in a court case and he the prosecuting lawyer. '... but how do you explain *this*?'

'Being in love doesn't mean you stop appreciating the aesthetic beauty of those around you.'

'Around you and *inside* you, I expect you mean,' said Georgie, with disgust.

'I see no point in us trying to score points over each other.' Sammy flicked him away. 'We're both in the same boat, quite literally. Don't be so annoying. We've been round the block enough times to have – finally – separated love from lust. Our lovely JD here,' he gestured towards me, 'must not be confused with the real thing. His carnal deliveries may keep us going, but he's just the irrigation system while we await the inevitable, deadly drought.'

'From the look of your skin that drought arrived some time ago,' spat Georgie.

Sammy's eyes were full of tears. 'You always have confused wit and cruelty,' he said.

So they went on, with their Oscar-Wilde-on-gin dialogue. Every week I gave them exactly an hour of my time each, rarely interjecting, then stood up and said how lovely the evening had been.

'See you next Friday,' Georgie would say.

'I'll see you out.' Sammy would pat my shoulder and lead the way to the front door.

I suspected that the conversations continued long after my departure, never resolved, never producing a victor, never giving way to silence.

'More whisky? You might be dead tomorrow.'

'You might be dead in half an hour, sister.'

CHAPTER TWELVE

'What on earth happened to you, Georgie?' I said, horrified by the swollen black eye he was sporting when he opened the door.

'Oh, don't.' Georgie rolled his other, still mobile, eye to heaven. 'Come in. We might have to be rather gentler than normal tonight. I've been in the wars.'

'What happened?' We sat down under framed photographs of the sparkling eyes and perfect complexions of Greer Garson, Joan Greenwood and Hermione Gingold.

Georgie looked rueful as he crossed his ankles. 'I was feeling a bit frisky so Sammy lent me some of his old videos. His tapes are never quite to my taste – he likes straight men being seduced by gay men, the less romance the better. I favour a story I can believe in. Call me old-fashioned but I like to see car mechanics understandably over-come with lust while working overtime in a greasy garage, or Ancient Greek slaves forced to perform sex acts in front of their sadistic but nevertheless gorgeous young emperor, that sort of thing.'

'Very plausible,' I said.

'Well, I watched a few of these with a bottle of Gordon's London Dry by my side and, after a while, it occurred to me to relive my glory days and go trolling.' He sighed heavily. 'I know it was stupid. Even in my youth, I wasn't exactly the pick of the bunch. I was never as good-looking as Sammy. But I went out pissed and took a walk along the towpath by Barnes Bridge, and when I saw a really lovely big chap, I asked him how about it. It turned out I'd misjudged the situation. He wasn't in the market for fun and games. In fact, he took offence.' Georgie touched his big purple eye. 'Ouch.'

'Oh, Georgie,' I said, concerned. 'Gay-bashed at your age! Why did you put yourself in that situation? You don't need to any more, not now there's me.'

'I know. That's what Sammy said. He said, "The next time you want to prove there's still life in the old dog wait till Friday. JD won't beat you up. For a mere hundred pounds he'll have sex with you and enjoy it. You can't troll down the towpath any more. You're past it." He's right, I am.'

'You're not past it. Coming up towards it, maybe ...'

'Oh, thank you, dear! How comforting.' Georgie leant towards me. 'Listen, JD. I want you to find that animal for me and give him a taste of what he gave me. Would you do that?'

I was astonished. There was a light in Georgie's eyes I had never seen before: a nasty glint of anger and glee. 'But how would I find him? The chances of meeting him are very small.'

'No, no,' Georgie insisted. 'I'm sure he's a regular. I've got a very good description. Give him a taste of his own medicine.'

'I'm going to, mate,' I said. I understood my punters' needs.

'Thank you, JD. You're a star.'

I knew there wasn't a hope of finding the man but it was clearly a fantasy Georgie wanted enacted, so I went down to the towpath and punched a brick wall a couple of times, then showed

Georgie my bloody knuckles. He almost came in his pants. 'Oh,' he sighed, 'you're a marvel, you really are. I shan't forget this, JD. Here – this is a tip for you.'

He handed over an envelope that contained two hundred pounds.

'Just be careful,' I said. 'You might not be so lucky next time.'

'Anything you say. You know how I love it when you come over all masterful ...'

When I got home, I told Catherine the story. She didn't find it as funny as I did, and she wasn't impressed. 'Two hundred is accept-able, Cowboy, but unless they're going to hand over the money they've earmarked for the cats' home I wouldn't waste my saliva on them,' she said decisively. 'Small potatoes like them might do for now, but do bear in mind that you and I have bigger fish to fry. Their days are numbered.'

I felt rather crushed. I was fond of Sammy and Georgie, and didn't like to think of our arrangement coming to an end, but I didn't tell Catherine that. Instead I wondered if anything I did would ever be good enough for her. My own achievements were so often dismissed, waved away with a perfectly manicured hand or snuffed out in an abrupt change of subject. She was hard to please, that much was for sure, but she was like my older, street-wise sister and it remained my ambition to win her approval.

Since our move Catherine's confidence had soared. She flou-rished as a high-calibre call girl. She was passed between business-men, recommended to first-time callers by Madame as 'Employee of the Month' and retained for a second hour by those who had enjoyed the first. The move upscale suited her, and her image evolved from dolly-bird nurse to sophisticated girl-about-town. Her clothes were still understated, but expensive and better fitting, while her makeup became bold but never tarty – russet tones took over from the frosted pastels and she styled her hair in loose ash-blonde ringlets instead of the old candyfloss bouffant. Several times a week she went for expensive facials, and her cabinet in our marble bathroom was full of expensive lotions, scents and scrubs.

'I wax the gash, Cowboy. My Arab gentlemen wouldn't go near me if there was a whisper of a pube.'

Once a month we went to be checked by a private doctor in Harley Street.

'Clean as a whistle, apart from the cystitis,' Catherine would declare afterwards, 'but that's an occupational hazard.'

Another occupational hazard, it seemed, was cocaine. We had long been accustomed to downers like dope, Valium and temazepam, but our new lifestyle required uppers, too, Catherine said. I'd had my first experience of cocaine on the day we moved to Camden. When we had unpacked our meagre possessions Catherine called me into the kitchen where six lines of white powder were lined up on a Tupperware plate.

'Prepare to snort your first line of cocaine, Cowboy,' she announced. 'Watch and learn.'

She inserted a rolled-up ten-pound note in her right nostril and blocked off the left with the forefinger of her other hand. She hoovered up the line with a flourish, then threw back her head, inhaling until her lungs could accommodate no more air. She froze, holding her breath for several seconds, then exhaled luxuriously through her mouth. She stood up, tall and suddenly Amazonian. 'Fucking fantastic,' she said. 'Now you.'

It took me a few attempts to grasp that I had to lower the

rolled-up note to the end of the white line while my lungs were empty. To blow instead of suck was very messy. Blocking off the other nostril and keeping my mouth closed was another lesson. To get the powder up your snout and hitting the back of the nasal cavity with a satisfying thud, an enthusiastic whoosh was required. At last I got a proper hit, and seconds later I was enjoying my first high. I felt regal and energetic. Suddenly I found it terribly urgent to articulate my euphoria.

'Do you know something, Catherine?' I said earnestly. 'You and I are fabulous. Let's face it, we're amazing.'

'I know, babe,' Catherine agreed. 'I've always known it.'

We chattered away, describing visions of our high-flying futures, fantasies of success that led, ultimately, to our joint master-plan for the saving of mankind. We were still talking at dawn, convinced we were going to change the world and that nothing else was as important. Until we ran out of cocaine.

'That's the last of the gear,' said Catherine. We'd been talking for twelve hours. 'Shall I phone up and get some more?'

'Has Robert Kilroy-Silk got a sun tan?' I replied.

After that I don't remember ever being without cocaine. Mind you, we only indulged in all-night binges once in a while. On a day-to-day basis we were far less greedy. We just topped ourselves up when necessary. Our cocaine supply was stored in a silver heart kept in a kitchen cupboard, and we would help ourselves to a line whenever we felt the need of a pick-me-up. Breakfast, even if it was in the middle of the afternoon, consisted of a cup of tea, a line of coke and a cigarette. It wasn't long before we had runny noses and suspicious minds, but fabulous cheekbones.

'I don't generally pay compliments,' said Catherine, one night when we'd got home from our respective jobs and were delving in the cupboard for our reward, 'and it might be the drugs speaking, but you look fucking gorgeous, Cowboy. I reckon you've lost half a stone.'

'I wasn't aware that I was overweight,' I said indignantly.

'You weren't. But it's a London thing. You can't be too thin or too rich in this town. I think it's more than that, though.'

'Am I pregnant?' I wondered.

'No. It's better news, even. You've aborted.'

'Well, that's nice talk.'

'Tim. You've aborted Tim at last. The sadness in your eyes has gone. That boring old toff has finally left the building. He slipped out when you weren't watching and now you're free.'

'Am I?' I asked doubtfully, reaching for the cupboard. I didn't feel as though that was true, but I'd been dwelling on Tim a lot less recently. I feared that meant he was only embedded all the more deeply in my heart.

As our drug consumption increased, the only real serenity in my life came from my Friday afternoons in Barnes. The fresh air, the predictability of my clients' demands and the regular financial rewards that came from such ordered lives gave a timetable, albeit vague, to my chaotic existence. It benefited me, I felt sure.

As the months passed we became comfortable with the routine. Relaxed after my clients' sexual needs had been seen to, I took an interest in the prodigious growth of Sammy's passionflower and expressed concern about the greenfly problem with regard to Georgie's mesembryanthemums. My knowledge of plants impressed the old boys. We sipped our drinks and chewed the cud, much like regulars at a country pub. We were a happy, carefree threesome, we enjoyed life in the moment, and by the time I left Barnes I had no doubt that I'd improved the quality of all our lives.

But not all of my clients were as easy or comfortable to deal with as Sammy and Georgie. By far the worst was another regular, a Mr Brown. He was a very troubled man and a bit of a psycho. For him, sex was an angry matter, and, for the hour he paid me, I was the focus of his fury. Spanking and restraint, bondage and S and M I could handle, but Mr Brown overstepped the mark. When he hit me it didn't feel like role-play. It felt like he wanted to beat the living daylights out of me.

He booked me through Madame, and always stayed in room 510 at Claridges. He was a handsome, well-groomed man in his early fifties. He was invariably naked when I arrived (apart from his wedding ring), and he handed me my money in silence. Then it was straight down to business. He made it clear that he preferred me not to speak. Not a hello or a goodbye.

'Come in, undress, bend over. You know what this is about,' was all he said. The punishment was administered with his bare hand. He slapped my naked bottom harder and harder until his palm was slippery with perspiration. Then he slid one, two and finally three fingers up my anus, swirling and jabbing them about like an angry plumber trying to unblock a sink. I could tell when he had come by his gorilla-like grunts, and sometimes from the splash of semen on my back. 'Now get out, you filthy slut,' he'd say, as if he meant it. His breathing would remain agitated while I dressed hurriedly, and left the room feeling that Mr Brown might lash out at me.

I muttered the traditional 'Remember me,' once I'd closed the door behind me.

'Look at the state of you,' said Catherine, when I got in one night, rubbing my tender rump. 'Life's tough enough without spending an hour with Jeffrey Dahmer every week. I'll phone Madame and tell her it's not on.'

'No, don't do that,' I said. 'It's only his fantasy. I can handle him.'

In fact, it wasn't anything to do with professional pride that made me carry on with my visits to Mr Brown. It was his connection to my true love. Although he clearly had no idea who I was, I knew him. Mr Brown was no less a person than Timothy's father, Lord Thornchurch.

CHAPTER THIRTEEN

My life had settled into quite a comfortable routine, with my regulars, my one-offs and my group bookings filling my days and nights nicely.

I didn't tell Catherine that I was servicing Tim's father. I hadn't realized it myself until the third visit, although I had thought he looked vaguely familiar. It was only when I was bent over the trouser press that I saw the label on his suitcase. He had obviously forgotten to hide it and I saw, plain as day, the words 'Lord Thornchurch'.

I almost collapsed with shock but remained professional. By the time he'd finished, I was fascinated by the idea of sleeping with Tim's father. It was both horrible and erotic – and also the perfect way to get even with Tim, despite his knowing nothing about it.

When I wasn't doing tricks, I was with Catherine, shopping, chatting or going out on the town. She enjoyed coming with me to the classier gay clubs. She would sweet-talk the bouncers into letting us into the VIP lounges, and while I went trolling about to see if there was anyone I fancied, she would order an expensive bottle of champagne and tell anyone who chatted to her ridiculous lies for her own amusement. When I returned to her, I had to catch on quickly or I might give the game away.

'I was just telling these lovely people how I'm Princess Grace of Monaco's illegitimate daughter,' she'd say, 'but enough about me. Johnny here slept with Boris Yeltsin last night. Why don't you tell them about his luminous semen?'

Then it was my task to improvise a vaguely feasible scenario. If she was feeling devilish she might interject halfway through with a further complication – 'Don't forget to tell them about the moment Sinitta walked in' – and sit back to watch me struggle.

If I was feeling frisky and picked someone up, she would give them the once-over. If my choice met with her approval she would pour him a glass of champagne. If not, she would say: 'No. Pig ugly. Goodbye, whoever you are.'

Tim – or, at least, the memory of him – still consumed my emotions, which freed me to have cold but convincing sexual relations with all and sundry. It was better than thinking too much.

It was ten minutes into one of Georgie's *après*-sex comfort cuddles that he mentioned a TV producer friend of his called Bernard. 'Do you think sex is good for the soul?' he began.

'Er, probably. What do you think?' Like any good therapist I had learnt to listen when my clients began to chat.

'I'm sure of it. My soul is singing now, you can almost hear it. I forget that I'm old and ugly. You've performed a very valuable service.'

'So glad to have given satisfaction.' There was a pause as Georgie sighed contentedly. I managed a surreptitious glance at my watch. Seven more minutes, then I'd be off.

'Bernard!' he declared, sitting up in bed. 'You're just what he needs! I wonder ...?'

'Does Bernard's soul require a bit of a sing-along too?'

'Oh, yes. He's been quite a worry. Bernard and Barry were a very happy couple. Together for fifteen years. But Barry died last year and Bernard ... He's not taken it well. A frolic with you would do him all the good in the world. Put a spring in his step again. Would you consider it?'

'Of course,' I said. 'He sounds like he could do with a touch of the JD magic.'

'How kind of me to share you!' Georgie got up out of bed and put on his dressing-gown. He picked up the soiled tissues that were, as well as his cheerful disposition, the result of our afternoon together, and moved towards the door. 'I'll give him a ring.'

I got out of bed and started putting my things together. As I neatly coiled the clothes line and popped it into my leather rucksack, along with the pegs and rubber mask, Georgie returned, all smiles, clutching a gin and tonic. He slipped a roll of twenty-pound notes into my pocket with a piece of paper.

'Bernard will be expecting you at six tomorrow evening. See if you can put a smile back on his face.' He gave me a knowing look.

'If I can't, no one can,' I boasted.

'One other thing, though,' he added, swirling the ice in his glass and turning ninety degrees from the fireplace to face me – very Katherine Hepburn. 'Bernard doesn't know you're being paid. He works for the BBC and he'd be horrified. I've told him you're cute and bright and that you're interested in becoming a TV presenter. Your job is to act the part and make sure one thing leads to a bit of the other.'

'I see,' I said, raising an eyebrow. 'And is the casting couch that much more respectable than using a prostitute?'

'It is as far as he's concerned.'

'I've never wanted to be a TV presenter, actually. The sets always look so cheap.'

'*Role play*, darling. Weren't you an actor once? Seduce him. I can see you now, sitting on his sofa with your legs spread wide, explaining how you want to become the next Peter Duncan. Don't take your bag of tricks – it might give the game away. Just do what you can to make the poor dear happy again. A glimpse of your beautiful cock would make a condemned man smile.'

'All right, Georgie. I'll do it.'

'And don't forget to let me know how it goes.'

The next afternoon I put some thought into my appearance. How would Bernard expect me to look? Masculine and youthful, obviously, but in an unselfconscious way, I decided. In the end I put on jeans and a pale blue shirt with the sleeves rolled up. I wore trainers and took the unusual step of shaving, moisturizing and deodorizing.

It was strange, making my way to a client's house and already feeling sorry for him. Perhaps, if I dealt with the situation carefully and acted my part convincingly, I could pull this grieving soul out of his misery – and wasn't that a good deed, whichever way you looked at it? It helped that I'd been paid handsomely in advance.

I could tell that Georgie was getting a weird thrill out of setting up the whole scenario. On his part, it amounted to deception although the lie had been born of empathy and concern. He had entrusted me with a dear friend's emotional well-being and I alone could cure him of his malaise. I could make him feel that life was worth living again. In short, I felt it my duty to ensure that Bernard felt ... if not the sun on his face then a similar sensation of warmth that can, with equal certainty, be declared a gift of Nature.

Bernard lived in a portered block of flats in St John's Wood, one of those seventies arrangements with large ashtray balconies that looked like they might fall off at any moment and that enjoyed limited glimpses of Regent's Park.

When I got there he was in slacks and a red v-neck cotton jumper over a white shirt. He looked sprightly enough, clearly in his late fifties, but his blotchy pink skin and home-dyed hair were a worry.

'You must be JD,' he said, when he opened the door. His 'Do come in!' was a little breathier than he might have hoped, but he skipped down the hallway to the open-plan lounge-kitchen-diner in a revealingly expressive way. 'Is it too early for a glass of Wither Hills?' he asked, opening the fridge and taking out a bottle of chilled white Sauvignon Blanc, which he held to his cheek as if it were a cleaning product and he a house-proud wife.

'What's that?' I said.

'Dry white wine,' he answered quickly, holding the pose.

'Yes. OK,' I said, sounding convincingly bashful, and Bernard relaxed his arms and put down the bottle. Two wine glasses were whisked out from behind the pine bread-bin and placed carefully on the counter that divided us. I perched on a stool and ran my fingers across my bristly head.

'Oriental snacks?' enquired Bernard, pushing a bowl of unlikely-coloured crackers in my direction. His hand brushed mine, and as I lifted the glass to my lips, I tilted my head downwards and engaged him in some serious eye-contact. He hesitated, looked away, and then, in one sweeping movement, brought his face close to mine and shut his eyes. 'So. You want to be a TV presenter, I hear?'

His depression was hidden far better than his erection, I thought. 'More than anything,' I lied.

'You have a very good face for television,' said Bernard, earnestly. 'Very photogenic. And, as it happens, I'm developing a show at the moment. We've interviewed dozens of would-be presenters but none of them quite fits the bill. Perhaps you could come in for an audition ...'

'Oh,' I said, 'this could be my lucky day.'

'And mine,' said Bernard, and I felt a bony hand creep along my thigh like a centipede.

The next morning Georgie met me for coffee, squawking with delight. Bernard had called him first thing and was brimming with excitement.

'He thinks you're adorable! And, of course, he's in raptures about your penis. Such a relief to hear my old chum happy again. I think he's in love.'

'Well, you know, Georgie, that isn't supposed to happen. Strictly speaking, this is a business transaction and nothing to do with love.'

Georgie's face fell. 'Oh.'

'It's breaking the rules. Bernard's already called me this morning. He's invited me for an intimate dinner on Saturday night. If he's not aware that I'm a working boy and is getting emotionally involved with me, I ought to say no.'

'Don't do that!' Georgie said hurriedly. 'Poor old Bernard. Rejection would be too much for him. Not now, when we've finally managed to get a sparkle back in his eyes!'

'I'm not in the business of deceiving people.'

'Let's compromise. You go along on Saturday and give Bernard another thrilling night of love, then let him down gently the next day. Would you do that?'

'I'm not sure ...' I frowned. The truth was, I had no desire to repeat the experience. Bernard had been all over me, slobbering and squeezing me, within minutes of my arrival. His girlish excitement over the phone seemed to indicate that there was a lot more where that had come from. Hours of it, no doubt. As he wasn't paying me, he was under the impression that I liked him. It seemed wrong and tedious. 'So who's paying this time? I told you, I'm a working boy, Georgie. I don't do freebies, I'm afraid.'

Georgie gave a short-tempered little moan.

'If I have to stay the night with Bernard, it'll work out as a rather expensive evening for you,' I warned.

'*Quel dommage*,' Georgie muttered. Then he roared with laughter and his eyes twinkled mischievously. 'I don't give a fig. Do it, JD!'

That Saturday night I arrived at Bernard's to find the table set for four.

'Hello, my dear. What joy to see you again. Now, I've got a surprise for you!' he said. He led me into the lounge. 'I want you to meet my two closest friends,' he announced, and there, sitting on the sofa, beaming at me and barely disguising their glee at my befuddlement, were Sammy and Georgie.

'Here he is!' said Bernard. 'Sammy, Georgie, meet JD. Isn't he a dream?'

They looked me up and down knowingly, their eyes resting on my crotch.

'We've heard so much about you,' said Sammy, standing up and shaking my hand manfully.

'Indeed we have,' added Georgie, following suit, though his shake was limp with mirth. 'I'm so glad you and Bernard have hit it off so well.'

I smiled uncomfortably. Clearly Georgie wanted to see how his money was being spent.

'I'll bring in the champagne,' said Bernard, oblivious.

'We'll chat to JD. What are your hobbies, what do you do, where do you live? Or don't you like to be tied down?' asked Sammy, brightly.

Bernard was out of the room just long enough for Georgie to slip a wad of notes into my hand and whisper, 'Now earn it, baby.'

Bernard returned with a tray of glasses foaming with pink champagne, which he passed round. 'Now,' he said, holding his aloft, 'I'd like to propose a toast. To JD. My new special friend.'

We chinked glasses.

I was silently cursing Georgie for getting me into this situation when Bernard made an astonishing announcement: 'JD is going to have a screen test!'

'I beg your pardon?' This was the first I'd heard of it. I'd assumed all the talk of a TV show had been Bernard's way of getting my trousers off.

'I can't discuss it at present – all very hush-hush – but this afternoon I called my commissioning executive at the Beeb and told her I thought I'd discovered the face for our new show!' Bernard beamed at me. 'She was very excited. And I do mean *very*.'

'Whoa there!' I said. 'Listen, Bernard—'

Georgie cut me off mid-sentence. 'You must be thrilled! What an opportunity for you!'

'I wasn't going to tell you until we were alone,' Bernard squeezed my knee suggestively, 'but I couldn't wait.'

'Good luck with your new opening,' added Sammy.

'Yes, indeed,' said Georgie. 'I'm sure you've got what it takes. In fact I think you'll be HUGE!'

'Thank you,' I said tartly.

'What a load of old bollocks,' said Catherine, when I told her about Bernard's plans for me. 'That's the oldest trick in the book. But allow him his casting-couch fantasy. It doesn't matter whose purse the money's coming out of – cash is cash. Our job is to make these old men feel good. We just say, "Yes, sir, no, sir, two bags full, sir. Allow me to empty them for you."'

'And if I find myself in front of a camera being screen-tested for my own TV show?'

'If that happens, I'll eat my own tampon.'

CHAPTER FOURTEEN

It was a week later when, after the usual session with Sammy, I went next door to find Georgie in a sombre mood. He didn't pass me any instructions or say a word as he opened the front door, just led me into the lounge and sat down.

'I've got some rather depressing news, JD. I've been to the doctor again. I haven't said anything to you – it would spoil the atmosphere so – but I've not been feeling right for some time. The reason for this has now become clear. It seems I'm positively riddled with cancer and there's not a thing they can do.' His black and white cat jumped on to his lap and nestled down. He stroked it listlessly. 'I've been advised to put my affairs in order rather quickly.'

I sat beside him and put my arm across his shoulders. 'Georgie, I'm so sorry. Is there really nothing they can do?'

'Oh, they could blast me with this and pump me with that but it wouldn't do a scrap of good and would make my last weeks positively hellish. The stupid thing is, I don't feel all that bad – just dull, nauseating pain here and there. I'm sure it'll get worse but they have a lovely thing called morphine for that. Any of their therapies would make me feel a million times worse and give me only a tiny bit more time, if I were very lucky. I don't think it's worth it.'

His lip trembled and I hugged him tighter. I felt sorry for him, and rather upset. I'd grown fond of him over the months I'd been beating him senseless.

'This has set me thinking ...' Georgie tried to continue, then stopped himself, hesitated, took some deep breaths and gave up.

'It must be a terrible shock,' I said, to fill the gap. 'I don't know what to say.'

'Can you see,' Georgie said, clearly choosing each word carefully, 'that if something is inevitable, one might as well embrace it?'

I gave him a sympathetic squeeze. 'I think that's a very healthy way of looking at it.'

'Healthy?' repeated Georgie, and threw back his head as he pretended to laugh.

'Well,' I said, 'acceptance is better than regret under the circumstances.'

'Exactly!' said Georgie, recovering himself. 'That's how I see it. And if death is on the cards, why not grasp the opportunity to deal the hand yourself?'

'I'm not sure what you mean, Georgie,' I said.

'No, no, no, you're not quite with me, are you?' He stood up, suddenly energized. The cat toppled off his lap and walked away crossly as Georgie paced the room. 'Can we not extract a little happiness, a little pleasure, from circumstances that are by tradition tragic and upsetting?'

'How?' I was baffled now. 'Are you talking about Jesus or something?'

Georgie went to the sideboard and poured himself a large gin with a splash of tonic. He took a gulp and closed his eyes, inhaling purposefully, summoning the strength to say something important.

'You know what I like sexually, JD. You alone know of my fantasies. Your hands round my neck, choking me. It's the only time I'm happy, to be perfectly honest with you. What I'd like to suggest – and I'm not sure how to phrase this properly – is that you do me a great favour.' There was a long pause. 'Murder me,' he said quietly.

I stared at him. He didn't open his eyes but talked on. I realized he was sharing with me some very private and important thoughts and felt strangely honoured.

'I have always dreamt of being strangled. It's the Mecca of my desires. The ultimate experience. I've wondered why, of course – I've questioned the genesis of my own fantasy – but I've never come up with an answer. I've gone as far as I can in acting it out, but life was always of greater importance to me. Ultimately I wanted to live. I still do, but my time is up. I could never seriously contemplate this before, but now ...'

I stood up and moved towards the door. What Georgie was saying had made sense and I was horrified. I needed to get out of this situation, stop listening to his ramblings.

He opened his eyes and leapt in front of me. 'Here is my choice. I let the cancer take its course, enduring the pain as it gets worse and worse until, eventually, they dose me with so much morphine that I slide into a coma and die. Or I pay you twenty thousand pounds to give me the sensational erotic finale of my choosing. Then I don't let the Grim Reaper have it all his own way!'

I stood there, staring at him.

He looked at me pleadingly, his hands clasped. 'Please, JD. It would make me happy.'

'Can I … can I think about it, Georgie? You must realize you've asked something very serious. I can't just say yes. I need time to think.'

'Of course, of course. But not too much!' he called after me, as I went past him to the door. He looked suitably tragic. 'I don't have much left.'

'It would make me happy.'

This sentence stayed with me all the way home, as I thought over the absurd thing Georgie had asked me to do. Kill him? How on earth could I? The last time I looked, the penalties for snuffing out a life were fairly stringent, no matter what the deceased party had had to say about it. I tried to convince myself that the whole thing was one of his elaborate ruses, but he had been far too convincing.

As soon as I got home, I told Catherine what had happened.

'Those old boys are full of fun and games, aren't they?' she said, laughing. Then, suddenly, she was serious and gazed at me with wide, excited eyes. 'Twenty thousand pounds, Cowboy … That's the important part. Is there some way of getting the money without doing the business?'

'That's called "clipping", I believe. A dirty trick and I'll have no part of it.'

'Such a good Catholic boy. You warm my heart. OK, then. If murder's the only honest way to get our hands on the lolly we'd better seriously consider it.'

'You're as mad as he is!' I said, astonished.

'Think about it. First, we need the money.'

Catherine was right. Our move upmarket was proving much more expensive than either of us had anticipated. Besides the constant need for grooming and clothes, the rental on our new flat was five times the amount we had been paying for the last place, and the Italian furniture we'd eyed up wantonly in Selfridges had been beyond our means but we'd bought it anyway, along with many other luxurious items that we couldn't live without. And there was our ever-increasing cocaine habit, which was now costing us hundreds a week. No matter how much we earned, the money melted away.

'Can't we just shag some more Arab princes?' I asked. That seemed a much nicer proposition than killing Georgie.

'It's bloody Ramadan, isn't it?' Catherine pointed out. 'They haven't got the energy.'

'Oh.'

'It's not just the money, though, sweets. Think about it. He's going to die anyway. Don't forget, I used to be a geriatric nurse and I've seen those poor old people suffering and dying in their hospital beds. Forget slipping gently away between clean sheets with your family gathered at your bedside. Think of horrible pain, sliding in and out of consciousness in a strange place surrounded by people you don't know as you listen to the sounds of a busy ward and the beeping and clunking of all the machinery keeping you going.' She eyed me meaningfully, as she swirled an expensive cognac round a cut-glass tumbler. 'Or die quickly, at home, in ecstasy, with someone you like. I'm pretty sure which I'd choose.'

She had a point. But still …

'Sleep on it,' suggested Catherine. 'Twenty thousand pounds! See how you feel in the morning.'

By breakfast Catherine had convinced herself that 'we' should carry out Georgie's wishes. 'It's his choice, after all. The way I see it, it's euthanasia for thrill-seekers.'

For a moment, we munched our muesli in silence.

She saw that I wasn't as enthusiastic as she'd hoped. 'I don't see what's wrong with the idea, when you think it through. He's going to die anyway. It's a compliment to you that he asked. Being able to make someone happy is no small thing. And we sure could use the dosh.'

'We? You're not the one who has to squeeze the life out of a little old man.'

'I'd be with you in spirit. I'll be standing by with some Wet Wipes.'

'You've just got your eye on the cash, Catherine,' I said plainly. 'It's really rather vulgar.'

Her eyes lit up. 'Cowboy, you're right! We're behind with the rent, we've got credit-card bills coming out of our ears and I've seen a fridge-freezer with a glitterball inside that turns when you open the door. We've got to have it. Please?'

I shook my head sadly. 'I just don't think I've got it in me.'

Catherine looked cross. 'He'll only leave the money to the other silly old fart or a cats' home. What a fucking waste! Do things his way and we're all winners. Don't be so mean. Anyway, I thought you cared about your clients.'

'The bottom line is I don't think I could kill a man. It's all very well for you, sitting at home planning the spending spree, but I'm the one who'll have to do the deed and live with it for the rest of my life.'

Catherine held up her hands to stop me. 'All right, enough! Let's forget it. Tell him he'll have to find someone else.'

I loaded our dirty bowls into the dishwasher and poured us some more tea. Catherine was sulking now, burying her face in a glossy catalogue of chic leather furnishings. I sighed. 'How much is the fridge-freezer?' I asked.

'Thank you! Thank you!' said Catherine, tossing the catalogue to one side to give me a hug.

'I'm not saying I'll do it,' I warned. 'I'm very far from that …'

But she could sense that something in me was weakening. By lunchtime she had made a list of our sudden new 'must haves' and precious little of the impending twenty grand was unaccounted for. The camp fridge, new sofas, a coffee-table and our rent arrears were neatly listed. A thorough make-over for our patio garden and a thousand pounds worth of 'miscellaneous' expenses had crept into the equation. A huge amount was noted as 'partying'. I assumed this was earmarked for Catherine's coke dealer.

'I've put aside three hundred for a holiday for you in Gran Canaria. You'll need a break afterwards, I should think, to come to terms with what you've done. You'll probably have night sweats or a spot of eczema. The sunshine will do you the world of good.'

'Three hundred pounds isn't much for a holiday,' I observed.

'No, well – have you ever been to Gran Canaria? Monte Carlo it ain't. If you want any spending money while you're there I'm sure you can earn it. The place is crawling with desperate old queens recovering from their exertions during the panto season.'

Somehow, as we talked, the money became more real and more difficult to imagine not having. Over the next few days, Georgie's proposition went from being an old man's ridiculous fantasy to something I had solemnly undertaken to carry out.

CHAPTER FIFTEEN

When I told Georgie I was prepared to murder him, he was delighted, then agonized over exactly when he wanted to make his exit.

'Does the seventeenth of September suit you?' he enquired, as if he was booking a manicure. 'I've had a look at the long-range weather forecast and it's likely to be cool but bright with sunny spells. Perfect, I thought. We can start in the early evening. You should be home for *Newsnight*.'

He seemed so rejuvenated by the prospect of his own violent death that it was hard to believe he was sick. It was as if he'd been waiting all his life for this extravaganza. The following Friday he clucked round his flat, excitedly instructing me on which restraints were to be applied where and in which order.

'I shall, of course, have all this written down for you, but we'll start with a little playful strangulation in the hallway. Handcuffs we won't bother with – they're so old hat – but I'm going to Bond Street tomorrow to look at some silk scarves. I'll treat myself to something expensive. As for the business round my neck, I think the leather strap from a Louis Vuitton bucket bag should do the trick, don't you?'

The execution was to be preceded by a marathon of sexual humiliation, plus S and M shenanigans.

I quaked at the prospect. Talking about it like this made it horribly real and I told Georgie I didn't think I could do it.

'Now listen,' he said, 'This is my last wish on earth. You're performing an act of great kindness, don't ever forget that. I won't have you torturing yourself – it's me that wants to be tortured, after all. Get a grip – in more ways than one, baby!'

He was very worried that his illness might cause some sexual dysfunction so he'd been on the Internet and ordered himself a quantity of Viagra, he told me. 'I got a few pairs of latex gloves too, for you, not me.'

I was touched by his concern.

'Well, dear, this will be a crime scene by the time you're finished. Remember, no fingerprints, no naughty DNA from you, my boy, or you'll be cursing me from your prison cell and I don't want that.'

Somehow he made it sound so reasonable and I was quite comforted. After all, if he could be so relaxed about it, surely I could too.

The date he'd set was two weeks away. He booked me to go round on Wednesday the fifth for, as he called it, a 'technical rehearsal'. He would pay for my time as usual, he added.

He met me at the door, that sunny early-autumn evening with a clipboard in his hand. An extravagant amount of lilac was arranged throughout the house. His nasal hair had been trimmed and he wore a little light foundation, I presumed, to disguise his yellowing skin. He smiled excitedly.

'You look good,' I said, because I felt a pang of sorrow.

Despite his remarkable enthusiasm for the event he was planning it occurred to me only now that, deep down, he was afraid of death. By taking matters into his own hands (or, rather, mine) he was 'dealing' with it, rather as he would the installation of a new conservatory. It would be messy, but worth it in the end when he was basking in eternal sunlight.

'I think I look drop-dead gorgeous,' he said, then laughed a little too loudly. He handed me three sheets of lined A4 paper, on which he'd listed things in capital letters. 'You must memorize all of this, then burn it before you leave,' he said, in a business-like tone.

I felt as if I was meeting a secret agent on Waterloo Bridge. It was hard to believe we were in earnest. The whole thing seemed like an elaborate charade.

'Early evening is a ridiculous time, I now realize. Far too cosy for what I have in mind. Let's make it three in the morning. This has advantages and disadvantages. On the plus side you're far less likely to be spotted entering the premises but on the other hand any, er, noises we make in the course of our endeavours may well be heard by your friend and mine, Mistress Sammy next door. I have ascertained that he is away at a wedding on the night of the thirteenth of September. I therefore propose that we bring our plans forward to the early hours of next Thursday morning. What say you?'

'Um ...'

'Now,' said Georgie, going all Katherine Hepburn, as he often did, 'our business transaction.'

He sashayed over to his desk in the lounge and snatched a bulging envelope from a drawer. He cupped it in his left hand and stretched his arm towards me slowly. There was silence between us. I knew if I accepted this mighty wad of cash I was committed to carrying out my side of the bargain.

'I can't,' I said eventually.

'This is only the first half!' he said teasingly, and walked towards me, hips swaying. He wafted the envelope under my nose and I smelt the funky, sexy aroma of used notes. The coppery taste caught the back of my throat like a hit of amyl nitrate, and I felt flushed and giddy. I snatched the money and heaved a mighty sigh.

'Thank you,' said Georgie, quietly, all acting gone now.

I sat down on the sofa and opened the envelope. I counted the money. Ten thousand pounds in fifty-pound notes.

'The second payment will be waiting for you. It's in the schedule. I'm going to add a bonus, too.'

'What's that for?' I asked warily.

'Dear Bernard. Could you carry on seeing him for a few weeks after I've – gone, as it were? Another death is going to be horrible for him. I'd like you to be there. A shoulder for him to cry on.'

'In for a penny, in for a pound,' I said, rather regrettably.

'Good. Now. A little champagne to celebrate?'

As we chinked flutes, Georgie said, 'A toast! To going out with a bang!'

Then we went through his notes together. This was how they read:

THE KILLING OF SISTER GEORGIE

TIME: 0300 HOURS ON THURSDAY 13 SEPTEMBER

LOCATION: THIS FLAT, 18 CASTLENAU GARDENS, BARNES, LONDON

COSTUME: TO BE PROVIDED BY GEORGIE. OVERALLS, SHOE COVERS, LATEX GLOVES AND BALACLAVA

PROPS: TO BE PROVIDED BY GEORGIE. TORCH, SCARVES, CLINGFILM, GAFFER TAPE, ASSORTED FRUIT AND VEG,

CLOTHES PEGS, CONDOMS, ELECTRICAL FLEX, CANDLES
AND MATCHES, CIGARETTES, LEATHER LOUIS VUITTON
STRAP, MIRROR, BIN LINERS

RUNNING ORDER
0255: GEORGIE WILL CALL PHONE BOX ON THE CORNER TO
CONFIRM THE PLAN
0300: JD TO ENTER THROUGH THE FRENCH WINDOWS.
GEORGIE TO BE IN BED AS IF ASLEEP
0302: JD TO ENTER BEDROOM AND UNZIP FLIES
0303: GEORGIE WAKES WITH A GASP ONLY TO HAVE A HUGE
ERECT COCK SHOVED IN HIS MOUTH

And so it went on, including a curiously amusing yet detailed list of sexual acts and fantasies, becoming ever more sadistic and violent. The entire proceedings were to last for one hour and forty-five minutes, but some leeway was given, as the duration of the final, fatal strangulation with the Louis Vuitton strap could not be accurately predicted. Ultimately even Georgie couldn't die to a precise schedule.

'I might pop off with excitement before the night, darling. Then you've got a nice little windfall for nothing, haven't you?'

I'm not sure if it was the alcohol or the strangeness of the situation but I was in a dream-like state. Georgie didn't seem to notice, he chattered away, salivating slightly at the corners of his mouth. It took me a while to notice that he was also, clearly, sexually aroused. His hands began to press and pummel, as if he was kneading dough in his lap. As I was paid to be there, my professionalism soon kicked in and I pulled myself together for long enough to pull my client together too.

Afterwards, Georgie recovered quickly and, now sitting in his dressing-gown, picked up where he'd left off. He snatched up his clipboard almost before his breathing had returned to normal and read out the last few items on the timetable:

'04.40: CHECK GEORGIE'S PULSE AND HOLD MIRROR TO MOUTH. IF DEAD, REMOVE ORANGE AND BLINDFOLD, ETC.

04.42: JD TO REMOVE CONDOM, PLACE IN SEALED PLASTIC BAG. CHANGE BED SHEETS, PUT SOILED ONES IN BIN LINER PROVIDED, AND PLACE IN HOLDALL.

LAY GEORGIE OUT ON BED IN DIGNIFIED MANNER. CLOSE EYES. RETRIEVE TEETH, COVER WITH SHEET PROVIDED. PUT ALL CLOTHES BACK ON, INCLUDING BALACLAVA, TAKE HOLDALL, COLLECT ENVELOPE CONTAINING REMAINING CASH AND LEAVE QUIETLY VIA FRENCH WINDOWS.'

At last, I thought, he's finished. But I was wrong.

'Then there's the aftermath to brief you about. Obviously there'll be a murder investigation. I sincerely hope the police won't want to interview you, but you never know. Be prepared! You will have your clothes, the sheets, the condom and all ropes, fruit and so on, in the holdall. Dispose of it as soon as you leave here. I suggest the incinerator in Wembley. On Wednesday night go out to one of your nightclubs before you come here. After you've finished, go to one of those recovery dos you told me about under the arches in Vauxhall. Take an E and make a spectacle of yourself. Make sure you're seen. That's where you were on the night in question. Don't act too upset. I was only a punter, after all.'

I nodded and smiled, touched that he'd thought everything out so thoroughly, even concerned about my alibi. He was right. If we were going to do this thing we might as well do it brilliantly. Georgie was being extraordinarily detailed, but at the same time he was invigorated by the planning and scheming. I started to play my part and think things out as seriously as the man planning his own departure.

I said, 'There's your semen to worry about. Don't come on me whatever you do.'

'I've already thought of that. By my calculations I should be face down at the point of orgasm. You will be very much on top, and thus free from any possible transfer of seminal fluid. As for faecal matter, I'm booked in for an enema that evening so no worries there either.'

'Lovely. Georgie, you've thought of everything.'

'I believe I have. My last piece of theatre – and this time I'm the director.' Georgie stood up and that was my cue to leave. 'Thank you for a lovely evening,' he said. 'We must do it again some time.'

I stood up, too, and shook his hand. It seemed appropriate to say something significant, but what? 'Until Thursday morning, then?' I said, awkwardly.

'Counting the hours!' said Georgie.

CHAPTER SIXTEEN

I must take responsibility for my own actions, of course, but Catherine and I discussed the plan to kill Georgie in great detail and without her encouragement – or, rather, insistence – I doubt I would have gone through with it.

'We must see this job as a military operation,' she coached me. 'You're a soldier following strict orders. Focus on making your benefactor's dream come true.'

'I will,' I vowed.

'Georgie's happiness is in our hands,' Catherine reminded me. 'I know you can do it.'

And she would reach for our silver heart and get me some 'medicine' to help me stay firm.

I still couldn't quite believe that it was going to happen. But as the date neared, it seemed no one was backing down.

In retrospect, I blame ambition for blinding me to the reality of my actions. The jockey who dopes his horse desires to win the race at all costs. He is wrong to do it, of course, but the dream of glory, the need to be the very best, is what drives him to it. So it was with me. I simply wanted to be the best fantasy-fulfiller the world had ever known. If that meant strangling my client, so be it. The circumstances were unusual, but the rules of the contract were simple: he asks me, I say yes. Could I be held responsible? Was I really a murderer? After all, anyone who kills someone else in cold blood must be unhinged in some way. Was I treading the path to madness? I didn't think so. I wanted to make Georgie happy, that was all. It didn't mean I was a sociopath, someone who experiences little or no empathy – on the contrary, my empathy was fully engaged with Georgie's most heartfelt desire. I didn't feel sorry for planning the end of his life because I was fulfilling his dearest wish. We don't have to share those desires or understand them, but neither can we dismiss them as unworthy of our consideration. I was in the business of granting people's wishes, not saying, 'No, I couldn't possibly!'

I suppose there is the fact that I was paid handsomely for the deed, and without that fee, I would probably never have done as Georgie asked. But I'm not Jimmy Savile granting wishes, or one of the Sisters of Charity, and I never claimed to be.

But don't allow the fact that I benefited from these circumstances to lead you astray in your assessment of my mental health, and don't condemn me as nothing more than a cold-hearted killer. There was so much more to it than that.

It was the night of Georgie's murder.

Catherine dropped me off at the end of Castlenau Gardens at two forty-five a.m. The streets were deserted and every window was dark. As the car pulled up, she turned to me. 'Good luck, Cowboy. Keep your nerve.'

We looked at each other for a moment, and I think Catherine saw fear in my eyes. She stroked my face. 'It'll be fine. You can do it. Don't worry.'

I got out of the car, longing to be anywhere but there. Then she drove slowly away.

I went to the phone box at the end of the street and waited. I was jumpy and nervous, certain I was being watched by a host of nosy neighbours who were already practising describing me to the *Crimewatch* artist. The phone rang, as arranged, at exactly two fifty-five. I knew it was Georgie, phoning to make sure there were no last-minute delays or unexpected developments. I let it ring only once before I picked it up.

''Ello, Georgie. 'Ow yer doin'?' I said, using the rough south-London accent that had turned him on so much in our more conventional encounters. I knew he'd like that touch.

'Ah!' He gave a little gasp of excitement. 'All set here. Ready to go.' He hung up.

I felt sick. So, this was it. Time to test my resolve. I took a deep breath. It was too late to back out. All I could do was give it my all, and try, in the strangest of circumstances, to remain the epitome of professionalism. I put on my black leather gloves and pulled my Vivienne Westwood jacket collar up around my ears.

No one was about but I managed a casual saunter just in case, looking, I imagined, like an innocent youth mooching home after a frustratingly chaste date with his frigid girlfriend. I had always been good at making up scenarios.

A few moments later I moved silently down the side of the house. There was a single lamp on in the lounge and the french windows were unlocked, as agreed. I climbed over the balcony and let myself in as quietly as I could, glancing round to make doubly sure that no one was about.

Inside, I drew the curtains and listened. There wasn't a sound except the ticking of a clock. On the sofa were the overalls, surgical gloves and shoe covers Georgie had bought for me. I slipped them on, exchanging leather for latex, amazed at how calm and collected I was feeling. I moved into the bedroom and saw the shape of a sleeping form under the duvet. When I reached the bedside Georgie stirred and said, 'Who's there?' just as arranged.

His acting's a trifle wooden, I thought. Never mind.

I had memorized the instructions he had given me and ticked them off in my mind one by one, needing just the occasional glance at my watch to check I was on schedule. The sex I could do with my eyes closed (and frequently did) and the moderate S and M wasn't unusual either. Once things began hotting up, though, I believe I went into automatic pilot. If someone asks you, pays you even, to hog-tie them and take a pair of pliers to their nipples, it's important to remind yourself that their muffled cries are really of satisfaction, not pain.

There was only one unexpected glitch: he choked rather violently on the lemon I pushed, as instructed, into his mouth. He went very purple and tears streamed down his cheeks. Should I remove the zesty fruit and offer him a glass of water, I wondered, or press gamely on? In the end the choking subsided and his cheeks returned to near-normal pinkness.

I was as ready as he was for the end when it came. I took a couple of deep breaths, wound the strap twice round his neck and pulled. I guess I hadn't bargained for how long it would take or the amount of thrashing about that ensued. I could see, as I looked into his eyes, that deep down, underneath it all, Georgie was having the time of his life, but that didn't stop the involuntary struggling as his body tried to overrule his wishes. When he finally slumped, dead at last, I realized we were no longer on the bed but halfway across the room. I continued to hold the strap tight with both fists clenched and counted to a thousand.

As a consequence I finished seven minutes later than intended.

I laid Georgie's body out as he had requested, and took the liberty of adding a squirt of Clinique's Happiness. There had been some loss of bowel and bladder control, as you might expect under the circumstances. I cleared this up with surprisingly little squeamishness (that's country folk for you) but a heavy faecal odour lingered in the air. Respectfully, I lit the incense and lowered the lights. I was hot and sweaty, but as my instructions were now to go out dancing it didn't much matter.

Before I closed the bedroom door, I stood back to admire my handiwork. I had done it, and it hadn't been as bad as I'd expected. Clean and serene (if a little red in the face), Georgie lay with his hands clasped across his chest and he was wrapped in freshly ironed antique linen, folded about his face; it gave him an unexpected – and, I suspect, unwanted – nun-like appearance. The blue smoke from the incense curled round him. It all seemed rather Victorian.

I smiled at the shrouded figure in his chapel of rest and considered my work well done. I packed the rubber gloves and the other paraphernalia into a small black sports bag and left the flat silently through the french windows.

'Remember me, Georgie,' I whispered.

Just as we'd arranged, Catherine was waiting outside in our new red sports car (she had already taken care of the first ten thousand pounds of my payment). She looked at me but I didn't say a word. We drove away in silence. When we eventually stopped at traffic-lights on Vauxhall Bridge she said, 'I don't know why *I'm* shaking. How did it go?'

Sounding rather like a doctor after a difficult operation, I said, 'As well as can be expected.'

'Good. Well done, I knew you could do it. How was he?'

'He went with a smile on his face.'

'That's just what he wanted. Now – everything in the sports bag?' she asked.

I nodded.

'Off you go and enjoy yourself, then,' she said. 'Here's a little pick-me-up for you.' She handed me a miniature plastic bag with three thick yellowish pills in it. 'Best to swallow them now to avoid any security nonsense. While you're shaking your stuff, I'll take the bag to the incinerator and watch it burn. Have you got the money?'

'Here it is.' I pulled the envelope of cash out of my pocket.

'Take a hundred pounds or so for tonight, and give me the rest. It'll be safer that way.'

'Okay.' I peeled off some notes and handed the envelope to her.

'Good.' She tucked it into the side pocket in the door. 'I'll look after it. Now go and have fun. I'll see you when I see you, Cowboy.'

I got out of the car. A light drizzle was falling but Catherine leant across, wound down the passenger window and said, 'It wasn't murder, sweetheart. It was an act of kindness.'

Then she roared off. I watched as the tail-lights of our whizzy new car disappeared on the Vauxhall roundabout, then headed for the dark doors under the bridge that led to the steamy world of a club called the White Swallow.

Once inside, I took my ecstasy and danced topless on a podium for a couple of hours, gyrating and gurning with the best of them. Drugged and delirious, I greeted even the vaguest acquaintance with uncharacteristic friendliness.

'Nicholas! You're looking fabulous!' I squealed at one. In reality, he was overdressed as usual, the stunted attempt at a Mohican he was sporting doing little to disguise his imminent baldness, but now was not the time to tell him the blindingly obvious. I wanted to escape reality, particularly on that night of all nights. 'It's so wonderful to see you!'

Nicholas wittered on and I pretended to listen. Suddenly, through the steamy haze, a figure emerged, swanning into my vision with a sinister smoothness. 'Well, hello, stranger,' it said.

To my astonishment, I recognized him. It was the unpleasant Sean from Lewisham School of Musical Theatre. 'Sean,' I said. 'How charming.'

He still looked bizarrely thin, his cheeks hollower than ever. He smiled, like a cheerful skull. 'It's been ages. You seem to be having a good time. Mind if I dance with you?'

The drug to make that an attractive proposition had not been invented, but here was another witness to my whereabouts, and I had to force myself. 'Of course! It'll be like old times.'

Off he went, giving it his all. Sean's step-ball-change style of dancing might have got him into the chorus of an Eastbourne production of *Dick Whittington* but it earned him few admirers on the dance-floor that night. Queens dressed as garage mechanics forgot their butch act and arched their backs, hurrying to get as far away from Sean's display as they could, as fast as their Dr Martens could carry them. Sean did a perfect double-spin and was suddenly up close to my face. 'You know something, Johnny?'

He was puckering up to me, I saw with horror. 'What's that, Sean?'

'We've had our differences, but I've always felt a special connection to you—'

I had to stop him right there. 'Sean, I once said to you that I thought anyone could sing or dance.'

'You did, but you regret it now, I expect?' He stroked my sweat-wet hair and gazed lovingly into my dilated pupils.

'I was wrong. Not everyone can dance. You can't.'

It was about noon when I got back to the flat, completely washed out and very depressed from the inevitable comedown. I had shaken off Sean, but it hadn't made me feel any better.

Catherine was busy on the phone to John Lewis. She mouthed, '*Ciao!*' at me as I slumped on to the sofa, eyes like saucers and a cold sweat on my brow. Then she went on, 'And have you got one in stock now? With the glitterball? How soon can you deliver? Great. We'll be in this afternoon to pay in cash. Thank you.' She looked me up and down. 'Go and have a shower, Cowboy,' she said, waving a hand under her nose. 'You smell like an abattoir. Then we'll go shopping. The Italian sofas and the fridge will be with us by next Wednesday. Doesn't that make it all worthwhile?'

'Not really,' I said.

'Oh, you'll soon forget about dispatching the old trout when we've got ice cubes at the press of a button.'

I left her to her shopping and went for a shower and a lie-down. I wouldn't say I had a clear head, but for the first time I allowed myself to contemplate my actions.

So. Now I was a murderer. It didn't feel as bad as I'd thought it would but perhaps that was because it was so hard to believe I'd never see Georgie again. The whole thing still felt like one of the games we played, where I was tough and merciless, punishing him in just the way he liked. Would he really never greet me at the door, paunchy and pink-cheeked, telling me what a saucebox I was and could I do it again next week?

Come on, I told myself sternly. It's not as though you're going to make a habit of it. This was essentially self-harming – and was what Georgie had wanted. He'd just done it by proxy.

I repeated this to myself until I felt innocent. I was almost able to forget what I'd done, but not quite. I felt a vague, distant sense of worry and regret, as if I'd run over a cat or been needlessly rude to a shop assistant. I must learn to live with this feeling, I thought. In case it never goes away.

But I very much hoped it would.

It was about four o'clock when Sammy called.

'I'm afraid I have bad news,' he said calmly. 'Our dear friend Georgie is dead.'

'Oh, Sammy, I'm so sorry,' I replied. I sounded convincing, even to myself. I'd done a very good job of persuading myself that I'd had nothing to do with it. 'That's a terrible shock. He told me he was unwell but I thought he had some time …'

'I've been away for the weekend and there was no sign of him on the veranda this morning. I was worried because his curtains were still drawn. I had an awful feeling that something—' He stopped, and a big sob of grief distorted the line.

'What do you mean?' I said carefully. I had to remember what I knew and what I didn't. 'What happened?'

'I went in and he was laid out on the bed, covered with a sheet. I had a little peep – it was awful, he was obviously dead – then ran back to my flat and called the police at once. There are dozens of them, forensics, photographers, yellow crime-scene tape everywhere.'

'Sammy,' I said, in a deep voice, 'how terrible. Whatever happened to him?'

'I think he was murdered. He must have gone out again and picked up someone dangerous. I told him not to, but he was always hot-headed. But, then, he was laid out so beautifully. Why would a thug go to such trouble? I don't understand. And no one will tell me anything.'

There was a pause.

'I'm just so shocked,' I said – rather believably, I thought.

'Georgie was my sister,' Sammy almost whispered. 'Why would someone want to hurt him?'

'Did he have any enemies?'

'Lots. But mainly silly queens he'd lacerated with his vicious tongue over the years. No one who hated him enough to lay him out like a dead pope. I wish you could have seen it, JD, it would have broken your heart. Poor, poor old Georgie ...' Sammy started to weep.

'How vile. He didn't deserve that.'

I felt rotten again. Poor Sammy. Right through all the planning and the execution of Georgie's fantasy, I had never considered him. Their lives had been bound together for so long and his 'sister's' death had come as a terrible shock. How was he to pass the long, lonely days? Who would he gossip and drink with now?

Come on, I told myself. He was going to be bereaved anyway, what with Georgie's cancer. Separation was inevitable. As it always is.

CHAPTER SEVENTEEN

Georgie's murder made the evening news and most of the next day's papers. It was reported in various tones. A broadsheet called it 'Suspicious Sex Death Of Retired Theatre Man'. A tabloid screamed, 'Killer Queen! Gay OAP Murdered At Home In Bizarre Sex Games Twist'. One even said that Georgie had died in a frenzied attack, which I was quite upset about: there had been nothing frenzied in my actions – I'd been most careful.

But it was rather terrifying when I saw on the news that the police had launched a murder investigation. I hoped we'd been careful enough, but after all my precautions and the evidence Catherine had incinerated, things ought to be fine. I'd been at the club that night, anyway. And they found it hard enough to catch genuine murderers, with proper motives, so why would they possibly suspect me? I just had to sit tight and keep quiet.

There were a few further reports, but mainly to the effect that Georgie had probably taken a stranger home for sex that had gone too far. That nothing appeared to have been stolen seemed to rule out robbery, and the calm nature of the crime scene meant that the killer had not acted impetuously after it happened. The general feeling was that it was one of those mysteries that would remain for ever unsolved, though the police said they were still investigating and hopeful of catching the person responsible. They always said that, though.

'You're home and dry,' Catherine said, when we'd watched the news that night. 'No one can really be bothered, can they? See? Just as I said. And to think you nearly turned down all that money! Honestly, if it were always so easy, we could open our own business putting the terminally ill out of their misery in a blaze of glory. Forget shoddy little hotel rooms in Switzerland and a paper cup of poison, think champagne, caviar, sex and an exit to be proud of.'

I tried to smile but it occurred to me that Catherine sometimes lacked a little in the good-taste department. 'Once is enough,' I said.

'Maybe you're right,' Catherine agreed. 'Shame, though.'

Because of the nature of his death, Georgie's funeral arrangements were somewhat delayed. Catherine and I had screwed our way through the sand dunes of Gran Canaria and were already lamenting our fading tans when Sammy called me. He couldn't bear to live in Barnes any more, he said, and was soon going to stay with friends on the Isle of Wight. 'Will you come to Georgie's funeral, JD? Only he left very specific instructions and you're on the invitation list.'

'Well, I don't know – I still can't believe he's gone.'

'Please. He'd be devastated if you weren't there. The police have finally released the body and after six weeks in a fridge drawer he deserves a good send-off. It's going to be quite a show.'

'Of course I'll come, Sammy. I wouldn't miss it.'

I didn't particularly want to go – in fact, I dreaded it – but Catherine said it would be suspicious if I didn't show up.

'I'll come with you. I've got a dinky little veil,' she said. 'It'll be fab with those jet earrings I saw in Old Bond Street the other day.'

Barnes Crematorium was done out with pink bunting when we arrived. The only flowers permitted were red-hot pokers flown in at great expense from somewhere exotic. 'It's Raining Men' was played at full volume as the coffin – shiny black gloss with yellow polka dots and marabou trim – was carried down the aisle by six Tom of Finland builders in overalls and hard hats.

'This isn't a send-off, it's a send-*up*,' muttered Catherine. 'Do you fancy a Valium? It might help you cry.'

'I'm managing without thanks,' I whispered back, wiping my eyes. 'I think it's rather lovely, actually. It's just what he would have wanted ...'

'And what Georgie wanted, Georgie got.'

The funeral was followed by drinks and camp food from Georgie's favourite era, the nineteen fifties, at a local pub. We dutifully tucked into Coronation Chicken, ham and pineapple on cocktail sticks, stuffed tomatoes and satsuma jelly.

Sammy said a brief hello and lingered only long enough to tell me that he was heading back to the Isle of Wight straight after the wake, where he would be staying in Sandown with a retired judge and his house-boy from Singapore until he had recovered sufficiently from the shock and could make plans for the future. He'd call me soon. Then he was off, circulating slowly and sadly like a grey carp in a murky pond. Sammy was chief mourner and organizer, however painful it was for him, so he had to comfort everyone and say a few appropriate words.

'Hello, JD,' said a small voice behind me.

Bernard was wearing an uncharacteristically sombre suit with a ghastly maroon tie and a pungent floral aftershave.

'Long time no see,' he said, looking a little flushed. 'You haven't returned my calls.'

'Haven't I?' Actually, I'd forgotten about Bernard in the last few weeks. My mind had been so occupied with Georgie's plans and then, afterwards, with what I'd done, that I'd forgotten Bernard still thought we were dating. 'Oh, sorry. I've been a bit tied up lately.'

'Have you?' Bernard said, breathing heavily. 'Not by anyone special, I hope.'

'No, no. Just with life.' I remembered that Georgie had asked me to carry on being nice to Bernard, for a little while at least, and that he'd left me some extra money to service his old friend. Well, it was the least I could do even if Bernard wasn't my cup of tea. I owed it to Georgie.

'It's because nothing's come of that audition I promised you, isn't it?' Bernard turned even pinker. 'I am trying, I swear. It's all bogged down in production meetings and boring old admin. We haven't got to the stage of screen-testing presenters yet, but when we do you'll be top of the list.'

'Yes, yes,' I said, rather impatiently. This was Bernard's only hold over me so he had to keep harping on about this fictitious job. 'Listen, I'll ring you, all right? And we'll go for dinner. Your treat.'

'Really? Fabulous!' Instantly Bernard looked more cheerful. 'Can I get you some Cliff Richard Thirst Quencher? It's a cocktail Georgie invented – Pernod, Grand Marnier and Lucozade. It's rather tart but slips down a treat. Georgie would have wanted to go out with a sparkle, wouldn't he? Poor old girl. I do miss him ...'

Everybody got spectacularly drunk, especially Sammy and Bernard, who ended up clinging to each other and reminiscing about their dear departed friend until Catherine could take no more. 'Let's get out of here,' she said. 'If I'd known how pathetic these people are I'd have killed Georgie myself, free of charge.'

The next day Sammy returned to the Isle of Wight. He called me from time to time, inadvertently giving me the welcome news that the police investigation was going nowhere and no arrest seemed likely. 'The murderer's out there somewhere, JD, but no one knows where. It's such a mystery, but Georgie would have enjoyed that, I'm sure. It's like the plot of a rather bad novel, don't you think?'

I did my best to keep the calls brief and my comments bland. Talking to Sammy made me feel dreadful, quite weighed down with the guilt I managed to escape the rest of the time by pushing Georgie out of my mind, getting sloshed or snorting some of our never-ending supply of cocaine. At night after I'd had a call from Sammy I'd wake up in a cold sweat, escaping a nightmare in which I was murdering Georgie, but however tight I pulled the strap, however many times I stabbed or suffocated him, he lived on, pleading with me to finish the job, to fulfil my side of the bargain.

'I'm trying!' I would say.

'Kill me! Kill me now!' gurgled Georgie, but nothing seemed to do the trick. Just when I thought he was finally dead, the corpse would rear up again, entrails flying about the room like bloody ribbons, severed hands pulling me back and Georgie's strangulated voice calling my name, begging me to put him out of his misery.

'It's dreadful! So real. I wake up in a terrible state,' I said to Catherine, after describing my night horrors to her.

'It's only a dream, Cowboy,' said Catherine, busy painting her nails and doing her best to stifle a yawn. 'Take no notice. What else can I say? You can hardly go for counselling, can you?'

'I need to clear my head. Mind if I take the car for a spin?'

'Ah, the car.' She stood up and walked to the window, flapping her hands to assist the drying process. 'I didn't like to upset you. I had a bit of a disagreement with a lamp-post yesterday.'

'What?' I said.

'Now don't worry. I've ordered another. I'll open a bottle of Cristal, shall I? Cheer us both up.'

Cars, champagne, Cartier watches, home improvements and drugs saw off our twenty-thousand-pound windfall within a matter of months. What I had assumed would be a life-changing amount of money had slipped through our fingers like sand.

I managed to retain two hundred pounds, which I posted to my mother for her birthday. She was thrilled, and called me up. 'Darling, what a lot of money! I'm going to treat myself to a "Rambling Rector" and some horse manure. Thank you, angel-cake, thank you so much! You're my favourite son by far!' She laughed excessively at her own joke, the mad, unpredictable sound fluttering down the line like a wildly coloured butterfly.

'That's all right, Mummy. I'm glad you're pleased.'

'They do pay well in London, don't they? I'm sure that if you were working with Help the Aged here you'd never be able to live so well.'

'I'm sure I wouldn't,' I said.

'Bye, bye, darling!'

'Bye, Mummy.'

I put the phone down, frowning, and tasted the bitterness in my mouth that seemed to have become normal lately. I supposed I'd just have to get used to the way the whole world seemed different now that I'd killed a man. I needed to lie down in a darkened room.

CHAPTER EIGHTEEN

With the money from Georgie gone, it was back to plying my usual trade. I was aware for the first time of a glimmer of dissatisfaction and a sensation of entrapment in a wearing occupation from which no escape seemed possible. Georgie's money had been like a Christmas bonus: much appreciated as it was (especially when the fridge-freezer and sofas arrived), it didn't last. Once gone, it underlined the treadmill of my existence.

I took down the details of each new booking with a weary heart. I even failed to turn up for a couple that had sounded particularly unsavoury over the phone. Catherine was furious when she found out. 'That is not on!' she shouted at me. 'We need cash.'

'I couldn't face them, Catherine,' I protested, trying to defend myself. 'I'm depressed.'

'Oh, well!' she said indignantly. 'I'll call the fucking emergency services, shall I? You'll be depressed when you have to move back to Brownhill Road and eat nothing but baked potatoes!'

I could tell she was building up to a lecture. I reached for the kitchen cupboard and our secret stash. 'I need a line,' I said.

Catherine dropped her voice to a tone that was almost menacing. 'I'm telling you something, Johnny' – she almost never called me that – 'there's no way I'm going back to how we used to live. I haven't spent the last few years on my back for nothing. We're going on, and that's all there is to it. So you've got to keep your end up – literally. Do you understand?'

I nodded. I wasn't really looking for a way out – in fact, I wasn't looking for anything right at that moment but a big, fat line of Charlie. It was the only thing that took away the fear and fug that were consuming me. I felt as if I was standing on a window-ledge high up on a city sky-scraper, teetering, hanging on for dear life, resisting the temptation to fall asleep and then to oblivion.

It was probably this feeling, with a certain recklessness that had possessed me since Georgie's death, that led me to shed many of my regular customers, despite Catherine's admonitions. Sammy was gone, of course. And then I got rid of another, more significant client.

It was only a few days after Georgie's funeral when I turned up for my regular session with the silent Mr Brown at Claridges.

By now our routine was set in stone. I arrived at room 510 at nine p.m. precisely on the first Monday of every month. He opened the door, naked and unsmiling, then handed me two hundred pounds. I undressed and got on all fours. He would spank me with his hand, belt or shoe, explaining in a low but colourful growl what a bad boy I was. He set the alarm for nine fifty to give him time to 'finish up'. This meant a royal fisting with one hand while he masturbated himself to a furious climax with the other. I was then told, 'Get out at once!'

I would dress as quickly as I could and leave, uttering the obligatory 'Remember me,' once I was safely in the lift.

In all this time, I had never so much as hinted that I knew he was not Mr Brown. I wouldn't have given him so much as a whisper of a clue that I was aware of his true identity. I was willing to suffer for this 'special' customer because being with him, I told myself, brought me closer to Tim, whom I missed more than ever.

I don't know why I suddenly decided to provoke Mr Brown. Perhaps I was trying to take out on him my anger with his son. Whatever it was, I couldn't help myself.

As usual, nothing was said when I arrived. I took the money, undressed and got into my doggy position. Mr Brown had only administered three or four preliminary slaps across each buttock when, as if from nowhere, I did a bad Barbara Windsor impersonation: 'Ooh, Mr Brown, whatever are you thinking of? Supposing someone should see us?'

His raised hand froze in mid-air and his eyes, fiery and familiar, glared at me. I turned and pulled his head towards me, then kissed him hard. He tried to pull away but I held him firm, swishing my tongue over his lips, which opened momentarily. I moaned encouragingly but without sincerity.

He got away, stumbling in his efforts to escape. He wiped his lips on the back of his hand and spat three times. 'You disgusting boy,' he said. 'Get out! And don't ever come back.'

I got up and began to dress. 'Thank you, kind sir. You don't know what it means to hear such words from a toff like yourself. A true gent, that's what you are, sir.' I sat on the edge of the bed to tie my shoelaces. 'I'll fink of you whenever I splatter me spunk on a gentleman's noble brow, so I will, sir, I—'

He shut me up with a vicious slap round the face. The force

knocked me to the floor on my hands and knees. His bare foot then pressed on the small of my back. I lay there, stunned, and felt the electric sensation of a stinging face against a nylon carpet. I heard it before I felt it, hot and wet, like blood. Mr Brown – or Lord Thornchurch, father of my one true love – was urinating on me.

Then he was gone.

If my inclination to endure being pawed, poked and punished by all and sundry was fast evaporating, then Bernard was next in line for the chop. He was as maddeningly needy as ever calling me all the time and trying to arrange dates when we could meet. Georgie's last wish had been that I should give him a good run for his money, so I went along with it for as long as I could, but it was getting a bit serious for my liking. I wasn't required simply to go to his flat any more, he liked to show me off in fancy restaurants. Rather embarrassingly, he had taken to clutching my hand at every available opportunity. I think this was partly to comfort himself: he, like Sammy, had taken Georgie's death very hard, and I had been given the irksome part of chief listener and amateur counsellor.

'The silly, silly queen,' he kept repeating, while sighing and shaking his head. 'It's such a cliché, and he'd have hated that! We all like a bit of slap-and-tickle but the source and pedigree of the slapper-tickler are obviously of paramount importance. You, for example, are a nice boy but so adorably butch with it. Georgie always had to have the *real* thing. Someone dragged up as a builder or a policeman didn't do it for him. Oh, no. He'd have to cruise the Underground staring at people's feet until he saw a convincing spattering of plaster dust or a nugget of Tarmac. Then he'd stalk him, the *bona-fide* builder on his journey, until success or failure won the day. I know he was punched on the District and Circle several times. I thought he'd grown out of all that at his age, but evidently I was wrong.'

'He got bashed on the towpath as well,' I added.

'Did he? Oh dear. He would have loved that. I do miss him.' His voice would crack, and his pale blue eyes would fill with tears and he'd drag a handkerchief across his nose in way I particularly disliked.

Bernard was irritating at the best of times, but Bernard the bereaved was worse. The constant references to 'poor Georgie' were more tactless than he, of course, could understand. It was hardly appropriate to keep changing the subject. My nerves were bad and my patience was wearing thin, but I couldn't seem to get out of those meetings. Bernard was driving me crazy. For my own sanity something had to be done. I tried to explain how I was feeling to Catherine.

'He's just a harmless old boot, Cowboy,' she said. 'You cannot afford to lose a rich, elderly boyfriend. He doesn't pay in the conventional sense, but he bought you a love bangle with diamonds for your birthday and that bloody well counts. If you think your life's tough, I'm off to star in a Bukake evening with the Lowestoft rugby team. Very good for the complexion, I'm told, but my hair will look like crème brûlée in a couple of hours. Now, go and earn an honest crust. Get some money out of Basil Fawlty before we have to resort to shop-lifting from Woolworths.'

I had learnt early on in our relationship that I ignored Catherine at my peril. She didn't give advice, she issued orders. But I was feeling so deeply unhappy that I was determined, for once, to do what *I* wanted. I had to finish with Bernard, and if Catherine was going to be cross about it, that was her look-out. She didn't really do happy or unhappy: she just was.

That night Bernard had invited me for dinner at a chic and discreet hotel called the Fox in Parker Street, Holborn. 'I've taken a room,' he said, with a leer. 'Well, it's been ages since we were ... together.'

We were dining on the veranda and I had decided it was my solemn duty to dump Bernard once and for all. I was about to begin what I knew would be a difficult conversation when he reached across and squeezed my hand. 'Look at the moon, darling. Quite stunning.'

It was full but partially covered by a solitary, lingering cloud stretched across its face, like a cat asleep on a window-sill. He sighed, happily for a change. Now was the time. 'Bernard,' I began, 'I need to talk to you.'

He turned to face me, alerted by my portentous tone, the serene expression slowly fading from his face.

I had given little thought to how best to proceed. It wasn't going to be easy, I knew that much. Bernard was blissfully happy and adored me. My words had to be final and leave no room for negotiation. Maybe that way I could get it over and done with as quickly and painlessly as possible. 'It's over, Bernard. I'm sorry.'

'Don't say that, JD.' His lower lip trembled, as I'd feared it might. 'You're the only thing that's right about my life. Without you, I'd be devastated. Don't do this to me. Not after losing Georgie and ...' There was a pause. I looked at him and his eyes turned cold. 'Don't do this to yourself,' he said, softly but finally.

I held Bernard's gaze dispassionately as tears rolled down his cheeks. I could do nothing but plough on, my only concession being to choose my words with a little more compassion. 'I'll always care for you, Bernard,' I said. 'I've really enjoyed our time together – but it's over. I need some space.' I placed my napkin on the table and went to stand up.

'No, no, no!' Bernard shouted, pushing me back into my seat. Then he covered his face with his hands and proceeded to rock backwards and forwards like a distressed child. Other diners turned to look, then leant towards each other, whispering animatedly. Bernard whimpered and sobbed louder still.

The waiter came over and asked if there was a problem. 'He's had some bad news ...' I muttered, hoisting Bernard up by his armpits. 'Come on, let's get you up to your room.'

I put an arm round his shoulders and led him, sobbing, out of the restaurant and towards the lift. Halfway across the tiled foyer, he let out a scale of sobs that culminated in a wolf-like howl of distress. A couple checking in jumped in alarm and the receptionist rolled her eyes, no doubt assuming he was drunk.

'There, there. He'll be fine in a moment!' I reassured her, rolling my eyes too. We understood each other – she nodded.

Upstairs, in the suite Bernard had booked for our fun and games, he pulled himself together somewhat. 'Oh dear.' He wiped his eyes with a tissue from the bedside. 'I really am a worry, am I not?' He tossed it into the bin with a flourish. 'Now. We'll have no more of this silly talk about it being over.'

'But, Bernard—' I tried, determined he wasn't going to put me off my mission.

He carried on regardless. 'We've both had a very nasty shock and we're not behaving rationally. We must make allowances for our bereavement and not do or say anything rash. I realize I haven't been particularly good company lately. I've been in mourning and that can't have been very jolly for you. But we belong together, you and I.'

He was gathering pace and confidence with this speech and my shoulders were slumping in surrender.

'Besides,' he said, clearly deciding the time was right to play his trump card, 'I have plans for you. You, Johnny Debonair, are going to be a huge ... *television star*!'

I put on my jacket and made for the door.

'Hear me out, my sweet. I've been working on this for some time.' He leapt up from the bed and blocked my exit, arms outstretched.

I stopped. 'Bernard, I've been hearing about this since the day we met. You've been telling me endlessly about how I'm going to be a television presenter and nothing's come of it. Forgive me if I simply don't believe you.'

'No, JD, listen. Please! I'm telling the truth. I'm the executive producer on a very top-secret project. The final casting decision is mine. We're looking for a bright, attractive young presenter with a certain *je ne sais quoi*. You are that person. I shall guide you, mould you, coach you. It's a huge opportunity and I'm utterly convinced of your suitability.'

I stared at him suspiciously. He sounded genuine, even though I'd long since decided that offering his young studs a job was Bernard's stab at foreplay. 'Bernard, you've said this before. How do I know that you're serious?' I asked, exasperated. This was obviously his last desperate ploy to keep me where he wanted me – in his bedroom for the night.

'I've never been more serious. I can spot star quality, you know. I discovered Jilly Goulden. She was working in my local Oddbins when I walked in for a bottle of Harvey's Bristol Cream and came out with the cream of British light entertainment for the next two years. I knew at once that the public would take her to their hearts.

But you – you have far more potential, JD. You have charm, wit, personality and, above all, sex appeal by the bucketload.'

'All right. But this is your last chance, Bernard, I mean it. Tell me what you've got planned for me. If I like it, I'll stay. If not, I'm leaving.' I took off my jacket. 'You've got five minutes.'

Exactly five minutes later, when Bernard had outlined (with uncanny accuracy, as it turned out) the amazing new career that lay in store for me, I called Room Service and ordered a bottle of champagne.

My depression had lifted like the morning mist. Fate had done it again. Just as my musical-theatre adventure had made way for a more exciting, lucrative career on the game so that dubious occupation had run out of steam just in time to accommodate the new challenge of a job as a television presenter. Life seemed to evolve in the most unexpected ways. Student, hooker, murderer, TV star. Bring it on!

That night I fucked Bernard as if my future depended on it.

It took Bernard a while to reveal it, but the exciting TV role he had earmarked for me was, strictly speaking, on a kids' programme. When he confessed, I was a little put out.

'You're being rather ungracious, darling, I must say,' he remonstrated. 'My kingdom only extends as far as the BBC children's-television department. Much as I'd like to introduce you to the British public as David Hasselhoff's replacement, it's not within my powers to do so.'

But this time Bernard was true to his word. Two days after our conversation I had my screen test in a bare little studio in Hammersmith, nowhere near the BBC. I was filmed talking to a glove puppet and pretending to introduce Mariah Carey.

'A sensation!' declared Bernard.

A week after that I was taken to lunch at an expensive Italian restaurant in Shepherd's Bush. It seemed I was moving closer and closer to Television Centre, which had to be a good omen. There, I was introduced to various suits and heads of departments who all seemed to have clammy hands and dry, flaky complexions. Over coffee and chocolate mints I was officially welcomed on board.

I could hardly believe it. Bernard had been telling the truth all along.

The BBC advised me to drop the JD and revert to my real name of Johnny Debonair. Then, after several high-level meetings, it was decided I should be known as Johnny D. I liked the change. It seemed to fit my new identity.

Bernard summoned me to his office to sign my contract. It had happened so quickly that I hadn't had time to consider what I would be paid – and there it was in black and white. Ten thousand pounds a week for every week the show was broadcast, plus rehearsal fees.

'That should keep you in condoms, my darling,' said Bernard, locking the door and moving determinedly towards me, unzipping the fly of his slacks.

Catherine will be pleased, I thought. We were in the money again.

I immediately withdrew my adverts from the gay magazines, phoned round my regulars, told them I was moving on and changed my telephone number.

Madame was gracious. 'It is good for you. You be happy. I always here if you need make money one day. Good luck.'

My mother was only slightly surprised by the news. 'My little puddle-duck, you're so pretty that it was only a matter of time before the world fell at your feet. I can't wait to see you on the television. Perhaps I'll buy one.'

And Catherine, as predicted, was beside herself with excitement at this sudden change in my fortunes. 'Blimey, Cowboy. There's a turn-up for the books. You lucky bastard.' She got that far-away look in her eye, thinking intently about how this news might benefit her. 'Of course!' she exclaimed. 'I can be your manager! You'd only fuck it up without me. I've been shagged by someone from *Hollyoaks* and he told me you can get a couple of grand for opening a supermarket. Imagine that! More than I get for opening my legs.' She looked quite serious. 'I'm not kidding – my snatch is red raw. I could do with a career change. Go on, let me be your manager. I'll get some stationery printed and change the answerphone message. I'll work from home initially, but offices in Holborn and a secretary called Kirsty are almost inevitable ...'

I had no idea whether Catherine would make a good manager or not but I didn't know how to go looking for a proper one – and, anyway, I trusted her. If anyone could work out how to get on in a crazy world, it was her. 'Of course you can be my manager, but don't get too excited. The programme might be a terrible flop for all we know,' I cautioned her. 'Steady yourself.'

'I'm going to need some new clothes,' she said, disregarding my warning. 'Power suits, designer briefcase, maybe some discreet platinum jewellery. Trousers will be a novelty.'

'It's only children's television,' I said. 'How successful can it be? Let's wait and see.'

My life as JD, prostitute *extraordinaire* and snuffer-out of old men, was officially over. I had a chance to be reborn.

I woke and we were sailing on
As in a gentle weather:
'Twas night, calm night, the moon was high:
The dead men stood together.

CHAPTER NINETEEN

When Bernard had said I was doing children's television, he hadn't really explained what he meant. It wasn't going to be quite as dreary as introducing cartoons at three thirty every weekday. Instead I would co-host a programme called *Shout!*, a hip teenage news show with live bands performing in the studio, broadcast on Saturday mornings.

'Are you really sure I can do this, Bernard? I haven't a scrap of experience,' I said, one night, as we lay in his bed together. I was being nicer and nicer to him as the reality of my new future sank in. Every day I woke with a feeling of pleasurable anticipation and excitement, as though I was about to get a particularly lovely present.

Bernard was blossoming under all the attention. 'Of course you can. It's easy as pie! Don't listen to those silly lies about how difficult it is to do television. If you can read aloud convincingly, you're almost there. Just practise on a newspaper or something – as long as you can do the autocue, you'll be fine.'

'I'm sure I can manage that.' I knew it wouldn't be a problem because I'd read all those books to my mother over the years as she reclined picturesquely on the sofa.

'Your job is to smoulder in a subtle, suggestive but, above all, *masculine* fashion for the camera. I want teenage girls to play with themselves under the duvet as they're watching you. Boys, too, if that's their inclination.'

I understood my brief. This would be a walk in the park.

Six weeks before the show went into production, Bernard summoned me to a meeting at Broadcasting House. The long corridors and the dreary public-school types who haunted them sucked the life out of me, but Catherine clicked alongside me in her killer heels, her blonde hair pulled back in a tight, business-like up-do, and a new shiny leather briefcase tucked under her arm. As my manager, she had insisted that she accompany me to the meeting, even though she had no real idea what a manager's job was. She seemed to think it meant being as close to me as she could get at all times and she steered me by the elbow as if I was partially sighted, and said a bright, 'Good morning!' to everyone we met. Much to my mortification she handed out business cards to the people we stood with in the lift.

'I think that was Esther Rantzen, presumably on her way to make-up,' she said excitedly.

'No, Catherine. It was Simon Fanshawe. After make-up.'

When we found our meeting room, she marched in confidently and shook hands with a bemused Bernard. 'How do you do? I'm Catherine Baxter, Johnny's manager.'

'Er, how do you do?' said Bernard, and raised an eyebrow at me. 'Please do come over and sit down.'

We joined the other people at a table laid with a jug of water, glasses and a plate of nasty-looking biscuits, still in their individual cellophane wrappers. Before we'd taken our seats Catherine tapped the water jug accusingly. 'Is this tap water? Not quite what one expects. My client's body is a temple, I'll have you know.'

Bernard coughed and patted the chair next to him. 'Of course it is, Miss Baxter.'

Next she lunged for the biscuits. 'What's this muck? Don't touch them, Johnny!' she cautioned me, as if she had discovered a landmine. 'He's wheat, meat and dairy free,' she explained to the room in general. 'He can't come within ten feet of a Scotch egg.'

'We'll see that all his needs are catered for,' said Bernard. 'Now, if we can get on. Everybody, this is Johnny Debonair, our new host for *Shout!*. Johnny, I'll go round the table and introduce you to everyone. This is Ruby. She's going to host the programme with you.'

A pretty and demure Asian girl gave me a warm smile. 'It's great to meet you, Johnny. I'm really looking forward to working with you.'

I liked her at once.

Next I met the series producer, an unfeasibly thin Geordie woman called Mo, who sat with her legs spread wide apart like a barrow boy.

Mo introduced us to a couple of assistant producers, four runners and a director called Maxwell. I had seen Maxwell out and about at gay venues that favoured military haircuts and camouflage trousers. 'Can we have pyros?' was all he seemed interested in. He clearly spent much of his time at the gym but had concentrated somewhat on his upper body 'T-shirt' muscles. Wisely, his spindly neglected legs were hidden under the table.

Catherine made lots of notes, which seemed to put everyone on edge. Then she lit a cigarette, which Mo told her curtly to put out. 'We don't allow smoking in this department.'

'Sorry, Mo,' she said, then dropped it under the table and trod on it. 'I suppose you go outside when you fancy a pipe, do you?'

Mo gave her a withering look. She explained the format. 'The show is basically *Blue Peter* with balls—'.

'My client won't work with dogs,' said Catherine. 'No disrespect to you, Mo.'

I nudged her hard. I was so used to Catherine, and so fond of her, that I hardly noticed how mean she could be, but suddenly I was seeing her as a stranger would. She couldn't help cracking jokes, no matter how cruel or inappropriate, and she always did it with a completely straight face. I could see that lots of people might not get her.

'Miss Baxter!' said Bernard. 'This is no place for cheap jibes. We're not at the WI now.'

'Sorry, Mo,' said Catherine breezily, but she shut up after that. She wasn't going to jeopardize this whole TV adventure of ours.

'Bernard, you carry on,' Mo said frostily.

'Very well.' He took a deep breath. 'Buzzwords for this show are: funky, energetic, unpredictable and sexy. Our research has shown that our target audience of twelve- to eighteen-year-olds is interested in music, comedy, sexy popstars and clothes. We're going to give them two hours of their favourite things every Saturday.'

As he spoke Bernard reached under the table and laid his hand gently on my thigh, his fingers undulating in what he imagined was a seductive fashion.

'Johnny and Ruby are to be *über*-hip, achingly trendy, gorgeous, clever and very "now". In fact, they sum up our show. Our viewers throughout the United Kingdom must want to *be* Johnny and Ruby, speak like them, wear their clothes, have their babies.'

Ruby and I looked at each other and smiled.

'I'll do Wales if you do Scotland', I scribbled on a notepad, then passed it to her.

'I'll toss you for Northern Ireland', she wrote back.

This was going to be fun, I could tell.

Straight after the meeting, Ruby and I were whisked to a photo studio in the basement. There we posed against the show's DayGlo logo while Bernard jumped about behind the photographer, shouting, 'Rest your arm on his shoulder, Ruby! Show us those beautiful teeth, Johnny! Think *pow*! Pizzazz! Hit series!'

The sight of this middle-aged man wearing M&S jeans and snowy white deck shoes punching the air and trying to do young-people-speak was too much: Ruby and I began to laugh, and the flashbulb popped away merrily. These were the photos that would soon be printed large in every TV listing in every newspaper and magazine in the country.

Slowly the form and shape of the show was revealed to us. The entire studio was to be done out in geometric black and white shapes. There were three performance areas – one in which the bands would play; another, cosier, interview 'den'; and a games-and-sketches playground where anything might happen. We had a resident troupe of ex-Cambridge Footlights types, who performed topical sketches making fun of current affairs. A live audience of two hundred carefully selected punks, Goths and bright young things would be hyped up to laugh at and cheer our every utterance. Standing, not seated, they would swarm from stage to stage to catch the action. Even the camera angles would be wild and crazy, with cranes and cameramen suspended from the rigging on bungee wires.

I looked at sketches, models and scripts but nothing prepared me for the scale and brightness of the reality. There seemed to be hundreds of people working on the show, climbing ladders, cradling cables as if they were new-born lambs or barking into walkie-talkies and calling for barn doors. It was madness.

My first experience of walking into the studio and standing on the set in front of all those cameras was pretty terrifying. It was only a rehearsal but my legs were shaking. Ruby had already done a series of *The Basil Brush Show* so she knew the ropes. She took my hand and must have felt how clammy I was. She gave me a squeeze. 'Television's easy,' she said. 'If Nicky Campbell can do this, so can you.'

Bernard had arranged for us to have an hour or so to practise with the autocue, and after five minutes I knew I had the hang of it. God bless my mother and those late-night reading sessions.

The floor manager was a tall, agitated man with a shaved head, and it was made clear to me quickly that I must keep my eye on him and follow his instructions. He would cue me, point to the relevant camera or signal for me to move on to the next item when the time came. My make-up artist, Anita, who smelt of exotic incense and had an elaborately tattooed neck, said I was so beautiful I only needed a light dusting of powder. She leant in towards my ear. 'And I have a variety to choose from, if you catch my drift.'

On our very first show we had the Backstreet Boys and Björk performing live, and Ruby and I chatted to M People about their new album and tour, joined in with sketches and improvised or flirted our way out of trouble. One of the quirky rules of the show was the klaxon: whenever a deafening fog-horn sounded, everyone had to join in a Mexican wave while singing a bastardized salsa version of Jason Donovan's 'Especially For You'. No one explained why.

The two hours of my television début flew by. With Ruby's calming influence and Anita's invigorating powder, I felt very comfortable indeed.

'You're a natural! A star is born! Words fail me!' said Bernard afterwards, wiping a tear from his eye.

Shout! was an instant success, lauded immediately as the epitome of cool, youthful broadcasting.

After the second week's show I found a gaggle of breathless, excited young girls waiting for me outside Television Centre, wanting me to scribble my name across a publicity still they'd got hold of. Next week the show was 'Pick of the Day' in almost every paper, and Ruby and I were on the cover of the *TV Times*. What was more, the *Daily Mirror* said I was the sexiest thing on television since *Starsky and Hutch*.

Fanmail began to arrive, scores of letters each day, and people on the street did double-takes, pointing, whispering excitedly and calling my name. As the weeks went by and fame crept up on me, the public's reactions became increasingly vocal and adoring. Catherine enjoyed nothing more than pushing my fans out of the way, acting as my bodyguard and informing them she had a black belt in origami.

I loved doing *Shout!*. The adrenaline high of live television was like nothing I'd ever known. Ruby and I sparked off each other beautifully and we were full of energy and raring to go as the clock ticked down to nine a.m., the camera lights went red and the stern floor manager made the hand signal that told us we were live on air. We felt confident and euphoric. We were a hit.

'This doesn't happen very often in a television career,' Ruby said to me, after rehearsals one week. 'We must enjoy it, savour our moment. Most TV is crap, after all.'

Viewing figures multiplied at a terrific rate. Our catchphrase ('Shout! Everybody, shout!') and games ('Call My Bluff' for obscure, mild expletives, and 'Name That Condom') were a national obsession. Our disrespectful version of 'Especially For You' was a playground craze in schools everywhere, and *Shout!* merchandise was quickly designed and rushed into the shops. Even though she was inundated with requests for me to make personal appearances, Catherine made sure I got twenty-five pence from each novelty mug that was sold and tenpence from *Shout!* toothbrushes.

In the evenings she and I would sit together in our flat, making plans, taking drugs, laughing and generally marvelling at the change in our lives.

'I can't believe it, Cowboy. You're famous! You're a star.'

'Maybe not quite yet,' I said modestly. 'More of a starlet.'

'Yes, but you will be. I can feel it in my waters, like the first tingle you get that indicates the mother of all orgasms is heading your way. The sensation is remarkably similar. I've got big plans. I'm getting those offices I told you about. We're going to be *mega*. Mega-mega!'

'Mega, smegma,' I said carelessly, shrugging my shoulders. But inside I was thrilled.

My only worry was that one of my clients might recognize me and decide to spill the beans, but I put that out of my mind. Most of them – particularly the married ones – wouldn't be over-eager to describe their sexual predilections, and the rest would either not recognize me out of *situ* or wouldn't care if they did. A few of my favourites would probably just think, 'Good on you, JD. Go and get a bit of the high life ...'

And why not? After all, I'd been lowlife for long enough.

Bernard basked in the glory that came with producing a hit show and finding the hottest new face of the year.

Those were our happiest times together – if you can call it happiness. If you can call it togetherness, come to that. I was so excited by what was happening, and so grateful, that I was some-times reasonably nice to Bernard, though with hindsight this might well have been a mistake. The thrill he got from making me a hit soon turned to possessiveness. He seemed to be with me all the time. At the studio he had a legitimate reason to hover at my side, and while I was on a steep learning curve I was glad of his advice and instruction. He watched me with an eagle eye, making sure I was always presented in the best possible way, with the best camera angles and lighting. But it wasn't rocket science and my natural, relaxed style was something I myself brought to the show. It wasn't down to him or even the original concept.

Out of the studio, he was desperate to be with me, showing off his discovery. He wanted to come with me to every interview, every photographic shoot and every personal appearance. That wasn't so bad, but he also wanted to come to clubs and parties as well, cramping my style horribly. Suddenly, wherever I went, I was fêted, spoilt and able to pull with even greater ease than before, sometimes several times a night – but it wasn't the same when Bernard was there, red-faced, balding and generating static in his nylon trousers as he burnt with jealousy. He still clung to the belief that I was his boyfriend – and even suggested moving in together. I managed to quash that idea at once, saying I couldn't possibly leave Catherine, but I slept with him on occasion to keep him happy. Of course I was grateful for the opportunity he had given me, but I began to feel as if I'd be indebted to him for ever.

Being famous was turning out to be great fun. The only thing spoiling it was Bernard.

CHAPTER TWENTY

Shout!'s initial six-week stint was quickly extended to three months, by which time I was a bona fide celebrity. My fame grew and grew, and I was soon a tabloid favourite, with stories about me appearing every day. Shots of me getting into the back of a taxi after a night out at a trendy Soho nightclub, or mingling backstage with the hottest bands, seemed to confirm my 'cool' celebrity status. I was thrilled when the press called me a 'TV star' for the first time, and indignant if they failed to thereafter. I was invited to music-awards shows, first nights and exclusive parties. Initially I went with Bernard, but he was not the most photogenic escort and was frequently edited out of the picture or, worse, pushed aside by ambitious starlets when the flashbulbs popped. When this happened I could expect punishment by pouts and sarcasm.

Once, as we were leaving a restaurant, we met Rachel Swooney, star of a tacky ITV show called *Bitches At Brunch*, going in. She squealed with excitement and threw her arms round me just as the paparazzi took their shots. Lunchtime celebs were generally to be avoided if there were cameras about. Even I knew that.

'Opportunistic little mongrel!' seethed Bernard, in the back of the taxi. 'She's never even met you before. Scheming Welsh cow. She's got a mouth the size of Tiger Bay. And those teeth! The only work she'll ever get is if they decide to do a remake of *Jaws*.'

Poor Rachel – she didn't deserve such abuse but I knew from experience that the worst thing I could do was defend her.

'The publicity's good for the show. Calm yourself,' I said.

The next day the *Mirror* had a picture of Rachel slobbering all over me with the caption: 'Swooning for Johnny! Rachel and Johnny nuzzle up together outside the Ivy. Is this the latest showbiz couple?'

As if!

I still felt obliged to have sex with Bernard from time to time, though I was doing my best to get out of this grisly chore. He was my producer, after all, with the power to pull the rug from under me, and if I declined too often, or professed more headaches than were believable, he just might replace me, unlikely as it seemed.

Bernard enjoyed the fact that I was lusted after by most of the female population. When I was voted top heart-throb in *Smash Hits*, he was delighted. 'Though it's the throb of your cock that interests me, dear heart,' he purred.

As long as I contained his jealousy as best I could, and sorted out his needs occasionally, all was well. I had enough of a life apart from him to keep me happy. I loved going out, drinking and taking drugs. I was popular and fashionable, and I was whisked into all the chic nightclubs, frequently exiting through the back door with a handsome youth at closing time. I had my own driver, whose job it was to see I got home at night. Roy was always there to keep me out of trouble. He was discretion personified. 'I've seen it all before, mate,' he told me. 'I used to drive Fanny Craddock.'

In interviews I became coy when journalists asked if I had a girlfriend. Officially I was looking for the right girl still, and the trick was to keep the tabloids at a fever pitch of speculation. Ruby, my co-host on the show, was happy to be my beard. (She'd known the score since she'd seen one of boy band Big Thing leaving my dressing room and spotted some jism on his shoes.) Catherine once arranged for her to be 'papped' leaving my flat at dawn so in the eyes of the general public my heterosexuality was beyond doubt.

The following year, with the second series of *Shout!* our ratings went through the roof. Catherine took her role as my manager seriously and worked hard at her smart new office in Fitzrovia. She read my scripts, helped me choose photographs for publicity and fantasized with me about the almost tangible excitement of what the future might hold. She learnt to deal with any request and made sure I featured in the right magazines. She was audacious when it came to discussing fees for colour spreads in the glossies, plucking figures out of thin air, doubling them and playing one editor off against another. The money was flooding in. I'd had no idea how lucrative it was to be well-known. You could get ten thousand for leaving the house in the morning, if you were canny – and Catherine was.

'I've got a vision, Cowboy,' she said one day. 'I really am an award-winning manager. I'm going to have to put my commission up, I'm afraid. I'm worth twenty-five per cent. And I mean of the gross, in case you're wondering.'

*

When it came to my interesting sex life, there was the occasional mishap but Catherine always smoothed things over. One Saturday night I was pictured leaving Heaven nightclub with a Puerto Rican hunk in a leather harness. Questions were asked; she countered them with a fabricated kiss-and-tell from an air stewardess with whom I had allegedly spent a steamy twenty minutes in the lavatory on a flight to Berlin. I was an insatiable but considerate lover, the young lady told the *News of the World* readers as she posed provocatively in underwear and jauntily cocked airline cap. I couldn't possibly be gay. 'Johnny D is *all* man, I can tell you,' she was quoted as saying. There was a handsome fee for this fictional tale, and I divided the money with the air stewardess. She got some cash, my reputation was restored, and everyone was happy.

The next week Catherine ensured that Ruby and I were seen walking hand in hand through St James's Park, and an 'insider' said we were trying to work things out.

In truth, of course, I was reaping the rewards of my sexy celebrity status in the gay clubs of London or wherever else I found myself. My sex drive was as demanding as it had ever been, but men were the beneficiaries, not air stewardesses. I needed the same sexual fixes as I had when I was for rent. I was quite a catch before, but with the added aphrodisiac of fame I had the pick of any night-club or party. The more famous I became, the more cute boys were queuing up for my attentions, and I wasn't about to disappoint anyone. Experienced as I was in such matters, I had the staying power and equipment to satisfy more than one lucky lad per night.

It was a dangerous game, perhaps, but I had little choice. I couldn't come out without risking everything – gay presenters were not as voguish then as they are today, particularly for children's shows – but I didn't feel too threatened. Kiss-and-tell stories were rare – too much was at stake for all parties – and in the small gay community, the avaricious queen who sold his story of a celebrity fuck was unlikely to get a pat on his perfectly toned back.

Even so, in retrospect, I was a tad reckless. Dark rooms, drugs, orgies – I was no stranger to any of them. In fact, I had a season ticket. I often turned up for work trashed from the previous evening but hung-over sleepy eyes only enhanced the come-to-bed subtext of my performance. I looked like I'd been having sex all night long – and I had. But even if mine was the name on everyone's lips, I was ostensibly a children's television presenter, so nothing could be too overt.

Then, at the Brit awards, Modesty's people suddenly announced that I, and my roving film crew, were to be whisked to the megastar's inner sanctum for a very exclusive interview.

'Oh, my God,' said Catherine, uncharacteristically flustered. She looked stunning that night, in a strapless red-silk number, and was drawing admiring glances. 'This is it. The big one! Get it right and you're made for life. I'll do the introductions. Do you think she'd be amused if I "strike a pose" when I walk in? Do you think it's all right to look her in the eye?'

'For God's sake, you don't have to walk backwards,' I snapped, wondering where I could get a line of cocaine to buck myself up for this once-in-a-lifetime opportunity. I didn't have to look far: Anita was loitering ten steps behind me, her bag of goodies at the ready. I had never been starstruck before; my boy-next-door manner had won over everyone from Diana Ross to Rick Astley. But Modesty was the most famous pop superstar in the world – with a fearsome reputation: she ate interviewers for breakfast.

Catherine trotted along beside me importantly as we were led backstage, saying loudly, 'I'm Johnny's manager,' whenever anyone caught her eye, but once we got closer to the inner sanctum, her way was barred by several security men. Ten minutes later the film crew and I were ushered into a muslin-draped igloo where Modesty sat waiting, small and serene, perched on a high stool, beautifully lit from behind.

'Hi there,' she said, reaching for my hand. 'I keep hearing about you wherever I go.'

'You're not unknown in my circles, either. What is it you're promoting today? Book, CD, fashion range or perfume?'

'I like your approach. Very fresh. Very Barbara Walters but without the hairspray. Have you been up all night being a bad boy?'

I had, yes. With one of her backing singers I'd met at a party, and a Nigerian taxi driver. The little devil had obviously told his boss about our free trip home to the hotel and the marathon night of sex and drugs that followed. Modesty was playing a game, letting me know that she was party to my secret.

'Up somewhere all night, yes. Now, enough about me. I suppose what my viewers want to know is – what's it like being Modesty?'

'Oh, it's fun. But complicated sometimes.'

'Do you need to sack people every so often to assert your authority?'

'Not especially, no. But they have to understand that I live on planet Modesty. That's my choice. I employ some to ensure my bubble never bursts and others to stop me taking myself too seriously. It's a balancing act, that's for sure.'

She was warming to me, I thought. She understood my cynical line of questioning, my lack of nerves, and was responding, I thought, honestly and intelligently. I'd try to push things a bit further.

'Lately you seem to be getting involved in world matters – peace, famine, plights and tragedies that beset the planet. Do you think that's appropriate for a pop star? Aren't you just there to entertain?'

Modesty pouted. 'Such insolence! I shall have you horse-whipped!'

We both laughed. Then she looked at me earnestly. 'Listen, Johnny. I started out as an ambitious dancer in New York. Things went well, then got better. I didn't know I was going to find myself in a position of great influence. What am I supposed to do? Churn out disco hits and keep smiling? If I'm on a world tour, performing to X million people, isn't it a good opportunity to make a few points about which I believe wholeheartedly? Where's the harm in that?'

'No harm at all. I guess music's the perfect medium.'

'I don't know about perfect, but it's a hell of a lot more effective than politics seems to be. Sex would be too exhausting, as I'm sure you'd agree.' She had laughter in her eyes.

'You're a naughty Modesty,' I said.

'I like you. Are you up for adoption?'

'Sadly, no. But you can always be my stalker if you want.'

She gave a good, healthy belly-laugh, looked straight into the camera and said, 'Johnny D is hot!'

'Are you flirting with me?' I asked.

'Flirting?' said Modesty. 'You're the most gorgeous creature I've ever clapped eyes on! And I've toured Brazil three times!'

'I'm glazing over, I'm afraid,' I said as one of Modesty's aides made vigorous wind-it-up signals at me. 'How much longer can you go on? Aren't you worried about becoming the Vera Lynn of pop?'

It was unheard of for anyone to be so irreverent to one of the most famous superstars of the day, but I felt I could get away with it.

'I'd be more than happy with such a title,' she said. 'Whoever the hell she is.'

The aides were apoplectic now, insisting we finish the interview at once. Then she grinned at me and said, 'See ya, Johnny. It's been fun.'

'Bye,' I said.

Outside, Catherine grabbed me.

'What was she like? What was she like?' she hissed.

I shrugged. 'Oh, you know. Nice.'

The interview was a coup for me, the programme and the BBC. The clip of Modesty saying, 'Johnny D is hot!' with her special brand of knowing sexiness was used to trail the show and as a kind of visual jingle throughout the series. Well, you would, wouldn't you? My sex appeal and cool-dude status were confirmed. If Modesty had said it, it must be true. The interview was declared one of the most revealing and sensational things to come out of that year's Brits. The press adored me. I was, without a shadow of doubt, the man of the moment. I was all the rage.

The only person who wasn't hugely impressed was my mother. Without a television and never reading the papers, she had no inkling of just how famous I'd become. She did notice that everyone in the village was being a lot nicer to her, all of a sudden, and asking when I might come to visit, but she couldn't fathom why.

I didn't let on to her the extent of my transformation. I wanted to keep one little part of my life untouched by the excitement and madness that had engulfed the rest.

CHAPTER TWENTY ONE

One night I was out on the town with a popular girl band of the time (five Liverpudlians called Rough, riding the crest of their success and on the hunt for Premier Division footballers before the moment passed). We were roped off from the hoi polloi so that we didn't have to sully ourselves with them but could enjoy our drugs and champagne in peace. Peace of a sort – Rough squealed and squawked and made raucous jokes as they got drunker and drunker while I smiled but wondered if there wasn't more fun to be had on the other side of the red velvet rope.

Then, to my astonishment, I saw a face I recognized. A man was talking to the burly bouncer guarding the VIP section, gesturing towards our table. He was handsome with short blonde hair. He was wearing – unusually for the kind of nightclub we were in – a suit of a distinctly Savile Row cut.

My heart began pounding and my palms were damp. 'Oh, my God,' I breathed. 'Tim!'

''Oo?' said Kelly, the thinnest member of Rough.

'Excuse me, girls. I've just seen someone I know.'

'Hurry back, Johnny,' shrieked Sabine, the classy one. 'I can't drink all this champers on me own. I'll fart like a rhino!'

I ignored them and hurried over.

'Do you know this gentleman?' asked the bouncer.

'Hello, Johnny,' Tim said, with a sweet smile, as though we'd last seen each other the other day, not five years before. 'How are you?'

'Fine.' I turned to the bouncer. 'Yes, he's a friend of mine. Please let him in.'

Once he was on the right side of the rope, we stood awkwardly in front of each other.

'Nice to see you, mate,' said Tim, giving me a manly pat on the shoulder. 'Life's been good to you, I gather.'

His straight-boy mannerisms annoyed me at some level, but seeing him rendered me speechless. Tim was really here, within reach.

He must have realized I couldn't answer him and had the social grace to witter on while I gathered my thoughts.

'I saw you on television the other day and the paper was full of pictures of you at the Brits. You've come a long way from gardening at Thornchurch! Who'd have thought it, eh?'

'Yes, well. I go with the flow, you know me.'

Just then a drunken member of Rough barged between us. 'Johnny, love, is this bloke getting on your tits?' She looked Tim up and down. 'Leave him alone, will ya, love? He's just having a quiet bevy. He's sick of being pestered by the likes of you.'

'It's all right, Lucy, we're old friends,' I said. 'Go and join the others and I'll see you in a bit.'

'I'm not Lucy. I'm Tammy, actually,' she said, offended, and staggered off.

'You're public property now, I suppose,' said Tim, a trifle sadly. 'I'd better leave you to your celebrity friends. Nice to see you again.' He signalled to the bouncer to let him back into the riff-raff area.

Suddenly aware that the man I had thought about every night for the last five years was turning his back on me again, I boldly took hold of his arm. 'No, you don't,' I said. 'We need to catch up.'

Emotion was fizzing inside me and I couldn't let him go. He looked down at my hand on his arm and gave me a slow, contented smile.

We left Rough gawping with displeasure and slipped away. Roy drove us to a quiet members-only club, hidden behind a nondescript green door in a Soho back-street. It was one thirty in the morning. Despite its modest entrance, the club was extremely exclusive. I'd been a member for only a few months, having been fast-tracked up the waiting list. The other members were either famous or accustomed to working with the famous – agents, managers, TV types, media executives and journalists – so it was one of the few places I could go without being stared at or hassled. Inside, the lucky members could enjoy a gourmet restaurant or choose between several quiet, dimly lit bars with discreet but attentive staff. Upstairs there were a number of luxury 'recovery rooms' where customers who had over-indulged could lie down until they felt more themselves. Or whatever. We chose the colonial-style Victoria Bar and I nodded politely to a shockingly inebriated Paul O'Grady and Sigourney Weaver as we made our way through it. Maybe this place wasn't so exclusive, after all.

'Anyone would think it was Pound-a-pint-for-Scousers Night,' I muttered to Tim, as we passed, ignoring Paul's shrill demand that I join them for a half of cider and a sniff of poppers.

We settled into a quiet corner, then ordered oysters and brandy Alexanders with fresh nutmeg as a Chopin concerto wafted soothingly over the sound system.

'Ah, that's better,' I said, beginning to relax. 'So, tell me about your exciting life. The last time we spoke you were off to Cambridge, weren't you?'

The mention of that meeting seemed to embarrass Tim, as I had hoped it would. My heart had never mended, and while I wanted to appear bright, happy and attractive, part of me wanted him to know how much he had hurt me, stunted me and, despite the trappings of success, ruined me.

He overcame his discomfort and answered easily, 'Oh, Cambridge was a hoot. I had a fantastic time. Made lots of great friends and finished with a first in Law, so Father was happy.'

'How is he?' I kept a straight face.

'Oh, busy on the farm and at the House of Lords, same as ever. Mother's thriving too. Regina has been married off to a rich South African and lives under armed guard at some sort of vineyard in Cape Town. How's your mum? Still as mad as a March hare?'

'Bloody cheek!' I said. 'She made you a lovely tea once.'

I studied Tim's face. His complexion was a little darker, his hair shorter, and the cute mannerism he'd had of tossing his fringe out of his eyes was now gone. But his eyes! They were the same expensive sapphire blue, and when I looked into them I was lost again, transported back to the summerhouse. I had wondered over the years if my love for him had been an illusion, a crush, somehow kept alive by willpower. Of course I'd imagined meeting him again, but what if first love had been simply youthful folly?

Now here I was with him, gazing into those heavenly eyes again, and all was well with the world. The twin towers of love and desire were standing tall and sturdy. Did Tim feel the same? I fervently hoped so – that would be my Mills and Boon fantasy fulfilled, but now was not the time to ask. Despite our looks and smiles, and the attraction you could almost see, like fireworks going off between us, we were still at the polite chit-chat stage.

'I'm working in the City now,' Tim was saying. 'Training to be a lawyer. Bloody hard work, doing my pupillage. I qualify in about five years' time.'

'An eternity,' I agreed. 'Where do you live?'

'Cadogan Square. Poky little mansion flat. More of a bedsit, really.'

We were on our third drink before either of us had the nerve to mention our love lives.

'I read about you and the air stewardess in the *News of the World*,' said Tim, grinning. 'Good on you. She gave you a very good report, you dirty devil!'

'Yes, I know,' I said flatly. 'I wrote it myself.'

'Oh, I see. Not true, then?'

'No.'

He seemed to feel the need to get the next bit of information out as quickly possible. 'I'm engaged to a cracking girl called Sophie. Her father invented laminate flooring.' He averted his eyes at the end of the sentence so I had time to recover.

'It'll never catch on. Where is she tonight?'

'Switzerland. Skiing with the Sandersons.' There was a pause. When he looked at me again my thoughts must have been obvious. 'You turned out to be gay after all, then, did you?'

'That's right.'

He glanced around to make sure no one was within earshot. 'Good lad,' he said quietly, and smiled his best, sexiest smile. 'Mind if I order a cigar to celebrate?'

I ordered it for him and brandy for both of us.

'Is there a recovery room available?' I asked the waiter, a thin, sad-looking man of about my age. More an out-of-work actor than a drama student, I thought.

'I'm afraid Mr O'Grady has just booked the last one, sir,' he said, rolling his eyes in the direction of Paul and Sigourney.

'Listen,' I said, slipping a fifty-pound note into his hand, 'tell Mr O'Grady there's been a mistake. He'd only honk in the sock drawer anyway.'

'Very good, sir,' said third chorus boy from the left, and walked towards the noisy duo on the other side of the room.

Twenty minutes later I closed the recovery-room door behind us and Tim and I were alone at last.

'I keep thinking this is a mistake,' were Tim's first words. He spoke quietly, without conviction, and almost before he had finished his sentence he pulled me roughly towards him and kissed me. Or, rather, we kissed each other. Five years of pent-up longing and missing found a fissure of expression in the volcanic rock of our fused emotions. It was the kiss of a lifetime, a time-travelling kiss. By the end of it, we were naked, satiated, empty and extremely sweaty.

We fell asleep almost immediately, as if we were anxious for another level of consciousness to take over and make sense of everything for us.

It was the dustbin men who woke me. It must have been about six. The window was open and the curtains were wafting in and out like lungs. I felt the heavy weight of a sleeping man on my left arm, and turned to see Tim, fast asleep and snoring through his open mouth. I studied the ridges in his lips, the bubbles of saliva gathering in the corners, and when I could stand it no more, I leant over and kissed him. I started by sucking his dry, dehydrated lips with my moist, succulent ones. I wanted Tim's to slide against mine, slowly arousing him so he would drift seamlessly from the calm lagoons of sleep into the deep, rocky waters of early-morning lust. But just as things were heading nicely in that direction, he opened bloodshot eyes and looked at me.

'Oh, my good god,' he said, stunned to discover where he was, what he was doing and who he was doing it with.

He bowed his head, exhaling noisily on my Adam's apple, then rolled off me unceremoniously.

'I'm a fucking idiot,' he said, running his palm over his forehead and banging the top of his head several times. 'Jesus Christ!'

He jumped out of bed and grabbed his clothes from about the room, getting particularly upset with his shirt, because it was inside-out – as if that was a painful reminder to him of our unbridled passion a few hours earlier.

Dressed, he stumbled into the bathroom. I heard him splash water on his face. 'Shit. Fuck!' he kept saying. Angrily he urinated, then slammed down the toilet handle with an almighty crash. He came back to the bedroom and stood beside me. 'I'm going,' he said.

'This is very sudden,' I said sarcastically. I was still lying naked on top of the bedclothes and tried giving my hips a suggestive wiggle. I wasn't going to let my lover walk out on me again, five years down the line, still protesting his indifference to my charms. Last night had put paid to that lie. 'You're scared of me,' I said.

'I know I am,' he replied.

'Is that it, then? Goodbye and thank you?'

He swayed from side to side, some internal pendulum rocking him one way then the other. 'Johnny, I'm going to marry Sophie.

Look, maybe we could meet up some time for a drink.' He pulled out his wallet and fiddled inside it. He took out a card and put it on the bedside table. 'It's been nice seeing you. Call me some time.'

'Remember me,' I said.

He smiled and left.

CHAPTER TWENTY TWO

Life was good, apart from two things. One, of course, was my secret love for Tim and the bittersweet memory of what happened between us that night. Whatever he had said in the morning, and however unceremonious his departure had been, I knew we had unfinished business to attend to.

The other problem was Bernard. Since I had tasted the pleasure of Tim, I had barely been able to tolerate him. Every ounce of affection I'd felt for him (and there had been only a couple to start with) had vanished. Instead I found him intensely irritating and did my best to avoid him. As a result, things were tense and his behaviour became increasingly erratic. He had taken to hissing things like 'I made you and I'll break you, you little shit! I know what you've been up to' one minute, then declaring eternal love the next.

When the show came to its three-month break, and I was on holiday from recording, Bernard suggested a trip to Nicaragua. I decided to go. He was thrilled. He thought this was our big romantic moment, and I let him, but in truth I felt it might do us good to get away and clear the air. I wanted to calm him down and get things on an even keel between us. I knew he was an important factor in my success, still, and I needed to keep him sweet. But he also had to understand that he wasn't my boyfriend and that I had to have a life without him in it. If we went away, I was sure we could sort it out. Besides, I was tired, feeling the effects of too many nights on the town. In the last few months I had found fame, fortune and Tim. I wanted to lie on a sandy beach and take stock.

All was well enough on the flight, but as soon as we landed in Managua, Bernard was clutching my arm like a maiden aunt, complaining about the heat, the food, the wine, and being more demanding and dramatic than ever.

Once we'd fought our way through the chaos of the airport we spent a night in the sleepy, dusty town of Granada, at the vaguely Arabic, colonial-style Villa Franca. Charming, dusky Latino boys were all around us, and Bernard guarded me jealously, placing a proprietorial hand on my arm whenever a handsome waiter, with white teeth and low-slung chinos, drifted past.

'Oh, for goodness' sake, Bernard, do calm down. If you're going to act like this the entire time, I'm going home right now,' I said crossly.

'All right. Sorry,' he replied sulkily. 'But no flirting!'

'I'm not flirting,' I said, exasperated. 'Now can you please stop, and let us both enjoy our well-earned holiday? Thank you.'

A day later we moved to the seaside resort of St Juan, where we resided in a hillside bungalow, dined in the alfresco restaurant and nodded at the security guards as we made our way up the hill in the evenings.

'Shall we go to the beach today, or stay by the hotel pool?' I asked, on the third morning, trying to snap us both out of a stormy mood. No matter how hard we tried, we couldn't relax together.

'I'm tired,' answered Bernard. 'I think I'll go for a lie-down. Go to the beach and I'll see you there in an hour or so.'

That was fine by me. If Bernard wasn't with me, for a while at least, I could forget about keeping him happy and concentrate on my own needs for a change. I was longing for a few minutes to myself so I could think about Tim. I wished Bernard a good rest and wandered slowly down the hill to the beach.

I stopped for a moment to take in the perfect view. The blue sky dominated a passive sea, and anaemic sand lay prostrate under both.

There was movement, and my eye was drawn to the fleshy tanned torsos of some youthful footballers. Aware of temptation, I tried to look elsewhere, to the trees that fringed the beach or the boats sailing across the horizon, but I was helpless to control my gaze. Like a street dog following a promising scent, I made my way to the beach and settled myself a few yards from the game so that I could watch easily.

There were six players, all clearly Nicaraguans, but one in particular attracted me. He was older than the others, about twenty-three, with wavy black hair. He seemed aware of my attention, glancing in my direction whenever the game allowed him to do so. I lay back on my towel and applied some sun lotion, flirting surreptitiously, and looking enigmatically out to sea whenever I was sure he had me in his sights.

As the game finished, I wandered to the sea and kicked the waves playfully. Suddenly my favourite ran past me and dived, dolphin-like, into the water. A few seconds later I followed him. Alongside each other, we took a deep breath and dived. Under water we held eye-contact for as long as we could, until laughter overtook us and we surfaced, smiling. We began a conversation, while doggy-paddling in the deeper water some yards out to sea.

His name was Juan, he informed me. He was twenty-four – I'd been almost right – and lived with his family in the resort. 'I have a car,' he said importantly, as if this qualified him in some way. His English was limited but understandable.

'Your friend? I have seen. Where your friend?'

'He sleeping,' I told him, and rolled my eyes.

'Your father?' he said, and laughed unkindly. Under the cover of water he stroked my shoulder, then swam towards the shore and joined his friends, who were still kicking the football about in the sunshine.

I felt a shimmer of excitement. Juan was a gorgeous creature. He'd driven my thoughts of Tim from my head, and that made a refreshing change. I returned to my towel and lay down, closed my eyes and relaxed for the first time in ages. Time away from Bernard was so much more enjoyable than time spent in his company.

My contemplations were disturbed by a shout of '*Hola*, JD!'

Juan's tousled locks were silhouetted against the sun and it took me a moment to focus. He was kneeling next to me and gave me a nudge in the ribs with his knee.

'I can drive you and your friend to the volcano in my car. You like? Tomorrow morning?'

Trips to Mount Massaya were popular with tourists. The hotel was offering a group trip in its minibus, promising to show us bubbling mud pools and impressive jets from geysers and blow-holes, but a private trip with a personal guide would be much nicer, especially if that guide was Juan.

'Yes, please. How kind.' I arranged to meet him at ten a.m. the next day at the hotel reception.

*

Dawn heralded another beautiful day. Part of me had hoped that Bernard would take to his bed again after breakfast so that I could go to the volcano alone with Juan, but Bernard had seemed pleased and excited by the prospect of the trip and bounced out of bed to get ready. As he came out of the shower I pushed him back on to the bed and did my best to wear him out before the day began, but to no avail.

'That's set me up nicely, Johnny,' he said happily, with a romantic sigh. 'Thank you, darling.'

Over breakfast he stroked his cheek with a white orchid from the table display and ordered a luxurious picnic for us to take with us to the volcano. 'I do hope we'll be safe!' he exclaimed. 'I've seen enough eruptions of hot lava for one day ...'

Over his shoulder I could see Juan, lovely in a tatty grey singlet and off-white shorts, waiting in the sunshine by his car. 'Our driver awaits!' I told Bernard, who turned to look. Juan waved.

Bernard seemed a little minty. 'That vehicle doesn't look the type that has air-conditioning,' he said, 'And I doubt he's fully insured.'

It was a bumpy journey, conducted mostly in silence. Juan asked me what I did in London, and I said I worked in television. Bernard's mood had taken a downward swing, and he sat in the back seat inhaling noisily and going 'Ugh!' every time we trundled over a rock.

As the car swung about, Juan and I knocked legs, creating a static both real and atmospheric. Each time the hairs on our outer thighs tangled momentarily, then stretched out longingly, like young lovers across a balcony.

After an hour's driving we turned off what, for all its shortcomings, was a main road on to a far inferior track towards Mount Massaya. The air became misty with heat, gravel and ash, while plumes of grey steam blossomed from nowhere. We were climbing the mountainside and Juan was gaining speed, despite the engine's protests, diving round hairpin bends in a cloud of dust and laughing with delight, presumably at our against-the-odds survival. I spread my palms on the ceiling of the car to stop me banging my head and kept my eyes closed. After some particularly violent bumps they opened involuntarily and I snatched a glimpse of treacherous precipices and spindly trees clinging to life at unfeasible angles.

Eventually we stopped at a deserted viewing-point and climbed out of the car, relieved to have arrived in one piece.

'Magnificent!' I said, gazing out at the view. Pale green and grey olive trees shimmered down the hillside, and scattered between them I saw the distant colours and heard the sounds of primitive villages going about their business. 'Isn't it amazing, Bernard?'

'I'm hungry,' said Bernard, turning to the picnic basket. He spread out our lunch on a fairly flat piece of rock, but Juan stayed in the car until I asked him to join us.

'Must he?' asked Bernard.

'We can't leave the poor boy sitting in the car all afternoon,' I said. 'There are limits.'

As soon as I invited him Juan leapt out happily and joined us. We ate sardines, chicken and coconut and drank beer. Nearby, ponds of thick mud simmered lazily.

'You look good in this setting, Bernard,' I said. 'Like something out of *Jurassic Park*.'

'Go fuck yourself,' said Bernard, but he was amused.

'I think I'll call you Jurassic from now on,' I continued playfully.

'Try it and see what happens,' said Bernard. 'It seems a shame to throw away your TV career when things are going so well.'

Before long he was yawning and saying he really shouldn't have drunk all that beer. 'I very rarely drink, you know,' he lied to Juan, who didn't know what he was saying.

After what seemed an eternity, he fell into a noisy slumber. I signalled to Juan to follow me. We tiptoed a few yards down a mountain path and sat under some olive trees. Our legs brushed together and we giggled nervously. I lay back and remembered my mother's trick of licking her lips and opening her mouth just a little. It worked and Juan rolled on top of me. I'm not sure how long our lovely encounter had been going on, but we were well into the heavy-petting stage and our shorts had just been discarded when we were violently disturbed.

'You bastards!' screamed Bernard, from twenty feet above us. 'You pair of absolute fucking, cunting bastards!'

He picked up several hand-sized rocks and threw them at us, missing by inches as we fumbled to get dressed. Juan ran down the hill and I ran up towards our attacker.

'Stop this, Bernard! We were only messing around! It's the altitude, it makes us light-headed!' Bernard was struggling to pick up a rather ambitiously sized boulder. 'You'll kill one of us with that. Put it down!'

'Well, I hope I do!' he said, trying to fling the rock at me but succeeding in dropping it an inch from his feet. 'Fuck!' he declared.

By now I was in front of him and I held his shoulders to prevent him gathering any more missiles. 'Calm down! It was nothing! Don't be so hysterical!'

But my touch seemed to recharge his anger. Suddenly he broke away from me and ran (rather nimbly for someone of his years) in the other direction, past the car and over a ridge, all the while flailing his arms like a mad Italian TV chef, half sobbing, half screaming.

'Oh, Jesus,' I muttered, and walked wearily after him. 'What a fiasco.'

When I reached the top of the ridge I stopped in my tracks. Bernard was standing on the edge of a grey mudpool, looking down into the swirling, steaming, bubbling mass.

'Bernard,' I said, serious all at once, 'what do you think you're doing?'

'I've been a fool,' he began. 'You don't love me, you've made that very clear. You told me so before I made you a star, but I wasn't listening. Now I've seen with my own eyes your contempt for me. It's too much, JD. There's only so much grief a man can take. My life, in many ways, is already over. I just have to catch up with that reality.'

I stood and stared, not sure if I was expected to speak. I sensed, with the benefit of experience, that Bernard was enjoying being the focus of this dramatic scene. Far be it from me to interrupt. His tone had been strangely portentous, Churchillian, even.

'I've enjoyed flashes of happiness in my life. I have loved – and felt, at times, that I was loved, but not any more. Who would want me now? I can't go on. I can't pick up the pieces and fight off loneliness any longer.' His chest heaved and tears flowed.

If I was going to plead with him not to jump, now was the moment. I didn't really want to witness such a grisly suicide. Apart from anything else, explaining his disappearance to the Nicaraguan authorities was bound to be a nightmare. And what of our considerable hotel bill? Familiar as I was with these histrionics, I knew I could talk him down. But curiosity got the better of me. I would say nothing and call Bernard's bluff.

He was still talking. 'It's far better this way. If I continued with this life, the image of you cavorting with our driver will be for ever branded on my mind. You, who mean everything to me, fucking about with a Nicaraguan slut under my nose! Who'd have thought it? How many others have there been, eh? The receptionist? The security guard? The waiter? You bastard!'

I was lost for words. Let the silly fool jump, I thought. At least I won't have to touch his withered old penis again. It was into the fiery mouth of Massaya that the Sandinistas allegedly threw their enemies and, according to the guidebook, sufferers of unrequited love weren't strangers to this dismally beautiful place. Jump, I thought. Go on, jump. I said nothing, just looked at him and gave a contemptuous half-smile.

There was silence. Was his speech over now? Would Bernard take an anti-climactic step away from the edge or jump to sizzling oblivion?

'Goodbye, and fuck off, world!' Bernard shouted. He bent his knees and raised his arms like a small boy on a diving-board. Suddenly, from a rock covered with singed grass a few yards behind him, Juan emerged. He moved forward stealthily and grabbed Bernard from behind in a bear-hug, lifting him off the ground and pulling him to safety.

'No, Juan!' I said, and rushed forward. This drama, of course, unleashed more cries from Jurassic, but now they were those of a damsel being abducted.

'Help! Help! Put me down, you brute! No, anything but that, you beast!'

I reached the wrestling couple and prised Juan's suntanned arms away from Bernard's torso. 'You don't understand, Juan! Leave him, please, leave him alone!'

'Consider yourself well and truly replaced as the front man of *Shout!*, Johnny, my boy! You just kissed your career good night!' screamed Bernard, a look of triumph on his face.

This cruel announcement pushed me over the edge, I'm afraid. My fists clenched and my leg darted out angrily, almost before I'd had a chance to know what I was doing. I caught Bernard sharply in the pit of his stomach. He fell backwards and tumbled head first into the mudpool. He resurfaced momentarily, looking suitably grue-some and shocked, but disappeared again surprisingly quickly. A grey, clay-covered hand reached up and out, then down again. Then, after a dull, slopping sound, there was silence.

Juan moved as if to rescue him but I held him tight.

'No,' I said quietly. 'It's too late. Leave him. He's gone.'

Bernard should have worn a St Christopher like me, was my first thought.

PART FOUR

PART FOUR

CHAPTER TWENTY THREE

The job of television presenting is a peculiar one, and if I can say anything with certainty, it is that I never fell into the trap of taking it seriously. Dear, departed Bernard had plucked me from a life of obscure prostitution and, with little or no ambition on my part, had put me in the right place at the right time. Nature and nurture had ticked some of the requisite boxes for my success: I had a pleasing face, a soothing voice and could read an autocue. Furthermore, I acknowledge, Bernard had wielded his influence and called in favours to get my shows commissioned. The rest, as they say, had been down to luck.

The trick to gaining high ratings is that you must have broad appeal. The show that made me, *Shout!*, had been aimed at teenagers, but was watched by students, young adults – anyone interested in youth culture and what was or wasn't 'cool'. The indefinable touch, the X factor of my success and the thing that I transmitted, without being aware of it, was sex. I smelt of it, exuded it and, through me, desire smouldered. My sexual confidence beamed its way into millions of hearts and homes. Being photographed at Heathrow on my return from Nicaragua made me realize I was seriously famous.

How was I supposed to cope with being gorgeous, rich, a murderer of two men – *and* famous? My ego, of course, became blissed out, hopeless at any detached assessment of my situation. I simply excused my actions and refused to feel guilty. I thought I was invincible and that fame had made me complete. I felt that everything had been leading up to it. Even if my life was a puzzle that would only be deciphered when it was over, I believed that God was on my side.

I had tried to call Catherine from Nicaragua but it was impossible. On the few occasions when I managed to get a line to England, there was no reply. I decided it was safer to leave the whole story till I got home. As soon as I was back, I sat her down and gave her the true account of what had happened up the mountain and how Bernard had died.

She frowned, then said, 'Most unpleasant for you both. Speaking as your manager, I suppose we could have put a bit more planning into it, but Bernard was becoming a serious drag. The important thing is that he's out of the way. Well done, Cowboy.'

She didn't like the sound of Juan, though. 'That was a bit careless of you. Witnesses are always a mistake. I'd have tossed him in too. It would have been a lot tidier.'

'I never thought of that,' I said. 'We can all be wise after the event.'

Of course I would never have dreamt of chucking Juan into the volcano. He was not only extremely beautiful but had provided me with exquisite pleasure. Most importantly, he had taken my mind off Tim.

Bernard, on the other hand, had expressed his wish to die – perhaps not as clearly and convincingly as Georgie had but, still, he had said as much – and would have jumped himself if Juan had not made the mistake of stopping him. By pushing him in, I might be technically guilty of murder but I knew I wasn't really. I had merely corrected a small glitch in the order of things. Killing Juan would have been something different altogether. It had never occurred to me. I wasn't that kind of boy.

'Well, you say this Juan can't speak English, and he won't have any idea of who you are, so perhaps we'll be all right,' Catherine said. 'I take it you gave him a massive wad of cash to keep quiet about what really happened? That should take care of him. What we have to focus on now is getting your reaction to Bernard's death just right. This, Cowboy, is what they call a key moment.'

Catherine had taken to media manipulation like a duck to water. After all, she had been manipulating those around her all her life so she'd had plenty of practice. 'The editor of the *Sun* likes me,' was all she would say. 'He's more important than the prime minister, as far as you're concerned.'

She had long since given up her life of vice and now moulded her image on Helen Mirren in *Prime Suspect*, wearing sharp, muted suits, high heels and a neat haircut. She was self-possessed and calm at all times. Now that she wasn't on the game, she had struck it lucky and was the (more or less) exclusive mistress of a married Algerian drugs baron. He gave her an excellent seeing-to every time he was in town, along with oodles of cash, a drawerful of diamonds and emeralds and as much cocaine as the pair of us could snort. Which was quite a lot.

Ali was of a jealous nature and not at all happy about Catherine sharing a flat with me, a man. But Catherine had put down her expensively pedicured foot. 'He's a woofter, Ali. He's not interested in me! You're being ridiculous. Johnny makes sure I come to no harm. We look after each other.'

Ali wasn't convinced and seemed to have no concept of homosexuality (unusual in an Algerian). He was only satisfied after he had sent round his personal physician to give me a rectal examination. After that, Catherine and he continued their affair, but when he wasn't in town, she made the most of her freedom and often went out on the pull.

'Aren't you supposed to belong to Ali?' I teased her.

'Fuck that for a game of soldiers,' she said. 'I may have sucked cock for cash, but I ain't kissing ass.'

After Bernard's death, she managed the press carefully and brilliantly, and although I was declared too upset to give any interviews, the 'Tragic Death Of Hero TV Star's Mentor' was front-page news. The story Catherine ('a close friend') had sold, needless to say, for a substantial fee, was that Bernard and I had been attacked by a band of ruthless robbers while visiting Mount Massaya. I had bravely fought them off but poor Bernard had been flung mercilessly into a mudpool before my very eyes. Traumatized as I was, I had fearlessly chased the murdering thieves for several exhausting miles, but they had eventually got away.

Of course, the one person (apart from myself and Catherine) who knew the truth of what had happened that afternoon was Juan. I had clung to him as I kicked Bernard that afternoon. He had seen what I'd done and had looked at me, stupefied with shock.

'It was an accident,' I had repeated to him, like a sort of mantra. And then he, in turn, clung to me. He had stayed with me for the remainder of my time in Nicaragua and confirmed to the police my version of events although it was probably my bribe of several hundred dollars that saved the day. I thought it wise to turn all my guns of seduction on him. I lavished him with affection and money, and saw to it that we were inseparable. Besides, sex with Juan was no great chore and, given his rudimentary grasp of English, one of the most effective ways of communicating. I feel foolish confessing it, but maybe I was a little in love with him, too. But only a little. And only maybe. Our bodies fitted together so well, and the raw, animal nature of our relationship obscured any wise, self-protective assessment of matters. By the time I left him crying at the airport he was well and truly under my spell, and I was sure that my secret was safe with him.

Now I could get on with my career. I couldn't help feeling refreshed and happy without the constant drain of Bernard's snipes and demands.

Despite the attempts of the Nicaraguan authorities, Bernard's body had never been recovered, nor the murderers apprehended (unsurprisingly), so Catherine thought it would be a good idea to hold a memorial for Bernard at the actors' church in Covent Garden. I was to be chief mourner. The press were alerted.

'Wear dark glasses and look as if you've been crying, please,' Catherine instructed. 'Stay up all night or something. But shave – show some respect. All eyes will be on you. I'll be there with smelling-salts if you feel faint.'

Bernard had worked with many celebrities in his career, but I was the hottest and the most famous. I stood on the church steps wearing black Prada from head to toe, smiling weakly (with,

I liked to think, a hint of allure still) and shaking hands with the many guests. The tabloids called me brave and broken-hearted. It couldn't have been better.

The best moment was the release of fifty doves dyed canary yellow – Bernard's favourite colour. A flock of seagulls swarmed in and attacked them as the mourners were gazing skyward. They were killed, every last one.

The public, however, saw another side of me and responded with genuine sympathy. I had hundreds of letters from people who wanted to express their sorrow, share their grief or send their best wishes and fervent hopes that I would be back on their TV screens soon. I was touched, and almost able to forget that I had pushed Bernard into a mudpool in the first place. Offers of work and magazine spreads poured in.

I was at home alone in the flat one afternoon (Catherine was having a long lunch with the editor of *Hello!* magazine) when I noticed that my favourite Gucci trousers had been returned from the cleaners. Stapled to the protective cover was a white envelope, the words 'contents of pocket' scrawled across it. I ripped it off and opened it. Inside was a small white business card, and across the middle was engraved '*Timothy Thornchurch*'.

Just seeing the name made my stomach quiver. I stared at it for a long time, running my fingers over the raised lettering. The urge to speak to him became unbearable. On impulse, I picked up the phone and, heart in my mouth, dialled his chambers in Fleet Street. 'Could I speak to Timothy Thornchurch, please?' I asked the unfeasibly posh-sounding woman who answered.

'Who shall I say is calling?'

My name was likely to cause a stir even in her plummy circles, so I said I was a Mr Bassey.

'Putting you through,' she said.

He sounded business-like when he answered. 'Timothy Thornchurch. How may I help you, Mr Bassey?'

'Meet me at a hotel tonight and make love to me,' I said.

'Er, who is this?' Then his voice changed. 'Johnny?'

'Do many of your clients ask you for a fuck?'

'Johnny, I've been so worried about you!' He sounded soft and friendly and I wanted to rush over to Fleet Street right there and then and fling myself into his arms. 'Are you all right? I've been reading about what happened to you. It sounded absolutely dreadful. I hope they catch the bastards.'

'I'm fine, a bit shaken. It's good to be home.'

'That poor bloke, drowned in boiling mud, right in front of you. It must have been horrible.'

'It was. He was such a dear old boy. I'm mentally scarred for life. I think I might be cracking up ...' I let my voice trail away.

'Listen. I have a meeting at six tonight but I could meet you afterwards. Would you like that?'

I managed a weak 'Thank you. I'll book a room at the Savoy.'

'Under the name of Mr Bassey?'

'Of course.'

'See you about eight.'

It had been so easy. Tim had responded sympathetically to my situation and now I would have him again. After all the years of silence and absence! If only I'd known that all I had to do was get famous and chuck some old duffer into a volcano, I'd have done it sooner.

When he tapped on the door soon after eight that evening,

I had to stop myself opening it with a big, happy smile. I rubbed my eyes a little and slumped my shoulders, presenting myself as distraught. He cradled me in his arms and I wept like a child. 'It's all right,' he whispered. 'I'm here now.'

The role of heroic saviour clearly appealed to him; his love-making was gentle and considerate and afterwards, I told him, I felt truly healed. Remarkable, really.

That was how our second affair began. We would meet every week when we could, usually at the Savoy, and spend a night together. I was so truly happy that I couldn't hide it, and within days Catherine had guessed my secret.

'I know what's happening,' she said in disgust. 'You're like a pig in shit.'

I didn't care. After all I had been through, the waiting was over. I had Timothy Thornchurch at last. Or, at least, I had part of him once a week. The only problem looming on the horizon was that, sooner or later, I would want the rest to go with it.

CHAPTER TWENTY FOUR

'*Hola?*'

'Sorry?' I didn't recognize the voice – the line was crackly and distorted.

'Johnny? Ees Juan!'

'Oh. Oh. Juan. Hello. How are you?' My heart sank. I had hoped never to hear from him again.

'Johnny, I meess you. I love you.'

My heart plummeted into my boots. 'I love you too, Juan, but we are forced to be apart for ever, sadly. My life is here, your life is there ...'

'No, no. Johnny – I no can live wizout you.'

'Is it money, Juan? Is that what you need? How much?'

'No, I no need money. I rich now. I sell my car for two hundred dollars. Buy ticket. Johnny, I come live with you. I meess you, I love you.'

'Oh, Christ.'

'You happy, Johnny, huh?'

'Ah – yes, yes, very happy ...'

'Me too. I see you next week. Come to airport, meet me. Next Tuesday, nine o'clock. Heathrow. Bye, Johnny!'

I reported this matter rather sheepishly to Catherine, who wasn't best pleased. 'Oh, for fuck's sake,' she said. 'That's all we need. Well, he can come for a week, then salsa back to the coffee plantation he came from. I've heard of "Fair Trade" but this is ridiculous.'

'He says he wants to live here.'

'I'll bet he does. But it's a quick trip round London – Leicester Square, Nelson's Column, Buckingham Palace – then home, with a bit of extra dosh as a sweetener.'

I felt relieved. If Catherine thought it would work out, I was sure it would. She always had my best interests at heart. And, in the interests of keeping Juan on side, I might have to force myself into hours of sweaty, pleasure-making sex. Perhaps this would have the added bonus of making Tim jealous. After all, he presumably slept with the laminate-flooring heiress, Sophie, although he was careful never to mention her and I didn't ask questions. It would all be fine.

The following Tuesday I stood, disguised in a baseball cap and dark glasses, in the arrivals hall at Heathrow airport. I was aware of a flutter of excitement and was cross with myself. The plan, as laid out by Catherine, was for me to be chilly and cold to Juan, not so much that he turned against me and decided to tell the truth about Bernard, but enough for him to want to return to Nicaragua on the return ticket she had so generously bought him.

But it wasn't that easy. When Juan emerged, gorgeous but bewildered, my heart melted. He seemed so innocent and lost. The frosty greeting she had instructed me to give didn't material-ize. Instead we threw our arms round each other like Romeo and Juliet, kissed passionately in the taxi on the way home and made our way straight to the bedroom when we got there.

When I came out several hours later, hair tousled, lips burning, Catherine was sitting silently in the lounge with her arms crossed.

'So,' she said crisply, 'I take it your special delivery has arrived?'

'Er, yes, he has.'

'And what happened to my instruction to drop him at the YMCA? I take it that went out of the window. From the grunts and groans coming from your room, you've either got Juan or a pot-bellied pig in there. And I know which I'd rather it was.'

'I didn't have the heart to be horrible to him. He seemed so vulnerable,' I said apologetically.

'Oh, I think you'll find it's you who's vulnerable, Cowboy. Anyway, he's here now. I'll have to skip to plan B. Get him out.'

'Plan B?' I asked.

'I shall keep it to myself. You'd only fuck it up. Chop-chop. Show Mummy what you've dragged home.'

'He's sleeping off his jet-lag. Let the poor boy rest.'

'I'll give him rest,' she muttered. 'You'll not be the first person to discover the short lifespan of a holiday romance. *Pick Me Up!* magazine is full of sad twats like you, although their fancy-men are mostly Turkish. I bet Juan thinks he's won the fucking lottery. Never mind love – these Latin Americans will do the business for a Diet Coke! He gives us former working girls a bad name.' She got up and hammered on my bedroom door. 'Come on out, *gracias*. Let's have a vada at you.'

A few seconds later, Juan emerged, sleepy-eyed and terribly sexy.

To my surprise, Catherine was very welcoming and outwardly pleasant. Of course, there was a barbed subtext to her words but mercifully it was lost on him. 'I'm so pleased to meet you!' she said. 'Johnny has told me so much about you. I've boiled some rice to help you feel at home. Would you like some?'

'Er, thank you,' said Juan, confused.

'Don't mention it, sweetie. And I'm going to teach you some proper English. I don't know what the Spanish is for "Fuck-face", but I shall make it my duty to find out. You'll find it an invaluable phrase, staying in London. Are you staying long, or is it just a flying visit? You'll be very cold here, I expect ...'

Juan turned to me. Sweat was glistening on his brow. 'I no understand,' he said helplessly, his golden skin glowing in the lamplight.

'Your poor mother will be missing you already, I should think,' Catherine went on, enjoying Juan's discomfort.

'My mother dead. I want be with Johnny,' said Juan.

God bless him for fighting back, I thought, touched. It occurred to me that Catherine was being a lot nastier than she needed to be, even if she was disguising it as niceness. Why did Juan rile her so badly? He was just a simple lad from Central America, and while he might hold the information that could destroy us, he had no intention of using it, as far as we knew. He liked me. Why would he want to turn me in?

Catherine lowered her voice so Juan couldn't hear her. 'Fuckofacio is here to stay, he thinks. It seems we have a difference of opinion. Shame.' She was leaning against the fridge, and stroked it affectionately. 'I'll give it a week,' she said to both of us.

Clearly Juan had other ideas. He believed we were at the start of a new life together. 'I love you for ever!' he said, about five times a day.

He was my constant companion and followed me around like a puppy. On the days when I was meeting Tim at the Savoy I told him I had to work and sent him to the cinema down the road: I tied the front-door key round his wrist on a piece of elastic so he didn't lose it. He was overwhelmed by the big city. Coming as he did from peaceful countryside, he was wide-eyed with wonder at the hustle and bustle of London life. 'Everything so fast!' he said.

'Ain't that the truth,' said Catherine. 'Apart from Johnny's arse, which is *sooo* loose!' She took delight in making jokes that he wouldn't understand.

'*Que?*' he said.

Catherine rolled her eyes.

When people stopped me in the street and asked for my autograph, he was amazed. 'You famous!' he said.

'Oh, well, yes. A little!' I said modestly.

'Aah,' said Juan, his big brown eyes wide with wonder. And adored me even more.

At first, it was lovely in a way. I revelled in his beautiful body, which was mine to enjoy at any time of day or night. He was sex on tap, always ready to please me, the other extreme to my secretive hotel love-ins with Tim.

But after a while, it began to pall. Sexual pleasure is all very well, but if you're going to carry on doing it with the same person time after time, you have to feel something for them, and as time went on, I felt less and less for Juan. The language barrier was more of a problem than I'd thought it would be. I was used to people laughing at my witty observations, but Juan just looked at me quizzically. I tried explaining and translating, with the help of a Spanish dictionary, but by then the moment had passed.

It might not have been so bad if he hadn't been around so much, but the only respite I had from him was when he took himself off to the English classes I'd arranged for him to have twice a week; otherwise he made it his duty to be at my side night and day, at the TV studio or a nightclub. At a time in my life when my every professional utterance was greeted more or less with unprecedented rapture, I found myself at home of an evening with a semi-literate foreigner who smelt of clay and didn't know what a TV remote control was, let alone a TV star of my calibre. A divine irony, you might think, but it was cruel and unendurable.

My desire for Juan curdled, in the familiar way. The cute face and open arms became irritating and I developed a permanent headache. I thought if we had a big row he might pack his bags and go, but that was wishful thinking. Juan refused to take the bait. If I snapped at him, he reached for my flies. If I shouted at him, he kissed me. Once, driven beyond endurance, I screamed, 'I hate you and want you to leave me alone! Fuck off back to Nicaragua, why don't you?'

He looked at me with sad, spaniel eyes and said, 'You no mean that. We live only for each other!' then took off his clothes and beckoned me to the bedroom.

I'm only human. What could I do? Sex and love, love and sex – it was all so confusing.

'Not for me, it ain't,' said Catherine, when I told her how I felt. 'I knew this would happen. I said from the start this was a mistake, but you wouldn't listen. He's like clingfilm. Doesn't his visa run out soon or something?'

I shook my head. 'He's applied for a student visa, now that he's at English classes. He'll be here for three years or more.'

'Holy Christ! No, he won't. Right. It's time for plan B.'

'What is this plan B you keep talking about?' I asked warily.

'Me learning Spanish,' answered Catherine.

'I'm not with you,' I said.

'Don't trouble your pretty head, Cowboy. Leave everything to me. It's a dirty business, but someone has to do it. However, I feel my commission may be going up to thirty per cent.'

With that, she picked up her handbag and made for the door. 'I'm off to the shops to buy some *Teach Yourself Spanish* CDs and a luxury sherry trifle. Do bear with me. I shall keep you informed. Dreary Juan should be out of your hair in a couple of days, tops. Don't you worry about a thing.'

'You're a saint,' I called after her, as I heard the front door slam.

I'd hoped that having Juan might fill the gap Tim's part-time love left. We were in love with each other and that love would endure for ever, but Sophie and Juan were facts of our lives, too. How grown-up we were being, how very modern.

It didn't work out that way. Now, ironically, I found I needed Tim more than ever. Juan had made me even more aware of how much I loved him.

One night I returned home after a much-needed evening with him to find Juan almost hysterical. 'Where you been, Johnny, huh? Where? I wait long time.'

'Out,' I snapped.

'You love someone else?'

'No,' I said, bored. 'I'm going to bed.'

'Someone else, Johnny? Huh? Tell me!'

At that moment, I hated him with all my heart. All the frustration and sadness I felt about Tim, and the way Fate had separated us so cruelly, built up inside me. Tim had Sophie who loved him, and I had Juan, but Tim and I weren't allowed to love each other. It was monstrously unfair.

'Stop it,' I said menacingly. 'Just shut up. I could kill you, I really could.'

There was a sudden look of realization in Juan's eyes. I could tell, clear as day, that he was remembering what happened to Bernard.

'Oh,' he whispered. 'You gonna kill me, huh?'

'Only joking,' I said lightly. 'Don't be silly. Come on, let's go to bed. I'll let you do all your favourite things to me and I won't make you wear a condom.' Desperate measures were called for.

Juan relaxed slightly but I cursed myself. Stupidly, I'd made him think about the very thing I'd worked so hard to help him forget. I'd given him the very weapon he needed to stay with me for ever. I couldn't bear it.

I decided that, whatever Catherine's plan was, I would go along with it.

CHAPTER TWENTY FIVE

The next day Catherine told me to make myself scarce in the evening. 'I shall tell Juan you're at a camera rehearsal. Stay away till about nine.'

When I got back, I heard voices from the kitchen. I listened outside the door for a while.

'Write this down in English, Juan. *Adios, carino,*' Catherine was saying, in rather bad Spanish. 'Have you got that?'

'*Si,*' said Juan.

'*Lo siento que todo tiene que terminar asi,*' Catherine said next.

'Er, *si,* I understand,' replied Juan.

'And finally, *Te amo,*' Catherine said conclusively. 'Got it?'

'I think so,' said Juan, tentatively.

'Read it back to me in English, then,' Catherine said encouragingly.

'Goodbye, darling,' said Juan. 'I'm sorry it has to end this ways, I love you.'

'That's very good!' said Catherine. 'We're both doing very well, I think. Let me see what you've written.'

I entered the kitchen and saw the pair of them huddled over

the table, which was covered with sheets of paper. Juan leapt up to greet me, wrapping his arms round me and awarding me a prolonged kiss. Catherine grimaced.

'I love you,' he said quietly, for the ninth time that day.

'You're a bit whiffy, Juan. I'm sure that's not very nice for your beloved. Why don't you go for a shower?' said Catherine.

Juan dropped his head and inhaled in the general area of his armpits. '*Bueno*, Catherine. I go for shower. *Momentito*,' he said, dragging himself away from me, blowing me a kiss just before he closed the door.

I felt cold and afraid. I knew that Catherine's plan was hatching before my very eyes.

'Whatever are you doing?' I whispered fiercely. The night before I'd wanted Juan out of my life. Now I was having second thoughts.

'Taking care of business. Taking care of you.'

'No, no, no, Catherine! Have some heart!'

'Let me tell you something you already know, but may have forgotten. He might be a poorly educated peasant from Nicaragua, but he knows right from wrong. He saw you kill Bernard. He could have you arrested tomorrow if he wanted to. Why doesn't he?'

'He loves me. He believes it was an accident.'

'No, he doesn't. You know he doesn't. He's come here to make his fortune and you, Cowboy, are the crock of gold. He's going to stick to you like a limpet.'

'He loves me, that's why.'

'I'm sorry?' said Catherine, angrily. 'You're not talking a language I understand. Love? Him? You? Fuck me pink. Let me spell it out for you. He's after your money and he'll not stop until he's got his olive mitts on every last penny and then the rest. It'll never end, will it? You'll be buying bloody farms for his cousins till you're blue in the face. Then they'll want tractors and garages and combine-harvesters. He'll bleed you dry for the rest of his life. But, with a little help from me, that will, mercifully, be just a few more hours. If I wasn't the caring friend and dedicated manager I am, his dreary existence might linger on for another fifty years. I would urge you to think about that. I have. I have thought it through and come to the conclusion that there is no alternative. The moment he stepped off the plane, his fate was sealed. Even so, I've given him six weeks, hoping he'd go away of his own accord and forget about you and what he saw – go and become a fisherman or a coffee-bean grower or whatever they do for a living where he comes from. But he's not going to, is he?'

I shook my head. I knew she was right.

'He's here for ever. You are rich and famous and he's holding a sword over your head. He's got all the aces. Apart from this one. Surely you must see that?'

'I wish he'd just go,' I said weakly. I was in danger of crying.

'So do I,' said Catherine, sincerely – which was so unusual in her that I looked across the table in surprise. 'I really do mean that,' she said, and I saw that her eyes, too, were full of tears. 'It's such a fucking mess. But it can't go on being a mess for ever. Can it?'

'I guess not. I don't want him hurt, though.'

'No. Leave it to me. That's what management is for.' Catherine's tone had turned business-like. She got up from the table and darted purposefully over to the fridge. She took out a large Marks & Spencer's trifle and put it on the table. She then laid out three dessert bowls and got some spoons from the drawer. I watched, intrigued, as she served three generous helping. She licked the spoon and tossed it into the sink.

'Delicious!' was her verdict. 'But I think something's missing. We want to impress our guest with our British cuisine, after all.' She reached into her black Prada handbag and took out a square box.

'What are they?' I asked suspiciously.

'A means to an end. A last resort. A ticket to ride. Call them what you will.' She slipped out a blister pack and began to pop the green, diamond-shaped pills on to the tablecloth. Slowly, fearing I already knew the answer, I picked up the now-empty packet and read it. 'Rohypnol?' I said, incredulous.

'Yes, dear. Rohypnol,' said Catherine, still counting pills. Then she added, 'The *date-rape* drug!'

'Oh, my God, you can't!' I said.

Catherine was now snapping the pills into tiny quarters and sprinkling them over one bowl of trifle. 'I can and I have,' she shot back. 'They're my favourite. Sleep on these is delicious. It's like sliding into a hot bath. And, what's more, I'm very kindly sacrificing my own personal stash. I've saved these from my days as the merry nurse of Greenwich Hospital. You never know when you might need them, I thought. Now needs must.'

'You are wicked,' I said, intending the traditional meaning of the word.

'Thank you, darling. I'm also thorough.' She waved the sheet of paper Juan had been writing on when I arrived, then read, in a mock Spanish accent, '"Goodbye, darling. I'm sorry it has to end this ways, I love you." I'm so fucking brilliant it hurts. You just make sure he eats it all.'

A tear ran down my cheek and I wiped it away, staring sadly at the killer trifle. From the bathroom I could hear Juan clapping as he sang a Nicaraguan salsa.

'Come on, you can do it. After all, what's one more to add to your tally?'

Juan bounded back into the kitchen like an excited puppy, with a white towel wrapped round his waist. His muscular torso was still speckled with water and his black curls were shining and tousled, framing his face so that he looked like a Pierre et Gilles model. He kissed the top of my head and joined us at the table. He looked at the offering before him and said, 'Mmm! What is called?'

'Oh, it's just a trifle,' said Catherine casually.

'Is it nice?' he asked innocently, picking up his spoon and taking a mouthful.

'It's delicious. So soft and sugary you don't need to chew. It just slides down your throat.'

'I like,' said Juan, nodding enthusiastically.

'I'm so pleased.' Catherine smiled at him. 'We'd be most offended if you didn't enjoy it. Tuck in.'

The three of us ate in silence. I glanced nervously at Juan, but he finished his in no time, appearing not to have noticed anything odd about it.

'Thank you. Is good,' he said, looking pleased.

'*Was* good, Juan,' corrected Catherine. 'The past tense has always been my favourite.'

It was only about ten minutes later that Juan began to slur. 'I tired. Was ... tired ...' He tried to continue but couldn't.

'Good boy, it's all right,' said Catherine, soothingly.

He stared into the distance for a minute, then began to sway. His head lolled from one side to the other.

'Let's move him to my bedroom while he can still walk,' said Catherine, getting up and moving to his side. She held him by the elbow and tucked her other hand under his armpit.

'Why your bedroom?' I asked.

'I know what I'm doing. We're going to say he was my boyfriend, stupid. As you may recall, you, Johnny Debonair, are a famous heterosexual. It's another example of my deep, caring nature. Now, chop-chop.' Catherine had a way of making me feel stupid. She was always one step ahead.

I moved to the other side of Juan and, mirroring Catherine's manoeuvre, helped to manhandle my unwanted boyfriend into her room where he flopped drunkenly on to the bed. Catherine arranged his legs neatly. The towel had fallen off on our short journey and she glanced at his genitals like a housewife considering the quality of a greengrocer's produce.

'I've seen better,' she said. 'Help me get the duvet out from under him. It's only fair to make him decent. There's no sign of him vomiting, which is a boon. This takes me back to my days on A and E.'

We stood back and inspected our handiwork. Juan looked as if he was in a deep sleep. It all seemed remarkably easy and painless.

'Now what happens?' I asked.

'It takes a while,' said Catherine, matter-of-factly. 'We need to move all of lover boy's bits and bobs into my room, wash up our trifle dishes, then you and I hit the town. Your job for the night is to pick up some Muscle Mary and go back to his place. We don't want you here for all the amateur dramatics later on.'

'What will happen?' I was gripped.

'I shall come home alone in the small hours, discover my boyfriend has topped himself and call the emergency services.'

We placed the suicide note tastefully by the bed, changed into our disco fashions, had a couple of lines of cocaine and took ourselves off to Soho.

In a club called Stretch, I left Catherine at the bar downing double vodka tonics and dutifully went cruising. It was an unusually quiet night for available trade, but Catherine's instructions were to pick someone up, come what may, so I made do with a dull little man from the East End called Rupert, who had weasel eyes and grey sideburns, and had made the unfortunate error of wearing white socks with black trousers and shoes. Still, it was not a night to be picky.

We caught a taxi back to his pretentious studio in Borough, and I had to listen to his tasteless selection of chill-out albums while he slobbered over me. When we stood up he was so short, his rock-hard circumcised penis could only jab at my upper thigh. To save his embarrassment, I lay down on the futon and he came eventually, crouched over my chest, huffing and puffing like a steam engine. You don't know how lucky you are, I thought.

He pretended not to be interested in my wonderful TV career, but the next morning I was paraded down the high street and forced to sit for a couple of hours in a trendy café while his equally dubious friends gasped and tittered behind their croissants, their eyes like saucers, partly from the drugs they had consumed the night before and partly in wonderment at seeing me in their local.

When I said it was time I went home, he scribbled his number on a menu and said, 'I really like you, Johnny, and I want to see you again.'

'Me too,' I lied. 'Thank you for a wonderful night. You're very special.'

'Maybe we could meet up in the week for a bite to eat?'

'Sounds great.'

'Wednesday suits me. How are you fixed?'

'Wednesday it is,' I said. 'I'll call you *re* where and when.'

I dropped the menu with Rupert's number on it discreetly into a wastepaper bin by the door and caught a taxi back to Camden. As I approached, I couldn't help feeling apprehensive. Would Juan be furious with a Rohypnol hangover ... or ...

If he wasn't, I was going to have to face some cold, hard truths about myself and the unfortunate fate of those to whom I became close. One murder might possibly be excusable. Two were beginning to look suspicious. Three ... Well, I could be sharing a cell with Dennis Nielsen by Christmas, if I wasn't careful.

I let myself into the flat. 'Hello?' I half hoped to hear that Spanish accent calling, 'Hey, Johnny, where you been, huh?' But instead I heard a faint 'In here!' from the lounge. I went in.

Catherine was huddled on the sofa in her dressing-gown, sobbing quietly, and a policewoman was sitting next to her with a comforting arm around her shoulders.

'What's going on? What's the matter?' I asked.

'Sit yourself down, Mr Debonair,' said the policewoman. 'I'm WPC Helen Jackson, a Bereavement Support Officer.'

'Pleased to meet you, WPC Jackson.' I took off my leather jacket and sat on the chair, aware that I smelt of stale alcohol and cigarettes. 'But why are you here? What's wrong with Catherine?'

WPC Jackson gave me a concerned look and tightened her grip on Catherine's shoulders. 'I'm sorry to say that Catherine's boyfriend took an overdose last night. I'm afraid it's not good news.'

'Oh dear,' I said. 'How awful.'

At this point Catherine leapt from the sofa and flung herself at me, crying hysterically. 'Why?' she wailed. 'Why, why, why?'

'It's all right, baby. It's not your fault,' I cooed, patting her back and stroking her hair.

WPC Jackson looked on, impressed by my sympathetic behaviour, I felt sure. 'When did this happen?' I asked her.

'Last night, sir. Juan wrote a suicide note, then took an overdose.'

'I've been out all night,' I explained.

'No law against that,' said Helen.

'I knew I shouldn't have left those pills in the bathroom cabinet!' wailed Catherine.

'It's not your fault, Miss Baxter, you weren't to know. If someone's determined to do it, they'll find a way.' The policewoman turned back to me as I rocked the bereaved, broken Catherine. 'The body has been removed by the pathologist and the police have examined the scene. I'll leave you to look after Catherine, Mr Debonair. We'll be in touch as we'll need statements from both of you. And may I say again how sorry I am?'

'Thank you,' I whispered. 'You're very kind.' I stood up to shake her hand.

'And, by the way, may I say, too, that I'm a very big fan of yours?'

'Oh, how sweet! Would you like a signed photo to take away with you?' From the sofa I heard a suppressed snort.

After the policewoman left, clutching her photograph, Catherine and I froze for a couple of minutes, still clinging to each other. Slowly Catherine began to vibrate with suppressed giggles. I joined her and we didn't break apart until we were helpless with laughter and gasping for air.

'I thought you were never coming home!' she said at last. 'I've been giving it the full Gwyneth Paltrow for about ten hours!'

This only produced a fresh wave of laughter in me. 'Oh, poor you!' I managed. 'But I've been on a labour of love, too. I've had to suck off some dwarf on your account.'

'It's like being in a Mike Leigh film,' said Catherine. 'God, isn't it beautifully peaceful? No more Carmen Miranda. No more "Johnny, I love you!" thirty times a day. I know it might look callous to an outsider, but let's celebrate.'

I couldn't stop laughing and crying at the same time and underneath it all I had the creeping feeling that some kind of line had been crossed. We really would stop at nothing, it seemed. I was exhilarated by our power and yet frightened by it. I felt sorry for Juan yet highly tickled by what we'd done.

Eventually we pulled ourselves together enough to snort a gram of cocaine and drink three bottles of Laurent Perrier rosé. The battle between Latino lover and Essex girlfriend was over.

CHAPTER TWENTY SIX

Fortuitously, just as my star was at its zenith, my contract with the BBC came up for renewal. The latest series of *Shout!* had been a riotous success, but Catherine decided it was time to move on. 'I want to see you interviewing Hollywood royalty, not East 17.'

'I like them!' I protested.

'You're bigger than that now. This is your chance and we must go for it,' she said. Now that I had 'suffered' over Bernard's terrible death in public, I was somehow thought to have grown up and matured.

'What else do you have in mind?' I asked. I wasn't sure how I felt about abandoning the goose that had laid such a spectacular egg.

'I'm thinking, Cowboy, I'm thinking. Maybe you could be the new Trisha – but without the Norwich fashions. It's time you were attracting an older audience. We should do a photo shoot with you dressed in black and looking serious – in fact, maybe you should say you're into classical music and listen to Radio 4,' she mused. 'Perhaps you should buy a place in the country.'

It sounded very exciting and, as usual, I was willing to go along with whatever she suggested. The two of us were bound up together now. Only one person on earth knew the deepest, darkest secrets in my life, and that was Catherine. She knew about Georgie, about Bernard and the truth about Juan's 'suicide'. There was no way that our fates could ever be separated.

The police had accepted Juan's death as suicide – after all, the medical evidence supported Catherine's story. And, in any case, why would they not? There was no one to care much about whether or not some Nicaraguan boy had topped himself. All the official channels accepted the outcome, and two weeks after his death Juan's body was sent discreetly home in a black ziplock body-bag. Even more amazingly, we managed to keep the whole thing out of the press. When one or two reporters sniffed round the story of another tragic death closely connected to Johnny D, Catherine did some swift trading to stop it coming out. Instead, I gave an exclusive interview to a Sunday newspaper about my battle with depression since Bernard's death.

'I sometimes wonder if you and I are part of a new super-breed of human beings,' Catherine said, when we grasped that we'd got away with murder once again. 'Can it really be so simple, or are we the clever ones?'

I was certain that Catherine, at least, was one of the clever ones. Everything she touched seemed to blossom. (Apart from Juan, of course.) The minute I was out of contract, she skilfully created a bidding war for my services to the television industry, with the BBC, ITV and Channel 4 slugging it out with their cheque books. The amount of money being waved around was ridiculous. You'd have thought I was a priceless painting by Picasso.

The winning bid was a Friday-night chat-and-music show on Channel 4, which included a satirical look at the week's news. It was a three-year deal that would earn me almost nine million altogether and leave me free to work on other projects with anyone I pleased. The new vehicle was simply to be called *The Johnny D Show*.

'You've arrived, sweetheart,' Catherine said.

'All thanks to you.'

'It is, rather. Lucky you to have clever me. I think I'm worth forty-five per cent, easily.'

I might have arrived but where was I? I still felt very much in transit. Maybe it was the drugs, but I felt as if I was forever chasing some elusive goal, be it Tim, celebrity, peace of mind or just the dealer. Wherever I was, it wasn't the paradise I'd hoped for.

It wasn't that I disliked fame – I didn't. I still loved the attention I got, and the way everything seemed to come to me so easily. But away from the razzmatazz, the parties, awards shows and restaurants, I was, to my surprise, still me. Catherine and I might have upgraded to a bigger and better flat, but I couldn't escape the memories. Sometimes I thought back to sitting on the veranda with Sammy and Georgie, sipping G and T while they talked about their glory days, and felt that that was when I had been happiest. The fact that Tim was in my life again should have made me delirious with joy – and, certainly, it was what I had thought I wanted. But, like so much else, the reality had proved different and the bitterness I felt that we couldn't be together outweighed the sweetness of our stolen liaisons.

And then there was the burden of darkness that I had pushed into the depths of my soul and tried to forget. But at night, as I tossed and turned and tried to sleep, the faces I wouldn't let myself think of during the day reared up in my imagination. Here was Georgie, breathless and desperate for me to kill him again. Here was Bernard, rising once more from his pool of molten clay, eyes wide with shock as mud dripped from his fingertips. And here was Juan, pleading with me, saying, 'But I love you, Johnny. Why you kill me, huh?'

Only now did I understand the phrase 'night terrors'. I longed to tell someone how I felt. But Catherine, with her steely heart, didn't understand and I couldn't risk losing Tim's affection by confiding in him. He thought I was a glamorous, successful star. How would he react if he knew that I was really a coke-addled killer? I'd lose even the small part of him I had managed to claw back.

So, I tried to lose myself in my constant companions – sex and drugs. The nightmares weren't so bad when I was in someone else's bed, their arms wrapped round me and the gentle rhythm of their breathing lulling me to sleep. And I could forget my depression and hopelessness when I was riding high on cocaine and speed, manic with alcohol. I took more and more to get the same fleeting feelings of release and happiness, sinking great wads of cash into my habits. In all senses, Catherine was my partner in crime, and as greedy for narcotic highs as I was. Together we went on extraordinary binges that sometimes lasted days, taking anyone with us who wanted to come along for the ride, dropping them and picking up new party pals for the next leg of debauchery.

The Johnny D Show went live to air for the first time at ten p.m. on a Friday night. I hadn't managed to stay in on the Thursday, but Anita the make-up artist was on hand with her magic wands and powders. Anyway, the heavy eyes and unshaved chin made me seem more grown-up. A new look for a new show. Tom Cruise was my first guest, and he patted me on the back as if we were old friends. He laughed and shook his head when I made jokey references to his height and to Scientology. 'Only you could get away with that!' he said, tears of laughter running down his cheeks.

Although some in the press predicted that I had bitten off more than I could chew in moving from children's to adult television, I handled the transition well. In fact, the later time slot allowed me to reveal more of the sex appeal that I had kept below the surface on *Shout!*. I flirted outrageously with the actresses I chatted to on my sofa, and was laddish with the boys. The strand of the show that was different, and which swiftly proved the public's favourite, was a part we called TLC. Here, I would chat gently to someone who was not famous but who had recently been involved in something either tragic or heroic or both: a policeman's widow or a burns victim, that type of carry-on. I coaxed the gruesome details from them by mining the still-raw emotions of my own recent experiences. I had been there. I was one of them. The reviews were unanimously complimentary. *The Times* said I had enough star quality to light up Milton Keynes for a fortnight. Even Jonathan Ross didn't get reviews like that. I enjoyed the shows, knew I was being sexy and enigmatic – but I wasn't excited or particularly motivated. If appearing live on national television in front of millions didn't get me going, what would?

To my surprise, I found my thoughts turning more and more often to Bernard. I missed him. Juan seemed like a distant bad dream, but Bernard had left a gaping hole in my professional life. I found myself looking for the fidgeting figure in the flowery shirt at the back of the studio, wanting his helpful advice after every show. He had always been first through my dressing-room door after a recording, smiling and nodding reassuringly. He had been bound up in *Shout!*'s success, of course, but it was me he had cared about. Now it was Catherine who came tottering in, wearing a power suit and brushing away my questions on how she thought it had gone.

'Whatever. We still get paid even if you look like Benny from *Crossroads* so who gives a monkey's?'

Or she was already there, racking us out a couple of celebratory lines of cocaine and opening vintage Cristal, as we pursued our endless quest for forgetfulness.

Before long, the results of our hedonism began to show. Forever hung-over and tired, I had long since stopped reading my scripts before a show. Sometimes it was as much as I could do not to sound surprised when I read out the name of that day's guest from the autocue. My mumbling, bumbling interviews were shocking and inept, but compulsive viewing nevertheless.

Elaine Paige even asked me during her interview if I'd 'been at the cooking sherry'.

'Cooking sherry? Fine Madeira wine, if you please,' I retorted, to a good laugh.

It wasn't long before the papers cottoned to what was happening and printed thrill stories about my show and my behaviour on it. They became more and more outrageous, thus creating more stories. I was becoming the king of car-crash telly and the more trashed I was the more my producers rubbed their hands. As long as my viewing figures flourished, everyone was happy. Shots of vodka were slipped to me during commercial breaks. I famously fell asleep while interviewing some old slapper from *EastEnders* and was considered a master of irony in the next day's papers. Simply, I could do no wrong.

Once or twice I told Catherine I thought I was cracking up. She stroked me under the chin and said, 'It's all rock 'n' roll, Cowboy. You just need a line.' She laughed off articles in the *Daily Express* and the *Mail on Sunday* that insinuated I was on a downward spiral. Photos of me looking wasted and much older than my twenty-five years appeared in the tabloids.

Roy, my driver, told me I needed a holiday. 'You're going at it all guns blazing, Sonny Jim. That manager of yours is flogging you too hard and you're going to be a dead horse before long. Get yourself home, have a nice cup of tea and put your feet up. No more nightclubs till four a.m. for a bit, eh?'

I was grateful he was looking out for me, but only a week later Catherine got rid of him. 'He was fiddling the books. Claimed you kept him waiting outside the Savoy for nine and a half hours,' she declared. 'I've got you an Addison Lee account instead.'

Taxi drivers, it turned out, were the real barometer of my celebrity standing. They no longer told me how great I was and how I'd made their wives fall about whenever I was on the telly. Instead they peered at me in the rear-view mirror, then didn't mince their words: 'You're losing the plot, mate, if you don't mind me saying. You want to stop burning the candle at both ends. You used to be a good-looking bloke.'

CHAPTER TWENTY SEVEN

One evening Catherine and I were dining in the plush surroundings of a private members' club called Ambulance – appropriately enough – discussing my career. In fact, we talked of little else, these days. I had no love life to speak of and couldn't bring myself to talk to her about Tim, who was more like a ghost in my life than a lover.

We had enjoyed several trips to the toilet and were cruising pleasantly on our usual high of cocaine and champers when suddenly a familiar figure shuffled past our table. I glanced at him, but l was used to avoiding the stares of people around me – lest they catch my eye and engage me in conversation – so I looked away. He had almost disappeared when I realized who I had just seen.

If I'd been sober, I would never have shouted, 'Sammy!' but I did. I was sure he had already spotted me – I was, after all, the talk of the restaurant.

He did a badly acted double-take, then came back to our table. 'JD, my dear! I didn't think you'd recognize me!'

'Of course I would. It hasn't been that long. How are you doing, you old poofter?' I asked boldly. He stood by my chair and I slapped the top of his expanded tummy gently. We hadn't met since Georgie's funeral, and Sammy looked awkward and a little upset. He was not the man I'd first met in Barnes those years ago – he appeared older, sadder, and broken.

'I'm fine, thank you,' he murmured.

'You've made it back from the Isle of Wight, then?' I said, his awkwardness contagious. 'Not everyone does, I hear.'

'Oh, yes,' he said, 'though I kept thinking I was going to fall off the edge.'

'Did you go back to Barnes?'

'No, I sold my flat. I've got a place in Hampstead now. Once Georgie was gone, I couldn't stay in the old place.'

'Such a tragedy,' I said softly.

'Yes.'

'Lovely, lovely man.'

'What I can't understand,' said Sammy, lowering his voice, 'is why the police never asked me who I thought was responsible. I know I was heavily sedated and distraught with grief for some considerable time, but I always had my suspicions, you know.'

'What were your thoughts on the matter?' I asked, clutching my steak knife.

'Well, it's too late now, isn't it, dear? Case closed. Nobody in a position of authority is interested in what I have to say.'

'I am,' I said, curious beyond words but trying to sound casual.

'I'm sure you've had enough upset to last you a lifetime,' said Sammy, patting my shoulder comfortingly, 'what with poor Bernard and those awful Nicaraguan ruffians you had to deal with. I really shouldn't distress you any further by bringing Georgie's unsolved murder into the equation. I saw the pictures of you in the paper at Bernard's memorial service looking so dreadfully … upset. I felt for you, dear boy, I really did. Let us change the subject.' He looked brightly about the table. 'So thrilled for all your success. I always knew, during your previous life, that you would make something of yourself one way or the other. I said as much to Georgie. "By hook or by crook," I said, "our JD – er, Johnny – has an interesting future ahead of him." Most fortuitous that Bernard helped you on your way, but I could see you were going places.'

'Could you?' I said politely. 'And I do hope you have a new arrangement to take care of your needs, these days.'

'Oh, yes, darling. A Bulgarian. I don't think he's illegal but he certainly ought to be, if you catch my drift. He lives in, as a matter of fact. I've never felt happy sleeping alone after what happened to Georgie. The middle of the night, you see, when it happened. Could have been either of us ...' He trailed off, then dabbed his eyes with the napkin. 'I really must be going. I've been dining with friends but it's well past my bedtime, and Big Boy, as I call him, will be wondering where I am. Good evening. Lovely to encounter you again so unexpectedly. Nice to meet you, Miss ...?'

'Catherine Baxter,' said Catherine, without a smile. 'Likewise.'

'Shall we meet up some time, Sammy?' I asked. 'Talk about old times?'

'Oh, JD – I don't know. There's been a lot of water under the bridge, hasn't there? Perhaps we should leave things as they are.'

I was taken aback. Not many people turned down an opportunity to spend time with me. 'All right, then,' I said, a touch coolly.

'Goodbye, dear. Take care.' Sammy wandered off.

'Well,' I said to Catherine, 'there's a turn-up for the books.'

'He doesn't look as well as he did at the funeral, does he?' said Catherine, pushing her lips into a thoughtful pout. 'Time hasn't been kind.'

'Perhaps it was my fault,' I said. 'He wasn't the same after Georgie went.'

Catherine was plainly exasperated. 'Change the record, darling! How many times do I have to say it? The old queen was dying anyway. Now, let's change the subject. I've had some new contracts through and various financial papers from the accountant. It's coming up to the end of the tax year and he's had some ideas about how you could limit your liability. There are various investments and trusts ...'

I found business talk desperately boring and let it wash over me while Catherine produced bits of paper for me to sign. My mind was fixed on Sammy and what he'd meant by saying he had his own ideas about who'd killed Georgie. He'd never given me the slightest inkling that he suspected anyone and that worried me, though I wasn't sure why.

'Well done, Cowboy,' said Catherine, when I'd signed the final document she'd put in front of me. 'Now, business over, let's go and celebrate. Anywhere you fancy?'

I felt jaded. I remembered what Roy had said about going home to a cup of tea and an early night. Maybe I should try it. I knew that heterosexuals often stayed in for whole evenings. Apparently they ate food covered with breadcrumbs and watched programmes about hospitals. Imagine.

'You disappoint me,' Catherine said, after I'd told her I thought I'd go home. 'Never mind. I'm up for it on my own. See you later.'

Back home, I found the unaccustomed silence strange. When Catherine was here, the television was usually blaring, so she could shout obscenities at the people she considered my rivals.

I wandered about, thinking of Sammy and Georgie, feeling very alone. I wished Tim would call me. If I ever felt the need of a booty call, it was now – not so I could get some release but so that I could feel his familiar arms, smell the warm, sweet scent of his hair and relish the deep rumble of his voice. The phone rang. I leapt to answer it. Had he psychically picked up my signal and called me? Perhaps Sophie was out of town and we could meet at one of our favourite places. Oh, I did hope so …

'Hello?' I said.

'I would like to speak to my grandson – Johnny,' said a haughty voice, with only a slight crack of age in its timbre.

'Grandma Rita?'

'Is that you, Johnny?'

'It certainly is.' My grandma Rita! To my great shame, I hadn't been in touch with her for a very long time. She seemed part of a different, distant life and I gave her barely a thought from one month to another. She had written to me when I became famous to say that she was pleased I had found success and that she'd always known that the Lewisham School of Musical Theatre would come good for me in the end, even if I had spent several years working for charity. 'Grandma, I'm so sorry I haven't been to see you for so long.'

'Don't worry, my boy. I understand. You're young, you're riding the crest of a wave. You haven't got time to think about an old woman, and why should you? But I do want to ask you a favour. I'd like you to come to Blackheath. Would you do that?'

'Of course!' It was on the tip of my tongue to ask her to phone Catherine's assistant, who managed my diary, and get her to find a window, but I brought myself up just in time. 'When?'

'As soon as you can. How about tomorrow?'

Something in her tone worried me. She sounded vulnerable, slightly shaky, and that wasn't like Grandma Rita.

'Of course I can, Grandma. I'd love to see you.'

'Good,' she said. 'It's boiled eggs and anchovies for lunch. Come at one.'

Her phone went down.

I stared at mine, contemplating it in the silence of the flat. Why, in all these years, had I never had time for Grandma Rita? I had always seemed to be so terribly busy, and going out to Blackheath had seemed impossible, just too difficult to fit into my diary. Couldn't I have put aside half a day a month to visit my wise, wonderful grandmother? Living with Catherine, guilt wasn't often allowed a look-in, but now it trailed over me like cold seaweed. The hours, days and weeks I'd spent coked up and drunk, dancing, flirting and fucking strangers …

Grandma Rita was almost my only family and I'd never bothered to go and see her. I'd only been back to Kent a handful of times – I'd always told myself I was too busy (as usual) and that my mother should come to London if she wanted to see me, forgetting how much she hated leaving her home and how much she loathed the city.

I'll do better, I resolved. I'll go and see Grandma Rita tomorrow, then every month from now on. I'll take her and Mother away on holiday. We'll have Christmas together. I'll become a grandson and son they'll be proud of.

CHAPTER TWENTY EIGHT

The house in Blackheath was exactly the same.

As the butler led the way to the drawing room, I expected to see Grandma Rita sitting there, straight-backed as she presided over a pot of tea, but the room was empty and had about it an air of disuse. We went into the conservatory, where the heat was turned up to boiling. Within seconds I was breathless and sweaty.

On a large wicker daybed there lay what appeared at first to be a pile of blankets and pillows until I saw in the middle, like a sleeping kitten, an oval white face. It took me a moment to recognize my grandmother.

'Master Johnny,' said the butler, in a low voice.

A strange sound came from my grandmother: harsh, rattly and rather frightening. I realized it was a long exhalation. Her eyes opened. The steel blue had gone, replaced by a watery-puddle colour.

'Grandma?' I said. It was awful to see her like this.

'Johnny, my boy. You've come. Good. Sit down.' She gestured with a movement of her bony wrist that I should take one of the wicker chairs near her bed.

I kissed her soft, cool cheek and sat down. The butler disappeared, bowing reverently, like a priest before the tabernacle.

'You can see that I'm not well,' Grandma said. Her voice sounded a little stronger, and I could understand now why I had noticed nothing on the telephone. 'Your mother is going to come here the day after tomorrow. I have plenty to talk to her about and, no doubt, when I've finished, she will not leave. So before that happens, I wanted us to have some time alone.'

'You're making this all sound very sinister.' I tried to sound as cheerful as I could, although it was obvious she wasn't long for this world. How like Grandma Rita to want her affairs in order before the time came.

Grandma flashed me a look that reminded me of her old self. 'I know you're very grand now, very important, but I'm going to ask you to shut up and listen.

'It must be perfectly obvious to you that I'm dying. I've not got long left. Organ failure, the doctors tell me. Apparently my darling kidneys are calling it a day. Then the liver and the heart. It's a one-out-all-out situation. I wasn't going to bother anyone – least of all you, with your busy, busy career – I was planning to disappear overnight, like a family grocer from the high street. And, in my experience, other people's diseases are very boring indeed. The doctors say I have about a month, which is generous of them.' She cleared her throat. 'I saw you on television the other night.'

'Oh, Grandma,' I whispered. I felt utterly bereft, even though she was still lying in front of me, alive.

Grandma's account of her illness seemed to have worn her out. She closed her eyes for a few moments. She looked like a frail, wrinkled child, her skin clinging to her cheekbones like a wet airmail envelope wrapped round a Queen Anne chair leg. My eyes filled with tears at the thought of losing her. I had left it too late to be the grandson she might have hoped for. Our tea-time chats, five-star holidays and Christmas dinners would never happen now. Just when I thought she might be asleep, her eyes opened and she looked at me.

'I don't like to see you sad. That's not why I called you here.' She gave me a grandmotherly smile, although her mouth was dry and her lips were pale.

'I lured you here on the pretence of lunch, but I've gone off eating. Maria will bring you a sandwich. Now, about this programme of yours.'

'Did you enjoy it?'

'No, I did not. People were laughing at you, not with you. Has no one told you?'

I was taken aback. 'Is there something wrong with your television set, Grandma? My producers couldn't be more thrilled. They threw a huge party for me straight afterwards in the green room. If there was something amiss I'm sure they'd tell me. I'm amazed that you should say that.'

'You made a fool of yourself in front of Liza Minnelli! Quite an achievement for anyone, given the competition. I saw you slurring and leaping about, your eyes wandering and your body quivering, and I realized that things are far worse with you than I could ever have imagined.'

I was surprised to find myself blushing.

'What's happened to you?' she went on. 'What about that lovelorn young man who arrived here at the age of seventeen and asked me what he should do with his life? Is this what he wanted?'

It wasn't easy to be cross with someone who wasn't long for this world, but I had a stab at it. I was understandably indignant.

'If you mean, did he want fame, recognition, money and luxury then, yes, he did! I've exceeded my wildest dreams. I've done better than I could ever have imagined. People would kill themselves to have what I have!'

I had raised my voice without meaning to, and she turned up the volume too, croaking rather than rasping. With a piercing stare she said, 'What do you have? Fame, money and an all-consuming addiction to narcotics?'

'Why, I– I—' How did she guess? Old ladies weren't supposed to know about such things.

She rested her head on the pillow, a shaft of sunlight suddenly illuminating her hair so that I could see how thin it had become. She must have noticed me looking. 'Like a tinderbox now,' she said, patting it as of old, but this time a couple of inches closer to her visible skull. 'Listen to me, Johnny. Your television programme and everything else will be taken away from you in due course if you carry on as you are. There is only so much patience everyone will have with a public figure who is out of their mind. Look at the Queen Mother.'

'No! My audience loves me! My producers are always saying how wonderful I am, how brilliant the show is ...'

'And they will go on telling you so until the moment your viewing figures drop, when they will tear up your contract and show you the door.'

'Everybody has a drug habit,' I said, a little weakly. 'It's rather fashionable.'

'No, Johnny. It's not a habit, it's a problem. What is fashionable is to *overcome* a drug problem, so I advise you to do just that immediately. Before you lose your looks and your sanity.'

I leant back in my chair, speechless. Maria came in with the tea-things, and laid them out neatly on the little table. A large plate of smoked salmon, egg and cress, and ham and mustard sand-wiches, with a generous garnish of healthy-looking salad, was presented to me.

'Have some tea,' said Grandma Rita. 'And eat. You need to. Now – there is something else I want to ask you about. Tell me about your friends.'

'My friends?'

'Yes, who are they?'

'Well, I – I've got *lots* of friends.'

'Name them. Name a friend who has nothing to do with you professionally but who is simply your friend for your sake.'

I thought. Celebrities didn't count. We were all de facto friends by virtue of our fame, a bit like the way all Labrador owners or MG drivers or real-ale drinkers feel kinship. But I knew plenty of people who weren't celebrities ... Name after name came into my mind, people who were kind, cheerful, polite, delighted to see me, thrilled with my jokes and my small amber phial, always on hand if I wanted someone to party with and yet ... they were all connected to me through my work or my fame. But how was I supposed to make friends with people who didn't know who I was? I'd have to go to deepest, darkest Peru or a high-security mental hospital.

'Catherine!' I said triumphantly. Of course! How could I forget her? 'She's been my friend since I was a student. She's been with me every step of the way. She shares a flat with me, she knows my secrets and she's my oldest and best friend.'

'Isn't this Catherine your manager?'

I blinked. 'Yes – and she's guided my career wonderfully, but she was my friend before she was my manager.'

'And this friend, your best friend, what does she say about your drugs problem?'

'Um...' I thought hard. The last time Catherine had mentioned drugs was to compliment the quality of our latest delivery.

'Nothing?' Grandma Rita frowned. 'Then she's no friend of yours, Johnny, I can promise you that. Get rid of her as fast as you can.'

I laughed. She didn't have the first idea what she was asking. Catherine was utterly entwined in my life and I wouldn't have dreamt of getting rid of her, as Grandma Rita so charmingly put it. It wasn't that simple. Catherine wasn't a dose of crabs: she was with me for life. We were shackled together by the unfortunate deaths on which we had colluded.

'My last question,' said Grandma Rita, before I could dwell too long on this revelation, 'what about love? Whom do you love?' She exhaled noisily. The energy she was expending on home truths was taking its toll on her. Even I felt as if I'd gone three rounds with a boxer. Wasn't there a rule about hitting a man when he was down? 'Or is there no love in your life?'

'Yes,' I whispered, as if I was pleading guilty.

Grandma Rita seemed relieved. 'Well, I'm glad to hear it. At least there's someone for you to cling to. Who is it?'

'It's ... Tim.'

'Tim?' She frowned. 'That name sounds familiar.' She thought for a while, her breath coming in long, slow sighs. 'Isn't that the name of the young man you were carrying on with when you were a boy? The one who broke your heart?'

'Yes.' My voice was so small it could barely be heard, but Grandma caught it.

'Well, that is good news.' She gave a happy chortle. 'So you two found each other and made it up? How very Barbara Taylor

Bradford! And now you're going to be together for ever?' She was perking up. This news had healed her spirits.

'Er ... no. He's engaged to a laminate-flooring heiress called Sophie. We steal the occasional night together when we can, but it's not really ... right.'

Despair crossed my grandmother's face. 'Oh, Johnny – no. No. That's too much. Laminate flooring ...' She dabbed her eyes with an embroidered handkerchief. 'And he has you on the side, like salad? He doesn't give you the love and care you need and deserve? Oh, my poor boy. That will never be good for you.

To my surprise, tears sprang to my eyes. Something she'd said had touched a nerve. I knew, at some deeper level, that my life was a sham and a charade. It was full of fun and excitement, sex and chemical thrills but it was lacking in something I longed for above all. Love. Real, true love. The sort we were put on this earth to experience. And the irony was that I knew who my true love was. I just couldn't have him.

'Johnny.' Grandma pulled herself up into a sitting position, panting, so that she could look me squarely in the face. 'I know you think I've disapproved of your mother, the way she's lived her life and, by extension, of you – her love child, the product of some animalistic rutting on a bed of hay, if she was lucky. But death is approaching. I'm thinking about what really matters – and do you know? The most surprising thing has happened. I have changed my mind. I think about Alice, and instead of feeling that she has wasted her life I feel that she has made the most of it. It is I who have missed out. Early on your mother freed herself from the chains that bind most of us. She saw what mattered and what didn't and, for herself and you, chose happiness. She didn't want material goods and money. She found happiness in her garden, her poetry and in watching her beautiful little boy grow up. I scorned it, you know. I thought she was ridiculous – an idiot! – when really, she's the wisest person I've ever met, despite the Hythe town-hall clock, the birds with names and the supermarket managers in her bed. She got it right.'

She reached out a long bony hand. 'Johnny, I'm dying. I see things more clearly than I ever have. I have to go with the knowledge that I wasn't brave enough to love my daughter. Until now. Learn to be brave before it's too late. Learn from my mistakes. I thought the sort of love I had for your grandfather was the only sort that counted: legitimate, respectable love, as witnessed before God. But you and Tim, that's just as real. You took a wrong turn-ing, but fate steered you back on course. You ignore the nudges of destiny, the correct order of things, at your peril. Love is a sacred egg that you must incubate. Sit on it, Johnny.'

'The times I've heard that,' I murmured. 'This is a death-bed speech and a half.'

She didn't hear me. 'And when you do, you will hatch the most wonderful gift that life on this earth has to offer. Doesn't that sound attractive? If you ignore the signs and fight against Nature, you take the consequences.'

'I'll try, Grandma,' I said, but she hadn't finished.

'Find love, find happiness,' she went on. 'Will you promise to do that? If you do, I can die happy, knowing that my daughter and grandson have found their true paths in life. My own loss won't seem so bitter.'

After such impassioned words from a dying relative, I could hardly refuse. 'Yes, Grandma,' I said. 'I will. I'll give it a go.'

A burden on my shoulders, one that I hadn't even known I was carrying, seemed to lift. I felt as though I was seeing the real state of things for the first time. Everything seemed so gloriously clear.

'Go out there, Johnny!' she whispered. 'Change your life. Make it what you know it can be.'

'Grandma,' I said, reaching out and squeezing her hand tighter than the terminally ill usually enjoy, 'I know what I have to do.'

I walked tall out of the house in Blackheath, gripped by a whirlwind of emotion, and hailed a taxi.

'Cheer up,' said the driver. 'It might never happen.'

I pushed the glass partition closed and had a good think. My grandmother was dying, and I was desperately sad, but she had inspired me, too, by showing me the way in which I could change the course of my life. It had taken a talking-to from Grandma Rita to make me see how miserable I was – and, of course, she couldn't even begin to guess at the homicides that also made my existence so hard to bear.

This was my moment of realization. I was going to turn my life round as of now. Stop all of it. I'd give up the drugs that could never give me up, and I would remake *The Johnny D Show* so that it wasn't car-crash telly any more but a wonderful, intelligent, fun show that everyone would want to watch and that would become a Channel 4 classic. I would turn into a British institution. What was more, *The Johnny D Show* would be hosted by an honest man. I would come out, in honour of my grandmother, and stop all the silliness about my love life and made-up girlfriends. It was time that my adoring public knew the truth. Incredible as it might seem, I was gay.

And, most importantly, I would tell Tim that neither of us could live a lie any longer. We would stop all the pretence. He couldn't stay with Sophie and I couldn't accept him doing so any more. We deserved to be together, to be happy. He had to let go and surrender to his desire for me.

This would be my true legacy from Grandma Rita, my future happiness – a tribute to her bravery and wisdom.

CHAPTER TWENTY NINE

I would come out, I decided, on next Friday's show. Not only would I be drug-free and clear-headed, but just before the closing titles Johnny D would stray from the autocue, and speak the words he longed to voice on air. He would stand up to be counted as a homosexual man.

'The truth is always beautiful. Do you still love me now?' I planned to say.

Catherine was not at home when I got in, so I couldn't tell her the glad tidings.

Instead I decided I needed to talk to Tim and, at the very least, set up a meeting between us so I could tell him of my resolution. I couldn't wait another moment to break the news to him about our happy future together.

I telephoned him at work. When his secretary put me through he sounded exasperated. 'Johnny, come on, we saw each other last week. I can't get away too often.'

'Please, Tim, it's important. Meet me tonight at Leonardo's.'

When we didn't go to the Savoy we chose this discreet but luxurious hotel in Poland Street, tucked away from the busy road behind World of Velour.

'Well ...'

He sounded as though he was weakening. Even over the phone I could tell he was smiling. He loved Leonardo's. 'I'll book the Mona Lisa suite,' I purred. 'Lobster, Cristal, stale rolls reheated just for us?'

'Sounds tempting,' he said. 'Guess I'll have to make do with you for afters.'

'Tell Sophie you're working late,' I coaxed.

'All right. But then we'll have to hold off for a while.'

'Absolutely,' I said, thrilled. If everything went according to plan, we'd be together for ever after tonight.

I was waiting for Tim, eager and excited. I had everything we wanted on tap for a marvellous night – the food, the champagne, the cocaine. (One last blast to finish what I had in stock. No more after that. For sure.) And, of course, the bed.

The minute he arrived, delicious and broad-shouldered in his Kilgour suit, a crisp Turnbull & Asser shirt and tie, I melted into his arms. 'That's better,' I said appreciatively, as he slipped off his dark charcoal jacket, and kissed me so ravenously I was pushed back against the wall. Eventually he pulled away from me, growled playfully and glanced round the room. 'Now, what have we here?' he asked brightly.

I showed him the food and champagne and the little silver cup of white powder. 'A few of your favourite things,' I said.

'You're in a good mood, I must say.' Tim moved away from me, sat down at the small oval dining-table and picked up a lobster claw.

'This is a special night. I want us to make the most of it,' I said, from the heart.

'Yes,' said Tim, suddenly pensive. 'Let's make the most of it, Johnny. Tonight is the night to taste all the delights we can.'

We toasted each other with our crystal glasses, then tucked into our lobster. Later we allowed ourselves a hefty dose of white powder. I took mine through the silver straw that Catherine had had made for me. On it were engraved the words of Hecate, from *Macbeth*: 'And I, the mistress of your charms, The close contriver of all harms.'

'Yum!' I said, with a hearty sniff. 'That's the stuff. I'm going to miss it.'

'Oh?' Tim said, surprised.

I nodded. 'I'm giving up the sauce. That's the plan.'

'Not you, Johnny. I can't see you without Charlie.'

'I'm going to get clean. Special occasions only. No more going on air coked up to the eyeballs and riding high for days at a time. It's wearing me out.'

'Good on you. Though I'll believe it when I see it.'

'It's all part of my plan for a new life.'

Tim raised an eyebrow. 'What plan is this?'

'Not now,' I whispered, pulling him towards me by his tie. 'Afterwards.'

We lay, exhausted, on the vast bed. We were on our backs, side by side, our arms hooked over each other's shoulders. Tim pressed his cheek to mine and kissed me sideways. Slowly to begin with, then faster and faster, over and over again on the same spot, until we were juddering together like lottery balls.

'Enough!' I said, laughing at the tingling, wet, giddying sensation.

He stopped and said, 'Now you know.'

My heart beat faster. This was it. This was the moment when I would tell Tim what I planned, and our new life would begin.

'How long have we been seeing each other?' I asked.

Tim shrugged. 'A year or so, isn't it? Unless you count before.'

'I most certainly do.'

'Then you've been on my mind for almost seven years. You're probably entitled to some of my inheritance.'

'Do you enjoy it? Us, I mean.'

He rolled over so he could look me in the face. 'You know I do,' he said softly. 'It's one of the things I live for.'

'It's the same for me, Tim. It always has been, since the first moment you spoke to me. I've always loved you. For me, you've always been that magical combination of love and desire, and I've never met anyone who makes me feel the way you do.'

'Maybe you need to get out more.' Tim grinned, evidently trying to make sure things didn't get too serious.

I pressed on regardless: 'No. What I need is to stay in more. With you. And I believe that, in your heart, you love me too. Tell me, do you really feel this ecstasy, this sublime pleasure, with Sophie?'

His eyes slid away from mine.

'There!' I cried triumphantly. 'I knew it. You can't possibly. You're only truly happy when you're with me. Listen, I've come to some decisions. I've suddenly seen what's really important and I'm going to change my life. I've earned a lot of money in the last few years. Millions. And I haven't known what to do with it, apart from stuff it up my nose. Now I have a vision. No more cocaine, and I'm going to buy a house in the country, in Kent, near my mother, and start to breathe again. I'll keep the London flat so I can come in for work when I need to ...'

'That all sounds like a good idea,' Tim said, frowning, 'but—'

'No buts.' I held up my hand to silence him. 'I want to be happy. Properly happy. And you're part of that, Tim. I can't be happy without you and I don't believe you can be happy without me. We're supposed to be together, two halves of a whole. I want you to stop living a lie, just as I intend to. I'm going to let the world know I'm not a ladies' man but a man's man – and I want you to do the same. Tell Sophie the truth, Tim. Don't let her marry a man who doesn't truly love her in the way she should be loved. Tell your family to go to hell – you've only got one life. Why should you sacrifice it because some bloke four hundred years ago happened to be given a title and a big house? Chuck it all in, and live with me. It doesn't matter if they disinherit you – I've got enough money for us both to live on. Come on, Tim, can't you see it? Don't you understand how happy and liberated we'll be?'

I was breathless and excited, eager to show him the vision of our future that was so clear to me.

There was a long pause. Then he said, in a low voice, 'My family would never accept it.'

'I know. I've allowed for that. But you can't live a lie for the sake of their old-fashioned prejudices.'

'You don't understand the pressure I'm under.'

'You're right. I don't understand why you can't be yourself.'

Tim propped himself up on one elbow to look at me. 'I came here tonight, Johnny, because I have something to tell you, too. It was fortuitous that you called me when I was thinking about how best to let you know. You see, Sophie and I have set a date for the wedding. Our parents want it to be sooner rather than later, so we've agreed that it should be this summer. The invitations are already being printed. There's going to be a huge marquee in the grounds of Thornchurch House—'

'Oh,' I said, remarkably calmly. 'That'll be nice for you both. Sophie will look good in a veil.' I got off the bed, went to the ice bucket and poured myself a glass of champagne.

'I don't want you to take it personally,' said Tim. 'I mean, nothing has to change.'

'I think you're wrong about that,' I said. 'You'll be taking vows and I've never been keen on messing with the sacraments.'

'I have to marry. It's expected. You know that, Johnny. I've never made any secret of it, right from the start.'

I tossed my rather flat champagne down my throat in one gulp. 'I suppose not. That's one thing I can say for you – you've always been honest with me, if not with everyone else. There are lots of reasons why we can't go on as we are, Tim, if you marry Sophie. One is that my mother always jumped at the chance of a married man, and I know what that particular choice did for her. I'd rather hoped for more from my own life.'

Tim sat up on the bed, watching me as I paced about the room.

'Another reason is that I don't want to live with odds and ends of your attention any more. I don't want a tiny piece of your life, a stolen night here and there, with the two of us dashing about all cloak-and-dagger, trying not to be seen. I want us to be able to do the things couples in love do: go for walks, go out together, be proud of each other. I'm not hanging about in hotel rooms for the rest of my life, waiting for you to tear yourself away from Vinegar Tits and deal with my aching two-week-old stiffy before I self-combust. I want a proper relationship, with love and respect and stability. I've never had one of those and I need it now, I really do.'

'You shouldn't have fallen in love with me, then.' He reached out to me. 'Come here.'

Instead I walked to the window and looked out. 'You're very confident about my eternal love. As you should be. But don't be so sure about me. I see a lifetime of snatched moments with you stretching ahead of me, and it depresses me. Sophie gets the main course and I get the scraps.'

'I have responsibilities to my family,' said Tim, pompously.

'Forget them!' I begged. 'Break off the engagement, Tim. I will be your reward. "Come live with me and be my love, And we will all the pleasures prove." Don't marry Sophie. Please.'

Tim stared at me for a long moment. Hope sprang in my heart. Perhaps my words had finally reached him and he had seen how fruitless, how pointless it would be to waste his life, with a woman he didn't – *couldn't* – love.

'I'm sorry, Johnny. I owe it to them, and to Sophie.'

A violent rush of bitterness welled inside me. This couldn't be the way it was going to turn out. I'd seen such a wonderful vision of our life together, and felt so sure it would come true. I longed for it so badly and the idea that it was to be snatched away was too much to bear. Bitterness curdled into rage.

'Oh, yes, you *owe* them all. That awful cold bitch of a mother, and your respectable father who is, after all, a pillar of society. You must follow in his footsteps. It's your duty. Provide an heir, pontificate in the House of Lords and keep your sordid proclivities hidden from the world. Like father, like son.'

'I don't know why you're suddenly reacting like this. We've always known the score.'

'I don't think *you* know the score at all.' For a moment I hovered on the brink. Then, fired up with fury, I jumped – what did I have to lose, after all? 'Suppose I told you the truth about your father?' I turned to look at Tim, sprawled on the bed, his glass in his hand.

He looked at me calmly. Posh people are often too polite to respond to provocation. He said lightly, 'The truth? Oh, I'm always interested in that. Go ahead, make my day.'

'All right,' I said, moved over to the bed and perched on the end. I didn't want to miss any of his facial reactions to what I was about to say. They always fascinated me. He would make strange puckerings with his lips when he was nearing his orgasm, and on the few occasions I'd seen him asleep, I'd watched his secret smiles for hours.

'When I first came to London,' I began, 'destitute and broken-hearted, thanks to you, I was a bit of a boy about town. I survived by prostituting myself. Yes, that's right. I was a rent-boy, and a rather good one at that. You had taught me well. I was rather accomplished for one so young. In demand.' I paused to let the full meaning of my words sink in. Tim put his empty glass on the bedside table. He paled a little.

'Your father, the mighty Lord Thornchurch, was one of my regular clients.'

Tim's hand darted out of nowhere and slapped me hard across the face, his signet ring crashing against my jawbone. I jumped out of his reach and went on: 'Quite a surprise, isn't it? Naughty Daddy, having his cake and eating it, paying his son's lover for sex! Leaves quite a nasty taste in the mouth. When he smacked me, spat at me, beat me, whipped me, fisted me, came on me and pissed on me, I often wondered which of us was thinking about you. Now I think I know. He was.'

Tim leapt forward and grappled with me, clearly attempting to stop the torrent of unwelcome words flowing from my unlocked mouth. We wrestled for a while, falling from the bed to the floor, but the tumble gave me the advantage. I pinned his shoulders to the ground with my knees and my hands grabbed handfuls of his lush blond hair. I held tight and pulled his head still. I hadn't intended to embellish the story – the facts were shocking enough. But I needed to turn Tim against his family in order to have him for myself.

'Your father told me he had always been gay, or "queer", as he termed it. He used to cry in my arms and tell me he had wasted his life. He doesn't love your mother and never has. He calls her the "mare" and you the—'

I didn't get any further.

'Shut up!' roared Tim. 'Don't say another word!'

With a furious grunt, he pushed me off him. Suddenly we were both on our feet, circling each other. He charged at me like a rugby-player and dragged me to the floor, crashing into the table and sending the plates flying with the remains of our food. He grabbed a lobster pick and held it to my throat. 'Shut your filthy trap! I would never have believed such disgusting words could come out of your mouth!'

'But don't you see, Tim? It's all been a lie, everything you've ever known. Your father's gay, just like you. He's had to live a sordid double life, just like you'll have to. Break the chain, Tim. Seize your chance of happiness.'

He stared at me, his blue eyes as cold and hard as flint. Then he said, in a tight voice, 'Idiot. Do you think I could ever be with you after this? Don't you realize what you've done? You've destroyed everything.'

'No, no!'

'Yes! I can't love you after this. I can't even see you again. I wouldn't want to! You bloody idiot. You filthy, low, disgusting, vile ...'

Each word was a knife to my heart. 'I wanted you to know the truth!' I protested. This had all gone horribly wrong.

'No, you didn't. You want revenge on me and my family because we won't do what you want. You're the most selfish man in the world. Well, I'm not going to let you get away with this. I'll make sure that everyone knows exactly what you are.'

'You can't do that,' I bleated. 'Besides, I'm about to come out. I'm going to tell the world I'm gay.'

'Well, bully for you. Gay is fine, no doubt, in your world, if not in mine. But how many people want to watch a former rent-boy on television? How many like the idea of a prostitute, and all the filth he got up to for money, swanning about getting rich and famous? Your career will be over, matey. Finished. You'll be all washed up.'

'You wouldn't do that, Tim ...'

'Why not? I consider it my duty as an upstanding member of society.'

'I'll take you and your father with me! I'll tell everyone about how I slept with you both, tell them what you're really like. I mean it, Tim!' Hysteria had gripped me. I started to shake. 'You don't know what I'm capable of.'

A look of disgust passed over Tim's face. 'I'm beginning to realize. God, you make me sick. All right. Do your worst.' He stood up and looked down at me contemptuously. I thought of that night in the summerhouse when he had broken my heart for the first time. 'A bit of boy action will hardly single out my father in the House of Lords. They'll all be slipping him hot skater lads who can be rogered for a very reasonable price. No one would have the bad taste even to discuss the matter. No, it's only you who will suffer long-term. It's not the kerb-crawler who disgusts society. It's the vile whore plying her trade on the street corner. How did I ever think I could love you? I don't know who you are. You're not the sweet boy I once knew. All the fame and success has turned you into a monster. You're crazy! You try to ruin my career and destroy my father, and you'll only dig your own hole deeper. Sophie will stick by me. She loves me, you see. But who is there for you, Johnny? Who will love you now?'

I said nothing. I had nothing left to say.

Five minutes later he left, silently and with no goodbye. I had a small cut just below my Adam's apple and a bruise the size of a sixpence on my jaw. I didn't mind. I felt strangely calm. So, now I knew the truth. Tim and I would never be together. And he was determined that I would suffer for what I had told him.

My life, as I knew it, was surely over.

CHAPTER THIRTY

A few hours earlier, I had skipped out of the flat I shared with Catherine, believing that quite soon I'd be leaving it to set up home in the country with Tim, my first step towards a blissful new future.

Now I dragged myself through the door, wilted and despairing, my dreams turned to dust.

'Holy fuck, Cowboy! What's wrong?' Catherine came rushing over to me, concerned. 'You look like you've been run over by a wheelie-bin.'

'Where have you been?' I asked. She was dressed to the nines as usual, her slender frame showing off her beautiful black dress. It occurred to me how different she looked from the crazy but lovable nurse I had met in the corridor outside the bedsits in Brownhill Road.

'Wheeling and dealing, of course. Feathering our nest a bit more. How do you feel about being the new face of Old Spice? Here, let me help you.' She put an arm under mine and supported me to the sofa where I sat down. She poured some brandy and handed it to me. 'Drink this. You look like you need it.'

I sipped, enjoying the burn as it coated my mouth and throat.

'After I've told you my news I'll be lucky if I'm offered the face of rat poison.'

'Come on.' Catherine curled up on the sofa next to me and put her hand on my arm. 'Tell me everything, Cowboy. What's happened?'

'It's Tim.'

'Oh.' Her expression changed to one of boredom. 'That dismal posh git. I thought it was something important.' She opened her bag and took out a nail file.

'It is. You don't understand. It's just about as important as it could be.'

'Oh?' Her eyes glinted and she put the nail file on the coffee-table. 'Go on.'

I told her about my visit to Grandma Rita and the revelation that my life had to change. 'I wanted to get clean, start afresh, make some changes ...'

'Get clean?'

'No more drugs.'

'No more drugs!' she exclaimed, as if I'd told her oxygen was to be rationed or clothes outlawed. 'Have you had a bump on the head? And what kind of changes, exactly?'

'You know – get some independence. We've lived together all these years and I thought it might do us good to have a bit of space ...' I faltered a little.

'Hmm. How does Tim fit into this?'

I told her about my decision to let the world know the truth about my sexuality.

'Oh, how fucking boring! You're not having a good day, are you? Why don't you just go to bed and stay there? I don't know how many people you thought still didn't know, Cowboy,' she said rather heartlessly. 'You might be the grannies' favourite but everyone else who's female and over the age of puberty isn't exactly sitting by the phone. What else? Are you going to reveal to the world that you're white, too? I wonder how they'll take it. The Riot Squad had better be standing by.'

'Well—'

'Tim,' she said impatiently. 'What about Tim?'

In a few words, I painted for her the picture of my future that I had seen so clearly: a proper relationship, a big house in Kent, a new beginning, free of drugs and drink.

'Sounds like hell to me, but go on.'

'But Tim wouldn't do it. He insisted he was going to go through with his marriage to Sophie, that he owed it to his family and his heritage – all of that terrible, life-destroying nonsense.' As I thought of it, my eyes stung and despair welled up in me. 'So I lost my head. I told him something I thought would change his mind.'

'Which was?'

'That his father was one of my most regular clients all the years I was a rent-boy.'

'No he wasn't!'

I nodded sadly. 'Yes, he was. Mr Brown.'

'Well, fuck me. Mr Brown was Tim's dad? And you carried on seeing him all that time? No wonder Tim was upset. He took it badly, then?'

'Just about as badly as he could.' I gulped. The memory of his face when I'd told him made me shudder. 'In fact, he's vowed to destroy me.'

'What?' Catherine's voice was sharp as a knife.

I nodded. 'He says that someone like me shouldn't be allowed to go on fooling everybody. He's going to let the world know about my rent-boy past.'

'This is serious,' said Catherine, getting up to pace about the room. 'Why would he do that? You'd just tell all about him and his dad in return, wouldn't you? It's like a nuclear war. One strike each and then it's over for everyone.'

'He says he doesn't care. He told me to do my worst.'

'Oh dear. Oh, dearie dear. Hell's bells, Cowboy. We're in the shit.' Catherine turned to me. 'I can't manage us out of this one. The press will love it. It'll be front-page splash for days. They'll dig up clients who'll tell them all about what you did – and once it starts, how many more will be climbing out of the woodwork, selling ever more lurid stories for cash? Mild cocaine abuse will only be the start of it.'

'But the producers love it when I'm naughty,' I ventured hopefully. 'At least, they always have before.'

Catherine shook her head. 'There are standards, Cowboy. Public decency. Regulatory authorities. As long as there was no proof of your darker side – no photos, no witnesses, no stories – it was fine. Once it's out in the open, they'll drop you like a hot potato. You won't even get work demonstrating electric vegetable peelers in Selfridges.'

I buried my head in my hands. 'How could he do this to me?'

Catherine came to stand in front of me. 'He hasn't yet.'

'But he will. I don't think I'll be able to persuade him not to. He won't take my calls.'

'Course he won't. But I'm not thinking of ringing him. No doubt he intends to get hold of the papers first thing in the morning. We need to act fast.' She went to the cupboard in the corner. 'Cowboy, we need a lift.' She took out a bulging mini cellophane bag of cocaine and started to prepare some lines.

'Not for me,' I said piously.

'Oh, Jesus Christ! You have tea with some old bag of bones and suddenly you're moving into an oxygen tent.'

'I'm just not sure that's the best thing for us at this particular moment.'

'Of course it is. It makes us invincible.' She passed the little mirror to me. I looked at it. 'Go on.'

I shook my head determinedly.

Catherine wagged a manicured nail at me. 'Do as you're told.'

Suddenly I craved that feeling of power and self-possession. 'Just one more won't hurt.' I hoovered it up obediently.

'Good lad. Now. There's only one way out of this.'

'Yes?' I looked up at her, hope in my eyes. Was there really an escape from this ghastly mess?

'You have to stop that maniac before he destroys everything. You have to kill Tim.'

It took a moment for her words to sink in. Then I gasped with horror. 'You can't be serious, Catherine! Kill Tim? I couldn't!'

'Yes, you could. You must. Don't you see? He's going to ruin us. We'll lose everything. I'm not prepared to let that happen. We did Juan in for less. Why would we stop at Tim?'

No. Not that. Never. She was asking too much this time. I'd rather lose everything than kill the man I loved. I'd rather kill myself.

'You don't have a choice,' she said bluntly. 'You have to.'

'No!' I shouted. 'Stop it, Catherine. I'm not going to listen to any more of this.'

'Yes, you are.'

'No.' I stood up. The cocaine was rushing through my blood-stream now, energizing me. 'If you're so keen to see Tim dead, you do it.'

'Don't be stupid. How would I be able to kill him? He'd over-power me easily. We don't have time to lull him into a false sense of security and drug him. It has to be quick and decisive. Let's see ...' She frowned. 'We could shoot him – but we don't have a gun. My dealer might. I'll think about that. We could stab him, but it would have to be fairly frenzied, or he might still have the strength to fight back. I think it'll have to be the unexpected blow from behind. It's quick and relatively easy. I've got an old hockey-stick in the cupboard. I once broke seven girls' legs with it in one afternoon.'

'I bet you won that game,' I said, happy for the digression.

'We didn't, actually. I broke their legs in the dressing room afterwards. Anyway, listen. Thwack. Hard as you can. He goes down, you finish the job off. Plop the hockey-stick in the Thames after, and it's thank you, good luck to you and your family.'

'This is madness!' I cried. 'What about witnesses, forensic evidence, DNA?'

'Cowboy, don't you see? We're immune to all that stuff.' She was busy cutting up more lines as she spoke. 'We have this thing called divine guidance. It's never let us down so far. High time we had faith in our infallibility. Tim won't have told a soul he's fucking you. Why would he? And who on earth is going to connect Johnny D with the mugging and murder of a City lawyer? No one.'

'But ... where would I do it?' I couldn't help myself. I was being pulled into Catherine's world, just as I always had been. She made everything sound so easy, so convincing. Without her I'd be lost, I thought. Without Catherine, I'd no longer have the super-powers I'd enjoyed for all these years. Maybe the secret of my success lay with her. But she would only stay with me if I did as she said. It had always been an unspoken part of our pact that I obeyed her orders – I could see that now. I had been her instrument all these years, first as a rent-boy when she'd wanted a partner who would help her get away from her nursing and the bedsit; then as a killer when she'd wanted the money on offer, or the freedom from an irritant; and finally as a hugely successful star who could give her the wealth and power she craved. How could I stop? I couldn't get off the train, even if I wanted to.

Now Catherine had set me the most momentous, unthinkable task she could ever have devised. To kill my beloved Tim. But I thought of the look on his face when I'd told him the truth and knew he was lost to me for ever. And why should Sophie have him? Why should his life go on in the way he had always planned, with his inheritance intact? Why shouldn't he lose everything, just as I would if he had his way? After all, I was Johnny D, a man who had carelessly swept obstacles out of my way when they threatened me. I could do anything I wanted. I thought of *The Importance of Being Earnest* and Miss Prism's line when she hears of Ernest's death: 'What a lesson for him. I trust he will profit by it.'

Killing Tim would teach him a lesson he'd never forget.

Catherine consulted her watch. 'It's late. Almost midnight. Where does Tim live?'

'In a mansion block in Cadogan Square.'

'Portered?'

'No.'

'Good. Then you must go and wait for him inside the block. There are always places to loiter and hide in those old buildings. When he gets back, whack him on his way into the flat – as long as there's no one about. Take his wallet. Off you go. We'll burn your clothes, just like before with Georgie.'

The plan seemed full of holes. 'What if there *is* someone about?'

'Then you'll have to wait till they've gone, knock on Tim's door and get him when he answers it. And if he's already inside, you'll have to do that anyway.'

'And what if Sophie's there?'

'I don't frigging know, do I? Kill her as well, if you like. What if the Queen of Sheba's popped in for tea and muffins? Use your fucking loaf! Now, have another line and stop putting obstacles in the way.'

We stopped talking to snort.

Catherine's eyes lit up. 'I've just had an idea! Forget the hockey-stick – it's too big and noticeable. Besides, it has sentimental value. Use a brick in a sock. Next door are doing a loft conversion and there's a pile of bricks in the garden. We can help ourselves to one of those. Now.' She looked pleased with herself as she chopped out another line. 'Let's give you a little more magic dust for the road and off you go. That's another fine mess I've got us out of.'

I stared at her. Had I really agreed to this crazy idea?

She gave me her strictest, sternest look, the one that sent icy chills all over me. 'Don't let me down,' she said, with soft menace in her tone. 'I mean it. Get this right and we can live happily ever after. Fuck it up, and everything is finished. *Capito*?'

'*Capito*,' I whispered.

CHAPTER THIRTY ONE

That was how I found myself standing outside a mansion block in Cadogan Square wearing a pair of dark glasses and a long black overcoat, carrying a brick in a sock and intending to batter my one true love to death. Who'd have thought it? It just goes to show you never know what life's about to throw at you.

A light was burning in Tim's flat. So, he was at home. That was annoying. I had envisaged him arriving after me. Then I would creep up behind him and brace myself for one almighty and, hopefully, fatal blow to the back of his head. I wouldn't have to see his face. But he was at home so, unfortunately, I would have to knock on his door. He would answer, no doubt, and I would be obliged to look into his eyes before I killed him. This wouldn't have been easy at the best of times, but eye-contact with the man I loved made dispatching him even more of a challenge.

I knew enough about murdering people by now to understand that the best-laid plans must be flexible. Most importantly, emotion must be kept out of it. However it was done, I must take his wallet and pick up a couple of bits and pieces so that the crime scene looked as though a violent burglary of the kind there sometimes was in an affluent area had taken place. I blamed the crack addicts from south of the river.

I just hoped Sophie wasn't there. After all, she was blameless. There was no need for her to be caught up in my drama.

The door to the block should have been locked but someone had left it propped open – perhaps so that a late visitor didn't have to buzz a flat to be let in. It was sign, surely.

I avoided the lift and instead climbed the narrow flight of stairs up to the fourth floor where Tim's front door was at the end of a spacious, carpeted hallway. There was a sweet, vanilla smell in the air, and the milky glass wall lights gave an expensive, filmic glow to the setting. No one had seen me. There was another front door but it was on the opposite side of the building, at the end of its own little hallway. Unless I was very unlucky, I wouldn't be witnessed at my grisly task.

Now all I had to do was knock on the door and begin. I took the brick, contained in its sturdy, speckled-grey boot sock, out of my coat pocket and wound the leg of it round my left hand. I swung the deadly weight from side to side, like an altar-boy with a thurible. I took a deep breath to clear my head.

Beyond this door, Tim was unaware of what I had in store for him. If I went ahead and did this terrible deed, I would truly be a thing of darkness. But what was the alternative? If I sloped off home without having followed her instructions Catherine would have a fit, Tim would ruin my career and marry Sophie, leaving me scorned, disgraced and penniless. If I could bring myself to kill him, quickly, painlessly, I'd be saved and Catherine would bow to me as a hero.

A voice seemed to speak to me. An inner dialogue, if you please. *Don't worry about Catherine. Think of yourself. Think of your soul. Think of your future. Could you really live with yourself if you did this? You mustn't kill the man you love.*

But he doesn't love me! I retorted silently.

That doesn't mean you should kill him.

He's going to destroy my career.

Let him. Find something else to do if it all ends. But don't destroy yourself with this terrible act. You've killed enough.

I was shaking with a strange energy. Catherine had given me some cheap Australian speed on top of the cocaine so that I would have the rush I needed to fulfil my task.

'You'll do anything on this stuff,' she'd said. 'I once let a dirty-minded East End gangster bring his highly excitable Doberman into the bedroom.'

'You didn't … do anything, did you?' I'd asked, horrified.

'No. Bloody dog couldn't get a hard-on. What a waste of videotape that was.'

My teeth were grinding together, but I still didn't think she'd given me enough. Or perhaps there wasn't enough speed in the world to make this easy.

Each man kills the thing he loves, I told the voice of my conscience, or whatever it was.

No, he doesn't. You're not Macbeth – you're not so steeped in blood that going on is easier than turning back. You've still got a chance to make things better. You love Tim. Let love win the day. Let him live.

I thought about indulging in a good, cleansing cry. What on earth was I doing here? How had I got into this situation? I seemed to hear Catherine hissing at me, 'Do it! Kill him! Do it!' and the voice of my conscience replying, 'No. Don't succumb to this madness. Save yourself while there's still time.'

I wavered between the two. Could I stand up to Catherine and disobey her for the first time in my life? I wasn't sure I had the strength.

Then my hours with Tim fluttered before my eyes like falling leaves – I saw the two of us gasping with pleasure, crying out with ecstasy, kissing passionately in the grip of fierce delight and softly in the luxurious aftermath. I saw us talking, laughing, bathing together. I knew that I would never – could never – kill him, no matter what. I lifted up the sock with the brick inside. I would take it out and leave it here beside his door as a token of what might have happened. It would puzzle him but that didn't matter. Maybe he'd use it as a novelty doorstop, never knowing its significance.

As I lowered my makeshift cosh, I heard a sound: heavy footsteps coming closer and closer. When I turned, a big, burly man in a black overcoat and leather gloves was charging towards me. In his right hand he carried either a sodden rag or a wad of cotton wool. I felt him grab me with incredible strength. Then he clapped something over my face. Darkness overcame me.

My head was throbbing and my mouth was dry, but the first pain I became aware of was in my wrists. I couldn't move them or feel my hands, and when I managed to open my eyes it became apparent that I was bound, wrists and ankles, to a wooden dining-room chair. Although it was light outside, the curtains were drawn. Silhouetted against the window, facing me, I saw a vaguely familiar shape.

'I'm sorry if Big Boy was a little heavy-handed. Bulgarian, you know. That's half the attraction.'

'Sammy?' I croaked. My throat was dry and I was desperately thirsty.

'Yes. You're in my flat in Hampstead. Welcome.' He moved

towards me and wiped my mouth with a tissue. 'Drink of water? I hear chloroform can leave you with a raging thirst. And Big Boy tells me you were sick in the boot of the car.' He leant forward and sniffed. 'Your breath isn't as sweet as it once was.'

'Sammy ... what's going on?'

'Well. What was I supposed to do? Everything seemed to be coming full circle. I felt it my duty to intervene.'

'Intervene? I don't understand.'

'Come on, JD. I'm not stupid. Let's treat each other with a little respect, shall we? I'll give you that glass of water – though you'll have to let me hold this straw to your mouth as I'm not going to untie you quite yet – and you're to stop pretending. You were intending to kill Timothy Thornchurch, weren't you? And I saw it as my duty to stop you. Or, at least, to send Big Boy to restrain you.'

He held the glass to my mouth and I sipped gratefully through the straw. When my thirst was somewhat slaked, I said, 'You can untie me now. There's really no need for these ropes. I feel as if I'm in some cheap, made-for-TV thriller.'

'I expect you're right,' said Sammy, dabbing my forehead with the tissue. 'It's just a precaution on my part. I wouldn't want you to lash out.'

'I wasn't going to kill Tim,' I said, desperate for him to understand the situation. 'I know it looked as if I was, but—'

'Please, JD,' interrupted Sammy. 'This moment isn't about you for a change. Allow me to speak.' And there, in the semi-darkness, Sammy began to talk.

'I require you to listen to what I have to say now. Much like yourself, JD, I fell in love as a teenager, also with a Thornchurch. David Thornchurch, Timothy's father. Isn't that a strange coincidence? We're more alike than we ever realized, you and I. We've both been enthralled by the gentlemen of Thornchurch House. We were at boarding-school together, David and I. Westminster. You can imagine. We used to meet in the gymnasium after lights-out. Terribly daring. Then we went to Cambridge, to the same college. I read English and he read Greats. There was no secrecy about it – we were a couple. David and Sammy. Everyone knew. We held hands in the refectory, we shared rooms. No one batted an eyelid.

'When we graduated, that changed. University life had been a strange yet beautiful hiatus in both of our lives, it seemed. Reality intervened. We had to part. I pursued my academic career while David became a farmer, businessman and politician. But our love didn't die. Being products of our time, we understood that we couldn't have it all – couldn't have each other. We made do. We made a pledge to each other that we would always be there. And we were, in our hearts at least.

'Soon David found the woman he would marry. Hilary was a beautiful débutante, a well-connected virgin who would blossom, in the fullness of time, into a Bible-bashing over-possessive partner. David went through the motions of pretending to love her, but we both knew our lives wouldn't be complete without each other. Nevertheless we made a decision. We would not see each other again. We had our final night together a week before his wedding, and that was the last time I was truly happy. I crystallized that moment and kept it locked in my mind for ever, like a priceless gem. We both suffered, I dare say, but I felt I suffered most.' He looked at me bitterly and said, 'After that, ours was a chaste love. Hard for you to imagine, no doubt.' He stopped to give me some more water.

Shocked as I was by his story, I hadn't yet decided how to react, and kept my face inscrutable, even in the shadows. After a brief stroll round the room, Sammy settled himself in the chair opposite me, by the curtains. I could hear traffic and rain outside.

He continued softly, 'I have seen David only twice in forty years. That's all. Once, seven years after he got married, I came face to face with him as I turned into Victoria Station. It was one morning, rush hour. We literally crashed into each other, briefcases and brollies flying.' He chuckled. 'We apologized profusely, in that very English way, before we realized quite who we were looking at. Then we just stood and stared, too aghast to speak. Eventually he raised his hat to me and walked on. I turned for another glimpse of him but he'd disappeared into the crowd. Just from looking into his eyes for those few seconds I knew he still loved me and I him.

'That was it for six years. Never a day went by when I didn't think of or long for him. Then, in the summer of 1979, Georgie and I went on holiday to Barcelona. At that time – what were we? Late forties – we livened ourselves up with dirty weekends away in Amsterdam, Madrid or wherever – the sex capitals of Europe, I guess. We felt so liberated, away from home, out of sight of prying eyes. We could have some naughty fun without causing a scandal.

'We went one afternoon to a gay sauna called Romeo's. Georgie and I took a shower and proceeded to wander around the labyrinth of corridors in our towels, through the crowded steam rooms and cabins, waiting for some man or other to catch our eye. These matters were never very prolonged for Georgie, bless her. She soon disappeared into a cabin with a dusky gentleman – carrying a manbag, doubtless, full of poppers and lubricants and who knows what else?

'I was always a lot more choosy. Classier, some might say. I stayed at the bar for a few gins. Eventually I got bored and went walkabout. I found myself on the top floor of the premises where a cinema was showing lurid gay porn. At the back, through a greasy beaded curtain, there was a dark room. I watched the film for a while then wandered casually into the pitch darkness. Just drifting, you understand, like the *Mary Celeste*. I could hear low moans and agitated breathing. Soon a hand reached out and lightly brushed my arm. Another stroked my buttock. A couple of mouths, a few more hands and – well, I was away with the fairies. Someone kissed me for the first time in years. Since David, in fact. I gave myself up to the moment in all its sordid, hedonistic glory. I felt alive again. Reborn. Once things had reached their inevitable conclusion I tidied myself up and rearranged my towel. As I slid towards the grey light of the beaded curtain I thought I heard his voice. I heard ... David ... quietly calling my name. Twice. "Sammy ... Sammy!" he said. Then there was nothing. I called his name but he didn't reply. I shouted, "David!"

'*"Callate, puto histerico!"* hissed an angry Spanish voice.

'I left the dark room and stood outside for a while, waiting to see him emerge. But he didn't. I cannot explain it. Maybe it was David, maybe it wasn't.'

There was another long pause. Sammy was staring into the middle distance, lost in thought. He gave a sigh.

'Time passed, everyone lived their lives. My dear friend Georgie and I became very important to each other. Sisters, as we always said. We understood each other. We shared our lives. As we grew older we enjoyed our sedate existence together in Barnes. We got to that age when you discover what an appalling hoax life has been. Just a bad joke, we both agreed. End-of-the-pier stuff. You're born, you fall in love, you suffer and then you die. We muddled on, a tad bitter but squeezing some enjoyment out of our lives. In the last few years we were almost approaching something called contentment. Time mellowed us, as it does everyone. We had each other, gin and whisky. Bowls. Bridge.

'Then you came along. Our indulgence, our folly. You were rather special. We both noticed it. There was your charisma, your charm, your sexual capabilities: all assets in a young man. But I knew you were hurt. Hardened, *you* liked to think. I analysed and understood you more than you could have known. You were our boy, after all. I was quite infatuated.

'Then one Monday evening a few years ago, I was leaving a posh gentlemen's grooming salon in Mayfair – I don't know if you ever studied my feet, but I have a pedicure every month. Immaculate, they are, especially the left one. I was attempting to cross the road when I saw a taxi pull up and a smart, silver-haired gentleman emerged. David Thornchurch – still breathtakingly handsome, I thought, in a foxy sort of way. I stood rooted to the spot and watched him, the man I hadn't clapped eyes on in twenty-odd years, walk down Curzon Street. I didn't think about it, I just followed him, diving into doorways if ever he glanced over his shoulder. I wasn't sure what I intended to do. It was unlikely that I'd summon the courage to speak to him. I wasn't thinking straight, just caught up in the thrill of the chase, studying his determined walk, inhaling the air he had exhaled.

'His brisk walk led him to Claridges. He'd always had expensive tastes. I stood outside, but the agony of losing sight of him was too much to bear. I covered my face with a handkerchief and crept into the hotel foyer just in time to hear the receptionist say, "Room 510, sir, enjoy your stay." Then he was gone, up in the lift. I went to the bar and ordered a large whisky. Part of me was hoping he would reappear and whisk me up to his room, but that didn't happen. I was on my third whisky, trying to pluck up the courage to send a note to him, when I spotted you arriving. You headed straight for the lifts, looking business-like and gorgeous as always. The two of you in the hotel at the same time ... It was too much. I had to know what was going on. I waited another ten minutes or so and caught the lift to the fifth floor. I stood outside the room and listened. Such an angry flogging he was giving you! He was much gentler in my day. Knowing your working routine, I waited downstairs and watched you leave exactly an hour after you'd arrived. I was filled with wonder at my discovery.

'I took to following you after that, sure you would lead me back to David. You were the key. Stalking you slowly became a sort of secret vice, a hobby. It gave me an interest in life, I suppose. I enjoyed the cloak-and-dagger aspect of the game: waving good-bye to you in my dressing-gown, then throwing my clothes on in twenty seconds flat to follow you home on the bus. I loitered outside your flat in Camden, waiting for you to go about your business. Quite in demand, weren't you?'

Sammy's voice took on an almost cheerful tone. 'The funny thing was that I really didn't mind about you and my David. Actually, I thought you might do each other good. I got a weird thrill out of the idea that I had you on Fridays and David had you on Mondays. Maybe, just maybe, some trace of my sexual fluid might mingle still with his. Pathetic, really.

'Then everything changed. Georgie died. It may surprise you to learn that I knew the truth about who killed him all along, and why. You did. For the cash. Georgie and I had shared our hopes, dreams and disappointments for decades. Did you suppose I didn't know everything there was to know? Georgie's death was so tailor-made to his very personal requirements that I knew at once someone was following his instructions. But, then, I hardly needed to be Sherlock Holmes. The morning before his death Georgie gave me a letter. "Darling, open this after I've passed over to the great behind. And please do as I ask for once." I didn't realize the ink would hardly have time to dry.'

I managed to speak at last. My tone was reasoning, not callous. 'He had cancer. He knew he was going to die. He wanted to leave instructions …' My voice trailed away.

Sammy clucked impatiently. 'Oh, there was no cancer, I'm afraid. He was lying about that. No cancer at all. That particular death was simply his ultimate fantasy, and a silly one at that. Thought you might have seen through his little ploy. Georgina was as fit as a fiddle. I'm surprised you were so taken in. You knew how dramatic the old girl was.'

I closed my eyes, refusing to allow Sammy the pleasure of seeing me shocked.

'When I found Georgie's body I went home and opened the letter. Would you like to know what it said?'

I didn't answer.

'He told me all about your arrangement and how he'd talked you into it. He pleaded with me not to mention your name to the police. Nor did I. You ought to thank me.' He waited. 'Oughtn't you?'

'Yes. Thank you, Sammy,' I said, without sincerity, like an insolent schoolboy. I was utterly hollow, unable to feel anything.

'It was against my better judgement,' he said quietly. 'But then you moved on to Bernard and superstardom beckoned. I went to the Isle of Wight and my ability to keep tabs on you lessened. But every now and then I would come to town and practise tailing you, just to see what my little JD was up to. And as you grew more famous and more successful, it occurred to me that you weren't truly happy. And why was that? You were no longer servicing David, or anyone else. You were living for pleasure, for the moment. Then one day in Nicaragua – oops! Another of my friends gone west. Quite the little butterfingers, aren't we? But you came home with Juan, so thank goodness for that. Your career continued to flourish. I saw the pair of you together one night, dining at the Ivy. Such a handsome, cheerful boy, I thought. But, no, it seems not. Poor Juan was full of inner turmoil and soon to take his own life. Who'd have thought it? One way or another anyone in your circle, as it were, isn't long for this world. You really are an unlucky charm.

'Then I saw you meet up with Timothy Thornchurch and the plot really started to thicken. What on earth were you up to? He was the one you loved, I could see that much. It was all so familiar.

'But everything was different now. I had begun to suspect you. After all, everyone you'd got close to – except for the awful woman you live with – had ended up dead. What would happen to poor Tim? I began to fear for his safety, and for the heartbreak David would suffer if anything befell his beloved boy. I was mad with worry. I should have gone to the police then but I didn't think they'd believe my theories about a BAFTA-award-winning serial-killer.

'When we met in that restaurant – and I intended you to see me – I recognized the light of hedonism in your eyes along with a coldness I'd never thought you capable of. After that, I knew Tim was probably not long for this world. I had you tailed – sometimes by Big Boy, sometimes by one of his friends – with strict instructions that you should be stopped if it seemed you were going to harm Tim in any way. And last night was the night, wasn't it? You were going to batter him to death, weren't you?'

'No! No!' I cried, suddenly able to feel again. It seemed

terribly important that Sammy believed me. 'I wasn't going to kill Tim. I admit, I went to his flat thinking I'd have to get rid of him. He'd threatened to reveal everything about me, you see, and I thought I had to stop him. But when I got there, I knew I couldn't do it. I was going to leave the brick outside his door as a secret sign for him. You must believe me, Sammy!'

'A likely story, JD,' Sammy said scornfully. 'You must think I'm a fool.'

'Listen to me,' I said, trying to convince him, speaking in a torrent in the attempt. 'I'm telling you the truth! I killed Georgie because death was all he had to look forward to, Bernard because it was what he wanted and Juan because he couldn't live without me. Believe me! But I would never have harmed a hair on Tim's head—'

Sammy cut me off. 'Thank you. That will do.'

He reached into his jacket pocket and I heard a click. For a moment I thought he had a gun, but he pulled out a Dictaphone. He pressed a button and I heard my last sentence repeated back to me: '... I killed Georgie because death was all he had to look forward to, Bernard because it was what he wanted and Juan because he couldn't live without me.'

Sammy stopped the machine. 'You can come in now, Detective Inspector Anderton.'

CHAPTER THIRTY TWO

Handcuffed in the back of the police car, I asked if it was really necessary to have the sirens on. To my surprise they turned them off.

DI Anderton turned slowly to look at me. 'I thought you might like it, Mr Debonair. Thought it might make you feel important.'

'My importance is in no doubt, Inspector. Where are we going?' I asked.

'Back to the beginning. Barnes nick.'

'Do I get my phone call there? I think that's my right.' As soon as possible I had to call Catherine. She'd get me out of this mess. She'd know what to do. I half expected her to have contacted my solicitor already. No doubt a team of legal wizards was waiting for me in leafy old Barnes. The less I said the better, until I could take their advice. 'No comment', I believed, was the correct answer to any questions, serious or casual.

DI Anderton was a bulky man, and I was directly behind him, studying the grey bristles on the back of his neck. I observed the way they undulated and fanned outwards, like a sea creature, as he moved his head from side to side.

'Are you arresting me on suspicion of murder?' I asked.

'Correct, sir. Your taped confession is a great help, pointing us in the right direction as it has.'

'But I might be lying. What if I simply say I made it all up to help an old man in his fantasies? Apart from the tape, you don't have any real evidence,' I said.

'As it happens, we have rather a lot of evidence, sir. Very obliging, your manager. She seems to know all your secrets. But, as she said to me, things aren't looking too good for her Christmas bonus.'

I had no idea what he meant. I told myself he was bluffing. I decided to keep quiet until I had a lawyer in the room, or at least had talked to Catherine.

'I'm thinking of pressing charges myself,' I said, a little sulkily. 'No one seems to care a jot that I've been kidnapped, drugged, tied to a chair and tricked into a bogus confession.'

'I shouldn't be so keen to mention drugs if I were you, sir. We'll be taking a blood test shortly.'

When we got to Barnes police station I was marched through the main entrance, past an Irish drunk and a woman, her hair scraped back into a greasy ponytail, in charge of a hysterical toddler. 'Johnny D!' she shrieked, stunning her child into momentary silence. 'What are you doing here? Has he been nicked? Can I have your autograph?'

DI Anderton and his colleague marched me past her, their minds clearly on the task in hand. They were not to be stopped by anyone. 'What's 'e doin' 'ere?' were the last words I heard in the free world. Seconds later I was shoved into a cell and the door was slammed behind me. Another, more genteel, noise interrupted the echo, as the cover slid from a slot in the heavy steel door.

DI Anderton puckered up to the narrow bars.

'It's not exactly the kind of luxury you're used to, Mr Debonair, but please bear with us. I must ask you to remain where you are.'

I heard a distinct snigger. 'I'm sure all this unpleasantness will be sorted out in no time. Meanwhile, if you do require anything be sure to make a mental note of it and your "people" will be only too happy to provide it for you the moment your liberty is restored.'

I was eventually granted my free phone call but every number I tried for Catherine went unanswered. I rang my mother.

'Mother, it's me. I'm in a spot of bother and I've been arrested. Could you get me a good lawyer?'

'Darling? Whatever do you mean?'

'It's quite serious. "Murder most foul, as in the best it is…" if you get my general drift.'

'Not really, dear.'

'I've been accused of murder, Mother.'

'Oh. I see. Whatever is going on with the world? I'd better phone Grandma. She'll know what to do, I'm sure. My geraniums are still blooming beautifully – isn't it amazing? Bye!'

Of course. My mother didn't yet know about Grandma Rita's condition and it was quite likely that when she discovered it she would forget about me. I would have to request a duty counsel, or whatever it was.

But before that, lay a cold and uncomfortable night in the cells, punctuated with sightseers opening the grille on my door to peer in at my plight. The great Johnny D, curled up on a nasty hard bed in a rank little cell. Who would have believed it? Goodness only knew how many policemen were on the phone to their contacts in the press, selling the story.

Grandma Rita must have had a burst of energy when Mother told her the news and used some of her connections in legal circles. The next morning, I found that Henry Vaughan had been appointed my solicitor.

'There hasn't been a more sensational case since Fatty Arbuckle's! You're all over the papers,' he told me excitedly. 'This could put me on the map at last! Things are moving at quite a pace. It's considered that there's enough evidence to prosecute you for three murders, although I believe that the CPS is still deciding about the third – that is, the death of Juan Castinello. I'm told there's also a possible charge for the attempted murder of the Honourable Timothy Thornchurch but no more news on that one yet. Anyway, you're to appear in court tomorrow to answer the first charges – the murders of George Hillington and Bernard Cohen – and then a trial date will be set.

'A little later in the day, your barrister will be over to meet you and set out your case. Is that all clear?'

I nodded, speechless. I still couldn't quite believe what had happened to me.

'Excellent. Lovely to meet you, Mr D. May I say that I'm a big fan? I really am! My wife is the president of the Essex Boxer Dog Rescue Association. Such a worthwhile charity. They rescue dogs, as long as they're boxers and as long as they're in Essex. Might you be so kind as to donate something for our fund-raising auction?'

Then it was back into my cell until later in the afternoon when I was brought out to meet my barrister, also appointed for me by Grandma Rita, a man of suitable pomposity called Richard Lipsmack, QC.

We faced each other over a battered old table in a cold little room lit by a fluorescent tube.

'I took silk in 1986,' he told me.

'That's nothing,' I said. 'I took polyester and cotton in 1992.'

'Very good. I was told you were a comedian. Now then. I wouldn't be surprised if you had no recollection of any of the alleged murders. Just a stab in the dark, but might I be right? At the time you were on a number of drugs, I suspect, and subject to blackouts both on that account and the terrible abuse, both mental and physical, to which these men subjected you ...' He was a wiry, eagle-like man in his fifties, and he eyed me beadily through his black-rimmed glasses, holding his head on one side as he waited for me to nod my reply to each question. This he wrote down, as if it were now established fact.

'Well, this is a miscarriage of justice and no mistake. We'll have to see what kind of evidence they've got but you're obviously innocent. We'll soon have you out of here and back on television where you belong.'

It was a long time since anyone had had such blind faith in me, and I was grateful for it.

I sat in my cell and tried to be optimistic about the future.

I appeared in court briefly the next morning and was charged with three counts of murder: Georgie, Bernard and Juan. I spoke only twice, to confirm my name and to plead not guilty. People in the public gallery jeered and swooned in equal numbers. I scanned the rows for a reassuring glimpse of Catherine, but she wasn't there, just hordes of scribbling journalists. The whole thing lasted a few minutes, after which I was remanded in custody and sent to Wandsworth Prison.

The paparazzi managed to capture one image of me looking rather Christ-like as I slouched, gazing heavenward, in the prison transit van. The following day it was on the front page of every newspaper. The *Sun* came up with 'Shout, Rattle and Rot!' which I thought was one parody too many. 'Shout Porridge!' said the

Daily Mirror, while the broadsheets said, rather obviously, '*Shout!* TV Star Charged With Three Murders Over Five Years.'

But where on earth was Catherine in my hour of need? I asked Richard to find out why she wasn't helping me or standing bail at least. Besides, I needed to see her so we could discuss the Juan story and get our facts straight. Would I be carrying the can for that one on my own? What evidence was there that his death wasn't suicide, besides my taped confession? Perhaps I could still get out of it.

I had to get used to the noise and smell of prison life: the constant banging, clanging, jingling, and the sound of feet on concrete. The smell was a mixture of piss, shit, sweat, paint and overboiled cabbage.

It's not for long, I told myself. I'll get out soon and write a bestselling book about my experience – *Don't Throw Away the Key* or *Snakes and Ladders – The Life of a Modern Celebrity.* All I needed was a happy ending and my suffering would be justified.

The next day Richard came to see me in my cell in the remand wing at Wandsworth Prison. He looked worried and not a little put out.

'I'm afraid I don't have very good news.' He opened his briefcase and took out several papers. 'Can you confirm that this is your signature on each of these documents?' He passed them to me and cocked his head while he waited for me to answer.

'Yes, that's mine. Why?'

He sighed. 'Mr Debonair, these are Deeds of Gift,' he said, as if addressing a small child. 'Your entire property portfolio was signed over to Catherine Baxter some six months ago. Legally you gave her everything.' He paused for dramatic effect and raised his eyebrows. 'Were you aware of this situation?'

I frowned. I had bought the Camden flat soon after I began

earning serious money on TV, and more recently I had purchased a stylish penthouse, overlooking the Thames in Docklands, and a rustic villa in Tuscany. 'That's ridiculous. I didn't know I'd given her my property ... I mean, I'm always signing things she asks me to sign. I expect this is a tax dodge of some sort.'

'You don't remember signing them?' Richard sounded incredulous. 'And these other papers, which relate to investments and similar matters?'

'I sign all sorts of papers practically every day,' I said. 'Of course I don't read them. That's the whole point of having someone like Catherine. She takes care of everything like that.'

'Oh dear,' he said, rather quietly. 'It appears that she's sold the lot, mostly to an offshore company called Cowboy Holdings.'

'Well, that's what I mean. It's probably a dodge. "Cowboy" is what she calls me,' I said, convinced all this would be sorted out the moment Catherine turned up. 'And I'm still living in the Camden flat.'

'That's true,' said Richard, 'but you've been renting the property from this company at the cost of ...' he consulted the papers '... five hundred pounds a week.'

I had to admit I couldn't see how that would help me save money. It was a spacious flat in a sought-after street, but even so, that was way above the going rate. But still ... There had to be an explanation. 'Well, where is Catherine?' I said.

'Gone. Somewhere.' He reached into his suitcase and handed me a bank statement. 'Along with the entire contents of your bank accounts. Everything was transferred to hers some weeks ago and almost immediately withdrawn. You've been left with nothing. All your assets have gone. Make no mistake, Catherine has sold you down the river. She has emptied your bank accounts, sold your properties, and it appears she has even disposed of your car. You haven't so much as a pair of cufflinks left to your name.'

I began to sweat.

'She left the country on the day of your arrest on a nine p.m. flight to Algiers.'

I could fool myself no longer. The full extent of Catherine's betrayal was now clear. I stood up, wiped my forehead and paced the cramped room as best I could, cold horror crawling all over my skin. 'I can't believe she'd do this to me,' I said. 'We loved each other.'

'It seems such feelings may not have been mutual,' said Mr Lipsmack, drily. 'If Catherine loves you she has a funny way of showing it. She has thrown you to the lions.'

So, we'll go no more a-roving
So late into the night,
Though the heart be still as loving,
And the moon be still as bright.

PART FIVE

PART FIVE

CHAPTER THIRTY THREE

I was in shock. I had lost everything. I had gone, in a matter of hours, from the nation's favourite TV personality to a penniless has-been, banged up with child molesters and murderers. It was hard to take in.

I felt so far from it all.

Because I was on remand I was allowed to wear my own clothes but I was still locked up for twenty hours a day, given the most revolting food and forced to grapple with my desperate need of a line. For years I hadn't gone for more than a couple of days without one, and now it was showing in my pallid, sweaty skin and shaking hands. I shared a cell with an old Albanian man called something like 'Nango', who spoke no English and had some sort of bowel disorder that saw him crouched over a bucket for most of the time. We had access to a toilet, but Nango's condition meant he required his own receptacle, his straining occasionally rewarded with a foul splutter against the plastic. I could only assume that putting me in with him was some sort of evil joke on the part of the screws. I was grateful, however, that Nango had no idea who I was. Prison is the one place where you don't want to be well-known. My famous face inspired shouts of derision whenever it was recognized. I was jostled and spat at in the lunch queue, punched and elbowed violently in the showers, and every night after lights out the entire wing would hum a discordant version of the theme tune to *Shout!*.

I tried to cope as best I could by shutting it all out. I couldn't think about what was happening and instead pretended it was a bad dream from which I would soon wake up. That wasn't easy, though, as I was plastered all over the papers every day as the press went into a feeding frenzy, delighting in all the facts of the case as they emerged – and emerge they did, as my life was dissected by scores of journalists. My rent-boy past thrilled them, my homosexual proclivities delighted them but my allegedly homicidal nature was the biggest treat of all, the icing on a cake of scandal.

I worried terribly about my mother, and prayed that reporters weren't camped outside the cottage in Cherry Lane, making her life a misery. After a fortnight or so, she came to visit me. She looked smaller and wide-eyed. I knew it must have been strange for her to venture out of Kent. She was wearing a pretty lace blouse with an oatmeal cardigan and a russet hemp skirt. People looked at her as she skipped towards me, their eyes lingering on her feet. Bless her, I thought. She was wearing red wellington boots, covered with authentic Kentish mud.

'I haven't seen you for ages!' was her greeting. 'Why haven't you been home to see me, you naughty boy?'

'A bit tricky at the moment,' I said. 'I'm in prison, Mother.'

'Still, it seems very nice here,' she said, beaming around the visitors' hall as if it were a dormitory at Eton. 'I can see lots of nice men with tattoos for you to make chums with.'

'How's Grandma Rita?' I asked. 'Is she any better?'

'Oh, no, dear. She refuses to get out of bed. What a carry-on. She's got bedsores and ...' she lowered her voice '... there's a terrible smell, like rotting meat. Who knows what's going on under that eiderdown?'

'Shouldn't she be in hospital?' I asked.

'Well, yes. But she's terribly worried the doctors might make her better. They're known for it, apparently, and it's not what she wants right now.'

'She wants to die?'

'Oh, yes, she's looking forward to it. She could do with a change.'

'Is she conscious?'

'Well, she speaks and moves her head about, but it's not very interesting. I'd say she's on a par with Gyles Brandreth.'

'It's all my fault,' I said.

'Oh, no, precious! Gyles has only himself to blame.'

'I mean about Grandma.'

'At least she rallied enough to arrange your legal representation. Grandpa was very high up in the Masons – he had to sit on Prince Philip's lap in one ceremony, he told me. Anyway, she made a few phone calls and got you the best lawyers emeralds can buy. I believe this Mr Lipsmack charges a great deal of money. Let's hope he gets you off.'

I felt deeply depressed by all the trouble I was causing. 'I'm sorry, Mother. I can't tell you what a ghastly mess it is. I feel terrible about bringing you to a place like this.'

'You're not to worry about me. A nice man from the *Daily Mail* drove me here.'

I covered my eyes with my hands. 'No, Mother. There are no nice men at the *Daily Mail*.'

'Well, this one is!' she said indignantly. 'He's giving me a lift home too, with his photographer friend.' Leaning towards me, she whispered, 'So. What they want to know is … did you do it?'

I had no idea how to reply. I had pleaded not guilty, but I knew I was guilty of something. I just didn't think it was murder in the way that everyone else seemed to think it was. And as whatever I said would be printed in the *Daily Mail*, I had to choose my words carefully.

'I've lost everything,' I said. 'Catherine's waltzed off with all my money.'

Alice shrugged. 'Life's easier without too many material possessions. Remember how we used to be?' For a fleeting moment, she looked sad.

I was glad when she left. It was too painful to know that my actions were intruding on her charmed life, exposing her to snooping hacks and cruel gossip. Whatever else I managed to wriggle out of, I would always be guilty of that.

The person I most wanted to hear from was Tim. I was desperate to explain to him that, although the brick I had been carrying that night had had his name on it, I had aborted any plan to kill him. He was to have been spared and I was, if he thought about it, his saviour.

It had come out in the press that we had been lovers, though, mercifully, my connection to his father remained hidden. I suppose Sammy hadn't spilled the beans on that one. I wondered if Sophie would still marry him, and whether his career could survive the revelations. I had so many questions. But there was no word.

All I could do was wait for my trial date.

'I'm quietly confident,' Richard Lipsmack said, when he came to visit and discuss the case. 'There's no real evidence – or, at least, the prosecution hasn't revealed it yet. There were no witnesses to any of the murders and the disappearance of Miss Baxter with all your money works in our favour. It gives the distinct impression that you've been framed. I don't think any jury could convict you beyond reasonable doubt of the murders of Bernard Cohen and Juan Castinello. The only difficulty is George Hillington. His death was considered at the time to have been murder and the case is still open. You're an obvious suspect, I'm afraid, and your confession doesn't help matters, but without any actual evidence … Well, let's just say they'll have to work hard to make a case stick. I'm a bit of a python once I get going in the courtroom, and I'm feeling mighty puckish.' He gave a thin-lipped smile.

'Thank you,' I said.

The few weeks I'd spent in prison had been enough to convince me that I really didn't want to stay any longer than I had to.

I needed to get out, explain myself to Tim, find Catherine and sort out my life. I spent the hours in my cell thinking about Tim and trying to come to terms with our separation, Catherine's monumental betrayal, and my future behind bars. I was also suffering from drug and alcohol withdrawal. If I began to weep, as I sometimes did, Nango would look over from his endeavours on the bucket and say something I presumed to be sympathetic in Albanian. Once he reached across, offering the hand of friendship, but as he rarely washed it, I turned over on my bed to face the wall, snubbing him in the interest of hygiene.

A few weeks later I heard that Grandma Rita had died and I was not allowed out to attend her funeral, which depressed me even more. I had to wait until my mother's next visit to hear all about it.

'How are you coping?' I asked, as we sat across from each other in the visitors' hall.

'I'm fine! The funeral was a great success. The whole of Blackheath must have been there. Who'd have thought she knew so many journalists?'

'Oh. Are you enjoying the attention?'

'Well, it's never been so busy in the village. They've had to order extra sausage rolls in the shop, and the pub has to be booked in advance for lunch, these days.'

Had it been someone else I might have imagined they were putting on a brave face for me, but my mother's excitement was genuine. I blessed her for it. It made things so much easier for me. 'I really meant, how are you coping now that Grandma's dead?' I said.

'Oh, I know,' she answered. 'Such a good innings. Sixty-three, you know.'

'It's my fault, Mother. We both know that.' I began to cry uncontrollably. 'I am ... so sorry!'

'Don't be silly,' said my mother, incredulous. 'I've inherited two and a half million. Isn't it glorious? I'm going to have crazy paving. And I'm thinking of buying the field at the back of the cottage for the sparrows to play in. It'll be nice for them to have somewhere to stretch their legs.'

I sniffed and dried my eyes.

'Oh, yes, and she left some bits and pieces to you. Not much. Some of Grandfather's things. Remind me to bring them in to show you one of these days. Not a penny, though. She said money hadn't done you any good so far.'

*

Apart from my mother and Mr Lipsmack, I had no contact with the outside world. My existence had shrunk to the prison routine and my dismal surroundings, and I sank deeper into a dark, murky depression. I lay on my hard bed for days at a time with my eyes closed, willing my heart to stop beating or my lungs to stop their pointless activity. When you reach rock bottom, it is but a short hop to thoughts of suicide. If I'd had access to any of Catherine's pills I would have swallowed them all, and if I'd been anywhere near a volcano I'd have dived in head first. As it was, my means of killing myself were limited. I even considered drowning myself in Nango's bucket but fortunately he was never off it for long enough. That was how full of self-loathing I was.

CHAPTER THIRTY FOUR

My depression continued during the months I waited for a trial date. From time to time my mother came to see me and chatted away, oblivious to my condition. Otherwise, there was no trace of my once-glamorous life. No one from the showbiz world showed their face. You'd think I'd done something terrible, like go out with Ulrika Jonsson.

I had a fleeting romance with an armed robber from A Wing, but it only amounted to a fumble in the gymnasium and, comforting as it was to feel the warm throb of an erect penis, I really couldn't be seen with his sort.

Then a visit from Richard Lipsmack brought devastating news.

'You'd better prepare yourself, Mr Debonair. According to the prosecution, your friend Catherine Baxter handed over some vital evidence before she disappeared. Detective Inspector Anderton received through the post a key for a left-luggage box at Euston Station. Further investigations revealed a rather dusty sports holdall, containing various paraphernalia, including the strap for a Louis Vuitton bucket bag, soiled bedsheets, degraded latex gloves, used condoms and the rotten remains of an orange.

These are all being tested for DNA but the prosecution is confident of finding enough evidence to link you to George Hillington's murder. In fact, they've dropped the charges with regard to the other deaths in order to pursue this.' Richard looked at me wearily, aware that my chance of achieving a 'not guilty' verdict had seriously diminished. 'I might also, at this juncture, remind you of the recorded confession and the original correspondence from the deceased, known as Georgie, passed over by the prosecution's witness, Mr Samuel Heyward, who, I might add, may well have to face charges himself for not revealing what he knew at the time of the original investigation. However, that need not concern us.'

'Things aren't looking good, then,' I said gloomily.

'Not particularly. And Miss Baxter appears to have left a signed statement attesting to her knowledge of your guilt.'

I was dazed by the extent of Catherine's perfidy. Clearly she had never taken the holdall containing the evidence of Georgie's murder to the incinerator. She had thought ahead, rather brilliantly, and made sure she kept it safe. She must have been planning my eventual downfall even way back then. But why? I had only ever been a friend to her. She had double-crossed me in a spectacular fashion, throwing me to the dogs.

The Jezebel!

And yet … a small part of me couldn't help being amused by what she had done – the thoroughness of the operation and the style in which it had been executed. The neatness of the stitch-up and the campness of the fleecing were so clever.

Catherine was a star, and even as I came to terms with the fact that my life from now on was likely to be lived behind bars, somewhere inside I managed to cheer her on her way. She was my kindred spirit, after all. Even in these, the worst of times, she could still make me laugh.

I had lost everything. The only thing I had more of was fame. Times being what they were, my starring role as a serial killer tipped me into mega-stardom. Adding infamy to fame is a powerful mix (see Roman Polanski, Mary Queen of Scots, et al.). When the trial at last began, it was hard not to feel important as I heard the helicopter hovering over the courtroom and the prison, or as I was blinded by an electrical storm of flashbulbs whenever I emerged. Photographs of me in prison would be worth thousands and the shot of me in the prison van achieved iconic status. The big-budget true-crime special on my life was, I heard, already being cast.

But by the time the trial arrived, I was already weary of it all. I'd thought *Songs of Praise* was boring, but legal matters nearly sent me into a coma. I spent five weeks in court listening to forensics reports, witness testimonies and psychiatric theses. My bored expression was reported as callous, and my stifled yawns during a pathologist's description of Georgie's injuries were considered an outrage.

Perhaps the worst day was when Sammy took the witness stand. He appeared frail and gentlemanly, and his description of my visits to Castlenau Gardens made me sound like a cash-hungry home-help, out to exploit two harmless pensioners. Georgie came across like a kindly vicar.

'He wouldn't have harmed a fly!' said Sammy, wiping a tear from his eye.

I hardly recognized his description of the manipulative old queen I'd known and serviced for so long.

Catherine's part in encouraging the murder of Georgie could

not, of course, be verified and the prosecution laid the full blame for everything with me.

'How convenient,' drawled the eminent QC for the Crown, 'that Miss Baxter is not here to confirm your account of events. I cannot suggest that you disposed of her in the way you have of anyone else who stood in the way of you and fame or fortune, but she has simply disappeared. Who can blame her, though, for taking flight and extricating herself from an existence entwined with that of a killer? She must have been frightened for her life.'

Naturally Richard Lipsmack objected vociferously to this appalling piece of supposition and blatant leading of the jury, but the damage had been done. It was lodged in the minds of the twelve good men and true that I'd probably done her in too.

Lipsmack tried to make the case that I'd been framed by Catherine, whose disappearance and theft of my possessions made her look more than a little shifty, but the fact that I had willingly signed the transfer papers went against this version of events. The DNA that linked me inextricably to Georgie's deathbed, however, was unarguable. Lipsmack parried with the defence that I had been unhinged at the time, subject to suggestion from Catherine, that she had plied me with drugs to make me submit to her will and urged me on in order to get her hands on the loot. I had also been horribly abused by elderly punters like Georgie, and was suffering from post-traumatic stress syndrome. I hadn't been responsible for my actions at the time of the killing. As I listened to his wonderfully smooth, persuasive and articulate argument, I was utterly convinced that he spoke the truth.

We changed my plea to manslaughter on the grounds of diminished responsibility. It was my only chance of escaping a life sentence.

'Johnny Debonair,' concluded Richard Lipsmack, with a timely quiver in his voice, 'is a man more sinned against than sinning.'

At last the trial was over. As I was led into the dock for the last time I was aware of a movement in the public gallery. I looked up and saw my mother waving. 'Yoo-hoo!' she called cheerily. 'You look gorgeous, poppet!'

The judge told her to be quiet in no uncertain terms. 'Any more disruption and I shall have the public gallery cleared.' Then he began his summing-up. He left the jury in no doubt as to where the facts pointed. They clearly agreed with him. Within twenty minutes I had been convicted of murder and sent down for life. Typical.

I was aware that all eyes were upon me. Should I remain emotionless, bow my head or go for the full Ruth Ellis? In the end I turned to the jury and smiled. It was not out of insolence, as would be reported, but because there was a fit young businessman type among them. We had enjoyed the occasional roll of the eyes during the duller testimonies and the odd half-smile, and it was my way of saying goodbye. I would miss his twinkling eyes and crisp, quality shirts. Gay men such as me are indefatigable, unable to resist cruising even in a court of law, even with those who convict us of murder. We can't help ourselves.

As I was led away, I could hear the crowds baying for my blood outside the courtroom. Hanging was too good for me, apparently. No one seemed to understand my point of view. The press were sharpening their pens, ready to have a field day. I was a fallen angel, a rotten apple, the devil incarnate. I had fooled everyone and now I would pay.

I was driven from the Old Bailey in a prison van, hollered at and battered on the outside by the general public until I was delivered to Pentonville Prison.

I was processed by the screws, given a rectal examination (during which I made a joke about not losing your wristwatch, but no one laughed), showered, then given some clothes and a number.

'Follow me,' said a tubby screw in black, who looked like an extra from *Emmerdale*.

I was dazed and exhausted, still to come to terms with the prospect of life in prison. I followed him for what seemed like hours, through sundry locked doors, along corridors and past cells where inmates screeched and cackled obscenities at me, promising they would see me soon and I would be sorry.

Abruptly the screw stopped, turned to his left and sorted through his keys. 'In here,' he said unceremoniously, and opened the battered steel door.

As I walked through into my cell, he guided me with his hand on my shoulder. I was, it seemed, at the end of my spectacular journey. I had travelled from nothing to the dizzy heights of fame and fortune and now here I was, the lowest I could possibly be.

Then he came up close and put his lips to my ear.

'Catherine says, "Hello,"' he murmured, and left. The door clanged shut behind him. I was alone.

CHAPTER THIRTY FIVE

I'd thought that Catherine had abandoned me but I was wrong. Everywhere I went, people whispered her name to me. In the dining hall I received extra helpings, with a muttered 'From Catherine.' When I was alone in my cell at night, there would be a tap and the door would open. A covered dish, containing delicious smoked salmon and quails' eggs, with a warm hollandaise sauce, would be passed to me: 'From the kitchens at the Mirabelle, with Catherine's compliments.'

On Christmas morning I even found half a gram of cocaine under my pillow, wrapped in a crisp fifty-pound note.

Screws would breathe her name in my ear as they pressed books, poems, CDs and other little luxuries into my hands. One day I went into my cell to discover a comfy new mattress with a nine-tog duck-down duvet and pillows encased in fine, antique linen.

It seemed that while Catherine had condemned me to a life in prison, she was determined to make that life as comfortable as possible and was constantly delivering goods she thought I might need or enjoy via her corrupted prison staff. The governor himself came to admire my stereo and spent fifteen minutes cooing to the pair of rare lovebirds I kept in a decorative bamboo cage. (These, I assumed, she had sent in the spirit of irony.) But from Catherine herself I heard nothing.

My mother was the only person who ever applied for a visitor's permit. One month she turned up wearing a maroon beret with a sprig of chamomile flowers behind her right ear.

'I've been meaning to bring you this for ages,' she said, after we'd exchanged the usual hellos and caught up on the state of her garden. She held up a slightly battered white envelope. 'It's a birthday card!' she cried.

'It's not my birthday,' I said, surprised.

'I know. Just look at it.'

I took the envelope and opened it. It was a drawing of a happy-looking boy fishing by a river, holding what might or might not be a glass of beer in his hand. *Now you are a man!* it proclaimed on the front. *Happy thirteenth birthday*.

'Oh! Is this …?'

My mother nodded. 'It's the card your grandmother refused to give you all those years ago. I wrote something in it that I felt you ought to know. Later she persuaded me that I shouldn't tell. In light of what's happened, I don't know whether that was right or not. I was going to take the secret to my grave. But Grandma particularly wanted you to have this card after she'd gone, and she's always known best. She went on about it, rather, before she died, and I've made my mind up. So here it is.'

Inside, underneath, *Happy birthday, angel-cake!* was written *and your daddy is … Peter St John McDonald. Many happy returns, love from Mummy.*

'Who?' There was a distinct sense of anti-climax. Was that it, after all these years? The name meant nothing to me. I wished she hadn't told me.

'You'll find out,' she said mysteriously. 'I met him at a folk festival.' My mother had that faraway look in her eyes, but for once I sensed she was telling me the truth. 'He was a beautiful, kind mandolin player, come to welcome in the summer solstice. It was love at first sight for both of us. We smoked opium and went swimming in a lake at midnight. He told me all about his family, particularly his sister, who he loved, but who had married unhappily. He wanted to marry me, truth be told, and I wouldn't have said no, though I was very against the whole institution at the time. But his family utterly forbade it, egged on by his sister, the one he loved so much. It seems she didn't want his happiness as much as he wanted hers. He never knew about you, my darling. He left me before you were much more than the size of a thumbnail, and went to travel the world. I never heard from him again.

'It was only coincidence that led me to live in the same village as his sister. I never laid eyes on the horrible woman but it gave me a distinct thrill when I realized our two sons had fallen in love ...'

I gasped. 'You mean ...'

'Yes. You're Tim's cousin. His uncle was your father.'

'Bloody hell.' I tried to think through the implications of this.

'Don't worry,' soothed my mother. 'It's not close enough to be incest. Not really. Cousins can get married, you know – though, obviously, not you two. What a shock it gave me when Tim turned up at our cottage! He looked nothing like your father, who was shorter, like you, and dark with your dreamy brown eyes and olive complexion. Nevertheless, he was a connection.'

I felt as though my whole life story had been twisted up with the Thornchurches, in all sorts of strange and quite gruesome ways. From my own father, through his sister, Hilary, Tim and Lord Thornchurch himself, to Sammy, who had brought me down to punish me and protect his true beloved.

'Thank you for telling me at last,' I said quietly. 'Everything seems to make sense now.'

'Does it? Oh, I am pleased. I should have told you ages ago, probably. But you were always so busy. Still you've got plenty of time on your hands now, haven't you? How are you, by the way?'

'Oh, very comfortable.' I didn't want to go into detail but it wasn't at all bad in my cosy, well-equipped cell. The latest little present to come through my door had been a Gaggia coffee machine and I had lots of fun frothing organic milk – sent in from a farm in Dorset – to make my own cappuccinos. I had a tidy business selling them to other inmates, too.

'And you'll be out in twenty-five years, I expect. Just when you're entering your prime. Must be on my way now, my little Scotch egg! I'm going to pop into Tiffany's to see if they can make me a platinum bird-feeder. My tits are ravenous this year, and it's no more than they deserve. I've got to get shot of Grandma's money somehow, after all. Cheery-bye!'

I went back to my cell and relaxed into my new Parker Knoll recliner. The final piece of the puzzle had fallen into place. I was at peace. I felt resigned to my life in prison – after all, I had killed three men, so I couldn't really complain – and determined to make the best of it. Now that I'd discovered the secret of my identity and accepted that I would be spending some years behind bars, everything was a great deal easier. I felt happier, far happier, than I had in years, in fact. I even had the occasional fling, just to keep my hand in. (One with a rookie prison officer who looked just like Brian Harvey, with the lights out.)

I occasionally heard of Tim through the social pages of the broadsheets – I saw over the years the birth announcements of three children, two boys and a girl. I just hoped, for their sakes, they were all heterosexual and conservatively minded. I guessed that his law career had flourished but he must have given it up eventually for I saw his father's death notice in the paper, then references to the young Lord Thornchurch began to appear. He was becoming a little more radical now that his father had died, and there was talk of his fronting protests against GM crops, then turning his entire estate organic and carbon neutral – all those modern obsessions.

I wished him well. I loved him still, even if he never gave me a thought.

As for Catherine, I was no longer angry with her. My feelings of forgiveness took me by surprise – after all, she had been double-crossing me from the start. But she knew I would get the joke. Cruelty could be hilarious if you saw things through Catherine's eyes and her complete destruction of my existence was all the funnier for its scale and grandeur. Besides, somehow I'd always known that my deeds would catch up with me eventually. So I cheered her on her way. At least one of us was free and rich. 'Go, girl,' I whispered each night, when I heard them lock my cell door.

A year into my sentence, I received a postcard from Dubai. The picture was of a beautiful, sandy, sun-baked beach. On the back Catherine had written, in wobbly pink fibre-tip:

Hi, Cowboy,

This might be a holiday hotspot for some, but it's a way of life for me. I knew you were on the way out and I had to look after myself. I'm sure you understand. It'll all be waiting for you when you get out. Miss you.

Hope you're getting as much cock as I am.

From Catherine xxx

PS.

'Thus, though we cannot make our Sun
Stand still, yet we will make him run.'

EPILOGUE

As you read this, I am still in prison, albeit a pleasant enough open one. Ironically, I'm working as a gardener once more. Otherwise I have filled my time with writing and this is my attempt to explain my story on my own terms, away from the media, the courts, the prison-gossip grapevine, and their warped interpretation of events. I want everyone to know the truth, because only those in possession of all the facts could begin to understand.

The person I most want to read it is Tim. Maybe once he has, he will think kindly of me in the knowledge of how it all came to pass.

I feel at one with the world now. I'd go so far as to say I feel cleansed. I no longer expect to live happily ever after with Tim. I know that will not happen. But I know what did happen. That he loved me once is enough. Life may disappoint, but its brilliance is that it teaches you the value of such meagre offerings. It is all we have.

> *The ring is worn, as you behold,*
> *So thin, so pale, is yet of gold:*
> *The passion such it was to prove;*
> *Worn with life's cares, love yet was love.*

Ebury Press Fiction Footnotes

*Turn the page for an
exclusive interview with Julian Clary...*

EBURY
PRESS

Interview with Julian Clary

What was the inspiration for MURDER MOST FAB?

Crime has always fascinated me, particularly the motivation for something as serious as murder. I wanted to write a novel where the reader could completely empathise with the murderer. They would have done the same thing themselves in those circumstances. Despite the serious subject matter I wanted the tone to be light and comedic, so before I started writing I re-read all of E.F. Benson's 'Mapp and Lucia' books.

Johnny is a celebrity driven to commit murder to protect his career – is there anything you would kill for?

I think I might kill for love, if that isn't a contradiction. I'd certainly die for love, if called upon.

You're a fabulously funny writer and comedian, but who makes you laugh?

E.F. Benson I've already mentioned, but I laugh out loud when I read Armistead Maupin's 'Tales of the City' books, and I smile a lot to myself when I'm devouring Muriel Spark.

Dream-casting time: who in your head would play Johnny in a movie of MURDER MOST FAB? And Tim? What about Catherine?

Both Johnny and Tim need to be impossibly good looking, radiating youthful charm and sex appeal, so it isn't easy...I saw an episode of *Hollyoaks* the other day and perused the bright young things there, but sadly found them wanting. I suppose a younger, slimmer, better spoken Chris Fountain type is what we're after for Tim.

Johnny has a touch of the Russell Brands about him: he is unconventional and slightly dangerous. I don't think he washes much, but he's so gorgeous no one minds much.

Catherine is easier to cast; beautiful but hard. Denise Van Outen, really.

Who are your favourite authors?

Edmund White, Muriel Spark, Adam Mars-Jones, Edna O'Brien, Neil Bartlett.

Which classic novel have you always meant to read and never got round to it?

War and Peace.

What are your top five books of all time?

Tess of the D'Urbevilles by Thomas Hardy.
Our Lady Of the Flowers by Jean Genet.
Portrait of a Lady by Henry James.
The Driver's Seat by Muriel Spark.
Monopolies of Loss by Adam Mars Jones.

What book are you currently reading?

The Collected Letters of Noel Coward.

Do you have a favourite time of day to write? A favourite place?

I've tried all sorts of times but it doesn't make much difference to me. Basically I start writing in the middle of the morning, once I'm up and dressed and have walked the dog and made some tea. I don't like silence and I love to be interrupted – anything to break the monotony. I don't really stop until I've finished my 1,000 words a day. Even if I go out, I then stay up late into the night until it's done. It's like home work. I can't sleep unless I've done my duty.

As for a place – usually in the kitchen: it's near the kettle and the biscuit tin.

Which fictional character would you most like to have met?

Scarlet O'Hara from *Gone With The Wind*. She sounds like my kinda gal – feisty and beautiful, and handy in a crisis.

Who, in your opinion, is the greatest writer of all time?

That's rather a lofty question for a camp comic to answer. I expect the answer is someone like Thomas Hardy or Dickens. Or some old Greek, perhaps. Or someone I've never got round to reading, like Proust.

Other than writing and performing, what other jobs or professions have you undertaken or considered?

I have a delightfully varied life: performing one man shows, writing books, appearing in West End musicals, going on *Just a Minute*, doing TV shows. I would hate to be confined to just one activity. I like all the challenges life throws at me, from ballroom dancing to revealing all in my autobiography.

Sometimes I envy people who have a straightforward 9 to 5 job. Once they go home their life is their own, while I'm nearly always pre-occupied with the current project. But I can't imagine my life any other way. At least I don't get bored.

I sometimes think it would have been nice to be a social worker or counsellor of some kind. I like listening to people off load their problems and then finding a solution. There is always an answer, life has shown me, it's just a question of winkling it out.

What are you working on at the moment?

My next novel, which is about evil in the guise of a sweet old lady. Or it is at the moment. By the time I've finished it might have changed. I'm terribly fickle.

A YOUNG MAN'S PASSAGE
Julian Clary

This is Julian Clary's story, in his own words - the tale of an awkward schoolboy who became a huge worldwide success on stage and screen.

After a sheltered suburban upbringing, Julian was sent to St Benedict's, where beatings from 'holy' men gave him some brutal life lessons, and other 'unholy' boys his first awakenings of sexuality. He had just one true friend and ally, Nick - to his other school peers, Julian's aloof demeanour made him an enigma or simply a figure of ridicule. In school he was just another pained adolescent, but inside Julian was a new Jean Genet or Quentin Crisp bursting to get out.

Leaving St Benedict's thankfully behind him, Julian went on to college where he found his true vocation as an entertainer with a peculiar comic brand of smut and glamour. At the same time, he was finding as much sex as he could, sometimes with remarkably less-than-glamorous characters.

Periods in community theatre and the singing telegram industry followed before Julian hit the big time with cabaret co-star Fanny the Wonder Dog as The Joan Collins Fan Club. Soon, the world was his oyster. But fame came at a price, as Julian struggled not only with the reality of being a high-profile gay man in the 1980s but also the pain of losing his lover to terminal illness.

Far more than just another celebrity autobiography or 'funny book', this is a touching, beautifully written and wryly witty account of a unique progression from shy child to comedy icon.

Turn the page to read more...

MALLORCA

No one told me I had become an old queen. I came to the dreary realisation all by myself. I'd been hanging around the Club Barracuda, raising my eyebrows at desirable Spaniards, and was finally about to make my way home in the certain knowledge that I was of no interest and there were no athletic off-duty waiters drunk enough to emulate lust for me, when I came across my 22-year-old nephew. He was at once happy to see me and curious as to what I'm doing out at this hour at my age. It is after all 5.25 a.m. and I'm the oldest swinger in town. If only I could clear the air by having a nervous breakdown, then look back fondly at my youth, embrace middle-age spread and attempt something along the lines of living in the moment. I'm sure that's the healthy way forward.

Forty-five. It sounds grave. It sounds like a punchline. A doctor might say it to you at the end of a sobering prognosis. 'You see, you're 45...' Or a psychiatrist, while demystifying your current crisis, a publicist explaining your unseemly behaviour, a personal trainer excusing the aching muscles. Eventually I say it to myself in the mirror. Forty-five. It feels important.

Good bones, careful diet and discreet Botox injections do what they can but facts are facts. I'd better start wearing dark colours and stop bleaching my hair. There need to be some other changes made in the pursuit of dignity, too. I've scratched a living for 20-odd years as a camp comic and renowned homosexual, bespoke Nancy boy and taker-of-cock-up-arse. That will all have to go. Soon. As did the rubber and the Lycra some years ago, replaced with corsetry and glamorous suits.

I'm pleased to note that I have evolved in some ways, even if I am still a single gay man living alone in a particular square mile of north London with his small mongrel dog. (The local services I require, incidentally, are minimal: a corner shop, an off-licence, a gay pub, a first-rate sushi bar and somewhere to walk the dog.) I'm happy now, primarily.

I knew instinctively, when I arrived here almost 25 years ago, that this was my destiny. It's as well to know. Ah, I thought then, I've come home. It's a different home now, and a different mongrel too, but this is where I belong in the great scheme of things. But why?

I feel honour-bound in the writing of this book to discover what the point of myself is. The universe is not as chaotic as it may first appear to be. Nature has a reason for everything. Why am I here? Did the world at that time really need an effeminate homosexual prone to making lewd and lascivious remarks? Does everything happen for a reason or did I just get lucky?

One theory, extracted from an essay I read during my formative years, goes along the lines that Nature produces a certain number of homosexuals in each generation. Their function is to stand aside from the rest of society (busy procreating,

eating food covered in breadcrumbs and living the family thing) and comment upon it. We are the outside eye, the constructive critic, diffusing with our insightful observations the inevitably tense and difficult moods that result from domestic heterosexual drudgery. This has always appealed to me. I prefer to think that gay men, lesbians and transgender folk are part of the great scheme of things. Everything has its place. I am a Catholic, after all, and it's a comfort to me to know that God moves in mysterious ways. (He's not the only one.)

It may be that Nature's reasons change with time, and the current crop of freaks serves a different purpose. But I hope that I can discover the wisdom of my own creation in the course of this book. Surely, if we take a slow, selective troll through the chapters of my life, the least we can hope for is an understanding of the finished product? I'm rather hopeful. Prospective husbands need only read the paperback and proceed with caution. It will save so much time.

So here at 45 I will tarry a while, casting a bloodshot eye back at what may or may not be the first half of my natural life, but what can, come what may, unarguably be called 'My Youth'.

That's my general angle. I think I'll put the emphasis on the comedy. I am a comedian, after all, so we'll all be looking for a bit of uplifting sauce and slapstick, but expertly combined, correct me if I'm wrong, with what is loosely known as 'light and shade'. You want the tears as well as the laughs, the lows, the traumas, the self-doubt, the drugs, the scandals. You want unexpurgated gay sex, and if you're a *Daily Mail* reader you'll want that followed by disease, death and loneliness. This may be just the book for you.

Once work gets a grip, depending on the work you do, it becomes the meaning of life for a while, as much an imperative as eating or sleeping. A career won't be denied; it chomps away at your allotted 24 hours and its hunger is satisfied only temporarily before the next urge, as sure as waves roll in from the sea. And even if your work is camp comedy, it's as all-consuming as a thesis. It has a life of its own.

In the throes of the early 1990s I might as well have been Sylvia Plath, so possessed was I. Buggery jokes, not bumble bees, perhaps, but I'd found my niche and took up the make-up brush as the poet does the pen, the teacher the chalk or the porno star the penis – i.e. with relish!

It doesn't last, of course. Things change: self-parody creeps in, laziness rears its sleepy head. Then there are well-meaning (or otherwise) TV producers who trust their own vision more than yours. Battle with them for a few years and your resistance may cave in, the path ahead obfuscated. By then you have tax bills and mortgages, expensive tastes and expectant friends to dish out for. What was once a joy becomes a job. You're not new and exciting, you're old and reliable, if you're lucky.

But why did I choose this particular line of work? It just happened, as things do. But here's how.

So prepare for a taste of a young man's passage.

It's not going to be easy for any of us.

LAMONT

One dull Sunday afternoon in December 1993 I lay on the carpet in front of the fire and thought about my life for a while. I couldn't indulge myself for too long as a car would be coming to collect me soon to take me to the British Comedy Awards. But the more I pondered my life, the harder it was to get up. My boyfriend had dumped me, my manager had lost interest, I was taking Valium during the day and sleeping pills at night. Even Fanny the Wonder Dog, while she hadn't exactly withdrawn her unconditional love, had taken to avoiding me: after 13 years of sleeping in my bed (under the duvet, head on the pillow), she now retired to a spare bedroom at night.

As far as I could work out, my life had gone pear-shaped two months previously when I moved house. Could it be that mere location coupled with bricks and mortar caused my emotional well-being to evaporate so suddenly? I lay on my back and looked up at the high ceiling. I tried to focus on the empty space, on the nothingness that hovered there. It was an unnecessarily large house. Detached, as I was, with a garage and a garden. This listed Victorian home was bleak, not impressive, as I had thought when I made the purchase. It was situated on a corner and the local Holloway youths congregated there, shouting unimaginative insults whenever they saw me, even heaving a brick through the kitchen window a few weeks earlier. It had been a mistake to buy it, but I was rich and it seemed a good idea at the time. I was trying to make sense of my newly acquired fame and wealth and saw 9 Middleton Grove, London N7 as an appropriate symbol of my status.

At the third attempt I managed to get off the floor and go upstairs for a shower. It was a black-tie event so I had better make an effort and pull myself together. These award evenings could be fun if you were in the right sort of mood. Of course, I hadn't been nominated for an award – I was presenting the award for the best comedy actress. Before I left the house I stroked a glum-looking Fanny and slipped a Valium in my pocket in case I had one of my panic attacks. I knew there was a lot of small talk ahead and I might get stuck talking to someone tiresome. In the cut-throat world of television, people sometimes enjoyed saying hurtful things. I had bumped into Chris Evans a few weeks before at the Groucho Club. 'How are you?' I said. 'Your career went off the rails a couple of years ago,' was his cheery reply.

When I got to the studio from where the bash was being broadcast live, I forced a smile and found my manager, Addison Cresswell, milling around the champagne reception. 'All right, mush? Our table's over 'ere.' He seemed happy and excited; maybe because two of his other clients, Jack Dee and Lee Evans, were nominated for awards. 'Should be a good night for the stable,' he said, talking out the corner of his mouth, as if he were a drug dealer discreetly offering a sale. His company, Off The Kerb, was hugely successful, and when he'd had a few drinks he would state his worth in no uncertain terms. Poking himself vigorously in the chest, he'd say, 'I'm a multi-fucking-millionaire, mate!' He was proud of the comedians he looked after, and viewed us a bit like racehorses. When he signed Jo Brand he said to me: 'It's good to have a female in the stable,' as if she might be serviced by Jeff Green and produce a mini comic genius.

I was presenting the penultimate award so I was free to watch the show for a while and think about what I was going to say. Before you read the nominations and opened the envelope to announce the winner, you had time for a bit of banter with the host, Jonathan Ross, and one quick joke. I hadn't thought of my joke yet, but there was plenty of time. I had some champagne and nibbled my Valium. I looked round the room. The set that year was an imaginative rural display of greenery, sprouting branches and scattered autumn leaves. A veritable Who's Who of British Comedy sat in the audience along with other television stars of the day. Near the front I spotted the Conservative Chancellor of the Exchequer, Norman Lamont. Fancy inviting him, I thought. How inappropriate.